RACHEL SCHORR

ZERO HOUR

THE DOUBLE LIFE OF MENDY THE ARAB

Zero Hour
Copyright © 2014 by Tfutza Publications
ISBN: 978-1-60091-345-7

Tfutza Publications
P.O.B. 50036
Beitar Illit 90500
Tel: 972-2-650-9400
Tfutza1@gmail.com

First printed in Hebrew as: *HaShavua HaAcharon*
Cover Design: Aviad Ben-Simon
Translation: E. Perkal

Distributed by:
Israel Bookshop Publications
501 Prospect Street
Lakewood, NJ 08701
Tel: (732) 901-3009
Fax: (732) 901-4012
www.israelbookshoppublications.com
info@israelbookshoppublications.com

Printed in Israel

Distributed in Europe by:
Lehmanns
Unit E Viking Industrial Park
Rolling Mill Road,
Jarrow , Tyne & Wear NE32 3DP
44-191-430-0333

Distributed in S. Africa by:
Kollel Bookshop
Ivy Common
107 William Rd, Norwood
Johannesburg 2192
27-11-728-1822

Distributed in Australia by:
Gold's Book & Gift Company
3- 13 William Street
Balaclava 3183
613-9527-8775

Distributed in Israel by:
Shanky's
16 Petach Tikvah St.
Jerusalem
972-2-538-6936

"They said no?" Shimon cried in disbelief. "It can't be! Do you have any idea how long I weighed up if they were good enough for *us*?"

A brief silence followed on the other end of the line, and the reply, when it came, was slightly defensive. "Well, they didn't exactly say 'no,' just that they want to think it over a bit longer."

"Reb Noach, pardon me, but Mendy has been in *shidduchim* for six months already, and by now, I know what 'thinking it over' means."

"Nu, nu…"

"But I still don't get it… Their daughter is hardly – well, anyway, you know what I mean. And they still don't want to consider Mendy?" Shimon's tone of voice clearly betrayed how insulted he felt. "They think we're not good enough for *them*?"

Noach Wallis, a veteran *shadchan* who knew the Brand family well, waited patiently for Shimon to absorb the blow. Finally, he said softly, "It'll be all right, Reb Shimon, you'll see. Things will work out."

The *shadchan's* words did little to comfort Shimon and he gritted his teeth in frustration before entering the kitchen to break the news to his wife. Shuli was finishing the dishes, and she turned around to look up expectantly toward her husband.

"So, did you give the go-ahead?" she asked him, smiling in anticipation.

"I did."

"And they're coming to see him tonight?" Her expression turned slightly anxious.

"No, they're not. I gave the go-ahead, but they nixed it," he dropped the bombshell, but seeing the devastated look in his wife's eyes, felt the need to soften it. "Don't take it to heart, Shuli. They really weren't good enough for our Mendy. They obviously can't appreciate a real *ben Torah* when they see one. Who do they think they are, anyway?" he added caustically. "A *chutzpah*, from such a family."

Since Shimon himself was still unable to come to terms with what had happened, it was clear that his efforts to calm his wife were doomed to fail. Shuli slammed down the last dish in the drainer and gave full vent to her feelings.

"You're not kidding! What's going on here? It's more than six months already, and not one suggestion has gone anywhere. Okay, I know – at first we were setting our sights too high, but that's normal for an oldest child. Lots of people make that mistake. But this Cohen girl… She was hardly the cream of the crop, and that's putting it mildly."

Shimon nodded morosely, recalling the doubtful expression on the *shadchan's* face as he outlined the various issues the Cohen family was grappling with. Despite everything, Shimon had decided to seriously consider it, never imagining the slap in the face he would be dealt.

"What are you trying to say?" Shimon asked after a long, uncomfortable pause. "Something's going on? Like what?"

"I'm saying that I think someone is lying. Maybe the *shadchan*, maybe the *yeshivah* faculty, or maybe even Men-" Shuli couldn't bring herself to finish the sentence.

Mendy. Her firstborn. The miracle that had transformed her into a proud, radiant mother. The child that had led them into a wonderful journey through parenthood. The bachur who was their pride and joy, and whom they now yearned to lead to the chuppah.

Could Mendy himself be lying? Didn't he realize that his word wouldn't stand up to scrutiny if it didn't match up to the truth?

"Mendy? I think more than anything, he's just frustrated and confused by all of this. You remember what he said last Shabbos, right? When he asked me why nobody was coming to check him out in *yeshivah*? He's hurting, Shuli, just like we are."

"Yes, I don't doubt that he is. But he's new to this, just like we are. Maybe he's lacking self-awareness, or maybe… maybe there's something he'd rather we didn't know about. And you know what, Shimon? It's been a long time since you spoke with anyone at his *yeshivah*. Maybe it's time to pay them a visit, and try and get a feel of what's going on there."

Shimon frowned. "We know Mendy's a good *bachur*. All the reports throughout the years confirmed it. Why do you assume it's him? Maybe it's us."

"Us?" Shuli bristled. "Being *baalei teshuvah* isn't enough to explain this. And there's nothing wrong with our family!"

Shimon nodded, deciding to keep his doubts to himself. From experience, he knew it was best to avoid arguing with his wife, usually a fruitless endeavor. The conversation was over, which meant that he was on his way to Mendy's *yeshivah*.

"Bye, Shuli. See you later," he said weakly and walked reluctantly to his car, suddenly feeling ashamed of what he was doing. Mendy was nearly twenty years old. He shouldn't have to check up on him like a little kid. What would his *mashgiach* think when he turned up and started asking questions? *What* questions, anyway?

The main roads were busy at that time of day, and Shimon turned into a side street to avoid the traffic. The *yeshivah* wasn't far away – *unfortunately*, he reflected, wishing that he had another half hour or more to figure out what to say. *No, on second thought, better to get it over with as quickly as possible,* he told himself, while keeping a look-out for a parking space. *As for what to say, I'll let the mashgiach do the talking. If there's something that needs saying, I'm sure he won't keep me in the dark.*

Just a few yards ahead of him, two *bachurim* crossed the street carelessly, not even looking where they were going. Shimon screeched to a halt to avoid hitting them, and a strangled cry emerged from his throat:

"MENDY!"

He was still trembling, having come dangerously close to hitting the boys, but he shouted again, "Mendy!"

One of the *bachurim* swiveled around, and his eyes widened in disbelief. "Tatty? What are you doing here?"

"I'm driving. But what are *you* doing crossing the street like that? I mean, what are you doing here in the first place?" he directed his question at both of them. Mendy's companion looked older than him, probably in his mid-twenties, Shimon estimated. Though also dressed in black-and-white, he somehow managed to look slightly disheveled.

Mendy smiled easily and ignored his father's question. "Tatty, meet Yehuda, my old-new *chavrusa*."

"Where are you going?" Shimon ignored his son's introduction.

"We learn in the shul down the block."

"Why not in *yeshivah*?"

"Because – wait, why are you asking?"

Drivers honked impatiently behind them.

"Get into the car. I'll drive you," Shimon said through gritted teeth. Mendy slipped into the passenger seat, and his friend Yehuda climbed soundlessly into the back.

"You know Yehuda Berman, Tatty, don't you? He moved into our neighborhood about a year ago. Remember the *yungerman* I told you about who was looking for a *kollel*?" Mendy's words flowed naturally; clearly he was completely oblivious to the tempest raging within his father.

Shimon tried to recall, but failed to retrieve the memory. "Maybe, and so?"

"So nothing. We were learning together in the mornings."

"What did they say about that in *yeshivah*?" Shimon had yet to exchange a single word with the man in the back who was looking decidedly uncomfortable with the direction the conversation was taking.

"Who's supposed to say anything? What's the problem? We're learning, and things are good. Yehuda found a morning *kollel*, so now we learn together for an hour each evening."

Shimon glanced into the rearview mirror at his passenger who nodded his head in agreement.

"Which Berman are you?" Shimon finally addressed the young man.

"We're related to the extended Berman family in Teveria. You know them?" Yehuda seemed quite friendly once he got talking.

"Teveria? No."

"I guess why would you? In any case, my parents moved to Borough Park a few years back, but *baruch Hashem*, I got engaged to an Israeli girl, so I moved back."

They reached the shul right then, and Shimon pulled to a stop at the curb.

"How long have the two of you been learning together?" he asked.

"Oh, a few months. Thanks for the ride, Tatty," Mendy replied.

Berman shook Shimon's hand and smiled generously. "You have a wonderful son, Rav Brand. *Yashar koach* for the ride."

For some reason, he avoided looking into Shimon's eyes, only adding to his misgivings. He watched the two disappear into the shul, made a U-turn, and drove back in the direction of the *yeshivah.* After a few minutes of impatient searching, he found a parking space, and slammed the door behind him before striding down the sidewalk and up the steps leading to the building.

Luckily for him, the *mashgiach* wasn't in the *beis medrash*, but in the lobby just outside. Suddenly he recalled their last encounter, probably about a year previously. Then, the *mashgiach* had heaped praises on Mendy, but the look in the man's eyes now forewarned him that this time, he wasn't about to receive a glowing report. Stiffening, he steeled himself for what was about to come.

"Oh, Rabbi Brand, your son just stepped out," the *mashgiach* began, his expression a mixture of surprise and confusion.

"I know," Shimon blurted out. "I came to speak to you, not him."

"Regarding?"

"Regarding *shidduchim* for Mendy."

The *mashgiach* exhaled in patent discomfort. "Did something happen?"

"No. That's the whole point. My son has been receiving pathetic suggestions, none of which match the reports we've always received throughout the years. Something is wrong, and I was hoping that the *mashgiach* could shed some light on what it might be."

"Shed some light?" the *mashgiach* repeated, his gaze both pitying and astonished. "Rabbi Brand, where have you been until now?"

Shuli stared at her husband with blazing eyes.

"Will you please explain what you mean by a 'change'? What exactly is the *mashgiach* trying to tell us?" she demanded, her voice already rising to dangerous levels despite the late hour and the fact that the windows were open.

Shimon lowered his voice, hoping his wife would follow suit. "He changed… It seems that he's become a different kid. He's been spending a lot of time on his own, and when people talk to him, he's not focused. Worst of all, he tends to change the subject a lot… to weird topics."

"Weird topics? *What* topics? Will you just be specific already? Or didn't the mashgiach give you any details? And why didn't you ask him?" Shuli's tone of voice was becoming more strident by the moment, although Shimon knew that it was a mask for the inner turmoil she was feeling. "Where is Mendy? Not in *yeshivah*?"

Shimon dodged the question, trying to focus on what he hoped was the more positive side of things. "He's learning with somebody called Berman. Do you know them? A recently-married young couple who moved into the neighborhood sometime during the past year. They're renting."

"I don't know…" Shuli had no patience to rack her brain trying to dig up the various Bermans of her acquaintance. "But if he's still learning, what's the problem? Why does the *yeshivah* care?

But what strange topics? You still didn't tell me. What does Mendy know about anything apart from *Gemara*? He was never into current affairs or anything."

"I know, but… he's acquired a strange reputation. He talks a lot about the *medinah*, the wars, and other stuff…" Shimon's voice trailed off.

Shuli shook her head. "This makes no sense. It doesn't sound like Mendy at all! Just do me a favor, Shimon – go get Mendy and bring him home. Somehow, we'll get the truth out of him. And then, we'll convince him to keep his mouth shut about his newfound interests until he's engaged and safely married! Doesn't he have any sense? What does he think he's doing?"

"Shuli," Shimon tried to reason with his wife, "I can't just drag Mendy home! He's not a little boy anymore. He's almost twenty! We can't just tell him what to do – I mean, he won't necessarily listen, so we have to find some other approach, and—"

"You have a better idea?" Shuli didn't even wait to hear his answer. "We have to try! Or, you know what… maybe he should find a new *yeshivah*, and make a fresh start there. Maybe it's something to do with where he's learning. Maybe he feels stifled there… Yes, we could try that, and take a break from *shidduchim* for a bit, and then start over…" Shuli's eyes were focused on somewhere far away, which was fortunate, as she missed the expression on her husband's face, which clearly conveyed how idiotic he thought her suggestion was, so much so, that he didn't even deign to reply.

After all, he had spoken to Mendy just now – she hadn't. He had seen the look in his eyes and heard his tone of voice, and he had noticed something he couldn't fathom why he hadn't noticed before. This was not his child of a year ago. The *mashgiach* was right. Mendy had changed. Sending him to another *yeshivah* wouldn't help – if he would even agree to consider it. Mendy had grown up suddenly, and had grown away from his parents as he did so. Although he had been an adult in *halachic* terms for years already, only now did Shimon see that he was embracing his maturity – and using it in ways that he didn't think were wise. Maybe this was just part of growing up? How much he would like to believe it… but wishful thinking had never been part of Shimon's nature.

Shimon sank despondently onto a chair at the kitchen table, and Shuli sat down opposite him.

"Shimon, how long has Mendy been learning with that Berman you just told me about?"

"A few months. Maybe a year? He wasn't really specific," Shimon admitted.

"So maybe this change has to do with him?"

"Maybe," Shimon agreed. "He seemed like a nice guy, but maybe he's just not the ideal friend for Mendy – who knows. But… they only learn together for an hour a day. I don't think we can chalk everything up to that." Uncharacteristically, Shimon found himself trying to forget his earlier misgivings about the young man he had given a ride to. "In any case, you're right that we have to talk to Mendy, and the sooner the better. At his age, this is no harmless game he's playing."

"And to think that just a year ago, he was the top boy in his *yeshivah*," Shuli whispered, tears forming in her eyes. "This doesn't make any sense at all…"

Jamil urged his black horse to speed its pace to a gallop on his way home through the village. The horse obliged, partially – it was already old and tired easily, and Jamil occasionally pitied the old beast, but it was the only horse that his father let him ride. As if understanding the situation, the horse remained faithful to him and allowed Jamil to push it to the limit of its strength, and Jamil gave it an appreciative slap on the back before jumping off when he reached home.

He entered the kitchen, carrying the parcel with him, and presented it to his mother.

"Did you get what I told you to?" she demanded, glaring at him. "What took so long?"

"There was a long line in the store," he apologized, retreating a pace as he did so. His mother eyed the merchandise coldly.

"Not very impressive, as usual. But I guess it's the best I can expect of you," she commented. "Get back to work. And be back in two hours, because I need to go out."

"Okay."

Jamil returned to his horse. He was almost twenty, but his life hadn't changed much in the last ten years, and, he reflected, was unlikely to change much in the coming ten years, either. For him, it was work, from dawn to dusk – not a respectable job for an employer who might treat him as if he was worth something, but a never-ending list of chores and random tasks given to him by his parents and older brothers, who seemed to regard him as the household slave.

Sometimes, he still found himself wondering why this was his lot, why his siblings had the privilege of education and prospects whereas only he had neither. Despite his father's fierce loathing for the Zionist country they lived in, he had saved up enough money to send his older sons to a Jewish college – but for Jamil, nothing had been provided.

The reason his father gave for this blatant discrimination – when he deigned to give one at all – was that Jamil was an ignoramus, totally block-headed, and that education would be wasted on him. Jamil mutely accepted this assessment of his abilities, although sometimes he did recall what old Yasser, the principal of the village's elementary school, had told his father, while brandishing Jamil's test results to underscore his point.

"This boy has potential!" he had said. "I'd even venture to say that he's got more brains than your other sons. I can see him going far."

Yet, for some reason, Yasser's words had only served to infuriate Jamil's father, Rashid, who had grabbed the older man by his shirt collar and shaken him violently.

"Nobody, you included, will tell me what my son is or isn't! I know him better than anyone else, and I'm telling you that he's a useless good-for-nothing, a lazy slob who can't even be trusted to look after himself, let alone anyone else. For *him* to waste his time on books? He'll work, like it or not, and earn his keep. That's all he's good for."

So Jamil worked. He labored from early morning until late at night, almost without respite. He was kept so busy that he rarely had time to reflect upon the misery of his existence.

Early on in his childhood, he had concluded that his father hated him. Sometimes, he even thought he glimpsed flickers of hatred in his mother's eyes, but he was unwilling to believe that her feelings extended that far, despite all evidence to support it. It was plainly obvious that both his parents extended themselves to make his life miserable and eliminate all prospects for his future, and things had reached such a point that he had become the proverbial black sheep and scapegoat not only in his own home but in the entire village. His brothers, along with the other village children, had taunted him mercilessly throughout his childhood, and the elders of the village regarded him with scorn. By now, there seemed to be little, if anything that could be done to turn the tide of feeling toward him. In his younger years, he had still entertained hopes that if only he would work hard enough, he would manage to please his father, and then he would finally be accepted, but gradually those hopes were crushed, and all he could visualize for his future was an extension of the present, a dull, monotonous, bitter existence.

On occasion, he would ask to be given tasks that would require him leaving the village, but his father always refused.

"You won't manage out there," he dismissed the idea out of hand. "If an accursed Israeli policeman asks you something, you won't even know what to reply. Forget it. Your place is here in the village. And don't bother me again with your stupid questions."

Jamil didn't ask again, until another period of uprisings began, and he thought he saw a chance to temporarily escape his confines. Surely his father would let him leave the village for the protests and rock-throwing? Wasn't that a worthy cause?

"You?" His father laughed contemptuously. "What can you do to help? Forget it. Your job is to work and earn money. And that's it! When will you finally get that message through your thick head?"

Jamil got the message. And yet, the hope still glimmered faintly within in. Maybe, somehow, some day, he would finally escape his fate and leave?

The news, when it came, was entirely unexpected.

Rashid arrived home early that day, when it was still afternoon. Jamil was already tired from a morning of hard physical labor, and he still had a long list of jobs awaiting completion before nightfall.

"You're coming with me to America, boy," his father shocked him with the sudden announcement.

"What?" Jamil's jaw dropped, and he was certain that he was dreaming.

"Don't ask questions! I said we're going, so we're going." Rashid narrowed his eyes, studying him critically. "You should be happy."

"I am!"

"We'll have to make arrangements to get you a passport, visa, and whatever else. It'll take time, but I think we'll manage. I've already received authorization."

"What authorization?"

Rashid's gray beard quivered as he laughed harshly. "You think I pulled you out of school for nothing, boy? According to Israeli law, you're defined as a special-needs child, and there are special educational methods in America for helping dumb kids like you. That way, we'll get whatever we need."

"What will we do in America?" Jamil asked innocently.

His father glared furiously at him. "I said don't ask questions. You'll see when we get there. Be happy that I chose you for the task."

The suitcase was small and so faded that its color was practically indiscernible, but nothing could quell Jamil's excitement as he stuffed his old clothing inside. His mother poked her head into his room on occasion to check up on him. His room was the small and drafty one, the ugliest in the house, and in desperate need of a paint job. But it was his own, if only because none of his siblings agreed to share a room with him.

"Have you finished?" she asked moodily.

"Yes."

She didn't even bother looking inside the suitcase. "What did you take with you?"

"Clothes. And… I'd also like to take my report cards."

"There's no point in doing that."

"Maybe, but I still want to. Why did the Israeli government agree to fund my education, anyway?" he asked, hoping to glean some information from his mother before he left. In less than two hours, he would be leaving with his father for the airport, departing the village for the first time he could recall in all his life. Couldn't she at least answer one question before he left?

"Why shouldn't they? They're all rich over there, and they have all sorts of philanthropic organizations. I don't know, and frankly, I don't even care," she added, frowning at him impatiently. "So, are you finished yet?"

"Yes, like I told you, but I'm already over eighteen," he persisted, trying to direct the conversation back to its starting point.

"What's the difference? They help out until twenty-one."

"What will I do there?"

"I don't know. Why do you always ask so many questions? Go and see for yourself. I'm sure you'll like it."

"How do you know?" his fury suddenly erupted from within. "Where am I going? What kind of school is it? Who are the teachers? Why in America? Why… *Aghh!*" he released a shout of pain.

His eldest brother had suddenly materialized behind him. Ahmad was already thirty years old, and as a youth, he had often beat Jamil to a pulp. By the time he reached his twenties, he had quit the habit, but he still stared at him with hate-filled eyes whenever their paths crossed. Now, he had just dealt a heavy blow to the base of Jamil's spine.

"Quiet, dog!" he shouted. "Keep your mouth shut and finish packing. How many times do we have to tell you to just listen?"

Jamil clenched his lips tightly together and his fists balled in his pockets. So he wouldn't get answers. But he would figure things out for himself. Despite them.

Not long after, a scratched, beat-up jalopy whose color might have once been white honked outside. Khalid, a friend of his father's, had volunteered to drive them to the airport.

"Time to go, Jamil," his mother announced.

He picked up his suitcase. "Isn't Father coming with me?"

"He's coming."

"All right, then… I'm going."

"Yes, go," she ordered.

He exited the house with mixed feelings, pausing as he crossed the threshold. In the distance, the Carmel mountain soared up to the heavens, its vibrant greenery contrasting starkly with the dull greys and browns of the village. And beyond it? What lay ahead for him?

He turned around briefly around and saw his mother staring at him from the kitchen window, his eldest brother at her side. Seeing him looking at her, she lifted her hand to wave, and for a moment, Jamil allowed himself to imagine that she was wishing him success, despite the coldness of their parting. His brother's dark eyes followed him until he was seated in the car. Rashid was already sitting beside the driver. Khalid floored the accelerator, turned onto the main village road and then onto the highway. From there, it was a two-hour drive until they reached Ben Gurion Airport.

Outside the terminal, Rashid and Jamil parted warmly from Khalid, and as they entered the huge building, Jamil's feelings of anticipation and fear intensified. They passed through the security check uneventfully, even though his father looked slightly anxious. Jamil did everything he could think of to please him, but even his best efforts were only rewarded with a constant barrage of curses interspersed with muttered criticisms.

At long last, they boarded, and Jamil could hardly suppress his excitement as the airplane soared gracefully into the azure sky. He felt almost like a prisoner who had just been released from jail.

"Where will I be going to school?" he finally broached the subject. "In what city?"

"What's the difference? You don't know America anyway."

"It's just... a bit weird. I don't know a word of English," Jamil replied.

"No, you don't. And that's the whole idea." Jamil was sure he detected a note of scorn in his father's voice, but then, that was nothing new.

"So where will I study?"

"You'll enjoy it there. Trust me. You're going places that others only dream of. Jamil, remember that your father did everything for you, okay? Don't hate me."

It was the strangest reply that Jamil had ever heard, and he had the bizarre feeling that his father's words concealed a riddle that he was supposed to decipher. All his subsequent attempts to engage his father in conversation failed, and then, Rashid closed his eyes and promptly fell asleep. Half an hour later, Jamil succumbed as well.

It was a twelve-hour flight, and the hours crept by slowly. Jamil awoke after six hours had passed and sat impatiently waiting for the ordeal to end. Gazing out of the window had long since lost its appeal, and his thoughts were beginning to torment him. Where was he headed? Would his life take a turn for the better now, or… or what?

A second meal was served, another movie started and then ended, and finally, the plane began its descent. When the wheels made contact with the runway, a smattering of cheerful applause filled the cabin, but despite his previous feelings of anticipation, Jamil didn't join in the excitement. The 'Fasten seatbelt' sign flickered off, and Jamil retrieved his carry-on bag and followed his father into the aisle. It suddenly struck him that his father's hands were empty. Hadn't he taken a carry-on onto the plane, as well?

He was about to ask him, when his father ordered him ahead. "Let's go, boy. People are waiting."

They disembarked and joined the throngs of passengers heading into the terminal.

"Where are we?" Jamil asked.

"In America."

"Where in America?"

"In New York, you idiot. Didn't you read the ticket or hear the announcements? I have an uncle here, which is the only reason I managed to bring you here." They proceeded ahead past passport control and then through Customs. When they finally emerged in the Arrivals concourse, his father stopped and took out his wallet.

"You see this, boy? These are dollars."

"I know."

"Take some. You'll need them."

Jamil accepted the money wordlessly, and his father started to glance around, his black eyes flitting anxiously in all directions.

"I don't believe it," he cried suddenly. "I forgot my carry-on on the plane! I'll have to go back and get it. Wait for me here, okay?"

"I'll come with you."

"No, wait here. It won't take long."

"How long do you think you'll be?"

"Ten minutes. Maybe fifteen. They probably found it already. If I don't come back you'll manage on your own!" Rashid laughed at his own joke.

Ten minutes passed, and then fifteen. A half hour turned into an hour and then three. It was only then that Jamil grasped that his father's last words had been no joke.

Jamil remained sitting on a bench in the Arrivals concourse, bewildered and trying to stifle his feelings of panic. Finally, he pulled himself to his feet and decided to exit the terminal. Maybe, just maybe, his father was waiting for him outside? He knew the answer already, but dragged his feet to the exit regardless.

Outside, it was evening, and the air was chilly, much cooler than it had been back in Israel. He paced around glumly, becoming more and more depressed by the moment. Unfamiliar strains of language wafted over him and suddenly he realized how alone and helpless he was. By now, six hours had passed since he had arrived here, and when his stomach began to rumble, he recalled that his father had stuck several bills into his hand.

He withdrew the money from his wallet and counted two hundred dollars. A quick calculation informed him that this amounted to approximately seven hundred shekels. *Seven hundred shekels!* Never in his life had he handled so much money. Any spare shekel that made its way into Jamil's hand was automatically confiscated.

But was money compensation for his fate? By now, he couldn't deny it. He had been abandoned, a foreigner in a strange country where he didn't speak a word of the language. There was no school waiting for him, no friendly uncle in New York to ease his transition. He had been led on a hoax to a faraway land, and now he had nowhere to turn.

He tried approaching several passersby in Arabic, but everyone shook their heads and quickly walked away. Worse yet, he noticed a security officer eyeing him suspiciously, and his instincts screamed at him to make a quick escape. But where should he go?

Reluctant to leave the only place with which he was vaguely familiar, he circled the huge airport terminal and entered again, mingling with the crowds. Then, he headed for one of the stores inside and bought a Pepsi, handing the cashier one of his hundred-dollar bills. As he counted the change, he swallowed nervously. Although two hundred dollars was a lot of money, it wouldn't last forever, and then what?

Sitting down on a nearby bench, he stared glumly at his surroundings, still desperately hoping to spot a familiar face. It was getting late, and he was tired, but he doubted that the airport personnel would allow him to spend the night on the bench.

Tears pricked at his eyes and he blinked them away. *At my age, boys don't cry,* he told himself savagely. Taking several deep breaths, he tried to regain his composure, sipping at his Pepsi and still keeping his eyes glued to the passersby. Every time he found his heart leaping at the sight of a man who somewhat resembled his father, he angrily quelled his feelings. *When will you get it through your thick head that he's gone?* he told himself. But why? Would he ever find out?

Suddenly, his gaze fell on a fellow Arab, and he sighed in relief. If nothing else, at least this man probably spoke Arabic, and maybe he would even offer him some practical assistance. From the suit and tie he was wearing, and the leather briefcase in his hand, Jamil surmised that the man was probably a well-to-do businessman, and he jumped up and approached him quickly before he had a chance to disappear into the crowds.

Embarrassing though it was, Jamil forced himself to spill out his sorry tale, and the man listened politely, only occasionally glancing at his watch.

"Well, it seems you are in America for a little while, at least," the man, who now introduced himself as Hassan, commented. "Why don't you stay over at my house tonight, and tomorrow, we'll see what we can do."

"A little while?" Jamil queried. "How will I get home?"

"I don't know, but your visa expires in three months, so you'll have to find a way," the man told him. "You'll find a job, hopefully, and earn enough to pay for your ticket back." Hassan narrowed his eyes. "Abandoning a son in a foreign country is quite a harsh thing to do, though. Your father must be very angry with you."

Jamil clenched his lips tightly shut. Of course it was his fault. Hadn't he been blamed for everything for as long as he could remember? No matter what he had done, he had never succeeded in winning even a modicum of his parents' approval, and now, they had given him a final slap in the face.

That very day, the old Jamil died and a new Jamil was born. The new Jamil was alone in the world, dependent on no one but himself, and determined, somehow, to make it. First of all, he resolved, he would defy his family's plans and return against their will. He would have his revenge on them. And then? Then he would be a free man.

4

At the Shabbos table, Shimon sang the *zemiros*, noticing with pain that although he could hear Mendy's voice from time to time, the boy's mind was clearly elsewhere.

Nachum and Suri, the two younger children, exchanged an uncomfortable look. Something was clearly going on; the atmosphere seemed heavy with unspoken words. Only Shuli deluded herself into thinking that somehow her ice cream cake would diffuse the tension.

"What's doing in *yeshivah*?" Shimon asked his son casually.

Mendy studied the remains of chicken on his plate. "Same old."

"How the same?"

"The same."

"You used to spend Shabbos in *yeshivah* more often in the past. What happened?"

"I just prefer Shabbos at home."

"Why?"

"I just do."

It was a fruitless exchange, Shimon knew, but he decided to draw it out regardless. "Mendy, how's your friend Yehuda, you know, your *chavrusa*?"

"Yehuda? *Baruch Hashem*."

"Why don't you invite him and his wife for Shabbos? We could get to know them."

"They moved."

"Where to?"

"Somewhere in Haifa, I think. He still comes to Bnei Brak pretty often, though, so we still meet up."

"You still keep your old *seder*?"

"Also." His tone was clearly evasive. *They didn't just maintain their regular seder, but "also." Meaning, they were spending more time together than in the past.*

"You're learning together?"

"Also."

"What do you do together when you're not learning?"

Mendy frowned slightly. "Tatty, what's this all about? And why now? I do things that I enjoy, that's all. Yehuda Berman is a great guy, and he has broad horizons. He's also giving me some advice on things that will eventually help me with *parnassah*."

Shuli, in the kitchen and listening intently, froze in the middle of slicing the ice cream cake. *Parnassah?* Why was her son filling his head with thoughts of *parnassah?* He had only just turned twenty, and he wasn't even engaged yet! How could he be thinking of leaving *yeshivah* so soon? What had happened to her *masmid*?

She was about to burst into the dining room and ask her son what in the world he was talking about, but when she heard her husband's calm, measured response, she decided to let him continue.

Shimon managed to maintain a cool façade even while pressing the issue further.

"Mendy, just who is this Yehuda? What does he do? I thought he was in *kollel*."

"He was."

"And now?"

Mendy shrugged. "Don't know. And, in any case, I don't think it's right to talk about other people, especially not at the Shabbos table."

Had the discussion not been so personally painful for her, Shuli would have burst out laughing. The "other person" under discussion, after all, was this Yehuda Berman, the one she suspected of wreaking havoc in her family, and yet those her son was trying to imply were in the wrong were herself and her husband, whose only motive was to rescue their son from… from what exactly? She didn't know, but she had to find out. She had to!

The ice cream was served, but Shuli barely tasted it. The black cloud that seemed to have descended over their home did not lift all that Shabbos day.

Sunday morning, immediately after *Shacharis*, Shimon Brand found himself in the home of Harav Michoel Katz. The neighborhood rav, a revered *talmid chacham* in his mid-fifties who was renowned for his listening ear, welcomed him warmly.

"Thank you for agreeing to see me at such short notice," Shimon said gratefully. "What I was wondering was, if the rav perhaps knows of a *yungerman* by the name of Reb Yehuda Berman who lived in the neighborhood for a while, although he recently moved away?"

The rav's countenance clouded over. "Yes, I've heard of him. And I also heard that he moved away."

"He was learning in *ko*—"

Uncharacteristically, the rav cut him off, his expression deeply distressed. "He wasn't learning in any *kollel*. From the very beginning, I discerned something strange about him. He seemed confused and unsettled. Then, I began hearing rumors. People assumed that he was a *yungerman* and had only recently married, but it emerged that he wasn't married at all. What he told people was that his wife had gone to America to visit her parents, but when we looked into it, we discovered that it was all bogus. He was unequivocally ordered to leave the neighborhood, and after repeated warnings, he did, *baruch Hashem*. Why are you asking?" the rav asked in sudden concern, noticing that all color had drained from Shimon's face.

"Because… my son… Mendy… The two became close, and… they're still in touch," his words emerged as a strangled cry.

The rav's expression turned instantly grave. "They're in contact, Reb Shimon? I don't know… This Berman is a strange fellow. At first, some people even suspected that he was a missionary, but it wasn't that. It took a lot of effort to get rid of him. How did Mendy link up with him?"

"I don't know, but I wish I did."

Rav Katz sighed deeply. "Reb Shimon, talk to Mendy. Find out what they discuss, what he thinks he's getting out of this relationship. And keep the lines of communication open with your son, whatever happens. He's a good boy, Mendy. He deserves better than this."

Shimon nodded slowly. "I will try – I am trying. But I feel like I'm not getting anywhere. Mendy refuses to divulge anything, and I blame myself for not realizing sooner what was going on. Though I don't even know what it is I'm trying to deal with! What is this Yehuda up to? What does he want?"

Rav Katz bit his lip. "I really don't know for sure," he admitted.

"Is he pulling boys off the *derech*?" Shimon persisted anxiously.

"No, no. No that. Honestly, if it were something like that, I'd be less nervous. It's something else, something strange, and I can't seem to put my finger on it."

Shimon was on the brink of hysteria. "Rebbi, what are you talking about?"

Rav Katz cleared his throat. "The trouble is that we really don't know. The man was proven to be a complete liar, and people kept their distance. I doubt that 'Berman' is even his real name. I can't figure out how he latched onto your Mendy. The whole story is very unclear to me. My gut feeling is that he's part of a cult or something like that, but I can't be sure," he added quietly. "It's possible that he's introducing Mendy to the cult… We can't really know."

"So what can I do?" Shimon whispered, the pallor on his face betraying his desperation.

"Keep Mendy as far away from him as you can," Rav Katz replied, but then he sighed. Mendy was twenty years old – how could his father keep tabs on him? How he hated sending a father away without being able to give him even the slightest hope to cling onto.

Shimon staggered out of the rav's house, heartbroken and feeling that he should be tearing *keriyah* on the loss of his eldest son.

His next stop was Mendy's *yeshivah* and, somehow, he wasn't surprised to discover that his son was nowhere to be found.

"He's been showing up less and less," the *mashgiach* answered Shimon's unspoken question. "This past week, he's hardly been here at all. I recently called him in for a talk and told him that if he doesn't shape up, we're going to have to ask him to leave."

Shimon's cheeks colored a deep red. Knowing there was nothing he could possibly say that would make any difference, he left the *yeshivah* with sagging shoulders and drove home, feeling as if his entire world had come crashing down on him.

Things seemed to be spiraling downhill so quickly. Just two days ago, Mendy had still been willing to speak to him, but today, as he punched in the numbers of Mendy's cell phone, he had an ominous feeling that his son would refuse to answer. Indeed, it took repeated efforts before Mendy deigned to pick up, and Shimon told him to come home right away, keeping his tone of voice firm despite his fear that Mendy would simply hang up on him and ignore the summons.

Mendy did come home – but the encounter was disastrous.

Shuli stared as her eldest child walked through the door – or swaggered, would be a more apt description. He seemed almost buoyant, exuding confidence and a tinge of scorn for his parents; the smile he flashed them was patently false.

"Please sit down," Shimon gestured his son to join him at the kitchen table.

After a moment's silence, he began. "I paid a visit to your *yeshivah* today. You weren't there."

"That's right."

"The *mashgiach* said that you weren't there yesterday either. You were with that Yehuda, weren't you?"

"That's right," Mendy repeated with an infuriating equanimity. The impossible calm he radiated buzzed like an annoying pest in the small kitchen.

"Mendy, are you aware that his name isn't really Yehuda?" Shimon asked suddenly, hoping to shock his son.

But his son's answer eradicated any hope he still harbored that he might succeed in saving his soul. "That's right."

Shuli lost control. "Mendy, what's wrong with you? We're your parents! Do you have any idea what you're doing to us? How can you hurt us like this? How can you destroy *yourself* like this? Why? What's going on? Mendy, we love you! Don't do this! Mendy, you're our eldest son, and we love you so much!" Tears trickled down her cheeks.

Mendy's reaction was bone-chilling. He lifted his head, opened his mouth and released an awful, raucous peal of laughter, laughing so hard that tears of mirth appeared in his eyes.

This was not their Mendy. It couldn't be their Mendy. This was somebody else. Somebody strange. Somebody different. Somebody… scary.

Hassan's amusement started swiftly to fade when the young man he had rescued from the airport made himself comfortable in his home. His mirth turned to concern and then anxiety as he listened intently to Jamil's side of his call home.

His mother answered the phone, and Jamil skipped all pleasantries, blurting out in a voice shrill with his feelings of betrayal: "Mother, do you know that Father disappeared on me?"

The only response was a sharp click, followed by the dial tone.

Hassan encouraged him to try again. "You probably dialed the wrong number by mistake, or maybe there was a problem with the line." But the next time, when Jamil called, whoever picked up the phone slammed down the receiver as soon as his voice came on the line. The message was crystal clear.

Jamil was heartbroken, and he found himself spilling out his woes to his hitherto sympathetic host. "They hated me from the day I was born. They deprived me of an education, and I wasn't even allowed to spend any of the money that I earned. And I was never even let out of the village! My brothers were allowed to, but they made me a prisoner! I always knew they hated me, but only now do I realize how deep that hatred runs."

"But why would they hate you?" Hassan tried to make sense of the story, but the despondent young man could offer no reasonable reply. It didn't take him long to grasp that behind the façade of this handsome young Arab who exuded a certain charm was nothing but a frightened little boy lacking even the most basic education and knowledge of the world. He had foolishly invited an ignorant, helpless foreigner into his home.

There was only one option Hassan saw as open to him: to get rid of the boy. He began with subtle hints, but when they flew right over the young man's head, he realized that he had no choice but to be explicit.

"It's time for you to leave," he announced clearly, leaving no room for ambiguity. His words were met with an expression of shock, betrayal, and worse yet, terror.

"But where will I go?"

"To the street," he replied, knowing that sympathy and kindness would get him nothing but a freeloader.

"What can I do there?"

"I don't know. Beg for pennies until you earn enough money to get back to Israel."

"How will I beg for money? What will I say? I don't speak a word of the language!" Jamil pleaded so pitifully and innocently that Hassan felt his defenses weakening.

"Well, what do you expect to do? Live off me for the rest of your life?" he demanded in aggravation.

Jamil might have been uneducated, but a fool he wasn't. "I was thinking that maybe you could help me find a job. If I work hard – which I'm accustomed to doing – I should be able to cover the cost of a ticket within a month or so. Then, if you help me make arrangements, I can get back home. Luckily, at least my father left me with all my papers," he added in relief, taking his passport and identity card out of his pocket to prove the point.

Hassan berated himself for being an old softie, yet he knew that if he threw the boy out, he would soon find himself condemned to a life of crime and drugs. While he had no inclination to adopt a grown man of twenty, there was something pathetically endearing about Jamil, and he couldn't help but pity him.

He weighed Jamil's offer for a long moment and then gave his partial consent. "Listen, kid, I can't let you stay here, but I'm willing to introduce you to one of my friends. Maybe he can lend you the money or offer you… some kind of job or something."

It was the most Jamil could have hoped for, and he listened in anxious anticipation as Hassan dialed an acquaintance and shared the story of the unfortunate cast-off who had landed on his doorstep. Apparently, he had called the right man, because Imani turned out to be a real family man who was aghast by the treatment a poor young man had suffered at the hand of his "dear Palestinian brothers," whose actions were obviously the direct result of the cruel treatment inflicted upon them by their Zionist oppressors. A good-hearted philanthropist, Imani generously sponsored the cost of Jamil's ticket back to Palestine and even had his secretary call his travel agent to make the necessary arrangements.

Jamil couldn't believe his good fortune. With the knowledge that he would soon be rid of his now unwelcome guest, Hassan graciously allowed him to stay in his home and gave him directions for touring the famous sights and attractions in Manhattan during the two days that remained until his departure. He even grew to enjoy the company of his young guest and surprised himself by offering to drive him to the airport on the morning of the flight. Jamil parted from his host with a bear hug and a profusion of thanks before he, with a final wave to the USA, boarded an El Al flight back to Israel.

Jamil settled himself into his window seat, peering out of the window with mixed feelings. He was returning home, but to what, to whom? To parents who had thrown him out like an old dog? To brothers who despised him and constantly abused him? How would the family react to his return? Would they accept him at all? What would he do once he arrived back in the village? Should he return home, at all? But if not, where would he go?

Unlike his flight to America which had mostly passed in excited anticipation with a long nap in the middle, Jamil couldn't sleep a wink throughout the ten-hour journey back to Israel. His thoughts turned constantly to his family back in the village, and gradually, his emotions morphed from anxiety and worry to a burning desire for revenge. In fact, he reflected, his return itself was his greatest achievement ever. After all these years of being a good-for-nothing workhorse, he was about to prove that he could take charge of his own life.

But would his mother be happy to see him again? Jamil didn't know, but he could hardly wait to see the look of shock on his father's face when he swaggered into the house. They had done everything in their power to get rid of him, and he had found his way back home! He had even managed to hold onto some of the money his father had given him, spending the minimum even while touring, and Hassan had also tucked a hundred dollar bill into his hand as a farewell gift before they had parted ways. He now had $224 in his wallet, which was almost a thousand shekels! With luck, it would enable him to establish himself independently, and then, the sky would be the limit.

Sentiments of sweet revenge flooded him, swelling larger and larger as he fantasized his imminent reunion with his family. His brothers would also, no doubt, be incredulous at the initiative their "stupid" brother had taken – never again would they so blithely dismiss him.

The hours passed, and at long last, the pilot announced that they were about to land. The plane touched down gracefully on the runway, to a smattering of applause. Jamil looked out of the window and was surprised to feel a feeling of warmth rush through him at the sight of his homeland. He soon found himself swept up in a tide of humanity – he, his small suitcase, and his precious dollars.

Jamil exited into the Tel Aviv heat and inhaled the familiar scent of his beloved Palestine. He spoke Hebrew, albeit not fluently, but he could definitely get by, unlike his traumatic experience in America. Nonetheless, knowledge of the realities of daily life was still beyond him and, unaware that there were cheaper ways to travel, he approached one of the waiting taxis, stammered through a conversation in broken Hebrew, and readily nodded his agreement to the asked price with a broad smile, failing to note the broader smile on the cabbie's face at having ripped off an unsuspecting customer.

When Jamil mentioned his exact destination, the cabbie's smile faded, and he wrinkled his nose in distaste. "I'll take you only as far as the highway. I don't drive into the village," he announced firmly, prepared to let his customer go, but his fears were for naught.

"No problem, but I pay ten dollars less." Jamil was no fool, or so he thought.

"You got yourself a deal," the cabbie agreed, still pleased that he was making a killing off this one.

Two minutes later, they were sailing northbound on the highway with Jamil's face pressed against the window. He could hardly suppress his excitement as he envisioned his imminent encounter with his family. As agreed, the driver dropped him off on the highway, and Jamil paid the $120 with a ready smile. That meant he only had $104 left in his possession, but he didn't care. He was home.

The village, located at the foot of the hills of the Galilee, greeted him with its eternal placid calm. Several dogs barked, and a hyena whined in the distance. Jamil strode in excitement toward his home, cutting across a field to get there quicker. From a distance, he could see that the house was dark, which was strange for that hour of early evening. It wasn't late enough for everyone to have gone to sleep already.

He knocked loudly and waited for someone to open, but everything remained eerily silent. He started to call out the names of his brothers and sisters, but no reply greeted his words. Frowning in growing consternation, he circled the house. At the back, there was a second-story window that could be easily accessed by shinnying up the drainpipe. He had entered the house dozens of times like that as a young boy, and even now, in the growing dusk, he knew he could slither up easily.

A minute later, he landed agilely on the floor of his older brother's bedroom, only to discover that the house was empty. Not only was there no one there, there was nothing there either. All the furniture, all the furnishings, everything was gone.

His former home was abandoned and desolate, and Jamil felt as if he had walked into a ghost house. The floors were black and gritty, and he briefly wondered if he was having some kind of crazy nightmare, but the longer he remained there, the clearer it became that this was far worse than a strange dream; it was a frightening reality.

Ten minutes later, after gloomily traipsing through the rooms, he exited the house in a daze, trying to make sense of the sudden disappearance of everything familiar to him. A moment later, he spied Jabbar, the next-door neighbor, whose house was separated from his own by a dusty dirt path.

"Jabbar..." he called out weakly.

The man leaped in fright, and his eyes widened in shock when he spied Jamil.

"Jamil! What are you doing here?"

"Where are they?" he croaked, suddenly realizing that he was parched – it had been hours since food or drink had passed his lips.

"Who?"

"My family! Where are my parents? Where is everybody?"

"Oh... They... they sold the house and flew to France. They're gone. But why did you come back from America so fast?"

"Why did I come back?" Jamil responded in disbelief. "Jabbar, do you know what they did to me? They abandoned me there!

Without anything! Without a place to go, without knowing the language! At first, I didn't understand why my father had to accompany me all the way there. It seemed like a complete waste of money, but now I get it. He wanted to make sure that I would stay there for good, didn't he?"

"How should I know?" the man replied tonelessly.

"You don't know, huh? Well maybe you can work a bit harder to remember, eh?"

Jabbar ignored him and started to walk away.

"Where are they? Tell me where they are!" Jamil screamed in fury.

Jabbar spun around, his expression transforming suddenly from indifferent to menacing. "Jamil, I recommend that you leave the village immediately, just like your parents did. Leave. Start a new life for yourself. You were foolish, boy. We gave you a ticket to America, and you could have made a life for yourself there. Now you're back here, with nowhere to go. Start over again, and make sure that no one ever finds you. Certainly no one in your family."

"Why not?"

Jabbar laughed, but his tone was mocking. "That's my advice, boy. And you know me; I'm never wrong."

"I know. So where do I go from here?"

Jabbar paused. "You don't really think that I'm going to invite you into my house… No, no. And don't tell anyone that you're back here in Israel. Listen, I suggest that you make your way to one of the Zionist cities and get yourself a job. Make some money and look for a cheap place to rent. It beats park benches."

"Jabbar, just tell me the truth. Why did they do this? Why do they hate me so much?"

Jabbar began running away, calling out over his shoulder, "Leave it behind you, Jamil. Take my advice, and forget about them. If you want to live, keep your mouth shut. Otherwise, you might just die in a car accident or something. It wouldn't hurt to change your name either. And don't tell anyone that we spoke! Get out of here, and never come back to this accursed village!"

He disappeared, and Jamil watched him go with hatred blazing in his eyes.

When Jamil exited the village, it was already completely dark. He stood at the side of the highway with his hand outstretched, hoping to hitch a ride to the greater Tel Aviv area. Unfortunately, but not to his surprise, not a single Israeli citizen stopped to pick him up – even at a distance, he was identifiable as an Arab. For what seemed like hours he stood there, waiting in hope. He was tired and worn out, and his house and previous life seemed to fizzle into oblivion before his very eyes. He was lost, alone and without family.

Where would he spend the night?

Shuli pushed a shopping cart into the neighborhood supermarket and couldn't help but notice a strange phenomenon. Everyone smiled politely at her or nodded in friendly greeting, but their expressions were tinged with pity.

"She's the one whose son…" she heard whispers from the next aisle, and the words pierced her like a thousand daggers. The secret was out, and Shuli felt like she was on a train plunging off a cliff, ready to explode.

Just yesterday, Mendy had returned home in the middle of the afternoon with a suitcase in hand. "They kicked me out of *yeshivah*," he announced with a broad smile.

Shimon hadn't been home, and Shuli thought she would faint, or drown in an ocean of tears of helplessness. "They kicked you out? What do you mean?" she shrieked. "Why are you smiling? You must be kidding, Mendy. You just came to do your laundry, right?" she asked, desperately grasping at straws.

"Nope, I'm not kidding," he smiled again, but his tone was sincere. "The *mashgiach* called me in and told me that I'm spending too much time learning with Berman and missing too many *shiurim*. He wants me to stay in *yeshivah* all day long, and I refused. So he told me to leave."

Shuli stared. "So why do you look so happy?"

"Because it came from them, and not from me," Mendy said

simply. "So now, you can't be mad at me. And, in any case, you don't have to worry, because I already found a new *yeshivah*."

"Another *yeshivah*? Where?" she gasped, unable to handle the onslaught of information.

"Up north," he replied, his words accompanied with yet another infuriating smile. "So, how soon can my laundry be ready?"

"Not until Tatty comes home."

"Since when does he help with the laundry?" Mendy's eyes started to dart uncomfortably around the room, which Shuli counted as a victory. So it did bother him that he had been expelled, she reassured herself; he still wanted to be a *yeshivah bachur*. Yet her moment of hope dissipated almost as soon as it had arrived.

"Mommy, I'm not sixteen anymore. I'm not a rebellious teen. I'm an adult."

"I know," her voice cracked in agony, but she swallowed her tears, unwilling for him to witness her weakness. Or maybe that was a mistake?

"What I'm saying is that Tatty won't be able to change my mind," he added.

Shuli grasped for straws. "Mendy, why don't you sit down? Let's talk this out rationally. I just made your favorite blintzes. I'll warm them up, and we can talk. Tell me what you're thinking."

"Mommy, I'm not a ba—"

"No, you're not, and you just said that we can't change your mind. Well, we're not trying to change anything. We just want to hear what's *on* your mind."

Mendy looked startled. "This has nothing to do with you… the change, I mean." He looked around, clearly desperate to make his escape.

"Of course not. You know how much we love you."

His mother's words caused his heart to melt, and he dropped his eyes. "I… I'm just finding myself, I guess you could say. In the beginning, when I started learning with Berman, he asked me a bunch of questions, like, why did the Yidden conquer Eretz Yisrael? Mommy, did you know that many of the homes in Haifa, and other cities too, once belonged to Arabs who lived there peacefully with their families? They didn't hurt a soul; they weren't out to hurt or kill anyone. But suddenly, Jewish forces appeared and they had to flee for their lives. Mommy, imagine if that was you, forced to run away and leave everything behind. Your clothes, your furniture, your jewelry. Everything. And then—"

"This is what that Berman has been telling you?" Shuli tried to make sense of her son's speech.

"No. It's just what I'm trying to tell you before you get mad at me. I'm trying to explain that there are always two sides to a story."

"Of course there are," Shuli agreed. "And you can also argue that the Jews of those days should have let the bloodthirsty Arabs run us all into the ocean or let Hitler, *yimach shemo*, have his way. Would that have been better?"

Shuli had always been hot-tempered, but as she had matured, she had learned to hold her tongue more often than not. This time, however, she couldn't stop herself and her words tumbled out furiously at her son.

Mendy looked momentarily confused. "That's not what I meant. I was saying that we could have made peace back then, and then no one – Jew or Arab – would have had to die."

"Mendy, you're being idealistic, and very unrealistic. It's like trying to make peace with Iran today. They'll gladly make peace with us, just as long as we leave our land."

"It isn't land that always belonged to us," he tried correcting her.

"Of course not. Arabs lived here from the time of Creation, and they never once harmed a Yid. They never once plundered or murdered, and they welcomed all Holocaust survivors with open arms," Shuli responded in disgust.

Mendy looked down again, and for once, he resembled her

Mendy, the one who would sit in the living room bent over his *Gemara* every Shabbos afternoon.

Just then, his cell phone rang, and he automatically reached to answer, his eyes suddenly illuminated with an excited spark. He gave several one-word answers, and then turned to face his mother.

"Okay, Mommy, I've got to go. You know what? Don't worry about the laundry. I'll work it out. Say hi to Tatty for me."

"Wait, Mendy! Where are you going?"

"Up north with some friends."

"Where?"

"I told you – up north."

"Mendy, wait!" she cried, but he was already on his way out.

"Don't worry. I'll call Tatty," he called over his shoulder.

"Don't you need money or something?" she tried desperately.

He was already at the threshold, but he spun around and met her gaze, his expression hazy. "I'm okay with money. I've got friends taking care of me." Then, he flashed that awful smile once again and disappeared.

The door shut behind him, and Shuli crumpled. The mask of toughness slid off her face, and she fell apart, weeping with the realization that the heartfelt *tefillos* and tears that she had spilled over her Mendy for the past twenty years, beseeching Hashem for his Torah, *yiras Shamayim,* and *middos,* now seemed to have been totally in vain.

As he had said himself, had her son been any younger, she could have hoped that it was just a temporary brown-out, a teenage rebellion. But Mendy was already twenty, old enough to live his life as he wished.

Whom had he befriended? Had he been kidnapped by a cult? A group of leftist fanatics? What did the history of Haifa have to do with his new chosen path? What *was* his new path?

By that evening, Mendy Brand was the talk of town. He had already been sighted wearing clothing contrasting sharply with a *yeshivah bachur's* wardrobe. Everything exploded at once, and the calls came with lightning speed. Even the *mashgiach* called; deeply distraught and apologetic, he explained that had he known the spiritual danger that Berman posed, he would have never allowed the two to learn together.

"He was a liar and a swindler," he said to a heartbroken Shimon. "He seemed so clean and innocent. Nobody ever dreamed that he was really a snake. No, Mendy didn't meet with Berman today; he met with others, and we have no idea who they are. We had no choice but to ask him to leave the *yeshivah*." There was nothing else to say, and Shimon muttered a weak 'thank you' to the *mashgiach* for his efforts.

Mendy had said that he was traveling up north, and true to his word, he called Shimon, but refused to shed any more light on his activities. "I'll be back some time soon," was all he would say. "Don't worry. I'm with good people."

There was no point in trying to hide the truth, because it was plain to see. The neighbors tried to mask their horror; Mendy's friends from *yeshivah* nodded in sad acceptance; family friends and relatives called the Brands to comfort and console with empty, meaningless clichés.

And Mendy, for his part, felt triumphant. Nobody had a clue as to his whereabouts, and he had all the money he needed. People assumed he was "up north," but that wasn't really the case. He let his cell phone ring ceaselessly until it got annoying and he turned it off.

The next morning, when Shuli was out shopping, the pitying looks were awful, but much less painful than her reality. She had lost her Mendy, and they didn't even know to whom or to what. Nobody could guess who was pulling the strings.

Mendy had simply disappeared.

"What are you doing here?" came a loud voice, the tone conveying annoyance tinged with alarm. Jamil started at the abrupt awakening and struggled to open his eyes before leaping to his feet.

"*Shu hada?*" *he asked in Arabic, before his eyes focused and he saw the sour face of a *Yahud* peering at him. Pulling himself together, he tried to appear respectable. This was his first opportunity. "I'm looking for work," he explained sheepishly.

"You're what?"

"I need a job. Do you have any work for me?" he tried again desperately.

"No, no work here," the grocer said quickly, eager to rid himself of the Arab youth whom he had discovered curled up on the floor beside some vegetable crates just outside his store. "Get out of here, now."

Jamil's pangs of hunger reminded him of the urgency of his quest for work. "Sir, I work. I need work. You give me apple. I work. Okay?"

"An apple? You'll work for an *apple*?"

"Whatever mister wants. I do everything." The hunger dulled Jamil's senses, and tears rose to his eyes, stirring the grocer's compassion.

---

* Who's there?

"All right then," he conceded. "You help me carry this produce over there," Max, the elderly grocer, pointed across the store.

Jamal nodded vigorously and immediately followed orders, working at a dizzying speed, blinded by the thought of food. He worked for half an hour straight, dragging crates of newly-arrived produce, stocking shelves inside and outside the store, and sweeping the dirty floor tiles.

"Now, apple?" he asked in his broken Hebrew.

"Now take your apple. Take three, boy!" the grocer agreed willingly. When he saw the way the youth attacked the fruit, he felt a surge of pity and handed him a fresh cucumber and tomato, as well.

"Mister, I work good," Jamil pleaded desperately. "I make floor clean, spotless! Your customers will be *mabsutim** with me. Please, mister, I work good and sleep here. I watch from robbers."

"And how do I know that *you're* not a thief?" the grocer asked suspiciously, but when Jamil's innocent gaze met his own, he had his answer.

Scratching his bald pate, Max sighed. "All right, then, boy. I'm not rich, and I don't earn much myself from this store, but I'll agree to give you a try. Take the scraper, and see what you can get off the floor."

As he had promised, Jamil proved to be a spirited worker, and he spent the next two hours scraping layers of grime off the floors. Then, once the store opened, he serviced customers with a friendly grin, helping an old lady to choose tomatoes and a little boy to arrange his bags in an empty stroller.

"You really are all right," the grocer complimented him reluctantly.

"Now I eat?" Jamil hungrily eyed the shiny produce and then the wall clock; it was already midday.

---

* satisfied

"Take whatever you like." Jamil chose a handful of fruits and vegetables, but not too many, and not from the better-quality produce.

"I have nowhere to live," he told the grocer. "My family threw me out. I have no money, nothing. Please let me work for money. A little bit. I just sleep here and work. Okay?"

"Let me think about it," Max said, and fell silent. For years, his wife had been begging him to close the store. How much longer would he manage to maintain his old, ramshackle fruit store on the outskirts of Petach Tikva? But he, in his usual obstinate manner, still wanted to work; he didn't want to retire and watch his days wither away. He didn't earn very much, but at least he kept busy, which was more than he could say for many of his friends. Lately, however, he had been suffering from back pain, although he tried to hide it. He didn't want to close his store, and he couldn't afford to pay a regular employee. And now, suddenly, this Arab was falling from the heavens to assist him.

"You got yourself a deal," he agreed finally. "Like I said, I'm not rich, and I can't pay much. But you can eat all you like, plus sleep here."

The two shook hands, and Jamil grinned from ear to ear. He had a roof over his head, plus a worn-out mattress and a blanket that the grocer generously added into the arrangement. It was a home. His roommates were tangerines and lettuces, but at least they wouldn't torment him as his brothers had. Not a bad start, as far as he was concerned.

If at first Max treated him with distrust, he eventually came to appreciate his worker's skill and eagerness to please. Jamil's Hebrew was improving by leaps and bounds, as well.

"In the village, I built with sheetrock. If Mister Max buys the materials, I can turn this place into a palace!" Jamil promised. Indeed, the young Arab proved himself and, with golden hands, renovated the store with a bit of plaster and moldings, enhanced the store lighting, installed mirrors behind the produce, and rearranged the shelves in a new eye-catching design that appealed to old and new customers alike. Max was gratified, and Jamil even more so.

And all the while, the young man wove a dream of revenge against his family.

His first month of work was rewarded with a thousand shekels, and Jamil felt richer than he had ever been. He was sure that he was finally making it in life when his dreams whooshed out of him in awful suddenness one morning.

"Here's what I owe you. Now, go!" Max said without introduction.

"What? Why? Isn't Mister Max happy with me?" Jamil gasped in astonishment.

"No, not at all. But, just go!" the old grocer told him firmly. "I don't like you or your friends around here. And I certainly won't let you bring your *chamula** here."

"Friends? I don't have any friends!" Jamil protested desperately, feeling like an alley cat being booted out the door. "And what family? Nobody knows I live here!"

"Someone does know. And you're right. You don't have friends, but you do have enemies. Lots of them. Just leave me out of your gang fights, and kill each other without me in the middle. Got it?" Max was clearly furious.

"No, I don't get it," Jamil replied plaintively.

"Take as much fruit with you as you like. Take whatever you want. They said that if I keep you here even one more night, they'll burn my store down. Do you realize what I'm saying?"

"No! Not at all! Why should anyone want to burn down your store?"

"Because of you. They don't want you here!"

---

* clan

Slowly but surely, understanding dawned on Jamil. "Who doesn't want me here?"

"Your friends. Your *chamula*. Your enemies' *chamula*, maybe. What does this have to do with me? Listen, Jamil, please go. I want to live. I don't want a part in your gang fights. Let me tell you something, though. I called the police and told them that you're being threatened. They said that they don't get involved in Arab gang fights until they're over. Listen, kid… I don't need blood in my store. Tomato juice is bad enough. Please go, Jamil."

"When? Where?" Jamil looked like a little boy.

Max sighed.

"Wherever you decide to go. You *have* to go though. And if you come back, I'll have no choice but to call the cops." As he said it, Max looked sad, and he felt it too. He had enjoyed the company and assistance of the friendly, capable young Arab, and practically for free. He had benefited from dozens of new customers who all complimented him on his newly-redesigned store and excellent service. It broke his heart to have to throw out Jamil after all he had done for him, but his life and safety came first.

Nodding in silent understanding, Jamil gathered his meager belongings and left.

Jamil boarded the first passing bus and sat down, wondering if there was any purpose left in his life. The suspicious looks of his fellow passengers made him uncomfortable, and he tried to make himself invisible. He wondered if he would ever get used to the feeling of being under everyone's eagle eye as they wondered if he was just an innocent pedestrian or perhaps a suicide bomber.

When he noticed two religiously-attired young men looking his way and then one of them reaching for his cell phone, he didn't hesitate, and leaped off the bus at the next stop. The last thing he needed was for someone to call the police on him. What would he tell them?

Only after he alighted from the bus did he notice its number, but it meant nothing to him. He had no idea where he was, but a quick look around indicated that he was in Jewish territory. Most of the men – and even women – were clad in black and white, and most of the men wore hats, which amused him.

He began walking, planning to try to locate the main street. The first grocery store he passed reignited his hope, and he approached the proprietor politely. "I've worked for several months in a grocery store, and I'm looking for work. Do you need any help?"

The owner shook his head.

"I have lots of experience. I clean, I organize, I fix things. I don't need a lot of money, just a job."

"No," the owner repeated firmly. "Please leave."

Sighing, Jamil continued on his way, walking aimlessly and trying his luck in several stores, but receiving the same reaction each time. At one point he stopped short and looked around; he had the strange feeling of being watched. Was he being followed? Who had it in for him?

He decided to play a game, walking a few feet and then turning around without warning, pretending to be looking into store fronts while scanning his surroundings. Finally, he spied them. Two men with Arab features were walking about fifty feet behind him, and Jamil was almost certain that they had been on the bus with him earlier. He quickened his pace and then slowed, keeping watch on them as best he could. He was right; they were clearly tailing him – now what?

It was clear that it wouldn't take them long to catch up with him, and then it would be two against one in an unfamiliar city where he didn't know a soul. Jamil didn't stand a chance.

His heart pounded wildly, and he wondered what they wanted from him. What did they stand to gain from his death? Had his parents sent them? What had he done to incite their wrath?

Suddenly, he saw them break into a run. The encounter would be cruel and bloody and its conclusion was almost foregone. Jamil turned and ran across the street, and then noticed a car stopped at the curb, the passenger door open. Taking a risk, he took a flying leap inside and slammed the door shut behind him.

The driver, sitting next to him, was rifling through a pile of papers. Without glancing up, he said, in Hebrew, "What took so long? It's late already." With that, he floored the accelerator, and they shot off.

Jamil glanced into the side mirror at the road behind them, watching with satisfaction as the two men left behind him stared daggers at the receding car, waving furious fists at him. His heart was still pounding from his near miss, but he forced himself to breathe slowly and deeply in order to calm down.

"What did you buy in the end?" the driver suddenly asked. Jamil didn't reply, and his heart suddenly lurched. Now what? The driver, as he had feared, turned momentarily to him, and his eyes widened in shock and terror. Slamming on the brakes, he screeched to a stop.

"Who are you? What are you doing in here? Get out! GET OUT OF MY CAR!" The driver leaped out of the vehicle, clearly presuming Jamil to be a terrorist. The young Arab grabbed the opportunity to beat a hasty retreat.

It was then that Jamil realized two interesting things.

The first was that he had quick thinking skills, and that he could get by in life. So far, he had managed to escape from two villains, most probably assassins, as well as find himself a job and arouse the compassion of others.

The second thing he realized was that someone out there wanted to see him dead. The wheels in Jamil's mind turned rapidly as he tried to make sense out of the puzzle, but to no avail. All his life he had been despised as a worthless human being, and now, virtually overnight, he was so significant that people had been hired to get rid of him. Why?

Why indeed? Jamil was a young, homeless Arab with just a few thousand shekels to his name. Who would mourn his passing? And yet, someone wanted him dead…

His cell phone rang, and Mendy rolled his eyes and shut it off.

Yehuda Berman lit up a cigarette. "Who was that?"

"My father," Mendy answered obediently. He had left *yeshivah* because he had felt he needed a break from life, but he was slowly discovering that he had bound himself to Berman. The man demanded regular reports about what seemed like every little detail of his life, and Mendy was beginning to feel stifled, especially as Berman supplied his food and the roof over his head.

"Why don't you pick up the phone? Answer them!" the latter ordered.

"Why? What should I tell them? That I'm in Haifa? Will that make them feel better?"

Berman blew out a plume of smoke and grinned. "Well, for one, you don't want them reporting you missing. Imagine what kind of mess *that* would make. I advise you to maintain a connection with them, but keep it low-key."

"Meaning?"

"Call them." Yehuda stubbed out the cigarette and gazed calmly at Mendy. "Call them, and let them know you're okay, but make it clear that you're starting a new life. Ask them how they're doing. You can even tell them that you'll probably pop in for an occasional Shabbos."

"Are you serious?" Mendy stared at Yehuda, trying to figure him out. "Why should I want to go back for Shabbos, at this point?"

"Oh, just for a visit, you know," Berman said casually. "If you object so strongly, then of course you don't have to go, but it will make them feel better just to hear it. Later, you'll figure out some excuse why it won't happen. What's with you, Mendy? Where's your head?"

Mendy didn't reply. Sometimes, when Yehuda was away, he reflected that the man seemed to have some kind of special power over him, a force that Mendy wasn't sure how to overcome. Not quite knowing why, he found himself punching in the familiar number, and his father answered on the first ring.

"*MENDY!*" Shimon shouted. "Where are you?"

"Up north. I'm doing good. Don't worry about me," he said with remarkable calm.

"*Don't worry?* Mendy, have you lost your mind? Don't tell when to worry or not! Tell me exactly where you are, and I'm coming to get you right now!"

Yehuda was listening to the exchange with narrowed eyes. "Tell him that you're an independent adult," he ordered.

"Who's telling you what to tell me?" Shimon sounded on the verge of having a heart attack. "Wake up, Mendy! Do you know who this Yehuda really is? His real name is I—"

Yehuda grabbed the phone out of Mendy's hand and shut it off.

"Hey!" Mendy cried.

"He's got to stop dictating your life," Yehuda said harshly. "You're responsible for yourself now. Enough is enough. If that's how he's going to behave, then it's time to break off contact."

"He'll cut off my cell plan."

"That's your concern?" Yehuda sneered. "I'll get you a new one. Unlimited. Listen, you're taking a major step in life. You need the freedom to choose."

Mendy was silent.

"Well, for that, I'd like to know your real name," he ventured bravely.

Yehuda Berman stared at him long and hard. He was tempted to deny it, but then said without blinking an eye, "Ilan."

"Why didn't you tell me before?"

"Because we'd never have become friends if I had," he replied simply.

Mendy thought about that. "And why was it important for us to become friends?"

Yehuda, or Ilan, closed his eyes momentarily. "It's a long story, Mendy. Very, very long. But we definitely wanted you."

"Wanted me?"

"Yes. You." Ilan smiled again, but this time, Mendy felt no comfort in the smile. Suddenly, there was nothing he wanted more than to escape back to *yeshivah*, open his *Gemara*, and forget this chilling episode. Nonetheless, he subdued his feelings, telling himself that it was important for him know why they wanted him. Specifically him.

"Would you like to tell me why?"

"Do you regret your decision?"

"No, but it does sound suspicious. Why do you want me?"

"Because of your past. Because of your future."

"Explain yourself," Mendy demanded, his eyes flitting in confusion. "What's interesting about my past?"

"A lot, Mendy. Much more than you could ever imagine."

"Will you just quit dodging my questions? Answer me already!"

Instead of answering, Ilan laughed, and it was then that Mendy suddenly noticed the transformation in his friend. When they had first met, Yehuda had come across as a typical *kollel yungerman*. They had begun to learn together after a chance encounter in shul, and it was then that Yehuda had revealed his secret: As a child, he had been diagnosed as dyslexic, and he had always struggled to make progress in learning, without much success. Now he was asking Mendy if he would be willing to help him, and good-natured Mendy was only too willing to oblige.

At first their learning sessions focused solely on the *Gemara*, but gradually, their conversation had begun to drift to other matters, and the *yungerman* who had initially appeared so timid and gentle now revealed himself as a charismatic leader with strong opinions on almost every topic. Mendy soon fell captive to his fiery words and idealism and drank up every word with enthusiasm. Gradually, they began meeting outside the *beis medrash*, wandering together through local parks and strolling through the neighborhood streets. Later on, Berman introduced Mendy to some of his friends, and Mendy started to wonder how it was that a married man spent so many hours out of the house – until he eventually realized that Yehuda was not married, after all – but by then, he was too caught up in events to question his initial perception.

Now, Mendy took a good look at his erstwhile *chavrusa* and noted each detail separately. The black hat was gone, as was the long jacket. The *tzitzis* were no longer visible – if he was wearing them at all – and the white shirt had been replaced by a colored one. Finally, the plain black pants had morphed into jeans – how was it that only now he was noticing?

Yehuda still wore a *yarmulke*, but perhaps that was only because to appear bare-headed would be to cross over a red line that would have set the warning bells ringing so loudly that even Mendy, entranced as he was with Berman, would have had to sit up and take notice.

Now, however, even Yehuda-Ilan's smile was strange, and Mendy began to fear him, while simultaneously feeling completely drawn to him and dependent upon him.

Did Ilan notice? Was that what he actually wanted?

"Look," Ilan began, still smiling, "I wasn't born Yehuda Berman, but at some point I decided to change my name, which is perfectly legal, after all. But let me tell you something else: Your name wasn't always Mendy, either."

"Will you quit playing stupid games with me?" Mendy spat out dismissively. "Just do me a favor, okay, and stick to the truth from now on."

"Oh, Mendy – I tell you only the truth," Ilan smirked. "Would you like me to prove it?"

A shiver ran down Mendy's spine. "You can't prove something as ridiculous as that," he countered, but his tone was uncertain.

"Yes, I can," Ilan replied calmly, keeping his gaze fixed on the boy. "Why else would I bring you here? I think you're mature enough to know the truth, Mendy."

"What truth?"

"You know your ID number by heart?"

"Of course."

"Write it down." Ilan handed him a blank sheet of paper and pen.

Mendy obliged, slamming the paper down on the table when he had finished. Ilan took the paper, without even glancing at it, and then withdrew an old identity card from his pocket and held it open for Mendy, covering the name with his hand. "Okay. Tell me who it looks like."

Mendy gazed at the image of a bare-headed man, clean-shaven, staring at him with serious dark eyes and light-brown hair combed neatly back.

"Recognize him?"

Mendy squinted at the photo. "I don't know... He reminds me of... somebody, but I can't put my finger on it. Hey! He looks just like..." he stopped short. "No, it can't be. Give me a minute."

"There's nothing to wait for. When you see the name, everything will become crystal-clear. Look a little closer, and you'll see it for yourself."

"He's so familiar..." Mendy fidgeted uncomfortably. "The eyes are... Wait a minute. Are you trying to say that this is... my father?"

Ilan leaned back in his seat, stretching out his legs comfortably. "Nice work, Mendy. You figured that out pretty quick, I must say. Today, your dad has a gray beard, but the eyes don't change." With that, he tossed the card on the table. "Your father's name wasn't always Shimon, nor was your mother's name always Shulamis. Your name wasn't always Mendy, either. The name-changing process that your family underwent was really quite simple, as was mine. If you'd like to know your real name, all you've got to do is look at the card."

Mendy picked up the card with trembling hands, gazing again into his father's eyes. It was true – only the eyes were the same, and somehow they seemed to be looking at him, pleading with him to return.

Then, he glanced at the name. Yotam Brand. Married. His mother's name wasn't Shulamis or Shuli, but Sheila.

His eyes flitted automatically to the paper insert on the opposite side, where the children were listed. Only one name appeared there, and the identity number listed underneath it matched his own. Gil. That was his name.

Nice to meet you, Gil...

Mendy burst out in raucous laughter and tossed the card across the table. "Cute, Ilan. Very cute. But don't expect me to believe you. If you want me to believe that you changed your name, no problem. But trying to convince me that my parents were once *frei* is ridiculous! You're simply a liar."

"That's what you think?" Ilan didn't react to the insult. "Haven't you ever heard of *baalei teshuvah*? What – someone who's *frei* can't become religious?"

"If my parents were *baalei teshuvah*, then everyone would know. There are some things that you can't cover up, and in the religious community, people would certainly know such a thing."

"True, but to their good fortune – if you can call it that – both sets of grandparents died young, and they were both only children. Which is why you've never met up with any *frei* relatives who would have aroused your suspicions."

Mendy froze, and he rose slowly to his feet and turned his back on Ilan, walking unsteadily to the window and gazing out into the darkness of night. Was this really happening to him? Until now, he had been sure that he was in control, making his own decisions, running his own life.

Whose life? Gil's, or Mendy's? The thought terrified him, and he swiveled around suddenly and fixed his gaze on Ilan.

"Yehuda, or Ilan, or whatever your name is, why are you telling me all this? What's the point? What do you want from my life?"

Ilan saw the fear in his eyes, and decided to pull out his sympathy card. "Mendy, Gil, however you want to call yourself, you don't have to be here. You're free to come and go as you please. But just remember this: I was a good friend of your dad's back in those days. He was a great guy. That's why I wanted to save his eldest son, who just so happens to be you."

It didn't take Mendy long to decide. "I need some money. I'm going home. Now," he announced.

"Money?" Ilan was smiling again. Now that he had blown his cover, he had finally removed his *yarmulke*, and Mendy found himself facing a secular, completely unfamiliar man. "You don't need money, Gil, I'll drive you home."

Mendy's eyes flashed in fury. "Don't you dare call me Gil! Certainly not until I tell you that you can." Suddenly, he felt his confidence return. He would find his way out of his mess, somehow.

"No problem, Gil, Mendy. Whatever you want. I'll give you a lift home, no problem."

"Why are you so determined to help me?"

"I told you. I was good friends with your dad."

"He didn't recognize you that time he gave you a ride," Mendy pointed out.

"Of course not. And you didn't recognize me either, the first time you saw me without *peyos* and a beard," Ilan reminded him. "Mendy, don't forget, this was *decades* ago. We were young, and time makes its mark.

"Anyway," he continued, "what does all that matter, if you're not planning on hanging around with me any longer? Get your stuff together, and let's go."

Mendy hesitated, but when he remembered that he didn't have a single shekel in his wallet, he relented. "All right. Drive me. But if I decide to stay at home, you don't come knocking at the door. Get it?"

"Got it," Ilan laughed again, clearly unconcerned at the possibility of this scenario. "But don't forget, I'm friends with your dad. I only want what's best for you."

Mendy ignored him, anxious to set out for home. Five minutes later, they were settled in Ilan's red Fiat. Ilan drove quickly, stopping only for red lights until he reached the highway. From there, it was a silent ride until five minutes away from Bnei Brak, when Mendy began issuing directions.

"I know the way," Ilan silenced him, and then drove straight to Mendy's house, parking right beneath the building. Mendy glanced at the clock; it was already close to midnight.

"I'm waiting for you, Mendy," Ilan said confidently. "But if you want me to leave, let me know. Okay?'

"Okay."

Mendy leaped out of the car, deliberately not bothering to thank the man for the ride, and then raced up the steps to his second-story apartment. He knew that his younger siblings would be asleep by now, and that his parents were usually still awake at this hour.

Shimon and Shuli were sitting in the kitchen, drinking coffee, when the door opened suddenly.

"Who's there?" Shuli cried in alarm.

"Me."

"Mendy!" his parents cried in unison, jumping out of their seats to greet their son. Shimon reached the foyer first, with a tearful Shuli close behind.

"You're back!" Shimon exclaimed in relief, and Mendy couldn't bring himself to look his father in the eye.

"Yes, but not permanently. I came to ask you something. Something I can only ask you in person."

Shimon stared at his son, suddenly sensing the tension in the air.

"Are either of you familiar with…" he wasn't even sure how to express it, until he simply dropped the bombshell, "…a couple named Yotam and Sheila?"

Shuli gasped and Shimon paled, and they exchanged a look of horror, feeling as if the earth had opened up beneath them. Shimon took a step closer to his son. "Come inside, Mendy. You don't have to stand in the doorway." Shuli disappeared into the kitchen, from where they could hear her weeping.

Mendy remained standing where he was. "So you do know them." He couldn't believe how calm he sounded. "So I guess you know a kid named Gil, too."

"Who spoke to you?" Shimon's voice was hoarse, and he cleared his throat as he tried to calm the pounding of his heart. "Who told you?"

"A friend of yours. Someone who knows you from back then. You've got wonderful friends, Father," Mendy said, his voice cold and deliberate.

"They don't give a hoot about me. Don't be ridiculous, Mendy. Who told you? Why? What else do you know?"

"What – that's not enough?" Mendy countered in disbelief.

Shimon's eyes flickered in manifest fear.

"Don't answer me with a question, Mendy."

"Gil."

Shimon cried out, "Mendy, when we were *chozer b'teshuvah*, we gave you a new name, Mendel, after the *tzaddik*—"

"I don't care," Mendy cut in. "It's too late to start with the truth now, at this point in life. But at least I know that there are *some* people I can trust, like my friends, or rather, like yours, Father, who want to help both of us."

"And who are these wonderful friends, may I ask, and how exactly do they intend to help?" Shimon asked, as he struggled to regain his composure.

Mendy laughed loudly, but there was no humor in his eyes. "There's no need for me to reveal all my secrets at once."

Shimon drew closer to his son. "Mendy… I want you to listen to me, and to tell you something important. My old 'friends' aren't allowed to make contact with me anymore. Not because of any reason you might be imagining, but because of something else, something completely unrelated. You have to trust me on this one."

"I do?"

"Yes – you do," Shimon pleaded. "Please, Mendy. Tell me who's presenting himself as my friend, so I can prove to you that he's lying."

Mendy glowered at him. "Yehuda Berman, for instance. Except his name is really Ilan. Remember him?"

"Berman, I remember, unfortunately. But I never heard of any Ilan."

"That's surprising, considering that he claims to know *you* very well. In fact, he was able to tell me all about you."

Just then, Shuli emerged from the kitchen, placing a gentle hand on her son's arm. "Mendy, who told you about Tatty, about us? Who?"

"What are you so upset about? That I discovered the skeleton in the closet? What's the big deal that you're *baalei teshuvah*? What are you so ashamed of?"

"We're not ashamed of anything, Mendy, and you're not answering my question." Shuli was no longer crying, and she seemed calmer than before, but Shimon looked terrible – Mendy noticed that he was literally trembling.

"This Ilan is not my friend!" he suddenly burst out. "How on earth could he be? He's years younger than me! And who exactly is he, in any case? Ilan what? Doesn't that interest you, Mendy? Why don't you care what type of company you're keeping?"

Mendy's eyes sparked in fury. "I'm going now," he said coldly. "It was enough to hear the truth. I'm more afraid of people who hid the truth of my life, of my *name*, my entire identity, than I am of someone who was willing to share the truth."

Shimon swallowed visibly as he watched his son spin around and exit the apartment.

"Mendy!" Shuli ran after him. "Mendy, wait! Don't go yet."

"The name is Gil," he called over his shoulder, not waiting to see their reaction. Hearing footsteps pursuing him down the stairs, he quickened his pace until he reached Ilan's car, when he flung open the door and catapulted in.

"Drive!" he ordered Ilan frantically.

"What's the hurry?"

"Just start driving! Now!"

At that moment, Shimon emerged from the building and cast a long, hard look at Ilan. "Mendy!" he cried. "I promise you! I don't know him. I never met him! You need to be careful! I need to tell you something important! I'm—"

But the red car zoomed out of the parking space and made an immediate left. Sitting beside a smiling Ilan, Mendy tried to collect himself.

"They contradicted themselves the whole time, and with a bunch of pathetic excuses. Now they're threatening me that—"

"They're still lying," Ilan cut him off. "Your father knows me well. We were good friends." For a second, he looked nervous. "Back home?" He purposely called the dingy apartment they had been staying in "home," another ploy designed to engender a feeling of dependence and belonging in his young disciple.

"Back home," Mendy agreed. Staring out the window into the dark night, Mendy knew that he was embarking on a new course in life. For a second, his father's terrified eyes appeared before him, and a feeling of uncertainty flashed through his mind. But then, he recalled the lie he had lived throughout his life and he smiled bitterly.

"Ilan, thanks for telling me the truth. I owe you one, friend. It's time I opened a fresh page in life."

Ilan laughed and echoed his words. "A fresh page. That's the way to go."

"It's them, Shimon. It's got to be them! You have to contact the department!" Shuli repeated over and over, pacing the house like a caged lion.

Shimon was still trembling. "I never thought I'd have to contact them again. I thought it was all behind us. But obviously, I was too naïve. But why would they do it?"

Shuli was silent. "I'm scared that—"

"Don't say it!"

But her voice grew louder. "Shimon, our son is in their hands. How could it be? Are they really so smart?"

"No. They're not. But I admit I can't figure out how that 'Ilan' got the information."

"Maybe we were underestimating them," Shuli insisted. "And Mendy's *there,* now! *Ribbono shel Olam*, Mendy's with them! We have to save him! Shimon, there's no time to waste! Call the department and tell them what's going on! This is not just a threat to us, but to all the kids. Our whole family!"

"I know."

Shimon's eyes clouded. "Hashem is my witness that I would never go back there if not for this story with Mendy. I just hope that Mendy isn't already in their hands. That he still has free choice. And I hope that this isn't some cruel form of revenge by—" A sharp pain suddenly clenched at his heart and sliced across to his left shoulder, cutting him off mid-sentence.

He collapsed to the ground to the sound of Shuli's hysterical shrieking.

10

Jamil spent that night sleeping on a bench in one of the neighborhood parks, terrified of shutting his eyes for more than a moment and yet so tired that eventually he dozed off. The next thing he knew, it was just after dawn, and he got up and stretched his aching limbs. The next project was to find something to drink; Jamil didn't dare to waste another shekel unless it was absolutely vital, and so he traipsed around from one park to the next until he found a water fountain.

The water quenched his thirst, but his real predicament was so much more complex. He was in deep trouble, and he had no idea where to turn. His first priority was to find out who was after him, and why; his second, almost as urgent, was to locate his family and discover the reason why they had abandoned him in a strange country and then disappeared themselves. That the two mysteries were intertwined he was convinced – but who would be the one to solve them? Suddenly he realized: Jabbar. It was time to pay the man another visit.

In the village, Jabbar was known as Abu al-Banat, literally, "father of the girls." He had nine daughters, but not even a single son for solace. It was a sore point for the man, and woe to anyone who dared mock him for it! Jabbar was known for his sharp tongue, and still sharper knife.

Unlike the other villagers, whose sons helped them out both financially and with their own physical labor, Jabbar had no one to help him and was always in need of extra manpower. He was poor, barely eking out a living, which meant that he couldn't just get up and travel away to some foreign country to escape whatever menace seemed to have frightened Jamil's own family away. No, Jabbar would have to stay put where he was, in the village, and he would also have to tell Jamil everything he knew.

He hitchhiked his way back to the village, no easy feat for an Arab youth, but Jamil was patient and he eventually reached his destination. On the way, he purchased a wide-brimmed sunhat and large sunglasses that made him appear ridiculous, but the main thing was that they concealed his features – and his purchase cost him a mere fifteen shekels.

He entered the village warily, wondering if his erstwhile neighbors would recognize him, but all that greeted him was the familiar barking of dogs. It was hot, and there was no one outside at that midday hour. Jamil knocked importantly on Jabbar's door. One of his daughters opened, welcomed him graciously, and asked him to wait while she called her father. She clearly didn't recognize him, which was a tremendous relief.

A few minutes later, Jabbar appeared.

"Who are you?" Jabbar peered at him suspiciously, deliberately omitting the traditional Arab welcome.

"Don't raise your voice," Jamil ordered, stepping inside and closing the door behind him.

Beads of perspiration appeared on Jabbar's forehead. "Who are you?" he cried. "Speak, or I shall summon the entire village!"

Jamil took off his sunglasses, and suddenly realized that his recently-grown beard gave him a wild, unkempt look. To allay Jabbar's fears, he also took off the hat. "It's just me, Jamil."

The expressions that flitted across Jabbar's face made him resemble a frightened chameleon changing its colors – first shock, then something that resembled panic, and finally, sheer terror.

"Why are you here? Why did you come? For revenge?" he stammered, retreating in fear.

A thousand thoughts spun wildly in Jamil's mind, and then he realized he had two options. The first was to get down on his knees and beg Jabbar to reveal everything he knew, perhaps even paying him handsomely for his information. The second was to squeeze the information out of him via intimidation – and, as the man was clearly already terrified, perhaps that wouldn't be so difficult. Jamil resolved to give it a try.

"They told me, and I decided to come here. To you."

"Why didn't you go to your brothers?"

What now? What should I answer him?

"They're not in the country," he replied bravely, hoping it would satisfy the older man.

"They're not in the country? You mean, you found your real family? The *Yahud* told you everything?"

Jamil felt dizzy. *The Yahud? Jabbar was talking about the Jews?* He tried desperately to make sense of the disjointed sentences, and all that rose to mind was that… he'd been born to a Jewish family.

"Jabbar, I want to know exactly how I ended up in this village, how I landed up with this family, and why they suddenly abandoned me and fled. That's all I ask."

"Yes. Even the *Yahud* don't know that," Jabbar agreed, but his eyes flashed with panic. "Is there someone outside waiting for me? Who sent you?"

"Nobody. I'm here on my own," Jamil replied with false equanimity. He took a deep breath. "Okay, Jabbar, I'm leaving now, but if you don't reveal my true identity before I go, then I'll be back. And the next time, I won't come in peace."

"How should I know who your family is?" Jabbar countered desperately. "You're a Jew, that's all I know. Go to the *Yahud* police and ask them! I've got nothing to do with this. I'm just a good neighbor, an old friend of your father. But they were smart to run away from you. They knew that you'd have your revenge on judgment day. I'm the only fool still stuck here."

Jamil put his sunglasses back on. "Don't tell anyone I was here," he ordered fiercely.

"As if I'd dare! If I make a peep, they'll kill me!" Jabbar was literally trembling in fear. "Don't come back here, Jamil. Listen to me! It's for your own good. Make a new life for yourself. You're a Jew. Enjoy our beautiful country. We're just second-class citizens here. You took our Palestine from us."

You're a Jew. If Jamil had been holding a gun in his hand at that moment, he would have emptied the barrel into Jabbar's skull. He despised the Jews, and he had been spoon-fed that hatred for as long as he could remember. How dare Jabbar call him a Jew!

Jamil spat in disgust and then turned on his heels and left Jabbar's home, slamming the door behind him. He strode down the dusty street leading out of the village, resisting the urge to turn around and check that nobody was following him, but once back on the highway, he realized he was shaking in fear. Now what? He no longer had a home!

With no other option presenting itself to him, he decided to head back to that strange city, Bnei Brak, not because he had enjoyed the night spent on a park bench, but rather in hope of finding a job on one of its main streets. Surely at least one storekeeper of the hundreds there would hire him?

To his good fortune, one of the first cars to pass him slowed down and then stopped completely when he saw who was waiting for a ride. The driver was an Arab, who told him that he was on his way to Lod and was glad to have some company on the long journey. He dropped him off at the Givat Shmuel interchange along with precise directions to Bnei Brak.

Jamil was worn out by then, certainly too tired to try and remember how to get back to "his" bench. Passing a falafel stand, he bought himself supper, along with a drink, and then entered the first park he found and sat down on a bench in a secluded area.

Now that his body was at rest, his mind started to whir and his thoughts gave him no rest. Was he really a *Yahud*? Were his real parents Jewish? Surely it was just a figment of Jabbar's overactive imagination – it was simply too bizarre to be true. Or was it? The more he thought about it, the more sense it made.

Arabs were after him, their expressions boding evil. Jabbar was terrified of him, and what other explanation could there be for that? And, what about the *Yahud* themselves? Did they know?

As he lay there, trying to make himself comfortable on the splintering wooden slats of the bench, he resolved to go straight to the nearest police station the very next morning, and tell them his story. The more he thought about it, the more the notion of being Jewish appealed to him. If he was a *Yahud*, then the whole country was open to him! He could abandon the filth of the village and settle in an affluent Israeli city, a tantalizing prospect. Hatred of the Zionist oppressors had been instilled in him since his early youth, but now that he had been deserted by his very own family, the notion of joining the enemy was suddenly appealing. The only question was… would they accept him?

Yoav's laughter speckled his conversation and, at first, his brother Yochai laughed too.

"It would have never happened to you guys at the GSS," he boasted.

Yoav was a seasoned police officer in the Dan region, and although life was rarely dull at the precinct, this story was so entertaining that he called up his brother, a GSS agent, to share it with him.

"I was sitting at my desk, with nothing much to do, when this Arab kid wandered in and told me, without any introduction,

'I'm one of yours. I'm not really an Arab.' I asked the kid what he meant, and he said, and I quote, 'My family adopted me. I'm a *Yahud*. They never told me the truth, but now I want to find my *Yahud* family.' Did you ever hear of such a thing? This kid just decided that he's adopted, with absolutely no proof to offer of the fact, and now he turns up, straight from one of the poorest villages in the Galilee, and he plans to go off on a crazy search after a Jewish family." Yoav chuckled as he leaned back in his swivel chair.

"Anyway, some of the *chevra* decided to play him for what he's worth. I'm telling you, Yochai, that kid has some imagination! He claimed that there's a hit team out to kill him, because he's a *Yahud*, and now he wants us to take care of him, as well as help him locate his Jewish parents. Did you ever hear of anything so nuts?"

"Maybe, maybe not," Yochai replied seriously. "Who's on the case?"

"*On the case?*" Yoav guffawed. "Yochai, are you crazy? This kid is not 'all there.' Even so, we acted all official and took down his details before sending him home. Problem was, when we tried to get rid of him, he replied that he doesn't have a place to go to, and that we – the *Yahud* – are now his only family. In the end, we had to threaten him to get him to leave. Guy said that he could stay with us if he really wanted – something like fifteen years behind bars. That got him moving all right."

A strange silence filled the line, raising Yoav's concerns. "Yochai, you still there?"

"Who wrote the report?"

"Who? Benny, I think. Maybe it was Amichai. I'm not sure. Why?"

"Was this information relayed officially to the GSS?"

"No, of course not! A story made up by some crazy Arab? What on earth for?"

"Yoav, you're not thinking!" Yochai retorted sharply. "When was the last time you heard such a story? People don't just make up stuff for no good reason. What's wrong with you cops? A kid comes in telling you that he's searching for his Jewish family, and that Arabs are after him, and all you can do is laugh? Did you at least make some kind of investigation?"

This time, it was Yoav who was silent.

"Yochai, are you serious?" he finally blurted out.

"Of course I am! In fact, I'm going to call my supervisor right now. I have a feeling that this information will interest him greatly. And, I really hope – for your sake – that you didn't chase that kid away for good," he added gravely.

Yoav was startled by the turn in the conversation. "Yochai…"

The line went dead.

Yoav banged his fist down on his desk as he berated himself for not looking beyond the surface. Yochai was right. The story was too bizarre to be false. The kid had been deadly serious, making the scene even more comic than it would have been otherwise – but, he clearly believed what he was saying. Could it be true? And if it was, how would they locate that Arab kid now, with no contact information whatsoever? Were people really determined to harm him? Who would reach him first?

11

The hospital staff looked on in puzzlement at the ten men who had suddenly materialized in Mr. Brand's hospital room, resembling a team of bodyguards. Unlike the patient, who was clearly a *chareidi* Jew with graying beard and skullcap, these men were bareheaded and clean-shaven. They had come in response to Shimon's call reporting an emergency, and now they stood around his hospital bed and listened quietly to what he had to say.

Yochai spoke first. "What happened, Yotam?"

"They came. Nothing happened, except the fact that they came," Shimon replied, sweat appearing on his forehead. "And I saw him."

"Who?"

"A guy named Ilan. First, he presented himself as a *chareidi* named Yehuda Berman, but everything about him was a pack of lies. He developed some kind of strange relationship with my son, and once things had progressed with them, he told him about my past. And who knows about my past, apart from them?"

The revelation came as a terrific blow to Yochai. The answer to Yotam's question was supposed to be "no one."

Years earlier, Yotam had served in the elite Duvdevan unit, as one of the hand-picked team of *mistaravim*, those Secret Service employees who disguise themselves as Arabs and infiltrate the world of their enemies. For years he had transferred valuable intelligence from the Arab world to his Israeli handlers, but one day, it all came to an abrupt end, when an Arab he had been working with blew his cover. Yotam barely made it out of the village alive.

Later, he was decorated by the department for his contribution to Israel's security, and his superiors advised him to have his appearance altered via plastic surgery and leave the country, but Yotam had adamantly refused. Instead, he grew a beard to disguise his features and reentered civilian life. Soon after, he met and married Sheila, an American *olah*, and his beard led many to assume that he was religious, although at the time, neither of them could be described as anything more than traditional Jews. Nonetheless, among his new circle of friends Yotam counted several *chareidim*, and gradually, he was influenced by their words and way of life, which he and his young wife began to adopt.

Yotam's newfound interest in Judaism became the brunt of every joke in his new workplace. Prior to his change in world view, he had been vocal in his espousal of leftist political ideology and totally secular in his outlook. Nobody could quite figure out what was motivating him to restrict his life so drastically, and when Yotam and Sheila tired of the constant questioning and the lack of supportive surroundings, they made the decision to relocate.

Their change in abode was accompanied by a change in name. Yotam became Shimon, after the *Tanna* Rabi Shimon bar Yochai, and Sheila became Shulamis – Shuli. Their son, Gil, who had been born before the revolution in their lives, was renamed Mendy, after Reb Mendel, a *rosh yeshivah* who had been instrumental in drawing them close to their heritage.

None of Shimon's new friends or acquaintances were apprised of his past, and all revealing details were prudently erased from the records. No one knew where the Brands had lived previously, and certainly nobody dreamed that there was an additional motive to their relocation – that it was literally a life-saving move for them. Surely, they hoped, Bnei Brak was the last place malevolent Arabs would search for an ex-GSS agent.

Therefore, when Mendy returned home and revealed the truth that they had struggled to conceal for so many years, Shimon had been petrified. The only people with any interest in rocking the boat were those he feared the most: the Arabs he had betrayed. The Arabs who had been so sure that Shimon was one of them. As the GSS had predicted, they hadn't been sitting on their laurels all these years. It had taken them time, but finally, after twenty years, they had caught up with him.

"I'm taking this very seriously, Yotam."

"Shimon."

"Shimon," Yochai echoed softly. "It didn't come from us – I can guarantee that. Your story is known only to those of us standing here now – or so we thought. I thought we'd done well, but now I see we were overly confident. In any case, we have to take urgent steps."

"What are you trying to say?" Shimon asked tautly.

Yochai bit his lip. "Shimon, these guys are not as dumb as people think. It's even possible that they are tracking you, and that they know that we're here. So, we have to break off contact with you right now. This is the last time that we'll meet in the open. Shimon, you have to be careful. If need be, we'll help you disappear."

"I can't disappear!" Shimon cried. "I have a family, with three children! I'm not single with a dog and two cats! Don't you understand the life that I lead?"

Yochai stared penetratingly at Shimon.

"I'll repeat myself, Shimon. You've lost your sixth sense. In fact, I think it could be even worse than that. It could be that they knew where you were all along, and for some reason that we have to find out, it's only now that they are choosing to exploit that knowledge."

Shimon paled. "What makes you think that?"

"I can't say for sure. Maybe because now they can use your son against you. So, first we have to find Gil, and then—"

"Mendy," Shimon corrected him irritably. "He's called Mendy, not Gil."

"Mendy, whatever. We'll find him and keep an eye on him. This is very complicated. You know that as well as I do, don't you?"

Shimon didn't reply. He felt as if his throat was being clenched with iron fingers. Mendy was in their hands… Yochai seemed to presume that it was Hamas, but the department was still investigating other options. To Shimon, it didn't matter. In his experience, an Arab was an Arab, *pere adam*, a beast in human form without compassion or decency. They had to find Mendy quickly, or else…

Ilan leaned back comfortably on the sofa and nodded in satisfaction.

"I didn't do it for money, and you know that," he commented to the dark-skinned man who stood facing him with a thin-lipped smile. "Only for the organization. A *chareidi* kid standing up for Arab rights in Israel – just think of the publicity we're going to get!"

The Israeli Arab's smile became broader. "You did a fine job and deserve to be paid. Enjoy it, *ya-habibi*!" *

Ilan frowned. "I already told you. I didn't do it for the money. It's an ideal that I'll fight for, one that I've been promoting for years. After all, we're all human beings, aren't we? Why should one human being rule over another? The Zionists stole this land from its rightful owners, and we have to right that wrong!"

"Yeah, yeah, we know your feelings on the matter already." The Arab yawned. "All right, Ilan, take your money and go." The Arab was obviously impatient, glancing frequently at his watch.

"I'm waiting for Mendy, Gil, or whatever that poor kid wants to call himself," Ilan replied.

* My dear one/friend

"I wouldn't advise you to wait here."

"Why not? He went out with Mahmoud to help him register. He'll be back soon."

"He won't be back, Ilan," the Arab said softly.

"What?"

The Arab smiled chillingly. "Forget about the kid, Ilan. Your contribution to the organization was outstanding, but the organization doesn't really exist."

Ilan froze. "Wh-what are you saying?" he stammered.

"Exactly what you just heard. I'm glad you believe that the land belongs equally to us, and that we have rights, but this organization was developed as a daughter organization of a Fedayeen organization. Get it?"

Ilan stumbled to his feet in shock. In his mind, "Fedayeen" and "terror" were virtually synonyms, and for good reason. He stared in horror at the tall Arab facing him, and his face paled. "You're not serious. Tell me you're not serious."

"Oh, but I am, Ilan," the Arab drawled.

"Then… what are you saying?"

The Arab smiled again, displaying his white teeth – suddenly, he reminded Ilan of a wolf. "All I'm telling you is the truth, my dear Ilan. You worked for us, and we appreciate your assistance. But from now on, people with whom you are unacquainted are involved in Mendy-Gil's case. Don't be concerned, he's in good hands. He's in *our* hands. We're saying thank you and paying you handsomely for your efforts. If you would like to help us out again in the future, we'll be happy to work with you. And that's one reason why we pay."

"I don't want your money."

"The money isn't for your help; it's to make sure you shut up and stay shut up. You can choose to talk, of course, but I wouldn't recommend it. The more you talk, the deeper trouble you'll find yourself in. If we ever find out that you exposed any of us, then… then we can find you. Easily."

Ilan felt cold sweat running down his back. Had he really been duped? He had been so sure he could distinguish between good Arabs and bad Arabs; between peaceful Arabs who only wanted to earn a living and coexist with their Israeli neighbors, and evil terrorists who caused untold suffering to Jews and Arabs alike. He had been so sure – and so naïve…

"What's going on? Where's Mendy?" he cried with his final burst of courage. Mendy had been the prize, the symbol of his success in building a bridge between Arab and Jew. He had lured Mendy away from his family, his neighborhood, his culture… for what?

All his illusions were shattered in an instant. The Arab glared into his eyes.

"Do you want to live, Ilan?"

"Y-yes, of course," the young man stammered.

"Then shut your mouth, and stop asking questions. Get lost."

"And if they ask me?"

The Arab laughed a long, callous laugh. "Think long and hard before you reply. If we're caught, they'll come after you, too. Ilan, you're a rich kid from Herzliya. You don't need trouble in your life."

Jamil was hungry. He found himself hanging around garbage cans outside supermarkets and kiosks in search of a stray roll or half-eaten sandwich, and try as he might to maintain a respectable appearance – without which he would never find a job – it was swiftly becoming a losing battle.

More than once, he had been forced to change location when people treated him to suspicious stares. His visit to the police station had been a total waste of time – nobody had taken him seriously, despite his pleas. He couldn't go on like this much longer; he needed a solution, and fast.

It was evening and he stood outside a grocery store, waiting for the owner to toss out the stale loaves. From there, he would make his way to the bakery. As he lingered outside the store like a stray alley cat, he heard a voice calling to him in Hebrew. His language skills had improved dramatically in the past weeks, and he immediately turned to reply.

"Looking for something?" A man with a black beard approached him. Jamil placed him in his late twenties.

"No. I'm just waiting for them to throw out the old bread," Jamil replied shortly.

"What do you want to do with it?"

"Eat it."

"You don't want to sell it?"

"No. I'm hungry. I want to eat."

The man stared at him curiously. "I'll tell you the truth. I've seen you around lately, and there have been a number of break-ins in the area. I don't think you're the burglar, but..."

"I'm not a burglar, mister. I was thrown out of my village, and I'm just trying to stay alive," Jamil said plaintively.

"Oh." The man could think of nothing else to say.

"They threw me out, because I'm really a *Yahud* like you."

"What did you say?"

"I'm a Jew. Like you. But none of the Jews believe me."

By now, the man looked intrigued. "You're Jewish? Who told you that?"

"People in my village. I used to live in the Galilee. I went to the police, but they sent me away."

"Why?"

"Because I can't prove it."

"Why do you believe you're Jewish?" The stranger seemed genuinely interested, and Jamil decided that the time was ripe to share his story. "It's a long story, but I can make it quick."

He shared his story in brief, beginning with the torment he had endured in his village. He described the cruel treatment at the hands of his parents and siblings, and the way they discriminated between him and his brothers – something he had never understood until the revelation of his Jewish origins. Finally, he related how his father had accompanied him to America, only to abandon him there like a worn-out piece of furniture, and certainly never expecting that he would succeed in returning.

"So, all this leads you to believe you're really Jewish?" the man asked. "Just because this neighbor of yours said so? And yet, on the other hand... why would he make it up? I guess he did have some reason for believing that."

"That's what I told the police. I went there and told them, but they just laughed at me."

The bearded young man sighed. "Listen, it's an interesting story. Let's meet tomorrow, same time, same place."

"Tomorrow?" Jamil was visibly disappointed, having hoped that his new acquaintance would welcome him into his home, and better yet, offer him a hot meal. As if reading his thoughts, the man fished in his pockets and extracted a twenty-shekel bill.

"Here, take this, and buy yourself something to eat." They parted, and the young Jew headed home deep in thought. Jamil, for his part, allowed himself to hope that this would be his last night on a park bench.

Shimon was released from the hospital two days later. Shuli took the day off work to take him home, and more importantly, to interrogate him.

"What did Yochai say?"

"Don't mention his name in the house!" Shimon retorted sharply. "It's bad enough that we've been exposed."

"But what did he have to say?" Shuli persisted. "The kids won't be home until later, and I want to know what's going on. It's only right, Shimon." Her husband fell silent. He didn't feel he had the energy to reply, but Shuli wasn't feeling sympathetic. Her thoughts were only with Mendy, and she was desperate for information.

"I can't understand him!" she cried suddenly. "We gave him everything! We love him so much! And look at him now! He doesn't even call!"

"Maybe he can't call," he pointed out wearily.

"Why do you say that?" Shuli pounced on him in fear.

Shimon wasn't sure what would be harder for his wife to take: the thought that Mendy had voluntarily broke off contact; or the thought that he was being held against his will by a hostile party and was unable to call them.

"Shuli, please. I'm very weak," he tried to put her off. "We'll talk about it later, but suffice it to say that it's very, very complicated. What we need to do now is *daven*."

"But why isn't he calling? Who isn't letting him call?"

Just then, the phone rang, and Shuli leaped to answer.

"It's not him, Shuli. Don't get your hopes up," Shimon tried to calm his wife.

But Shuli didn't hear. "Mendy!" she wept. "Mendy, where are you? What are they doing to you? Why can't you call?"

To Shimon's astonishment, it really was Mendy, who answered slowly, "Of course I can call. Why did you think I couldn't?"

"Where are you?" Shuli asked in shock.

"Back in the world that you left behind."

"Mendy, where are you?"

"Why are you shouting, Mommy?" Mendy asked quietly. "Mommy?" he tasted the word, as if hoping that the conversation wouldn't end so quickly.

"Mendy, I want you to come home!" she sobbed.

"I'm calling to say that I won't be back. Don't look for me."

"What are you saying?"

"That this is goodbye."

On Shuli's end, Shimon gestured frantically at her to continue the conversation, while he whipped out his cell phone and dialed a number he only used in emergencies.

"What do you mean?" Shuli cried. "Why – what for? What happened to you? Who are you with?"

"I need to find myself in a new world, the world you turned your back on."

"Mendy, you don't even know our side of the story!" she cried.

"I heard enough. What else do I have to hear about Yotam and Sheila?" Mendy's tone was anguished. "Just know one thing: They're letting me call you, but from today, *I'm* the one deciding not to call. Is that clear?"

"I don't believe you, Mendy. You would never do that to us! Just tell me where you are! Tatty was hospitalized because of you. He had a heart attack!"

"It wasn't because of me! That's the life that he chose for himself, a life full of risks."

"How do you know all this?"

The coldness of his tone of voice caused her heart to skip a beat. "I know a lot of things now that I never knew in the past."

"From who?"

"It doesn't matter. I just know."

"Mendele, listen to me. You can't just break off contact like this. Please, come home, and we'll talk it out. Please come." Her plea was so innocent, filled with faith that he would give in and come home.

Mendy laughed, but his voice took on a menacing tone. "I'm not coming back, Mommy. Obviously, you didn't hear a word I just said."

"Mendy..."

"No – I've got to go now. Maybe I'll call again, but then again, maybe I won't."

"Mendy, do you need help?" she asked desperately.

"No. You do. You and the—"

The line went dead.

Shuli's face was gray, but Shimon didn't try to console her. "Yochai's men assumed that he'd call at some point, and they were on the line," he said tonelessly. "I hope they found him. I really, really hope so. I assume that they must have sent a squad there. We'll know the results within the hour."

With that, he took a *sefer Tehillim* and sank onto his bed. "Now, we *daven*," he said.

Shuli was speechless with shock. When she was finally able to speak, she croaked out, "The past has come back to haunt us."

"Not the past. Them. They captured Mendy, but I trust Yochai.

He's a *shaliach* from *Shamayim*. He's committed to the mission, and he won't rest until he brings Mendy home."

"Where are you meeting?"

"I have a check-up in the hospital in an hour. We'll meet there."

"I didn't know the hospital was a rendezvous point for—" she stopped short upon noticing her husband's glower.

"Go, and come back with good news," she sighed. She wanted to come along, but Shimon refused.

Shimon's five-minute check-up stretched to five hours. When he returned home, the house was lively with the boisterous chatter of the two younger children. A weary Shimon dragged himself into the house and sank onto the couch. Shuli followed him and shooed the children away, saying, "Tatty needs to rest now."

"What happened?" she demanded.

Shimon's voice sounded like a stranger's. "We have to get used to the new facts on the ground, Shuli." His words caught in his throat, and a tear escaped his eye. "Mendy isn't coming back. At least not in the near future."

13

The *Yahud* was waiting for him, as he had promised, but this time, he wasn't alone. Another man, dressed in similar garb – black and white, as the inhabitants of this town seemed to favor – had accompanied him. Jamil approached them warily.

The *Yahud* recognized him immediately and waved to him. Anxious that Jamil could panic and flee, especially after his experience in the police station, he quickly told him, "Don't be afraid. We're your friends, and we want to help you."

Jamil nodded and even mustered a smile; the other men returned the smile.

"First of all, my name is Meir," the young man tried to break the ice. "And this is my friend Chaim." They shook hands all around. It was a strange meeting, indeed.

The young Arab had intrigued Meir Landsman, a *kollel yungerman* and father of three, and he hadn't been able to stop thinking about his strange story since their first encounter.

Naomi, his wife, had rolled her eyes. "Do yourself a favor, Meir, and forget about him. He's just a dumb Arab who wants money and sympathy. Arabs can't tell the truth to save their lives."

Meir had disagreed. "Listen to me, Naomi. He was serious. I could tell."

"So he's hallucinating," Naomi said dismissively. It didn't even occur to her to believe anything this Arab said. Even when it came to her fellow Jews, she was chronically suspicious – it was simply her nature. Meir, on the other hand, was innately trusting and naïve, really her polar opposite. He saw only the good in others and ascribed to them only the purest of motives, even when presented with evidence to the contrary.

The expected first clash had come only several days after their *sheva brachos* ended. As Naomi unwrapped the decorative porcelain dish that they had received from Meir's great-aunt Zelda, the young *kallah* noted wryly that the old lady had simply wrapped an old dish of her own in wrapping paper and placed it in a bag from an expensive store in order to make it look like she had bought them a nice gift.

Meir was horrified by the suggestion, and he couldn't fathom why his wife would want to investigate the history of a porcelain dish given as a gift by a woman in her seventies. However, since his young wife insisted, they had headed to the exclusive housewares store whose name was emblazoned on the bag and asked to switch the gift.

"Sorry, miss, but we don't carry that kind of dish," the proprietor informed her primly, and Naomi celebrated her victory.

"See, Meir!" she said proudly, "didn't I tell you? It was just an old dish she didn't like!"

"Well, at least she went out of her way to wrap it," Meir replied, slightly upset that his rosy view of the world had become a little clouded. Naomi had found his naiveté amusing, but she had also realized at that point that it was best to be wary of her husband's good heart, or, to be precise, to take care that his "good eye" was not exploited by others. Meir, for his part, had resolved to make every effort to instil in his wife a basic trust of humanity – with little success, he sometimes admitted, although that didn't stop him from trying.

Now, hearing her husband's bizarre tale of an Arab with possible Jewish roots, Naomi's defenses sprang up. "Meir, trust me – all he wants is to get money out of you. Don't fall for it!" she pleaded.

"He didn't even ask for money," Meir protested. "All he wanted was something to eat. He was hanging around the garbage cans looking for food. And if his story's true," he returned to his main point, "then – what a *zechus*! To bring back a lost soul to his people – just imagine!"

Naomi frowned. "But even if he really does have Jewish ancestry – then so what? I mean, he's an Arab by upbringing, and they don't exactly teach their children to be nice and friendly to Jews, do they? I don't know… I don't like it. To be honest, it scares me."

"You know what? If you're scared, then I'll take a friend along with me. We'll take him to the police station – what could go wrong?"

"What could go wrong? Lots of things," Naomi insisted, sighing as she realized her husband was determined to do what he could to help this weird Arab kid he had come across. "If you do go, then I want you to call me every fifteen minutes to make sure you're okay."

"Every fifteen? Don't you think that's going a bit far?" Meir protested.

"Okay, so every half hour."

"Every half hour, more or less," Meir offered.

"Meir, please! I'm nervous about you! How will I know that he didn't stab you?!"

"All right, all right, so I'll call once an hour or so."

"Or so?" Naomi called after him, but Meir was already gone. On the next street, his friend was already waiting for him, intrigued by his story no less than he.

And now the two of them stood facing Jamil, who looked like a frightened mouse.

"Jamil, you say that you're a Jew, but the police don't believe you," Meir began softly. "So, I thought the best thing we could do to help you, is to accompany you to the police station and try to persuade them to rethink things, to at least open an investigation. What do you think?"

"They'll be mad. They warned me to stay away," the Arab youth said nervously.

"Okay, so this time, they'll have to deal with us too. We're with you," he smiled encouragingly at Jamil.

The three of them slipped into Chaim's car and headed to the police station. There, Chaim remained in the car, while Meir escorted Jamil inside and approached a bored-looking officer behind a desk.

"Hello, good evening. We would like to verify that this young man, Jamil, submitted a claim regarding his alleged Jewish origins. He comes from an Arab village—" Meir began.

The officer interrupted him mid-sentence. "Jamil, eh? You're the kid who came by a few days ago?"

"Yes."

The officer grinned. "Call Yoav!" he shouted over his shoulder, and then turned back to the youth. "We didn't know where to look for you! Someone here wants to speak to you. And who are you?" he turned scornful eyes upon Meir, who stood up straighter.

"I'm a friend of his – I convinced him to come back here. He claims he's Jewish, and I think it's vital to investigate the claim. There are major ramifications if—"

"Skip the ramifications. You're already imagining him becoming a *baal teshuvah*, right? I get it. Let's first verify that he really is a Jew, so we won't spoil the party."

Meir and Jamil sat down to wait, for what turned out to be over twenty minutes, which seemed interminable for Jamil who fidgeted constantly and at once point asked to go outside for some fresh air.

The officer barred his exit. "You're staying here, my friend."

"Why? I just want to go out for a minute."

"You're not going anywhere. We've been looking for you, and we need you here now."

Jamil grew hysterical. "I didn't do nothing wrong! I didn't steal. I didn't lie ever! I came here of my own free will, and I want to leave now!"

"Sit down! And the same goes for you, too," the officer added, nodding in Meir's direction. "You're staying here till I tell you otherwise."

Jamil trembled like a fish in a net, and he turned accusing eyes on Meir who motioned for him to be seated.

"Don't make them angry. It's not worth it. Let's wait a bit longer and see what they want from you," he whispered encouragingly, although he too was beginning to feel ill at ease. Suddenly, he remembered that he was supposed to have called his wife, who was no doubt frantic by now – over an hour had passed since he had left home. Indeed, his phone, on the "vibrate" setting as usual, displayed "seven missed calls" when he opened it. He had been so preoccupied with Jamil and his story that he hadn't even felt the phone in his pocket.

"Naomi?" he whispered, the moment she picked up the phone.

"Meir! Where are you? What's going on?"

"I'm still in the police station," he whispered back, aware that the officer posted at the door was listening in to every word.

"Still? And why are you whispering? When are you going to be home? It's been almost two hours already!"

Meir sighed. "I don't know when I'll be finished here. It might take a while."

"What might take a while? If they want to investigate, then fine. But you can come home already! This has nothing to do with you!"

Meir cringed. "I… I can't… whatever. I'll be home as soon as I can." And he ended the call abruptly, before Naomi could offer another protest.

Another half hour passed, during which Naomi called Meir back no less than four times, but all he would tell her was the same refrain over and over: "I'll be back as soon as I can," before ending the call, hoping that she would eventually tire of asking the same question.

Finally, just when Jamil thought he was going to go out of his mind from boredom, a tall, olive-skinned officer strode into the room. His nametag read "Yoav Stern."

"Jamil, nice to see you again," he approached the Arab youth directly. "And you are?" he turned to Meir.

"Meir Landsman. I met Jamil, and he told me that he's Jewish, and that when he came here alone, nobody would take him seriously. So I thought—"

"Wait here. I'd like to speak to Jamil privately for a minute first," Yoav interrupted him. He motioned for Jamil to follow him into a small cubicle. The latter followed obediently, turning around at the last second to shoot another accusing glare at Meir, who was no less frightened than he.

"Why are you saying that he won't be back?" By now, Shuli wasn't crying; she was angry. Furious, in fact, and her tone rose to unprecedented octaves.

Shimon felt his throat tighten. "Please, Shuli. You don't have to shout. The next thing we'll know, all the neighbors will be here. I'm telling you that he won't be back, and it's the truth."

"How can you know such a thing? Okay, so Mendy is confused right now, mixed up and afraid. But he'll calm down sooner or later! And then, he'll come back. We're his family! He can't just leave like that."

"We're not… Whatever. It's not that simple. You don't get it, Shuli." No, Shuli didn't understand, and Shimon pitied his wife deeply.

Shimon's voice cracked as he struggled to break the truth to his wife. "I know where he is, Shuli. But he's in a place from which he can never escape. What we need to do now is find that Yehuda Berman, that Ilan, or whoever he is. We need to figure out how they trapped Mendy, how he agreed to link up with them. We need to—"

"Shimon, where is he?" Shuli cried.

"I'll tell you, but only if you keep believing that somehow, he'll still come back to us," Shimon said suddenly, in a total reversal from his previous forbidding statement. "Don't lose hope. Hashem can always—"

"*Where is he?*" Shuli was at her wits' end.

"Do you promise to stay calm?"

"Not if you don't tell me the truth!" Shuli exploded. "Where is he, Shimon?"

Shimon lowered his head. "In Gaza. Mendy is in Gaza. They traced the call, and there was no doubt about it. So there won't be a rescue mission, for obvious reasons. If Mendy wants to leave, it's possible, even, that they'll let him. But if he wants to stay there, then there's absolutely nothing we can do about it."

14

Yoav opened the interrogation in a friendly tone of voice, doing his best to keep Jamil calm and amenable to answering questions. He needn't have worried so much – Jamil was only too eager to talk, now that he had a receptive audience. Yet suddenly, Yoav realized that he had no idea what he was supposed to be doing with the information.

"Okay, wait here," he said finally to Jamil. "I'll be right back." He left the room, not bothering to lock the door behind him, and headed straight to Guy's office to deliver his preliminary report straight to the chief.

"Guy, it's a strange story."

"All stories that make it here are strange." The chief was unimpressed, and he kept his eyes glued to his computer screen. "Talk."

"I need your attention, sir."

"Talk, Yoav." Guy deliberately continued staring at his screen.

"There's this Arab kid who claims to be Jewish."

"So? I remember the story."

"But that's just the beginning." Yoav found himself losing his tongue. He would have liked to treat the episode with the same indifference as Guy, but Yochai's harsh words had shaken him up. "Listen, Guy, maybe this is all some stupid hoax, but then again, maybe there really is something to it. The first time, the kid showed up alone, and we laughed him out of town, but this time, he came with a *chareidi* friend."

"Oh, Yoav, don't start up with *chareidim*!" Finally, Guy tore his eyes away from the screen. The last thing he needed was a *chareidi* protest outside the station.

"I didn't start up with anyone! All I said was that he came along with a *chareidi* friend. Anyway, I've been listening to his story for the past half hour, and I'm telling you, we could make a thriller out of it. This Arab says his family abandoned him in America – and he doesn't know a word of English – and that somehow, he made his own way back to his village, only to find that his family had disappeared into thin air. I told Eitan to check out the family, and he should have some answers for me pretty soon."

Guy still looked amused. "Yoav, don't be a fool. Most likely, after spending much too long on this, we'll find out that he's just a smart village kid who wants to live the good life on the Israeli side."

"But what if his story really is true?"

"That's a big 'if,' and why don't you just wait to see what Eitan comes up with? Let me know when you have some hard facts," Guy emphasized.

"And what do I do with the kid until then?"

"Leave him here."

"Under arrest?"

Guy shrugged. "Call it what you want."

"What about the *chareidi*?"

"Him you can release. There's no reason I can see to keep him here. And, by the way, if Eitan uncovers even a hint of a lie in the kid's story, we ship him right back to his village."

"Yes, sir."

Guy lifted his eyes again. "And Yoav?"

"Yes?"

"This doesn't suit you at all," he shook his head in displeasure at the officer, who shrugged helplessly. The chief was right, and he knew he wouldn't be doing this if not for his elder brother. But

Yoav had always idolized Yochai, and now he didn't dare ignore his words.

Eitan, the officer assigned to verify the facts, was hungry. He trekked down to the cafeteria, bought himself a sandwich and a coffee, and prepared to take what he was convinced was a well-deserved break. When his cell phone rang, he didn't hurry back to his desk either, preferring to spend another half hour chatting to his colleagues. When he noticed his boss enter the cafeteria, however, he beat a hasty escape and hightailed it back to his desk.

"Hey, Eitan. Any news?" Yoav called out to him.

"Soon," he replied vaguely.

"How soon?"

"As soon as I can. Take it easy, Yoav! What's your issue with this Jibril?"

"It's 'Jamil.' And I want to know what to do with him. And with his *chareidi* friend too. In the meantime, Guy authorized the friend's release. Do you know where he is?"

"Yeah – in the large waiting room on the first floor."

Yoav took the stairs two at a time and found Meir Landsman pacing back and forth with obvious impatience. He had already said the better part of *sefer Tehillim* and was hoping that the merits he had accrued would serve to placate Naomi for the hours he had spent away from home.

"Mr. Landsman?" Yoav approached the young man. "Thank you for bringing Jamil in. His story is going to take a while to check out."

"How long?" Meir asked.

"I don't know yet. I've got an investigator on the case as we speak, but it's not a matter of minutes, and maybe not even hours."

"So I can go now, and you'll let me know when you find something out? But what about Jamil?"

"Don't worry – we'll take good care of him."

"You mean he has to stay here? Well, I guess... maybe that's not such a bad option. After all, he told me he doesn't have anywhere else to go, in any case."

"Right. So, yes, you can go. And we'll be in touch. Just fill out a form with your contact information at the front desk before you leave, okay?"

Yoav sighed in relief once Landsman had left. That was one less headache to worry about, at least. Back in his office, he picked up the phone and dialed Eitan's number.

"Nu? What's taking you so long?"

Eitan frowned, uncomfortably aware that he had wasted too much time before getting down to work. "I'll have something for you soon," he promised. "I'll call you, okay?"

Yoav grunted his displeasure and slammed down the phone.

Mendy studied himself in the mirror and was pleased with what he saw. He practiced pacing back and forth and smiling coldly.

"Gil Brand. Nice to meet you," he told his reflection. The false smile spread across his lips, but didn't touch his heart, which was, of course, his intention – he had to remain cold and calculating in order to survive in the new world in which he found himself.

It had been obvious to him almost from the outset that they would want to recruit him as a double agent, since nothing could be better than a man in deep with the enemy. But even they didn't know how determined Gil was to remain faithful to his true homeland.

"And now, you head out to your mission!" he ordered himself. He was alone, so alone, but he was determined to use the loneliness in order to draw upon his reserves of inner strength.

His parents were imagining the worst: Gaza, Arabs... They didn't understand his real mission, his true motivation. And it was better that way.

When the hour hand on his watch touched nine, Gil left the apartment and slammed the door behind him, instinctively checking to see if he was being followed. Of course; the answer was clear.

Stop that. Don't be afraid, Mendy. Whoops: Gil. Enough fear!

He took the elevator down to the lobby and exited the building that faced the scenic Haifa port, stepping into the street to hail a passing taxi. The cabbie pulled to a stop, and Mendy dictated the Tel Aviv address. Then he leaned back against the headrest and fell asleep for the duration of the journey. Less than two hours later, the driver roused him and announced that they had reached their destination.

Mendy opened his eyes, and his first waking thought was that he was about to begin a new chapter in his life. It was a daunting thought, but one that exhilarated him; he could feel his heart rate speed up and he enjoyed the sensation, one that told him that nothing would ever be the same again.

He entered a small, quiet café. When the owner, an older man, approached him, Mendy knew that he had just crossed the point of no return.

"Are you alone?" came a quiet, measured voice from behind him.

Mendy-Gil spun around. "You can see for yourself."

As expected, it was Yochai, who smiled at the young man's quick response.

"Not bad, kid. You've grown up since we met last. Come, let's have a drink and I'll hear what you've got to say."

"What do you want to hear?"

The GSS officer settled into a seat opposite Mendy, positioning himself so he had a clear view of the entrance, and asked the proprietor to close the windows and turn on the air conditioning. "It's unusually hot today, you know," he added by way of explanation.

The proprietor actually thought it was quite cool, but he said nothing and switched on the air conditioning, aware that these were his first and last customers for the day.

"First of all, I'd like to know why you insist on your parents not knowing that you're free," Yochai began.

Gil stared back at him harshly. "You'd like to know, but it's none of your business. For your purposes, it's enough that you yourself can see that I'm free. Nobody's holding me against my will."

Yochai nodded, his eyebrows raised a little. "Okay. Let's say I believe you. What do you want from me now?"

"To join the GSS."

Yochai burst out laughing. "That's a good one!"

Gil's expression, in contrast, was completely serious. "Listen, Yochai, my parents chose a different way. I respect that. And I also know that if my parents knew my intentions, they would never let you accept me into your ranks. But look at me, Yochai. I'm Yotam Brand's son, and I've got every chance of succeeding. I inherited a lot from my father, and I advise you to make good use of my talent and potential."

Yochai stopped smiling. "I see that you inherited your father's rhetorical skills – that's for sure."

"Indeed I did. So what's the word?"

"I'll think about it. But on one condition: We let your parents in on the secret. They're both living in terrible fear, Mendy. It's cruel."

"As far as I'm concerned, you can tell them that they can calm down. But don't give them any hint that we've been in contact. I don't want to lose the opportunity of a lifetime because some family member decided that I don't belong in the Security Service."

Yochai nodded. "I hear you. And now I've got a question for you."

"Ask away."

"I understand that after you left Ilan, you made contact with Arabs."

"You mean those people who try to bridge the gap between Jews and Arabs? I helped them out a bit and made a mint."

"Yes, I know that," Yochai grinned.

"So, do we have a deal?" Gil-Mendy seemed anxious to end the meeting.

"We'll see. I'll get back to you."

The two rose from their seats and shook hands. Gil left the café first, followed shortly after by Yochai. Both men were smiling in satisfaction, and when Gil settled into his taxi, he knew that he had taken an important step toward his life's goal.

To his truth.

15

Shuli needed to talk to someone. She felt like she was going crazy, and her thoughts were tormenting her unceasingly. Her husband had become a shadow of the man he had once been, and the children tiptoed around the house, as if afraid to make a noise. Their happy home was falling apart, and she was powerless to do anything about it.

Ten minutes ago, Shuli had pulled out a chocolate-fudge cake from the oven, and when Suri walked in from school, she inhaled the heavenly aroma.

"Yum! I love that cake. It's Mendy's favorite, right? Does that mean he's coming home for Shabbos?" Her expression was so eager that Shuli's eyes filled with tears. The younger children were still oblivious to everything that was going on – she and Shimon never discussed the situation within their earshot – but sooner or later they would have to be told something.

"No, Mendy isn't coming," Shuli finally replied.

"Why not?" To Shuli's surprise, Suri burst into tears.

"Why not?" Shuli was tempted to cry along with her daughter, but she grabbed a tissue and blew her nose loudly to hide the tears. "Because… he can't."

"Mendy is learning," Nachum called from the living room. "When *bachurim* learn, they can't come home every week. You know that Rabbi Akiva didn't come home for twenty-four years?"

"Can't be!" Suri retorted.

"Can be! Ask Mommy!"

"I mean, it can't be that Mendy is like Rabbi Akiva. Right, Mommy?" Even seven-year-old Suri was old enough to figure that out.

Shuli preferred not to answer, turning around instead and busying herself with the cake. "Nachum," she called to her ten-year-old, "I have to run out for half an hour. Keep an eye on Suri, okay?"

"Don't worry, Mommy," he replied in his most mature voice, and suddenly, Shuli wondered how aware he was of their fears and the drama unfolding in their home. Trying to contain her tears and halt the stream of frightening scenarios playing out in her mind, Shuli walked quickly to the Rebbetzin's house.

Rebbetzin Miriam Greenberg, who had been her mother, grandmother, best friend, and confidante during the period of her return to *Yiddishkeit*, greeted Shuli with open arms.

"Shuli, my dear, what's happening?" the Rebbetzin welcomed her, ushering her inside and embracing her warmly. Shuli was about to speak, but the Rebbetzin stopped her, and guided her to the kitchen. "First, you need a hot drink. And then, we'll talk." The Rebbetzin placed the ancient tin kettle that had been part of her dowry on the stovetop and turned on the flame. "I'm making you a nice, relaxing chamomile tea. It looks like you need it," she added, frowning slightly.

Shuli swallowed hard. "You're right – you could always see on my face what's going on. It's… it's Mendy. He's gone!" Shuli almost choked on her tears, but struggled to compose herself and continue: "He said he's not coming back. Somehow, he found out… about our past, that we weren't always religious, and it really threw him. I never imagined…" Shuli's voice trailed off. Could she share every detail with the Rebbetzin? She knew she could trust her, and yet, it wasn't her own secret – it was Shimon's, and she had no right to reveal it without his express permission.

On the other hand, she so desperately needed to unburden herself, and when Shimon himself was under so much pressure, it was impossible to talk to him. Instead, she had called Yochai, on numerous occasions, but his assurances that "everything possible is already being done" and "for now, there is no reason to worry" did nothing to assuage her fears.

"I never imagined that he'd take it so hard," Shuli continued slowly, trying to think clearly. "But… it's not as simple as you think. Shimon used to have an important job for the State, and he made some enemies in the process." Shuli stopped short, knowing that she had already said too much. In any case, the expression on the Rebbetzin's face told her that the older woman had already grasped what she was saying – there was no need to add another word.

"I see." Typically, the Rebbetzin's response was calm and understated. "Has your husband spoken to the Rav?"

"No."

"So tell him to make an appointment. And *daven*. It may not be as bad as you fear. We have a great Father in Heaven, Shuli! He does so many miracles for us, and He is only waiting for us to ask.

"And you have to try and take better care of yourself," she added, smiling gently and taking Shuli's hand in her own. "I know it's hard, but try to get more sleep, and to eat healthfully. You don't look so good, and you have your other children to think about. And, remember, Mendy is such a special *bachur*. The Rav was always impressed with him. *B'ezras Hashem* you'll yet have much *nachas* from him."

"Amen," Shuli said fervently, struggling mightily to keep her tears from overflowing. She got to her feet, and the Rebbetzin accompanied her to the door, giving her a warm hug before she left. And yet, the older woman's words were little solace to Shuli, who returned home as brokenhearted as before. Moreover, now she was also worried about what her husband would say when she told him what she had done, and requested that he speak to the Rav.

She wasn't wrong to worry.

"You told her?" The words exploded like lava from a volcano, and Shimon began pacing the room like a caged lion, trying to contain the angry words that threatened to gush forth. "You knew it was forbidden, Shuli. We swore never to tell a soul! What did you do it for?"

"What did I do it for? Our son is in danger! Do I really have to spell it out to you? I don't care about the rules anymore! I want my Mendy back! I want him home!" Shuli wept, trying to keep her voice down so the children wouldn't hear.

"In any case, what on earth can the Rav do to help? What does he know of the GSS? You've endangered not only me, but Mendy too, not to mention the Rav and Rebbetzin themselves! If someone finds out that they know things, they may have to pay the price for that information. You know that, Shuli!"

Shuli closed her eyes briefly, and they flashed angrily when she opened them again. "Shimon, I don't care! My son is there, and I'm not to blame for that. It was all about you, and your devotion to the State! I never said anything back then, even when we sacrificed everything. But I won't sacrifice Mendy! It's time that you went to the Rav and heard *daas Torah* on this!

"I was patient until now," she continued her tirade. "I called Yochai dozens of times, but all he offers me is empty platitudes. And why should he care? After all, it's not *his* son whose life is at stake. But let me tell you one thing, Shimon: If it *was* his son who was over there, he'd turn the whole country upside-down to get him back. But it's only our Mendy! The son of an anonymous agent who's been off the payroll for the last fifteen years. Shimon, is there anyone out there helping us, anyone at all?"

Shimon reacted in intense frustration to his wife's outburst. "Shuli, I don't think you have a clue what you've caused through this pointless discussion with the Rebbetzin, but you're right about one thing at least. Now, I've really got no choice but to speak to the Rav." With that, he donned his hat and jacket and was gone.

Shuli didn't walk him to the door, as she usually did. Instead, she remained sitting on the couch, clutching a *sefer Tehillim* in hand. Nachum chose that moment to wander into the living room.

"Mommy, what's happening to Mendy?" he asked bluntly.

So he's not oblivious, Shuli realized to her dismay, although she was not really surprised at the fact. She took a deep breath before steeling herself to simply tell him the truth, hoping that a partial account of events would satisfy him. "Mendy is going through a hard time right now. He's left us for a while. He wants to figure some things out, and it may take time for him to understand what he's thinking and return to us."

"How long do you mean?"

"As long as Hashem wills it."

"But he'll be back?" Nachum's expression was so innocent, his tone of voice so hopeful. Shuli gazed into her younger son's eyes. Nachum resembled Shimon so much, with his innocence, faith, and fervor. Mendy had always been much more laid back, calm, and accepting.

"He'll be back, *im yirtzeh Hashem*," she said as convincingly as she could. "Want to help me make supper? What would you rather? Eggs sunny-side up or an onion omelet?"

Shuli recited one last chapter of *Tehillim* and then headed to the kitchen, busying herself there for the next half hour. She jumped when the door opened suddenly.

It was Shimon, and he looked happier than she remembered seeing him in a long time.

"Nachum and Suri!" he exclaimed to his wife. "They're the key!"

Grabbing his surprised children by the hands, he began to dance with them. "Nachum and Suri! I can't believe we didn't think of it earlier! They'll help us restore contact with Mendy!"

It didn't take Gil long to make up his mind to call his parents. At first, he had been determined to distance himself as much as possible, but twenty years of a loving relationship had made its imprint on his soul, and he knew that he couldn't leave them suffering indefinitely. Primarily he was motivated by his feelings for his mother, unable to live with the knowledge that she was possibly mourning his death already. For a while, he had derived a sense of satisfaction from knowing that he was punishing them for lying to him for twenty years, but the moment his imagination conjured up a picture of his mother's tear-stained face, guilt and regret wormed their way into his heart, no matter how hard he tried to quash the feelings.

And yet, on the other hand, the situation was quite amusing, he had to admit. Yochai, once his father's good friend and colleague, was now allied with his son against him, and Gil was determined to live up to the man's expectations. He had already gleaned that Yochai resented his father's decision to disappear into the religious world, seeing it as a betrayal of the Service, and even of the State itself. Even though many years had passed since then, Yochai's willingness to keep Gil's secret from his father was proof that the resentment still smoldered – or so Gil thought. Otherwise, why would he have agreed to abide by Gil's stipulation?

He timed the call for half-past-nine at night, an hour when his younger siblings were usually fast asleep already. He planned for a ninety-second call, but things turned out differently.

"Hello?" he said, as soon as he heard someone answer.

"MENDY!" a delighted voice exclaimed. It was his little sister Suri, the last person he had expected to be up at this hour. "Mendy, is it really you? I miss you so much! Mendy, when are you coming home? What are you bringing me back from America?"

So that's what they told the kids.

"Um, we'll see, Suri. Can I speak to Tatty or Mommy for a second?"

"They're not home. Mendy, talk to *me!* What are you doing in America? What's your new *yeshivah* like? I miss you so much!" Suri didn't let him get a word in edgewise.

"Who's babysitting?" he finally countered.

"Nachum. He also wants to talk to you!"

Mendy's heart beat rapidly, and he was tempted to slam the receiver down. He knew he had to maintain the coldness in his heart, but with Nachum, his one and only brother, he knew it would be impossible.

"Mendy? How are you? I miss you. It's hard at home without you. Mommy is so sad," Nachum said plaintively.

Mendy's heart melted. Nachum's voice was a poignant reminder of home, of loving family, of happier times. But he was strong now, and he needed to overcome such weakness.

"It's hard for me too," he choked out, and the image of the family sitting around the Shabbos table practically overwhelmed him.

"Remember when we used to play chess, and you checkmated me with your bishop every time?" Nachum asked suddenly.

"Yeah. So?"

"So I finally figured out how to stop you from doing it! I've got three new strategies to protect myself! When you come home, I'll show you!"

Oh, those evenings when they had spent hours playing chess! Tatty would sometimes cheat and whisper a new strategy to Nachum, and usually, Mendy would still win, but sometimes, he had let his little brother win, to the boy's delight.

"Are you coming back soon?" Nachum persisted. "By the end of the *zman*?"

"Not so soon, and we'll see exactly when. Tell Tatty and Mommy that I called, okay?"

"No," Nachum replied in a serious, mature voice.

"Why not?"

"Why not? Because every time someone mentions your name, Mommy bursts into tears. Mommy's become the biggest *tzaddekes* you've ever met, sitting and saying *Tehillim* all day long. Do you know that Tatty cries too? Did you ever see him cry, Mendy?"

Tatty? Crying? No, Mendy had never glimpsed even a stray tear in his father's eyes. Tatty was strong and virtually impregnable; he never cried.

"Mendy, I don't know why you left, but if you want to make them happy, speak to them yourself. I can't be the one to make them cry again. It hurts enough inside my own heart."

A long silence stretched across the line as Mendy wondered when his little brother had grown up.

"Oh, Nachum. Come on. I never came home more than once in three weeks. It hasn't been that long yet. You're blowing this all out of proportion."

"You think so?" Nachum shot back. "That's besides the boys in my class who point at me and whisper behind my back, and the guys who won't even talk to me because I've got a brother off the *derech*! And then there's the do-gooders who say that it's all a *nisayon*… Forget it. I'm sorry I said anything. You left a big *peckel* behind you, Mendy." The ten-year-old exhaled the sigh of an old man.

"Nachum, what I do with my life is my decision."

"Yes, but don't forget who your real family is! Don't forget that we'll be the ones to come to you if you ever get hurt. Don't forget that we're the ones *davening* for you!"

As Gil listened to his brother's words, spoken with such intensity, tears blinded him. "And don't forget who—"

Mendy's other cell phone rang just then, and he glanced at the caller ID.

"Hold on a second, Nachum. Just a sec, okay? Hello?"

Mendy listened for a moment to the voice. "Ignore him. Your parents are dictating his every word."

Gil's tone was harsh as he resumed his conversation with Nachum. "Nachum, enough already. Stop talking. This isn't you talking in any case. This isn't coming from a ten-year-old. Somebody's feeding you exactly what to say. Tell Tatty and Mommy and whoever is with you in the room that this is the last time I'm calling. They've lost me for good this time!"

He slammed the phone down, and the boy stared in fright at the receiver and promptly burst into tears. Shimon entered the room and embraced his trembling son.

"Don't cry, Nachum," he comforted him. "You were a tremendous help, and you did an amazing job."

"No I didn't! He said he'll never call back again!" Nachum wept.

"He will. Mark my words, Nachum. He'll call again. He'll miss us too much. You know Mendy. You know that he'll call."

"I know that… he was very angry," the boy stammered, trying to choke back his tears. Overhearing the exchange, Suri started crying too.

Shuli hugged her children tightly. "Don't cry, *kinderlach*. Everything will be okay, *b'ezras Hashem*. Don't cry."

Yochai's voice interrupted the family drama as he exited the kitchen along with two of his colleagues.

"We managed to do something at least," he told Shimon. "And I hope it'll help us in the long run."

"Yochai, is the boy safe?" Shimon asked fearfully.

"I hope so. I believe so."

"Is there anything you can do? Has anyone seen him?"

"Not yet," Yochai stared at the floor, unable to meet Shimon's gaze with the secret burning inside him. He needed to show Shimon that he was dealing with the issue, even if he wasn't divulging the whole story. If Shimon ever discovered the truth, he'd never forgive him. He was better off playing the part of the anxious, hardworking agent and trying to push Shimon's anguish to the back of his mind.

17

A pale-faced Naomi opened the door for her husband, her cheeks still damp with tears. "I told you not to go!" she wailed. "I told you it would be dangerous! Do you have any idea how petrified I was?" she wept, as she continued her tirade. "I was frantic! You can't imagine what I went through. No, you really can't!" Naomi kept repeating, intent on arousing a guilty conscience in her husband.

"No, I really can't," he murmured, ever the good husband.

"You're too naïve, Meir! You were so sure that you'd show up with some Arab who claimed to be Jewish, and they'd award you a certificate of merit for your service to the State. And what happened? They probably wanted to arrest you for wasting police resources or something like that."

"Yes, something like that," Meir agreed. "Close, but not quite."

"What?!"

"They held me—"

"They held you?" Naomi turned ashen.

"Not for long," Meir added quickly. "As you can see, they let me go in the end. They just wanted to know how I met up with Jamil, and what he told me, and if I thought someone was really chasing him. Poor Jamil was a wreck."

"Poor *Jamil?* I'm talking about you, Meir! And what about your poor *wife*, waiting at home without any idea what was going on?" Naomi's voice grew hoarse, but then suddenly her eyes lit up with a glint of curiosity. "Do you really think his story is true?"

"I really don't know," Meir sighed. "But Jamil himself is convinced that it's true, and the police are actually taking it very seriously – they aren't even letting him go for the time being. He was devastated when he found out. The way he sees it, everyone's out to get him, Jew and Arab alike. Poor guy."

"What – he's really afraid that there's some Arab hit squad on his tail?"

"Yes, and he should know better than any of us what they're like, and what they're capable of doing. After all, his own father dumped him in America and tried to get rid of him forever."

"Well, if his father could wash his hands of him, then you certainly can. Meir, you've done enough now, okay? You got the police to take this seriously, and now you can leave it to them. Right?"

Meir frowned. "Well, not quite. I mean… I told Jamil I'd be back tomorrow."

"What did you go and do that for? I told you – you did enough already. Just drop it!"

"But I found him."

"Big deal! You think that makes you responsible for him? He's not a minor! And, he's perfectly capable of taking care of himself."

"But he's Jewish – I mean, he could be, and so—"

"And so nothing, until this gets proved one way or another."

"Naomi, please, try to understand. This isn't so simple. I have a strong feeling that there is really something going on here. The police wouldn't be taking it so seriously otherwise. It's hardly their first priority to make sure that any lost Jew returns to his People. They have something else in mind, which is why Jamil is still in custody. And since I took him there, I feel like… a sense of responsibility to him, to make sure he's okay."

Naomi frowned. "Forget the sense of responsibility stuff. You don't even know he's a Jew yet, and since, as you pointed out, the police don't really care about that side of things so much, there's another reason why they're taking an interest. It really is bizarre," she said thoughtfully.

A long silence passed between the couple.

"So tomorrow you're going back to visit."

"Definitely. I need to know what's going on. There *is* something going on; I feel it. It's big, Naomi."

"If you say so," she said doubtfully. "I just hope you don't get yourself arrested. If someone is trying to kill that Arab-Jew of yours, maybe they'll go after his friends too…" Exhaling a hopeless sigh, Naomi attacked a laundry basket. "I've got a night of work ahead," she yawned. "I was so nervous I didn't manage to do anything the whole time you were gone." She glared at the sight of her husband's eyes fluttering closed on the couch.

Yoav called Yochai excitedly. "Yochai, you were right!" he exclaimed.

"I'm always right. So what's new?" Yochai asked his younger brother condescendingly.

"That Arab kid, the one I told you about—"

"He came back?"

"He did, and this time, we took him seriously. Yochai, this is something big, I'm telling you. Gideon's been called in."

"Gideon?" Yochai uttered the name in admiration. Gideon Bar was one of the highest-ranking officers in the national police force.

"Gideon came down earlier this morning," Yoav confirmed. "Something's going on. The Arab had a very strange story to tell, and it's under official investigation now."

"Good." Yochai's response was typically understated; he was curious, but there was no sense in getting excited about something that might fizzle out before it even got going.

"Yochai, I didn't call you just to share the news," Yoav added seriously.

"So why then?"

"So far, I haven't breathed a word to anyone else."

"A word of what? Sounds pretty much like you got the whole national police force involved."

"No – there's something else." Yoav took a deep breath. "There's this group of *shnorrers* hanging out suddenly outside the station, and… I'm not sure how to say this, but…"

"But what?"

"They don't look like *shnorrers.* They look more like… I can't help but think that maybe…"

"Yoav, I'm calling you back in a few minutes. We'll meet and talk it over for real," Yochai cut him off.

Thirty seconds later, Yoav's phone rang.

"I doubt anyone's listening in on you, but never talk about these things on a cell. I'll be seeing you in half an hour. Okay, little bro?"

"You think there's something to it?" Yoav suddenly sounded uncertain.

"I think it's worth discussing," his brother said firmly.

Had Yoav known of the meetings Yochai cancelled on the spot in order to meet with him, he doubtless wouldn't have called, but since he didn't know, he spent the next twenty minutes pacing restlessly around the station, waiting for Yochai to arrive.

Jamil was still in a holding cell, where, unlike the other detainees, he was receiving five-star treatment. He was summoned on occasion for questioning, when he was interrogated by senior officers, those who usually dealt only with counter-terrorism operations. One by one, the details of his story were being verified by Eitan and two other officers who had been assigned to the case.

Thirty minutes later, Yochai walked in and headed straight for Yoav's office. Placing a finger on his lips, he motioned to his brother to follow him and then walked quickly down a corridor, and then another, until they reached a quiet area near the cells where they wouldn't be disturbed.

Yochai turned to his brother, his expression threatening. "Okay, are you a police officer, or are you just playing cops and robbers?"

"What?" Yoav was caught off-guard.

"What's going on? What kind of games are you playing? You have a suspicion. Why don't you tell your superiors? Didn't anyone else notice those *shnorrers?* You're the only bright one around here?"

"No – some of the officers actually approached them to ask what they were doing here, but they just claimed to be collecting money for some charity. I still thought it was suspicious, but nobody was interested in what I had to say."

Yochai continued staring coldly at his brother.

"Do I have to share my opinion about you, or do you get it on your own?"

"I get it," Yoav admitted, his cheeks blushing in shame. "To me, they look like Arabs. But the boys at the station are sure they're *chareidim*, because they said something about a *yeshivah* and raising money *l'ilui nishmat* someone or other. You know what? I'll try and speak to Gideon, and see what he has to say."

"Yes, you do that, and get moving. You don't have all day, and neither do I." Yochai started to walk away.

"You're going already?" Yoav asked.

"Of course. I'm supposed to be at work as we speak. What about you?"

"Me too," Yoav stammered and followed his brother back down the corridor, wondering what to make of this strange encounter. It was obvious that Yochai wouldn't have left his office if he didn't think this was serious. But what should he do?

A second before Yochai slipped back into his car, he murmured something indistinct to Yoav. "Bear in mind that your little Arab interests many more people than the police."

Yoav nodded, and then turned the corner to check on the *shnorrers*… "No way!" he exclaimed, stopping in his tracks. The group was gone.

Reentering the station, he strode up to the front desk in a fury. "Where are they?" he yelled.

"Where's who?" Yaron, a junior officer, asked.

"The *shnorrers*."

"Oh, them?" Yaron laughed. "About ten minutes ago, a minivan pulled up outside and the whole group piled in. I guess they can afford more than they want people to think!"

Yoav didn't laugh. Why had the group disappeared precisely during his discussion with Yochai? Were they being watched? By who? Beads of cold sweat broke out on his body as Yoav suddenly grasped how menacing the situation had become.

"It's a good story," Gil mused aloud, keeping his eyes averted from those of his guest.

The dark-skinned man stared at him with a penetrating gaze.

"It's a fascinating story," Gil continued. "Riveting, actually. It fits more into a thriller than it does into real life."

"What are you trying to say, Gil?" the dark-skinned man asked softly. "That you don't believe me?"

"That it's too crazy to be true," Gil said, almost apologetically. "First you sent Ilan, then you brought me here; first you told me one story, then another, and now yet another… Then, you even got the GSS involved. What do you want from me, exactly? Will you just tell me the truth for once?"

Dark-face stretched his lips into a smile, revealing crooked teeth. His sharp, piercing gaze was undoubtedly one of the factors that had catapulted him to his unique status, evoking the nickname Laser. Laser's eyes seemed to bore right through a person and read his heart and all his secrets.

"We want you to join the GSS," he said calmly.

"You already told me that, but you still haven't explained why."

"Isn't it obvious? You will serve us from there."

"How so?"

"You'll join them, but you'll tell us everything you learn. You'll be our mole. Now do you understand?"

Laser leaned closer to him, and Gil began to feel dizzy. For a moment, he saw himself back in front of a *Gemara*, swaying over the familiar, comforting black letters, listening to the melodious voice of the *maggid shiur* as he explained the *sugya*. *Go back, Mendy! Go back before it's too late!*

The image faded as quickly as it had appeared, and the dark-skinned man was back, unyielding, unforgiving, baring his crooked teeth. His canines were particularly jagged, giving him the look of a wild beast.

"I don't know how to be a mole. Who said that I'll be privy to anything important anyway? The GSS trains its operatives for specific missions. You're sending me blindly into a job that I don't know how to do," Gil replied defensively.

Laser kept his eyes glued on him. "You're talented, Gil. If you weren't, we wouldn't be having this discussion. We don't take chances with operations that won't meet with success."

Gil bit his lip. "What else do you know about me?"

"Only everything. How else do you think we got to you?"

"Did my father ever suspect that you—" he stopped short and looked nervously into the eyes of his guest. He knew the question was inappropriate.

"All right. I'll do it," he said finally. "I already took the first step, although I'm not sure they'll accept me. We'll see how it all ends."

The dark-skinned man rose and, without a word, headed to the door. On the way, he dropped a huge wad of bills on the table. A quick glance revealed that they were all 200 shekel bills; the total equaled well over 10,000 shekels.

"Wait," Gil called to him. Laser turned around slowly.

"What if I fail? What if they expose me? Will you help me?" Gil was no longer as naïve as he had once been, and he understood the inherent danger in the mission.

"You won't be exposed."

"But if I am?"

"If you are?" A chilling smile appeared on the man's face, and his eyes suddenly acquired the glint of a beast of prey. "If you are, then you won't need our help anymore."

"Meaning?"

"Meaning that you can't help a dead man." He tossed the words over his shoulder as he left, his laughter echoing in the stairwell. Involuntarily, Gil shuddered. With his own two hands, he had thrown himself into the deep end of a murky world he was only beginning to understand – and the more he understood, the more his instincts told him to flee, while he still could.

Can I still escape? Or maybe it's too late already?

If he declined to "be of assistance" to Laser, then it would surely not be a case of, "Okay, so long friend, let's part on good terms." That much was already crystal clear. Meanwhile, Ilan, his only Jewish liaison with "the group," as he privately termed them, had disappeared, and nobody would tell him where to. Presumably, he had already served his purpose and had been reassigned – or worse.

Will that be my fate, too? Even if I do succeed in my mission for them, will they let me free afterward? That was all I wanted – freedom, to discover what my life is all about, to decide how to live it in the future. Instead, I only ended up trapping myself.

Gil stood up and stared gloomily out of the window. In the street below, he saw Laser striding to his car. As if reading his mind, the man glanced up, and their gazes locked. Laser lifted his hand in a friendly wave, which Gil didn't return. Laser then stuck his hand into his pocket and withdrew his cell phone. He called Gil, who answered reluctantly.

"What now?"

"Imagine for a second what could happen if you approached your parents with the truth. Think hard about how they'd react. Get it?"

"Yes."

Gil ended the call, reflecting that Laser was in the wrong business; he would be better off as a psychologist. How indeed would his parents react? What would they say? What kind of future awaited him back in Bnei Brak, if any at all?

"Shouldn't you have left by now?" Shimon asked his wife, glancing in concern at his watch.

"Where to?"

"To work!" he exclaimed. "It's late already."

Shuli was usually as punctual as a Swiss clock, and her boss could count the times she had arrived late at work in fourteen years on one hand.

"I called to say that I'm not coming in," she replied, taking Shimon by surprise.

"They were okay with that?"

"I didn't ask them. I just told them. I said I had an emergency and can't come in today."

"What kind of emergency is there?"

Shuli lifted her chin defiantly, glaring at her husband. "I'm not going anywhere, Shimon. I'm quitting my job. I told them I'd be gone for a week, but I'm really planning on tendering my resignation."

Her husband would have been less astounded had she said that she was planning a trip to Mars. He gaped at Shuli and then closed his mouth like a fish.

"Why? You can't just quit your job! And you can't just take off a week without good reason."

Shuli narrowed her eyes, ready for a fight. "I'm not a baby, Shimon, and I know exactly what I'm doing. I'm not ready to work now. I'm not even ready to leave the house. Wherever I go, I see people pointing and hear them whispering behind my back. I can't take it! Everyone's talking about us! Everyone's talking about Mendy going off the *derech* and joining a leftist cult, advocating Arab rights. 'Poor lady,' she mimicked. 'Just look what that boy did to the family! They used to be so happy and confident, and she's losing it, the poor mother. Going off the *derech* is one thing, but joining the leftists – that's really going too far. Before you know it, he'll be advocating animal rights too!'" Her tone was so perfect that Shimon actually laughed.

Shuli wasn't laughing, though, so he immediately grew serious.

"Shuli, you can't let these people get to you. People are always looking for something to talk about – that's just the nature of things. We'll be the talk of town for a week, two weeks, a month at most, and then people will lose interest, and find something else to talk about. But if you do this now, if you leave your job, then later, when life goes back to routine, what will you do? And apart from that, the kids need you to keep up a strong front, to keep a regular routine. Do you want them to start staying home from school because 'they can't take it' either? Or do you want to set the right example?"

Shuli's eyes filled with tears, but still she refused to let her husband's words penetrate. "It's easy to say," she replied bitterly. "But let's see you doing it. You're not as exposed to people as I am. So don't give me *mussar* until you really know how I feel.

"And, what's more," she continued, "I didn't even tell you the worst part of it all. Do you know how many people are only too eager to attribute it to our 'humble' origins? After years of being accepted, of no one even suspecting that we weren't once religious, some stupid, evil-minded person had to go and dig up our past and tell everyone? Can you believe it?"

Shimon winced. For him, too, it had been a painful revelation to discover that their secret was out – it certainly hadn't been something he had expected.

"It's so unfair!" Shuli continued, after the briefest of pauses. "Most *baal teshuvah* families have wonderful kids!"

"Of course, Shuli," Shimon agreed wholeheartedly, "but try not to take to heart what every idiot has to say on the topic. In any case, it's well known that kids go off the *derech* from the best FFB homes too."

Shuli nodded, relieved to see that finally, her husband seemed to be taking her seriously.

"The only thing is," Shimon added thoughtfully, "that we really do need your salary right now, and who knows if we won't need even more money in the future, with Mendy's… issues." He turned imploring eyes to his wife, begging her to reconsider.

Shuli froze. Maybe Shimon was right. Maybe she was being too impetuous. And what would she do at home all day, anyway? She sighed and nodded in slow agreement. A second later, loud knocks sounded at the door.

19

The telephone rang in the Landsman house. Naomi dried her hands, stole a peek at the cake baking in the oven, decided to leave it in for another two minutes, and reached for the cordless.

"Hello?"

"I'm on my way home," Meir announced jubilantly.

"Great!" Naomi wasn't sure why he was calling to tell her that.

"With a guest," he added deliberately.

Suddenly, Naomi forgot all about the cake.

"What kind of guest?" she asked suspiciously.

"You know, Jamil."

"Meir..." Naomi looked around anxiously, as if a dozen knife-wielding Arabs had suddenly materialized in her kitchen. "No way! I'm not letting any Arab into my house, even if he claims to be a Jew. Just like I wouldn't allow any *goy* into my house!"

"I asked a rav," Meir interrupted her.

"What did you ask?"

"I told Rabbi Feiner the whole story, and I was accompanied by a police officer named Yoav. He confirmed everything that Jamil says, and it seems very likely that the boy really is a Yid. What he needs now is to be somewhere he feels comfortable. He's not going to stay with us. We'll just give him a hot meal and then I'm taking him to a *yeshivah*."

"A *yeshivah*?" Naomi exclaimed in disbelief. "So the police are done with him?'

"Not totally, because it seems that there's more to the story than meets the eye. I can't talk about it over the phone."

"So we'll talk at home?"

"Yes. Do you mind having lunch ready for us when we come?" Meir pleaded. Naomi murmured something indistinct, which Meir took as reluctant agreement, and they ended the call.

The chocolaty aroma suddenly reminded Naomi about the cake, and she hastily yanked it out of the oven before it started to burn. Without wasting a second, she set the table in the dining room, microwaved a frozen vegetable soup, and added salad to the menu, all the while wondering what someone who was less of a *balebusta* would have done in such a situation. Luckily, the chicken was already cooked, and the rice would be ready in precisely four minutes. All she had left to do was to melt the chocolate glaze and pour it over the cake… but for an Arab she should go to such lengths?

Just over ten minutes later, light knocks sounded at the door. Meir entered, followed closely by a slovenly-dressed youth.

The boy took his seat at the table and ate with gusto, showing no embarrassment at being the recipient of their charity. From the kitchen, Naomi looked on in distaste as her culinary delights were polished off by a scruffy Arab who didn't even bother to offer a word of thanks.

"He's a *tinok shenishba**," Meir whispered to her, trying to comfort his wife.

"*Right.*" Meir didn't miss the irony in her voice. "And just how was he *nishba* exactly? You promised you'd tell me, remember?"

"Not now," he murmured. Meir was perspiring as he waited on the young Arab, offering him a drink, a second portion of food, and then a piece of cake to complete the meal.

---

* A Jew who was kidnapped by non-Jews and raised by them, without any knowledge of his Jewish heritage

"I didn't say you could give him cake!" Naomi hissed angrily, but Meir ignored her. "And I want to know for sure that he's a Yid!" she added, as soon as Meir reappeared in the kitchen.

Meir nodded. "From what I understood, it seems that his mother – meaning, his adoptive Arab mother – gave birth to a stillborn and stole a Jewish child in its place. Later on, she admitted the truth to her husband. It's not clear how she pulled it off, but they were too scared to tell the police. Recently, they abandoned him abroad and ran off to France, which has become a haven for Arabs and terrorists. That was after they dumped Jamil in America, never expecting to see him again. Well, actually, he hasn't seen them again. They're gone, but he returned here to discover the truth. That's the basic story."

"Nuts."

"I know," Meir agreed.

"No, I mean to say that this whole thing is nuts. The story makes no sense at all! It's impossible."

"What do you mean?"

"Because you can't just steal kids out of hospitals these days. Don't you remember what it's like? The plastic tags, the double and triple checks… This crazy story is one hundred percent baloney, and that's why I don't want this Arab in my house. Who knows what he has in mind to do? Get rid of him now!" she begged.

Meir wiped the sweat from his brow. "Please, Naomi, don't get so hysterical. I promise you there's nothing to worry about. He'll finish eating, and then we'll be on our way. Like I told you, I'm taking him to a *yeshivah*."

"Meir, you're making a big mistake. He's not some innocent little kid like you think. He's a conniving, lying Arab, nothing more. You have to be careful!"

Meir sighed. "Naomi, you're worrying for nothing. You're just too suspicious by nature. Please, give someone a chance, for once. It'll be okay."

"And if it won't be? Meir, you're too naïve! Besides, why would he want to join a *yeshivah*?"

"He said he doesn't mind investigating Judaism, at least until we have something else to go on."

"That's ridiculous. And what if they discover that he's really an Arab?"

"It'll be okay."

Naomi made a face, indicating her true feelings.

The whole story was ludicrous, fantastical. It stank of Arabs. And to make things worse, that Arab had eaten her food, the lunch that was supposed to have sufficed for the whole family. Naomi grimaced; what a waste. Now the kids would have to eat fish sticks. At long last, near the end of the meal, Jamil remembered to thank her sincerely for the hospitality. He added that he had been homeless for a long time, and that they were the first people who had offered him a hot meal in weeks.

Naomi cringed at the thought. Who would have ever thought that she would open her door to homeless Arabs? Why, oh why, did Meir have to be so gullible? He was too good-natured, too naïve and trusting. Her thoughts turned back to the time when they had been on their way to visit her brother and sister-in-law in Ashdod, and a car had stalled near the bus stop where they were waiting. The driver had gotten out of the vehicle and asked for help, and who had volunteered if not her Meir, of course?

Meir spent the next hour helping the man fix whatever was wrong with the motor, getting himself smeared with engine oil in the process, and meanwhile, three buses came and went. Meir let them pass, glad at the opportunity to do a *mitzvah*. When the car was finally back in working order, the driver mentioned that he was on his way to Ashdod. Naomi had jumped at the opportunity to get a ride, and Meir exclaimed that it was *hashgachah*.

However, instead of happily accommodating them and their small children, the driver had mumbled something about having to make several important calls on the way, which meant that unfortunately, he couldn't offer them a ride. "The next bus should be here in about ten minutes," he added, before slipping into his car and driving away.

Naomi had been livid. "Meir, why do you always have to do favors for everyone?" she cried. "I've been standing here for the past hour with Yanky crying his head off, and the guy just took advantage of you and then left us here in the dust!"

"You're right, but at least I had the *zechus* of helping another Yid," Meir had replied. "Although I probably should have told you to go without me," he added, somewhat shamefaced. "But, not everyone is like him. Most Yidden are *makir tovah*, and we have to be *dan l'kaf zechus*. We'll never really know why he couldn't take us."

At the time, Naomi had refrained from any further complaint, instead trying to rise to her husband's level and judge the man favorably. But on other occasions, it wasn't so simple. Meir didn't just respond to requests for help – often, it seemed, he actively sought to volunteer for all the kinds of jobs nobody else wanted to do, and sometimes, in her opinion, he went way too far, such as the time when he signed on the authorization for their neighbors' building permit, even when the extension severely limited their options to add to their own home in the future. Naomi had been furious then, and so frustrated at being unable to do anything about her husband's ridiculously good heart.

But this time, it was different. This time she wasn't just feeling powerless or angry. As she watched the Arab youth munching her food in satisfaction, she felt terrified.

Hearing the knocks, Shuli jumped and Shimon turned pale. Before either of them could react, the door opened abruptly, and Yochai walked in, eliciting cries of protest from Shimon and Shuli.

"It's customary to wait for someone to open the door after knocking," Shimon said tightly. "Why didn't you call to say you were coming?"

"Why do you ask irrelevant questions?" Yochai answered bluntly. The men shook hands, and Shuli gestured for him to join them at the table.

"We're hoping for good news," she said quietly, the expression on her face making it clear that she was prepared even if the news was other than good.

"Well, I have good news for you," Yochai said, flashing a quick, taut smile. "We've made thorough inquiries, and believe me, we didn't leave a single stone unturned. At this point in time, I can tell you this for certain: Your son is not in any danger. Yes, he's in their hands right now, but he's safe. They have a purpose for him, and once they implement their plan, they have no reason to harm him."

Shimon raised his eyebrows. "What plan? Do you know the details?"

Yochai exchanged a significant glance with Shimon, which Shuli somehow missed. "Not yet," he replied. "But, the point is, that they need your son for the plan, so they'll be taking good care of him, don't worry. The only thing you have to keep in mind is that Mendy needs to feel that he is still welcome here. That you're waiting for him to return, and that you'll greet him with open arms."

"What's the question?" Shuli replied, clearly offended. "He's our son! We never gave him the slightest reason to believe that he wouldn't be welcomed back here."

"Of course, of course," Yochai tried to placate her. "I didn't doubt it."

"Thank you for this," Shimon said quietly. "I hope you'll give us more details the moment you have them."

"Oh, there is one other detail," Yochai added. "Mendy has asked to be accepted into the GSS. I haven't approved it yet, but it's very possible that I will at some point in the near future. It will certainly keep us in frequent contact, an advantage for you."

A long silence passed in the room, until Shimon spoke up again. "Yochai, don't you dare let my son do anything dangerous."

"You know how many years of training he'll need to undergo before I dream of such a thing," Yochai replied with a smile.

"I know, but still…" Shimon pleaded desperately. The past that he had left behind was returning to haunt him. His son, his own flesh and blood, now aspired to face the same dangers and challenges that he himself had once confronted, only to abandon later. The fear he had felt for himself back then didn't approach the fear he felt now for his son.

And yet, along with the fear came an overwhelming wave of relief.

Jamil was delighted with all the attention. After the sumptuous meal, he was now cruising along in a police car, sitting back comfortably in the upholstered seat and enjoying the air conditioning.

"Where are we going? To make a new identity card?" he asked eagerly.

The officer in the driver's seat didn't even bother to answer. Meir, who had been instructed by the rav to escort the Arab-Jew wherever he went, blushed at the silly question, the latest in a string of inane comments.

"I want the card to say that I'm Jewish," Jamil added.

"No one's proven that you're Jewish yet," Meir commented. "Until they do, we can't make any kind of official declaration."

"So when will they know?"

"I guess when they locate your parents."

"Parents? What parents? They're dogs! They threw me out like a…" Switching to his native Arabic, Jamil began cursing the people who had raised him, the anger in his eyes and the ferocity of his gesticulations making his feelings quite clear, even if the language was unintelligible.

"I get the point," Meir interrupted him, unable to listen to the abhorrent words, even though he didn't understand any of them. *Jamil's going to need to learn how to watch his mouth*, the thought flitted through his mind. A long silence followed.

"What now?" Meir turned to the officer, whose only reply was an indifferent shrug.

"He's no longer under our jurisdiction, so I'm taking him elsewhere for questioning."

"And then?" Jamil, who had calmed down by then, asked. Needless to say, the officer ignored him yet again.

At long last they reached their destination. The car entered a small settlement surrounded by barbed wire and parked outside a one-story building that was guarded by watchdogs. A young man exited the main entrance and approached the driver. "Let the kid out. You can go home now," he added to Meir.

Meir stared. "They told me that he'll be coming back with me when they finish questioning him," he protested.

The man leaned forward, speaking through the window. "Mister, this investigation could continue for the next few weeks. Were you planning on sticking around that long?"

Meir swallowed nervously – what would Jamil say to that? The boy turned accusingly to him.

"Hey! You said that everything would be fine!" he complained. "A few weeks? I don't want to stay here for that long!"

"Don't worry – you'll enjoy it here," the man told him soothingly. "Come on, let's go. This isn't a prison, you know," he added, winking at the officer in the car, who grinned back at him and started up the engine.

Still muttering under his breath, Jamil got out, and before Meir even had a chance to wave goodbye, the police car had made a swift U-turn and was speeding off back in the direction from which it had come.

"If you knew that I wouldn't be staying, then why did you schlep me all the way here?" Meir challenged the officer angrily.

"You're helping your country," the driver kidded good-naturedly. He seemed more relaxed now that he had completed his mission. "You didn't serve in the army, or even do national service.

So you helped your country for two hours in a different way. You brought the boy to us, and reassured him enough so that he was willing to stick around. You did your job well, and now, I advise you to go home and forget the entire episode."

"You mean, forget about Jamil?"

"It's for your own good," the officer said gently.

Meir swallowed. The situation had become worse than strange; it had become positively scary.

Twenty years previously, in Gaza

At twenty-four years of age, Marwan al-Buraq was just starting out. After almost eight years of working all kinds of jobs, from construction to frying falafel to teaching in the local Islamic school, he finally decided to hitch a ride with the nascent Hamas organization.

Soon enough, he was recognized as one of their rising stars, and his ascent to a position of leadership was assured once he devised a certain brilliant scheme that helped to put the new organization on the map.

At that time, al-Buraq was still employed as a teacher in an elementary school in Gaza operated by the UNRWA, the relief and work agency for Palestinian "refugees." As such, he was permitted to enter and exit the region at will, making him one of Hamas' most precious assets. It was during one of his trips over the border to the "Zionist entity" that the kernel of the idea for his plan took root, and although at first it seemed far-fetched to the point of lunacy, once he figured out the details, he realized that it could actually be implemented relatively easily.

Al-Buraq sat on his low chair, smoking a *nargila*. Beside him sat Laser, his hair and beard still jet-black in those days, his eyes piercing and full of malevolent intent.

"Hamas is just starting out, and the battle will be long and painful. We will liberate Palestine with our very blood!" al-Buraq exclaimed. Silence followed as Laser absorbed the man's words with reverence.

"I am in the process of developing a plan, one that will succeed regardless of whether or not I live to see the results. The point is to strike the Zionist security forces right in the heart, and then, our victory will be assured."

Marwan al-Buraq raised glinting eyes, as if looking into the promising future.

"Just imagine, Muhammad," he turned to Laser excitedly. "Imagine the day when all the secrets of the GSS are revealed to us. When it happens, the Israelis will eat dirt!"

"How do you plan to integrate moles into their system? It's very tight," Laser pointed out. "The Israelis aren't stupid, nor are they traitors to their own. You can't buy them with money," he continued.

"Money? When did I say a word about money?" al-Buraq smiled cunningly. "I'm telling you that the blow will come from within, and it will strike them in the heart. They won't even know what hit them, they'll be so shocked. Get it?"

No, Laser didn't get it at all.

"I'm sending you now on a mission. Take a trip through the villages. Find a simple, preferably poor family that thrives on the spirit of jihad and the prophet Mohammad. A good Palestinian family which is still licking its wounds from the war – people who long to return to their homeland. And one more thing…"

He finished his sentence and grinned triumphantly.

Muhammad returned a perplexed stare, but eventually, understanding dawned on him, and a slow smile spread over his face.

His first step was forging contact with the father, Rashid. They met in a small, dingy café in the Israeli-Arab village. He spoke at length with Rashid, trying to gauge his commitment and ideals.

"The woman doesn't need to know. Is that clear? Women are fools and can complicate matters. She doesn't need to know now, or even in the future. Is that clear?"

"Yes, it's clear." Rashid suddenly appeared restless. "I don't know… We're simple folks; I'm not sure we're fit for this mission. My wife… If she finds out…"

"She won't find out, and you are bound by your oath to Hamas. Do you really want to renege on that oath?"

Reneging on the oath was tantamount to immediate death, and Rashid shook his head vigorously.

"Very well, then," Muhammad smiled. "We will meet again when you accompany me to Marwan al-Buraq." He articulated the name reverently. Rashid had no choice but to attend the meeting.

"Rashid, my friend," al-Buraq welcomed him graciously. "You know why you are here."

Rashid fidgeted nervously. "Not entirely."

Al-Buraq smiled generously, his tone velvet. "Rashid, do you know where I was born?"

"No, sir," Rashid shook his head, trying to stop himself from trembling. The other man's eyes seemed to bore through him, and he sat in terror.

"I was born in the Shati refugee camp in Gaza. We were refugees, banished from the village of Al-Jura. Have you heard of it?"

Again, Rashid shook his head.

"Today, they call it Ora; it's right outside Jerusalem."

Finally Rashid nodded; the name indeed rang a bell.

"The town was founded by Jewish Yemenite immigrants. They built their houses on the ruins of my parents' home, my grandparents' home, my family's dwelling place for generations. I'm the son of refugees, and I wish to return to my family's rightful land. That is my dream as a true Palestinian. Are you also faithful to your country and your people?"

Rashid nodded quickly, too overwhelmed to utter a sound. Terror silenced his vocal cords.

"Good," al-Buraq continued with evident satisfaction. "And that is why I have devised a plan, one that you will have the privilege of implementing. You will sacrifice your unborn child in favor of our homeland. It is a small price to pay for our freedom and land."

"What if the plan doesn't succeed?" Rashid dared to ask.

"You will do your part, and we will do ours. With the help of the prophet, we will succeed! You will have given up a son, but we will have given our lives for jihad!"

"My son?" Rashid croaked hoarsely.

"Just one child," al-Buraq said soothingly. "Just one."

Samira was blissfully unaware, too absorbed in the excitement of the moment. Concerned with finding someone to watch the children at home and anxious for her mother and sisters to visit her in hospital, she failed to notice how tense her husband was. Certainly he did not share in her excitement, even though she had just given birth to another son, which surely should have filled him with delight.

It was still only several hours after the birth, and Samira simply could not fathom why her husband was so uncharacteristically glum.

"Rashid, what's wrong?" she asked.

He sat in the plastic chair at her side, his shoulders slack.

"Nothing. I'm just tired. It's been a long day."

"I'm the one who just gave birth, not you!" she reminded him jokingly. But he didn't respond to her playful tone, instead motioning for her to be quiet.

"What should we call him?" she mused aloud. "I was thinking of—"

"Jamil," he said suddenly, his tone rough.

"Jamil? Why?"

"That's his name."

"I was thinking of—"

"He'll be called Jamil," Rashid said severely. "Enough talk, woman. I need some quiet."

Samira fell silent and stared in confusion at her husband. Rashid was clearly lost in thought, and she wondered what could be the problem. Why wasn't he rejoicing upon the birth of another son? Samira laid back against her pillow, hurt and angry.

A nurse entered and informed her that the infant was hungry.

"You stay in bed. I'll bring him," Rashid replied hurriedly.

Samira stared. "Why should you go? I can get him myself, or the nurse can bring him," she said.

"Yes – you should go and get him," the nurse concurred. "It's actually good for your wife to walk around a bit and not stay in bed the whole time," she added, turning to the father.

"I'll bring the baby," Rashid repeated stubbornly. Samira sighed and resigned herself to wait. While Rashid followed the nurse to the nursery, she turned tear-filled eyes toward the window, wondering what was going through her husband's mind. She heard the bassinet rolling down the hall, and Rashid speaking to the nurse, but she couldn't catch what they were saying.

A moment later, Rashid returned with the newborn in the bassinet. Samira rose from her bed and approached her infant lovingly, but her expression grew confused, and she double-checked the name on the bassinet.

"Rashid, he looks so different from right after he was born," she exclaimed.

"All babies change," Rashid replied irritably.

"But he changed so much! His eyes are so much bigger, and even his skin tone—"

"What kind of mother are you that you don't recognize your own son?" he attacked her sharply. Samira paled and bit her lip, feeling every bit the primitive village wife. Indeed, how could she fail to recognize the child she had just borne?

The more she stared at the bundle in her arms, the more familiar he seemed. "You know, Rashid, now that I'm looking at him again, I see that he really does look like his brothers. Even the birthmark on his hand; it's just like Halil's."

"Good."

"But he definitely changed. He doesn't look at all like he did when he was born," she added quietly, cuddling the infant in her arms. Just then, the baby opened its eyes and let out a piercing wail.

"Before, he slept so soundly, and I said that he's a calm baby. But look at him now; he's all red, a real screamer." She cradled him gently. It was her fourth son, the fourth son she had given to Rashid. Where was his gratitude? In place of happiness, all she saw was fury.

Samira passed the baby to Rashid. "Look how darling he is. He's a carbon copy of Halil," she exclaimed as brightly as she could, trying to draw her husband into the joy of the moment.

"Take him from me," he grunted, his expression downcast. Confused, she took the baby back from him.

"I haven't seen you like this since Ranya was born," she said, referring to when she had given birth to a third consecutive daughter. "What's your problem?"

"Don't ask me questions, woman, and don't remind me what happened when Ranya was born. I'm happy with every child that we have. It's time to go. We're taking him home with us right now."

"Now?" Samira gaped at her husband in disbelief. "But I'm supposed to stay here in the hospital for the next two days!"

"You're entitled to leave after seven hours. I can sign a waiver declaring that we want to return home and that we take responsibility for your health and the baby's."

"But why? And we can't take that kind of responsibility on ourselves! There's no hospital anywhere near the village! I'm not ready to go home yet! I just gave birth, and we have seven children at home! I need to rest!"

"You'll get your rest. They'll help us out. I already spoke to your sister, and she agreed to watch the boys for the next few days. I'm going to take care of the paperwork now. Get your things together, Samira. We're going."

"But..." Samira was so stunned, she didn't know what to say. But she knew her husband well, and when he was this determined, there was no changing his mind. She didn't dare defy his authority.

Everything moved at a rapid pace. A doctor entered the room, checked Samira, and authorized her release. A nurse appeared immediately afterward to help her check out. She gazed curiously at the Arab mother of eight, noting the exhaustion evident on her face, the lines of worry around her eyes.

"It's not good for you to go home so soon," she asserted. "A mother needs to rest after birth, especially at your age." However, the moment she noticed the fury in Rashid's eyes, she fell silent, and began dressing the baby quickly before sending them off with a wave.

Rashid was silent throughout the ride home. When they entered the house, he turned to his wife with a strange expression.

"I don't want to see this child or even talk about him," he told her coldly. "Raise him and do whatever you want with him, but I'll have nothing to do with him. As far as I'm concerned, he can take ill and die."

Samira gasped. "Take ill and die?" she repeated, her eyes filling with tears. How could he speak like that of his own child, his flesh and blood? How could he be so cruel to her, a woman mere hours after birth! Why wasn't he grateful for this beautiful, healthy child?

"And make sure he doesn't cry at night," Rashid added. "I'm tired."

Samira watched her husband stalk out of the house, feeling as if her world had come crashing down on her. How in the world was she supposed to prevent a newborn from crying at night?

Shuli dragged her feet home wearily from the supermarket, where once again, she had been the object of stares and whispers. She was so sick and tired of it all, sick of being the center of negative attention, tired of people stirring the pot and analyzing her relationship with her eldest son.

Without even trying, and certainly without wanting, she had managed to overhear the conversations of two of her neighbors. One, who lived a floor beneath them, claimed that Mendy had gone off the *derech* because the *chinuch* in the Brand home was too strict; the woman who lived one flight up argued that the problem was that Mendy had always been too spoiled.

On the other hand, the grocer's compassion had shone through. "I just got a delicious shipment of dates. Dates give a lot of strength. Should I include a package in your order?"

Shuli had smiled her thanks, while bitterly reflecting that she didn't need energy from dates – all she needed was to have her Mendy back. And that was something no one, and certainly not the grocer, could give her. Only Mendy could make it happen.

She entered the building, stopping in the lobby to check the mailbox. Her fingers brushed against something which she pulled out and then turned over in her hands. The envelope was completely unmarked, and for a moment, she wondered if it was really for her, but, of course, only if she opened it would she find out.

She started up the steps, tearing open the envelope on the way. A single sheet of plain paper was inside, folded in half.

"Dear Mommy," she read, her eyes filling with tears at the sight of the familiar handwriting. It was crooked and a bit shaky, as if his hand had been trembling when he penned the letter, but it was still unmistakably Mendy's.

You're the only person in the world I want to share some of what's been going on in my life with. You were always the wonderful mother figure in my life, and you raised me with so much love, and I want to thank you for that.

The day will come when you will understand. No matter what I do, no matter who my friends are, no matter what direction my life takes, whether I remain with a yarmulke on my head or not, I know that you'll always be my mother, and that you'll always accept me back.

I know that you never gave up on me, and that you'll never give up. And I also know how much you davened that I should become a tzaddik and talmid chacham. Who knows? Maybe, one day, your tefillos will be answered.

I don't know if I'll ever share the complete truth with you. I don't know if I'll ever write you again. But if you read this, then I ask that it remains between us, just the two of us.

To reassure you – I'm doing well, starting to feel comfortable with myself and the man I've become. I force myself to look into the mirror and accept myself as the person that the Creator of the world made me. That is our goal in life, isn't it? To believe that He created us in the way that is best for us, and to choose the right path in life.

It's hard for me, but I'm trying to do my best and fulfill my purpose and mission in life.

My heart aches for you, Mommy, because you really aren't to blame for what Tatty did to us.

Please don't ever try to find out how this letter got to you, and don't tell Tatty about it. If someone tries to track the source of these letters, I will easily find out about it; and then I won't be able to contact you again. And I still want to keep in touch. More for myself than for you. The truth is that for you, it would probably be easier if we broke off contact completely. It would be easier for you if you accepted the truth that I am gone forever. But I still need you, Mommy… I still feel that you're my mother, and I still want you to love me. I want to express my gratitude to you, something that you always taught me to do.

Like I said, I'll know as soon as you tell Tatty. I have my ways, so please don't tell him, please.

Give me the chance to unburden my heart once in a while, and maybe, just maybe, one day I'll share the secret of my life with you. When you discover it, it will hurt you as badly as it hurt me. It will wrench at your body and soul with a pain you've never felt before. Still, it's a truth that you deserve one day to know, and I won't hide it from you forever, because revealing it – painful though it will be – is still for the best.

I love you, Mommy.

Yours forever,
Mendy-Gil

Rashid stood submissively before al-Buraq, like a dog facing its master.

"Master," he ventured, his voice trembling like a dying machine, "I would like to know when my baby will be switched back with the Jewish infant."

Silence.

Al-Buraq turned significantly, and his black eyes bored into Laser.

"What switch is he talking about?"

Laser lost his tongue.

"What is this man talking about? Who's switching who? What is the man talking about?" Marwan al-Buraq spoke so softly that one might have been fooled into thinking that he pitied the man who dared to question him, but even Rashid, simple villager though he was, could detect the danger in al-Buraq's tone of voice, and even he could sense the imminent explosion. Nonetheless, the urgency of his question forced him to continue, regardless of the peril inherent in asking.

"Master, I left my baby in the hospital, and I am now raising a Jewish child in my home. I would like to know how long this will continue. Samira, my wife, keeps on repeating that the child bears no resemblance to us, and obviously, the older he gets, the more this will be apparent. As far as I'm concerned, you can take him and kill him."

"Kill him!" Al-Buraq exclaimed, his gaze murderous. "You will guard him with your life! And, if I hear one more mention of a

Jewish child, someone *else* in this room will be dead! You will raise him as your son. Your *son!* Understood?"

"Very well," Rashid lowered his eyes. "I just wanted to know… when… because originally, you said it would be a month," he stammered, his words emerging like a pathetic wail. "But it's been much longer than that; it's been half a year already!"

"Yes, and it will be twenty years."

"Twenty years?" Rashid gaped in disbelief.

"Yes. If we told you one month, then… let's say that I apologize. And now, accept that the plans have changed. You will raise him until he is twenty. But even then, you will not dare to tell him of his true origins, and you will most certainly not kill him. You will set him free. Understood?"

"I…"

"Take him away!" al-Buraq ordered Laser. "Take him. He tires me with his whining."

Rashid left, his lips trembling, his entire body trembling in distress. He had never intended to hurt Samira, and he knew that if she ever discovered the truth, she would never survive the thought that she was raising a Jewish child. And if she then demanded to know where her own child was, what would he tell her?

Rashid felt his heart plummet as he realized that his last glimmer of hope had just been extinguished. Why, of all men, had he been chosen for this mission? He had no need for a stolen child! He had no desire for drama in his life. Rashid leaned against a rickety fence and began to weep, accepting that he had lost his son forever. When Laser returned, he found al-Buraq staring out of the window at the weeping Rashid, with the majestic Galilee as a backdrop behind him.

"I must return to Gaza now," al-Buraq announced abruptly, gazing around through narrowed eyes. "Listen well, Muhammad. Aside from the father, you are the only one with knowledge of this. The years will fly by, eighteen, twenty years. When the Arab child joins the Zionist army, you will make sure to track him and do whatever is necessary. Is your mission clear?"

"What about you?"

"I will perish first for the land. I will die when I liberate the land, and I will die with Jewish blood on my hands." An awful laughter filled the room. "But if I live, I am not sure that I will have the energy to deal with this mission. Right now, I'm just a simple teacher, educating innocent children in Gaza to live the Palestinian dream of glory. But one day, I will be a leader in Hamas, and this plan will be the one I am most proud of. We will have a mole. A real mole that no one will ever identify. And nobody ever succeeded in such a thing before. Nobody – but me!"

Laser spoke deferentially, "Marwan, your plan is truly genius. There is just one thing that I do not understand. Why do you insist on keeping the Jewish baby alive? Why not kill him?"

Al-Buraq turned back to the window.

"Why, you ask? When will an ounce of intelligence penetrate that thick skull of yours?" he sneered. "One day, the police may come in search of the child. If they realize that he died, or worse than that, what do you think will happen then?"

Unable to answer the riddle, Laser chose the route of silence.

"And yet, I am afraid that we erred," al-Buraq changed the subject without warning. "We chose the wrong man. Rashid is weak; he's too much of a family man. Palestine is not his supreme goal. He agreed to cooperate, but only because he feared for his family, not because he was inspired by the mission. If the child dies, his conscience will plague him, despite what he says, and if the police investigate the death, he won't be able to keep his mouth shut. Then, neither of us will remain to carry out the mission. It is best that he raise a Jewish child, who will anyway grow up to be a Jew-hating Arab. You know what, Muhammad?" al-Buraq bared his tiger-like teeth, his eyes glinting with sudden elation. "I think we should also create a mission for our little Jew! When he comes of age, we'll send him on a suicide mission to kill Jewish soldiers! What do you say to that?"

Their gazes locked, and the men burst out in raucous laughter.

Al-Buraq turned and headed for the door. "I'm going now, and I don't yet know when I'll be returning to this side of the fence. Perhaps not even until Palestine is free. Meanwhile, I will disappear in Gaza and bury myself in other duties. Keep this secret safe, Muhammad *habibi**; keep it locked away in your heart. And when the day comes, you will find our son, tell him the truth of his roots, and recruit him to serve us. Understood?"

"Understood, Master Marwan."

They clasped hands, clapped each other on the backs and parted.

Laser never saw Marwan al-Buraq again, but the memory of the Arab infant who had been switched with the Jew by an Arab nurse paid handsomely to carry out the mission never left him for even a day.

Incidentally, the Jewish infant hadn't been chosen at random either. Al-Buraq had done his research well and deliberately chose the newborn son of Yotam Brand, a senior operative in the GSS. It was a hilarious twist of fate, but also vital, that the future Arab mole be none other than the son of a GSS man. More than it was amusing, it was actually a fundamental basis of the game that would only commence twenty years later.

"What's going on?" Shimon asked for the thousandth time.

Unlike the previous times, Shuli finally agreed to answer. "Nothing."

He rolled his eyes. "But you're smiling!" His tone was almost accusing.

"Right!" She paused for a moment but then decided to share her thoughts. "I have good reason to think that Mendy will come

* My dear Muhammad

back eventually, maybe even sooner rather than later. He'll see that the outside world is empty, and that Torah is what really counts. He'll come back. He'll get engaged, and we'll be *zocheh* to see him build a home and raise a family!"

"Amen!" Shimon exclaimed, but he looked worriedly at his wife. If Shuli was becoming delusional, her emotional state must be worse than he had imagined.

"Shuli, maybe we should think about getting help?" he tried delicately, deliberately using the plural.

"Help?" she stared at him perplexed. "What kind of help do you mean?"

"You know..." he stammered, "like, emotional. Maybe it will help us to look at the whole picture differently. We need a lot of support now, and—"

"Shimon!" she interrupted him, impatient with his lack of understanding yet still hoping that she could tell him something without actually telling him. "Look at me, Shimon. I'm doing good. I'm fine. I'm really happy. In fact, I want to sing and dance and thank Hashem. I feel like our troubles are finally reaching their end, *b'chasdei Hashem*!"

She turned to head toward the kitchen, and Shimon watched her, his heart performing a wild dance. Shuli was losing it.

"Why don't I make you a cup of tea, and then you can lie down?" he suggested hoarsely.

"I'm not tired. I don't need anything." Shuli could hardly contain her smile, but when she noticed Shimon's frantic gaze, she lowered her eyes.

"Shimon..." she whispered, her voice trembling. She so badly wanted to tell him, to lessen the burden upon him. When she had read Mendy's letter, she had understood that he was confused, standing at a crossroads, and leaning back toward them. She desperately longed to share the letter with Shimon, to tell him everything that Mendy had written, but she was too afraid to do so.

Mendy had explicitly told her not to breathe a word, fearing that his father's messengers would catch up with him. It was torture, but she would keep the secret safe inside her heart, at least in the meanwhile.

Her heart ached to tell her husband the truth, but Shuli also knew that if Shimon knew that his ignorance could potentially lead Mendy back home sooner, he would gladly surrender the opportunity to know more. She was confident that Shimon would allow her to harbor Mendy's secret in exchange for Mendy's safety and future.

It took superhuman effort, but somehow Shuli managed to contain her smiles, contenting herself with the comfort of the wonderful truth. Mendy would come back! He would return home, to *yeshivah*, to Torah. Shuli accepted that *shidduchim* would be a challenge, but Hashem would help, as He had helped them until that day.

"Shuli..." Shimon's voice drew her back to the present, his tone pleading. "Shuli, I'd really like you to take a break. Go on vacation for a few days. We both need a vacation. In fact, let's take the kids too! They've suffered throughout this whole episode. Let's all get away for a bit." Shimon sounded so miserable that Shuli's heart wrenched. He needed the vacation far more than she did.

"Okay," she agreed on the spot.

"So we'll get away and forget it all for a while?" Shimon said hopefully, though he inwardly laughed at his words. As if they could ever forget...

Shuli also contained her laughter. She stuck her fingers into her pocket where she had hidden the letter and fingered it, warmth flooding into her heart.

Come home already, Mendy. Before our vacation, after the vacation. It doesn't matter when. Just come home...

Jamil was terrified as he stared with wide eyes at the investigator who treated him to a wisp of a smile.

"You have nothing to fear, Jamil. We'll do our job, and you'll do yours."

"What am I supposed to do?"

"Just talk. Tell me whatever you know," the investigator, who had introduced himself as Yochai, replied. "Tell me about your childhood, whatever you remember."

"There isn't much to tell."

"Just start. We're listening." Yochai crossed his legs and leaned back as he fixed his gaze on Jamil, gesturing for him to begin.

Jamil sighed but began to talk. "So, I was born in an Arab village in the Galilee. I'm sure you know that already."

"Correct. How did your father relate to you?"

"He was okay," Jamil replied tonelessly, but even an untrained eye could easily detect the storm of emotions that crossed his face at the mention of his father. "He was a bit… cold to me… Um, sometimes even mean. He never let me study much, and he called me stupid and lazy. He made me stay home instead of going to school, and I worked…" Here, his voice cracked. "Some of my brothers went to college, and I even have a brother who's a nurse in a hospital," he added with a note of pride. "He's not in the country now, though."

"What about you?" Yochai guided the dialogue back to his target.

"Me? What about me? I was just dumb and lazy, so I worked

at home. I did deliveries; I sold a bit in the market. You know, household stuff."

"What about your mother?"

Samira, his mother. There were times when Jamil commiserated with her, and times when he felt he actually hated her. He, himself, wasn't sure which feeling should prevail. Samira always seemed angry either at him or because of him, but she also pitied him on occasion, which was more than anyone else did. Sometimes, way back in the past, she had gazed at him, her dark eyes overflowing with compassion, "Jamil, *habibi*," she would murmur. "Love all your children. Love them all unconditionally. Oh, Jamil, *habibi…*" And he had understood, or, at least, he had thought he did.

Samira also did her best to shield him from his father's wrath. "Run, Jamil," she'd whisper. "Father is home. The look of you just annoys him. Get going!" she'd urge him into bed every night when he was young, and Jamil hadn't understood why. Why did Abu hate only him? Why did he embrace his brothers and express his pride in them, but spurn only him?

"Take him away!" Rashid would shout. "The sight of him repels me." Little Jamil would bow his head, wondering what he had done to incite his father's wrath.

Now, Yochai wanted him to speak the truth, to share all the pain and loneliness he had endured throughout his childhood, and eventually, how even his mother had turned against him and, anxious to please her husband, began abusing him.

"You used to tell me that I'm all right, and that Abu hates me without reason," fourteen-year-old Jamil had once dared to complain to his mother.

Samira had turned blazing eyes upon him, and well did he remember the sight. "It's not without reason," she had retorted angrily. "You're a lazy creature. Just look at you standing there and whining while your brothers are working hard to study and succeed in life!" But they had never given Jamil a chance to study, nor was he allowed to mix with his brothers and enjoy the pleasures of growing up in a large, loving family. His brothers beat him often, and instead of protesting, his father would egg them on, and usually join them. "Hit him! Hit him harder! Let him know the meaning of pain and suffering."

Jamil knew it all too well. His screams of agony would slice through the quiet of the Arab village, and no matter how many times he endured the ordeal, he could never bring himself to fight back, despising himself for his weakness even as his brothers must have equally despised him. As he grew older, he learned, at least, to hold back the tears, and he even began to pride himself on his stoic acceptance of his lot.

Once in a while, Samira's heart would still feel for the boy. When he staggered to his bed, bruised and bleeding, she would tiptoe into his room, really a storeroom that was just larger than a broom closet, and hand him a wet rag and a bandage. "Wipe the blood away, *ya-habibi*," she would whisper. "Soon, the pain will go away. You're a man now. It's not your fault Abu isn't happy with you."

On other occasions, she only stared at him mournfully. "He never liked you from day one. Why? I'll never know. From the day you were born, he hated you. What did you do to make him hate you?"

Yochai interrupted his reverie. "Jamil, I need you to express your thoughts, not just relive them. Please, tell me. By the way, do your parents have acquaintances in Paris?"

"No, not that I know of." How would his father, a simple villager, know someone in Europe? The whole thing made no sense to him.

"Did your father ever talk about moving to Paris?"

"Never."

"What did he tell you during the flight to America?"

"Not much… That he was worried about me. That he wanted what was best for me. Something about qualifying for special education. At the last second, he even looked like…" His voice trailed off.

"Like what?" Yochai leaned closer.

"Almost like he was apologizing for the way he treated me all those years. At least that was the feeling I got then. I didn't dream that he was planning on disappearing on me."

Yochai stretched. "Jamil, if I find your father and bring him back, would you like to meet him?"

"No!" Jamil said decisively, but then reconsidered. "Well, maybe."

"What would you tell him?"

"Something that I'll never tell you."

Yochai's eyes widened. The young Arab who claimed to be a Jew had suddenly become an enigma. What secret was he hiding?

Naomi was in her element preparing for Shabbos, stirring pots and polishing the silver, but Meir seemed restless.

"I wish we could invite him for Shabbos. Who knows what they're doing to him over there. He should have a break for a day, even two," Meir said, frowning as he spoke.

"We still don't know for sure that he's Jewish," his wife replied stubbornly.

"Maybe they found out already."

"And maybe they didn't. Until I hear proof, I'm not interested. And, in any case, what kind of a Jew would land up being raised in an Arab village? There's a ton of unanswered questions here. So, until I get some answers, he's not coming here for Shabbos!"

"Well, in any case, they're not letting him out, so you don't have to worry. They won't even let me contact him," Meir complained.

"I've called so many times, and they just hang up on me! 'It's not your concern,' they say. Such chutzpah! I brought him to the station in the first place, and now they're ignoring me!"

"Maybe it really isn't your concern," Naomi suggested.

"You think so too?" Meir looked hurt.

"Well, not necessarily, but I do think that... at least, let's wait to confirm that he's a Yid."

"He is. I feel it."

"Meir, you're always feeling things." Naomi couldn't contain herself.

Meir fell silent, feeling beaten. *Was she right? Did he always have 'feelings?' Were they usually wrong?* Once, he had had a feeling that they should invest their savings in the Iraqi dinar, like many of his friends. He had purchased a fortune in Iraqi dinars, and then closed the account in a savings plan, only to be informed that the suicide bombings in Iraq had negatively affected the economy there. He'd had a good feeling about it, but the Landsmans' savings were now depleted. Ultimately, the money was still there, and hadn't gone completely to waste, as Meir frequently reminded his wife, but it hadn't exactly made them a mint, as she never failed to remind him. In any case, his 'feelings,' in that particular case, had gotten them nowhere.

Another feeling he had had was that if they told their landlord that they were leaving because the rent was too high, he would lower the price. The problem was that when they informed him of their plans, the landlord turned out to be delighted as he had already found a renter willing to pay even more than them. With no other option, they had moved into a much smaller apartment, and Meir had been forced to admit that his feeling had really let them down that time.

But, of course, there were also times when his feelings had been right on target, and they were amazed each time anew by his incredible intuition. One afternoon, he had returned home earlier than usual. "I came to help out," he had explained. "I had a feeling that you needed help cleaning up." Naomi had cast a grateful look from the filthy floors and remnants of dinner still on the table, and handed her husband a mop. She had thanked him endlessly, but even more so when her grandparents popped in for an unexpected visit that evening, excusing their sudden appearance by telling them that, "We didn't want you to go out of your way for us!"

Ultimately, Meir determined that his feelings were more or less fifty percent on target, and fifty percent off. This time, he was convinced that he was on target.

Jamil was a Jew; there was no mistaking it as far as he was concerned. Even the actions of the police seemed to bear out his intuition – why else would they be taking such an interest in him? Why, precisely, the police were in fact so interested in the story of a Jew who had been brought up in an Arab village, was still a mystery to him, but Meir's interest was of an entirely different nature. If Jamil really was a Jew, then he, Meir, felt obligated to introduce him to the rich world of Judaism and restore to him his stolen heritage.

"Kol hamatzil nefesh achas mi'Yisrael ke'ilu kiyam olam malei!" he announced fervently. "Naomi, I'm going to save this boy! I'm going to show him Yiddishkeit, and bring him back. I have no idea how he landed up with Arabs, but his eyes are Jewish. It's clear as day."

Naomi still thought otherwise, but she held her tongue. Despite her husband's occasional lucky strikes, as she privately termed his occasional intuition, she was still inclined to dismiss her husband's feelings, and not only because they had led into so many blind alleys in the past. By nature she was pragmatic and unemotional, and, moreover, usually determined to believe that until proven true, everything was false. Still, the fire in her husband's eyes caused her to pity him a little and soften her approach.

"Listen, Meir, maybe you have a phone number for that police officer? Call him directly. He seemed a bit more approachable than the others you described. Ask him what's going on, and if your little Arab really is a Yid. My guess is that you'll be able to figure out the truth just from his tone of voice, even if he doesn't give you a straight answer."

Meir didn't waste a second. He searched through the contacts in his cellphone until he located the number.

He was just about to press 'Talk' when the phone began to ring. His eyes widened when he saw the number, the same one he had just pressed to dial. Yoav was calling him!

"Hello!" Meir exclaimed, already celebrating his victory. As he had known, his feeling was right on target!

24

Yochai greeted the young man who entered his office with a benevolent smile.

"Come in, Gil. I see you know your way around here."

"More or less," the young man replied, his brow furrowing in concentration as he cast a hard look around.

"Good, because it's new. The State pampers us, as you can see. Would you prefer a couch or a chair?"

"Chair." Gil sat down, and when Yochai rose to get him a coffee, Gil discreetly withdrew a tiny sticker and attached it to the underside of Yochai's desk. His hands trembled slightly, but he worked to steady them. Once the sticker was firmly in place, Gil exhaled slowly, as if he had just accomplished a difficult task. Luckily, it took Yochai two minutes to return, during which time Gil managed to calm his stormy emotions.

"Here's your coffee," Yochai said generously, "and some cookies too, on the house."

Gil took the coffee, and his lips automatically mumbled something as he raised the mug to his lips. He noticed Yochai's amused gaze and chuckled uncomfortably. "Old habits die hard, eh? You don't just stop thanking G-d for granting us sustenance."

"Maybe. Can't relate to that, but I know what you mean about habits dying hard." Yochai was a die-hard secularist, with no intention of being broad-minded enough to consider the opposite approach, but he knew well enough when to keep his opinions to himself.

Embarrassed, Gil took a cookie, mumbled something again and bit in hard. "I just can't stop! See what my parents did to me?" he said in annoyance.

"You're right – it really is hard to quit old habits," Yochai agreed. "Anyway, let's get to the point, Gil. What makes you want to join the GSS?"

"It's a mission. Until now, I served in the ranks of the *yeshivah*, but now I feel my place is with my country. I never served in the army, and I'd like to do my part for the security of the state."

"So why not join the army now? You're still the right age. Do your service like everyone else does," Yochai suggested.

"Because I want to study too. I want to make it in life and advance. Here, I feel that my father's service will work to my benefit," he admitted. He smiled, his expression a mixture of hypocrisy and arrogance.

So he finally mentions his father, Yochai mused.

"You know that there are certain criteria for acceptance," Yochai replied seriously. "First of all, you've got to pass some rigorous tests. Then, we decide. Based on your scores, we also decide where to place you. Your father's reputation will only take you so far. First, you'll undergo intensive training, and you'll start out as a rookie. Sometimes, it's tough stuff. Slowly, you advance, but only if we're satisfied with your investment and efforts. But the first step is to see if you even qualify."

"Meaning what, exactly?"

"There are cognitive tests you'll have to pass, but more important is the assessment of your personality traits. We need to see that you can exercise discretion and remain cool under fire. Your organizational skills are also important, and your ability to follow orders even when your own mind might tell you otherwise. But not everything we're looking for can be quantified. If we reject you, we won't tell you why." Gil frowned but remained silent. "So, let's get the ball rolling, shall we?" Yochai suggested. "I'll recommend you, despite the fact that you never served in the army. You're right, people here still have good feelings about your father."

"Why?"

Yochai grinned. "You really don't know?"

"No," Gil admitted frankly. "I know that my father served in the GSS, but I don't know in what capacity."

Yochai's grin grew even broader. "It's quite an amazing story, kid. Your father did the impossible. Had he wanted, he probably could have been the chief today, but he chose a different life for himself."

"You've managed to pique my curiosity."

"It's an old story, but a good one. Your father was born in Jerusalem, close to an Arab neighborhood. He befriended Arab kids his age, and learned the language fluently. His dark features also worked to his benefit. When he was recruited by the GSS, he was dispatched as an operative to collect intelligence from the Islamic principalities. He flew to New York and created a new identity for himself as an affluent Arab merchant. From there, he traveled to Arab countries where he befriended various political figures and managed to uncover vital state secrets. When we realized that they'd caught onto the game, we staged his arrest and threw him into the Nafcha prison where security prisoners are held."

"And he agreed to all that?" Gil asked, overwhelmed by the tide of information.

"That's the way things go here," Yochai answered casually. "Like I said, following orders is key. We don't take rebels here. We're not looking for trouble." Yochai pierced the young man with a sharp gaze. "Anyway, your father was thrown into prison, and even the wardens didn't know he was one of us. We had only one contact man, the jail doctor, who knew that your father was there as an agent, and he relayed instructions back and forth. Yotam – your father – had a rough time in there, but he succeeded beyond estimation.

"The prisoners trusted him and treated him with respect bordering on reverence. Don't forget, he was a rich real estate magnate with connections to the Saudi princes. They ended up spilling many of their secrets to him. With your father's help, we managed to locate and raid terrorist cells, and we arrested dozens of terrorists who had carried out major attacks. We also managed to avert two planned attacks and prevent a prison break."

"How did you pull him out of there?"

"Eventually, he was released for weekend parole, but he was pretty depressed. Jail can do that to anyone. It took us all by surprise. He wandered into a Chabad House and spent a Shabbos there, enjoying the atmosphere. He returned to jail for a period of time, but eventually decided that he'd had enough and wanted out of the GSS."

"So who exposed his real identity?" Gil asked curiously.

"No one. We just made sure that he got 'sick' in jail, and the records show that he eventually died there. We took him out in an ambulance, and he walked away, a free man. Usually, people like that undergo plastic surgery to alter their features but your father refused. He preferred to grow a beard, which changed his appearance completely."

"Why are you telling me all this?" Gil asked, suddenly suspicious.

"Because you're his son. And the story is twenty years old. Plus, it's not quite accurate," Yochai chuckled. "I'm not worried about him being exposed now."

"You're not worried about anything happening to him now," Gil repeated, his eyes narrowing like a lion preparing to attack its prey. Was Yochai really his father's friend? Could he trust this man at all?

"In any case, let's set a date. You'll undergo testing, and we'll see if you qualify past stage one. Then, we'll take it from there. Agreed?" Yochai concluded, ignoring the anger on Gil's face.

"Agreed." They shook hands, and Gil made his way to the door. At the last second, he exchanged a glance with Yochai, and Gil felt a chill run down his spine. He was a traitor, and he felt sullied.

During their short vacation, Shuli's mood relaxed even further from quietly relieved to openly contented. Despite their residual unease at the situation surrounding their older brother, Suri and Nachum allowed themselves to be pulled into her upbeat mood, letting themselves believe their mother's frequent reassurance that "Mendy will soon be home."

Shimon, in contrast, was more reserved, his expression as worried as ever.

"I'm glad you're still so hopeful, and it's wonderful to see you coping so well with the challenges, but I still don't think you should nurture unrealistic hopes," he told her, his brow furrowed as he tried to fathom what had come over his wife.

"I know," she nodded. "You're totally right."

Shimon released a worried sigh. "Shuli, I hope you're not going to crash."

"I won't. You'll see that I'm right."

Her last sentence was definitely cause for concern. Shuli had never been known for her optimism; in fact, she was the cynic and realist of the two. She was also hopeless at keeping secrets, especially from her husband, who immediately latched onto her tone of voice with suspicion.

"What will I see, and when?" he asked slowly, fixing her with a penetrating gaze that told her that he would tolerate no more excuses.

Shuli paled, immediately grasping her error. "Shimon, whatever. It's not for now. Let's just enjoy our vacation, okay? We can enjoy the fresh air, the beauty of nature, the birds and flowers—"

"Shuli, stop!" Shimon cut her off. "What is going on with you?"

The words stuck in her throat. "Listen, Shimon, the point is that I know something that is important for both of us. But you've got to understand that if we want what's best for Mendy, then…"

"Then what?"

"I can't tell you," she whispered. "It's not like a secret or anything… You know what?" she sighed, realizing that her husband would not be fobbed off any longer. "This is going nowhere. Shimon, don't tell a soul, but… Mendy sent me a letter…" She reached into her pocket where she had been keeping the letter since receiving it, and handed it to her husband.

Shimon froze, but then took the letter. His eyes flitted nervously across the paper, across the words that had been intended to bring solace to his wife. He read it again and again, and then turned the sheet over. Then, he stuck his hand into the envelope and withdrew it again immediately, a shout of terror emerging from his throat as if he had been bitten by a snake.

"What happened?" Shuli paled in concern.

"Nothing… nothing." Cold sweat broke out all over his body, and he began hyperventilating.

"Shimon! *Shimon! What's happening to you?* You're not having another heart attack, are you? SHIMON!" Shuli began to scream.

"Shuli, I'm fine… You don't have to shout. Listen, I… you… You didn't…" he choked and broke out in a violent coughing fit. Finally, he regained his composure, burying his forehead in his hands.

"It's okay. Everything is fine. I'm all right. I was just overcome when I saw that, *baruch Hashem*, there's been a change."

"So you see?" she exclaimed triumphantly. "He'll be back!"

"Yes… In the end… He'll be…" the sentence emerged disjointed, and Shimon's expression was completely shattered. It was one of those rare occasions when Shimon Brand allowed a tear to fall.

Although he tried to regain his composure, Shimon's shoulders began to tremble violently, and he broke down in wracking sobs as Shuli looked on, shocked and terrified. She had been so sure that her revelation would reassure her husband and instill renewed hope in him, and she had no idea how to interpret his actual reaction.

Yet Shimon refused to listen to her comforting words, and the envelope shook between his limp fingers, until he let go of it and it fluttered away in the breeze only to land in a nearby brook.

"Shimon, look what you did! We lost the letter!" Shuli cried, berating herself for not keeping it to herself.

"Never tell me anything about those letters again, if they come. Keep in touch with Mendy, but don't tell me anything! Do you hear?" Shimon told her sharply, the color returning to his face. "I don't want to see another letter like that again."

"Why not? I don't understand! It shows clearly that Mendy still cares! I… I thought it would make you happy to read it," Shuli said, her voice trembling. "Why, Shimon, why?"

"I can't explain," he replied shortly. "But I don't want to see his letters. Not even one."

Shuli nodded slowly, realizing that it was pointless to press her husband any further.

Had she only known what Shimon knew, her heart would have doubtless broken. Concealed inside the envelope had been a paper-thin listening device and transmitter that broadcast their conversation directly to whoever was listening, but the drowning of the letter in the brook had ruined it. Somehow, Shimon had managed to refrain from revealing the terrible information from his wife while firmly warning her to avoid future disclosures.

No, Shuli must not know – the news would break her. With his discovery, Shimon had realized that virtually all hope was lost. Mendy had defected. He was no longer one of them.

It wasn't long before Shuli was put to the test. Several days after the family returned home from their three-day vacation, she found another envelope awaiting her in the mailbox. This time it was addressed to her, and she recognized the handwriting immediately, her heart beating faster in anticipation. It was unmistakably from Mendy, and she knew what it would say: He missed them; he yearned for the closeness of home and family; soon, he would return.

Although the suspense was almost unbearable, she determined to wait to read it until she was alone. She urged the kids into bed early that night and then escaped to the privacy of her bedroom to open the letter. Shimon was learning in shul and wouldn't be home for another hour.

Taking a deep breath, she slit the envelope open.

Dear Mommy,

I see that you kept your word, and I'm happy about that. I hope that you will keep my letters, so if I return one day and want to read them, I'll be able to look at them again.

It's interesting, Mommy, but now, looking back, I'm beginning to recall images from my childhood that were long buried in my subconscious. I remember you dressing differently, I remember Tatty without a beard, and I think even without a kippah. I think I even remember the first time you lit Shabbos candles. I was very young, but you spoke to me about the kedushah of Shabbos, and you said that Shabbos will give us a good life.

Shuli stopped reading, and stared unseeingly at a plant in the corner of her room. She, too, remembered this discussion now, and it amazed her that Mendy recalled it so clearly.

You talked about leading a happy, meaningful life and being close to Hashem. I remember liking the sound of that. You talked about sweetness, and I waited for the sweetness to envelope me. But now I'll admit the truth: I never tasted the sweetness of Shabbos; I only wanted to please you.

Why am I telling you all this?

Why, indeed? Shuli paused her reading. To hurt me? To break my heart more than you've already broken it? To tell me what a horrible mother I've been? She returned to the letter, fearing what she was about to read.

You told me that if we keep Shabbos, then something good will come of it. But you know what? Only bad came of it. You can't even understand what I'm saying yet, but one day, you will.

Daven for me, Mommy. I feel that your tefillos are the only thing that can help me now. Daven that I choose the path that Hashem destined for me. Please don't be angry at me. Every person has his mission and destiny in life.

You will always be my mother,

The letter ended there, as if Mendy had abruptly stopped writing. Shuli read the last sentence several times and sighed heavily, feeling that she hadn't reached the end of the 'conversation' with her son.

Reading the letter again, she felt that he wasn't just telling a story, but also crying out for help. Why was Shimon being so stubborn about not knowing about the letters? She so longed to discuss it with him, to have him help her decipher them, to figure out what exactly was going on in Mendy's mind and to gauge if he would really be back.

As she read the letter for the third time, she noticed the positive hints sprinkled throughout. It was almost as if Mendy was saying,

"I'll be back home soon!" The fourth reading, however, inexplicably filled her with doubt. Did Mendy have an ulterior motive with these strange letters? What was he trying to achieve?

Gil gazed moodily at the map spread across the table.

"You're sure? I'm sick of sending letters!" he complained, his expression like a little boy's.

"I couldn't care less about your feelings on the matter," Laser glared at him. "And I need those letters to be less emotional, more factual, with less feeling. I want the letters to talk about your parents, not you."

"But you said that my mother shouldn't show them to anyone, in any case, so what difference does it make?"

Laser looked irritated. "There are things that you write to your mother, and there things that I expect – from you. Don't start making trouble, okay?"

Gil sighed. "So what now?"

"Now, after sending the second letter, you'll send a third one. In the end, she'll discuss the letters with your father. She'll have no choice, once you bring up the fact that you know something about your origins. You won't state it outright – you'll just hint, and that will confuse her even more."

"What are you saying?"

Laser pierced him with narrowed eyes and waited for Gil to understand of his own accord.

"Look, my mother knows that I support left-wing organizations, but what else should I write?" Gil was genuinely confused, but then a spark of emotion suddenly ignited in his heart. "The truth is, I'd rather keep my mother out of this. I'm quitting the letter-writing."

"You will not!" Laser leaped to his feet and slammed his fist down on the desk, almost causing it to topple over. "You will involve your mother in every stage of the process. You will tell her exactly what you're experiencing. Your mother has to suffer such emotional upheaval that she'll have no choice but to involve your father, and then we'll really hear what he thinks of all this. Based on the fact that he drowned the letter, we've got good reason to suspect that he's onto us, but I want concrete evidence of that."

"And if he does suspect something?"

"Then it could interfere with the implementation of the plan."

"Which is?" Gil pressed, determined to reach the crux of it.

"The fulfillment of our plan is the reason you're here, a goal that we've invested twenty years to achieve."

"You didn't ask me first." There was a note of rebellion in Gil's voice.

Laser took a menacing step toward the boy and pierced him again with those frightening eyes. "What were we supposed to ask, and how exactly, would we have gotten an answer from a day-old baby?" he barked. "To you – Mendy, Gil, or whatever you call yourself, it makes no difference. You are really Jamil. And you, dear Jamil, were destined to restore Palestine to us. We will redeem her with fire and blood!"

A weighty silence filled the room.

Had Gil, the erstwhile *yeshivah bachur*, been able to, he would have switched off the lights and announced that the play was over. There were no more actors, stage, or props. But here he was, trapped into playing a role against his will, the strings holding him by the neck, their strangling grip forcing him to continue acting in this dreadful play of life.

"I need a small break," Gil managed to say. "I need to think it all through." Doubts raced dizzyingly through his mind, and the questions rose like steam from a cauldron. What if Laser's stories were all fabricated, and he was being manipulated like a fool? What were the true purposes of this organization he had become involved with?

"And just what, precisely, do you need to think through?" Laser's voice was suddenly dripping with honey.

"Everything," Gil replied, wary to speak the truth – that he was terrified of Laser. But the other man had no intention of making it so easy for him.

"You can't think anything through, until you hear certain things that were said by your parents at various points along the way. Here, listen to this recording, and tell me if it's your father."

Laser removed an old-fashioned tape deck and pressed "play." There was a slight hum, followed by the familiar sound of his father's voice.

The conversation, which had taken place at an unknown time and place, caused Gil to shudder, and a sharp pain sliced through his heart. Was it really his father? When and why would he have spoken with such loathing for his eldest son? And the words were directed at him!

Which was worse – Laser's treatment of him, or his father's attitude, so cleverly concealed until now?

Once again, Gil felt powerless, and Laser celebrated his victory.

"I told you so. There are many other things that you're still unaware of. Want to hear another one?"

He didn't, but he agreed anyway, curiosity getting the better of him. When he heard his father telling an unknown somebody that he was dissatisfied with his son and was considering sending him off to an orphanage, he wished he hadn't listened.

Was it really his father? Or was one of his new "friends" playing a mind game on him, in order to manipulate him toward some nefarious end?

The third tape made Mendy's blood run cold.

No, home would never be a haven again. But neither was this place a refuge – a place where people rejoiced at his misfortune and exhibited a total lack of consideration for his feelings.

Was there any place he could escape to?

"Get up," somebody woke Jamil. "Wake up. Yochai wants to speak to you."

"Now?" Jamil rubbed his eyes, confused, struggling into wakefulness.

"Now," the young man repeated firmly.

"But it's two in the morning!"

"What are you? A human clock? Who asked you what time it is!"

Jamil got out of bed meekly, freshened up, and followed the young man out the door.

Yochai greeted him with a friendly grin. "Listen, Jamil! We located your family in Paris. You won't believe it. They have a beautiful house, and they all changed their names. Even their first names."

Jamil tried shaking his head clear, still half asleep and half wondering if he was dreaming.

"Where are they?" he finally articulated.

"Paris," Yochai repeated. We also discovered a bunch of fascinating things about them. Would you like to meet up with them?"

"No."

"Too bad, because your dad is here now."

Jamil stiffened. "My father?" he gaped. "Did he say anything about abandoning me?"

"He didn't abandon you, Jamil. You're a big boy, and he claims that he did it for your own good. In order that you could make something of yourself and earn a decent living."

"How? Without knowing the language? Without a roof over my head? They could have killed me there, and no one would have even cared!" Jamil shouted.

"I suggest you tell him what you just told me. One more thing: I want you to face him off and tell him everything on your heart."

"You mean, everything that I suffered in my life?"

"Exactly. About the way they raised you. I want to see a full-blown confrontation between the two of you. Okay?" Yochai was warm and encouraging.

"Why?"

"It's important to have closure."

Jamil glared at the GSS officer. "Closure? Close what? Close off the way to everything? You should be opening up opportunities for me!"

Yochai stared in confusion, and then held himself back from laughing at the Arab kid's ignorance of such a simple concept. And yet, Jamil was not stupid, just woefully uneducated. Most probably, he was also learning fast.

"Whatever. In any case, prepare yourself, Jamil. In two minutes, you'll be meeting the man whom you believed to be your father for twenty years. This may be your last opportunity to tell him what you want him to hear, so make good use of it."

The two minutes passed way too quickly, and Jamil, still in shock from the unfolding of events, began perspiring heavily. Then, the door opened and Rashid was ushered inside.

"We have a surprise for you, Rashid," Yochai announced jovially. "You must have really missed your son!"

Rashid was silent, clearly just as shocked as Jamil.

"What are you doing here? We tried to get rid of you! How do you keep on cropping up?!" His father's words were spoken furiously, belying the claim Yochai had previously made. "You've got more lives than a cat! What are you doing here?"

Jamil sat in silence for a moment, trying to compose himself, and then, suddenly, his words began to spill out like molten lava.

"You were never my father! Why did you abandon me?"

"I was always your father."

"No, you weren't. They told me that I'm a Jew."

"Don't be a fool. You're my son, *ya-habibi*."

Jamil grew confused. "One minute you hate me; the next minute you love me. What's going on?"

"You were always a difficult child. People thought you were retarded," Rashid's voice softened, and he affected a sympathetic expression. "I was angry. When you're a father and you discover that your son is retarded, you'll be angry too."

"I wouldn't abandon my son in New York."

"I didn't abandon you. I sent someone to take care of you."

"What are you talking about?"

"The same man you met. What did you think? That a random Arab would take a street rat into his home out of the goodness of his heart? We needed to get away, to give Mother a break from you. You're getting older, and likewise, your needs are increasing."

Jamil closed his eyes and shook his head. "I was always the despised son, the only one who succeeded in school and wasn't allowed to continue to high school and college. Why?"

Rashid swallowed visibly. "Do you deny that your mother loved you?"

"No," Jamil was honest enough to admit the truth. "But perhaps Mother didn't know what you did know," he added in sudden inspiration. A moment's wait, followed by, "If I was really your son, you would have called an ambulance."

Rashid's face paled, yet he quickly recomposed himself. "What ambulance? What are you talking about, boy?" But his terror was confession enough, and Yochai observed the exchange in growing satisfaction. Neither Jamil nor Rashid was aware of it, but there were trained investigators and psychologists watching the entire confrontation through one-way glass, as well as a close-circuit camera documenting every word and nuance of their conversation.

"When I was ten, I came down with pneumonia," Jamil reminded him tightly. "I could hardly breathe. Remember?"

His question was met with silence.

Jamil rose and began pacing anxiously. "You said there was no reason to go to the hospital. I lay in bed, gasping for breath. Mother sat beside me and wept, scared that I would die. Remember?"

"You're hallucinating, Jamil."

"You told Mother that it would be better if I died at home. Remember?"

Again, silence.

"You left the house, Mother crying loudly. You told her you were going to work and to eat your pita outside with the neighbors. I wanted to live. I climbed out of bed, and I called an ambulance myself. Remember?"

Rashid was so nervous, his beard twitched.

"The ambulance came, and you couldn't understand how it got there. I went out of the house and told them that you summoned it. You followed me in and told Mother that I was the devil, and not human. Remember? You called me the devil... What kind of father talks about his son like that? Even Jabbar treated his daughters better than you treated me! When Anuar was sick, you sat at her bedside day and night! You took her to the hospital three times when her condition worsened, even though she didn't need it. If I hadn't called the ambulance myself, I'd be dead today, and you'd have been glad. What kind of father are you?"

By now, Rashid was trembling from rage, and he too rose and screamed so loud that Jamil retreated. "I was the best father you could have had, under the circumstances!"

"Some great dad tries to kill his own son!"

"No, I was a father who took care of you, even though I didn't have to! Don't you get it?"

Yochai decided it was time to intervene. "Why didn't you have to? Tell him why not."

"I didn't want him."

"Why not? How was Jamil different from your other children?"

"I didn't want him. They forced me to raise him! They threatened that they'd kill my family and all my children! Leave me alone! I don't want to talk about it. Let me out of here. I have French citizenship, and the French government won't permit you to hold me. I'll send all your cousins after you," he threatened Jamil.

"You can't send anyone to 'take care of him.' We'll be doing that," Yochai replied firmly, casting a glance at the petrified Jamil. "I just want to hear you admit that he's not your son."

"He's my son."

Yochai sighed and shook his head. "In that case, we'll have no choice but to take care of one of your *real* sons, the way you took care of our precious son, Jamil."

"You won't lay a finger on any of my children!" Rashid roared. "It's enough that they took away one of them!"

That was enough for Yochai, and Rashid realized his blunder. His face paled, and his eyes began to dart frantically in their sockets, revealing his long-kept secret. "Have mercy on me!" he began wailing. "Don't hurt my family! It wasn't me! I had no choice! It was them! I'm not related to Jamil at all! They took the real Jamil from me! Don't hurt me..." His screams resembled those of a wounded animal.

Jamil stared disbelievingly at his father. Never had he seen the man, whom he had always believed was cast of iron, breaking down and weeping like a baby.

"Would you like to cooperate with us and get your son back?" Yochai asked him, his tone matter-of-fact.

"If I cooperate with you, they'll kill me and all my children too. They're much stronger than you."

"That's what you think," Yochai leaned forward. "But I'm assuring you full protection, and to your family, as well. We'll relocate you to a different European country that accepts Moslems with open arms. All I need is the information."

"What information?"

"Whom you met with. What happened. Which family. Everything you know."

"I don't know who the family was," Rashid replied immediately.

Jamil was following the exchange in confusion. "What's going on? Am I Jewish? Is it confirmed?"

"Nothing is confirmed yet," Yochai replied bluntly, and he motioned for two of his men who were standing at the door to take Rashid away.

"Jamil, nothing is final yet," he repeated. "And until you're otherwise instructed, you'll say nothing about all of this. There is only one thing that we know beyond a shadow of a doubt: The couple that raised you are not your biological parents."

"So who are they?"

"That we still have to find out. Trust us. We'll do our best. But I don't want this getting around. It's still possible that you're an Arab from another family."

Jamil's shoulders sank. Over the past days, he had come to enjoy the thought of being a Jew, and now he suddenly felt as if the opportunity had been lost.

"So what do we do in the meantime?"

"In the meantime, you keep quiet," Yochai replied, just as he was flooded by inspiration. He would exploit this until the very end, thus assigning Jamil the mission of a lifetime.

27

Yochai returned to Headquarters, took a seat at his desk, and withdrew the pack of cigarettes that he kept in the top drawer. He lit one, drumming his fingers against the desk as he inhaled and then blew out short puffs of smoke. A moment later, two men wearing serious expressions burst into his office, interrupting his peace. One was short, fair and seemed restless, while the other was tall with a thick black beard.

"If he really is Jewish, we need to identify his biological family," the tall one spoke first.

"We have a lead," Yochai replied evenly.

"Meaning?" the fair one asked.

"Meaning, we wait and see."

"What on earth for? We have to move quickly!"

"No. First we have to know who, exactly, concocted this wild plan."

The blond one muttered something under his breath: "I didn't think they were so cunning."

"It's not a 'they'; it's a 'he.' It was all concocted by one person, but like all criminals, he messed up along the way," Yochai said, his gaze distant.

"Where exactly did he go wrong? What do you know about Jamil that we don't?"

"Nothing. I'm just assuming."

The taller man straddled the chair opposite Yochai. "All right, Yochai. Spit it out. Should we leak this one to the press?"

"Absolutely not. It's too sensitive. You don't know everything, boys, despite being certified investigators. You're missing a lot of pieces of the puzzle."

"How much is a lot, in this case?"

"All my suspicions. Again, this is a very vulnerable situation. If it leaks, it's possible that a family will identify Jamil as their son, when it's not really the case."

"How bad is that?" the tall one challenged. "If they're wrong, then we just move on."

"Think about it. Rotate all those wheels in your brain to try to think what you'd feel like if you discovered – from a random news article – that the son you raised as your own for twenty years isn't actually your own, and that your real child is some Muhammad in an Arab village. How would you react?"

"Well, since I'm not a father yet, I can't really relate," the tall one replied nonchalantly.

Yochai answered for him. "For a parent, it would be a devastating blow. On the other hand," he mused, closing his eyes to think harder, "to break the news to a family face-to-face isn't much better, so maybe it isn't actually such a bad idea for the media to soften the blow in advance."

"Will you just spell things out, Yochai?" the blond man said, his tone frustrated. "Make up your mind already."

"I will. And, I'm going to need your investigative talents here." Yochai leaned forward and spoke seriously, detailing all he knew. The more the men heard, the more their interest was piqued.

The short one, who had a family of his own, looked shaken, while the tall dark man still managed to appear amused. "I hope insurance covers that," he joked, with black humor.

"What kind of insurance covers the loss of a child in such a way?" his colleague retorted.

"At least let them earn a mint off this story."

None of them laughed again, and a frozen silence hung heavily in the office even after the department investigators had left to get on with their jobs.

Shimon returned home with the day's newspaper tucked under his arm. After *Shacharis*, he always spent the half-hour before setting out to work eating a light breakfast and skimming the headlines. The house was quiet then, with the kids already on their way to school and Shuli, as usual, cleaning the counters before heading to her office.

His breakfast was already set on the table, a tuna bagel and a cup of coffee minus the hot water.

"Good morning," he greeted his wife, dropping the newspaper on the kitchen table before washing his hands.

"What's doing?" she asked. As both of them knew, her question had nothing much to do with the newspaper, but everything to do with their lives – or rather, to do with Mendy.

"Nothing," he replied, and they both sighed.

Shimon skimmed the headlines. "Same old. Apartment prices are still rising. Protest against unfair tax hikes. Terrorist bombing in Syria. Hey! This is neat." He read something and fell silent.

"What?" Shuli asked curiously. It was Shimon's lack of response that piqued her interest.

"What does it say?"

"That… it doesn't matter."

"Yes, it does. I hear it in your voice. Something happened!" Her tone rose in hysteria. "What's going on? What does it say there?"

When Shimon still didn't reply, she nearly ripped the paper out of his hand, and her eyes flitted automatically to the small article on the left-hand side.

Switched At Birth?

State security agencies are investigating a suspected case of Jewish and Arab infants who were switched at birth twenty years ago, as the basis of a long-term terrorist plot. Leads are currently under investigation by senior officials. No further information has been released to the public.

"Why is that so interesting to you?" Shuli demanded.

"Who said it's interesting?"

"You did. Or rather, you didn't. But I know you well enough to read right through you, Shimon. What does this have to do with us?"

Shimon's face was expressionless. "Don't be ridiculous, Shuli. It has nothing to do with us."

"Yes, it does."

Shimon turned to his wife. "What in the world could it have to do with us? The only reason I noticed it was my security background, as a former agent. That's all, Shuli. Honest."

Shuli still looked thoughtful. "We always said that Gil looked like your father." For some reason, she reverted to his original name.

"Mendy!" Shimon corrected her, aghast at the error.

"Yes, Mendy. But there's something else that I'm remembering now, something I never told you, because I was too ashamed," she whispered. Shimon had never heard his wife sound so meek, and he stared at her, waiting for her to continue.

"It's… such a strange thing. But I remember it like it was yesterday. When the midwife placed Mendy in my arms that first time, right after he was born, he screamed and screamed, and opened huge gray eyes at me, and I thought to myself, 'Yotam, your eldest son looks just like you!' And the midwife was also amazed and said, 'Why, he's a carbon copy of his dad!'

"You weren't there, because your phone rang just then, and you went to the bathroom to answer it." In those days, only men in Yotam's position had enjoyed the use of private cellular devices, and they had been huge, cumbersome instruments with weak signals that cost a fortune to operate.

"I remember. I was so upset at the interruption, but it was important," Shimon recalled. At the time, he hadn't been able to apologize enough to his wife, and even now, twenty years later, he still felt a need to apologize.

"Then, they gave me a blood infusion, because I'd lost a lot. I was so weak, and so they didn't give me Mendy for another six hours or so, despite my protests. But, when they did finally bring him..." Shuli paused and lowered her eyes. "It was so strange..."

"What?" Shimon played along.

"He seemed to have changed completely. What did everyone tell me? That I was just overwrought, and that all babies change... I saw it with all my children. They change, but so much that a mother shouldn't be able to recognize her own child? But since he was our first child, I accepted what they said, especially because everyone was laughing at me. What should I have said? That I don't recognize my own child?"

"What does this have to do with us now?" Shimon asked carefully.

"I don't know," said Shuli. "Nothing, right?"

28

Mendy's third letter arrived, and Shuli couldn't contain herself any longer.

"it's so weird," she confided in Shimon. "On one hand, he refuses to come home, but on the other hand, he sends these mushy letters."

"What's weird?" Shimon asked.

"Mendy is reminiscing about his childhood in a way that doesn't suit him at all. He's too down-to-earth for that."

As soon as she had whispered that she had received another letter, Shimon had slipped his hand inside the envelope and felt around inside until he found something and removed it. Shuli didn't ask questions, preferring not to know.

"Okay," Shimon said heavily. "Read it, and then I'll read it. Tell me if you think it's his style, or if someone else dictated it to him."

Shuli opened the folded paper and began to read:

Dearest Mommy,

Dearest Mommy? Since when was Mendy so sentimental? Now that he was far away? It really was out-of-character for him to write that way.

I want to share with you a little of my life, so you'll know that I haven't forgotten you or our family, and that I'm still following in your ways. You'll still be proud of me, one day, Mommy, like you were when you were raising me. But only in the world of truth will you fully appreciate the truth, even though I'm no longer pursuing the goals that you laid out for me when I was a child. But I'm still fulfilling an important role and mission in life.

I never forget to daven in the mornings, although my prayers are different from yours. I'm happy that I've finally been directed along the true path of life.

I'm learning a lot and trying to follow Tatty's path. I hope that you will be happy and proud of me. What do you say about meeting in person, so we can talk more, and in person?

--Gil

A baffled Shuli handed the letter to her husband, exhaling a heavy sigh. "I don't get him, Shimon. He says that he wants to speak about his life, then says nothing about it. He wants to tell me that he hasn't forgotten the family. That's obvious, if he's still writing to us. And why would I have thought that he would forget? A person doesn't just forget!

"He says that I'll be proud that I raised him, but when? After a hundred and twenty? Gee, that's encouraging. What about down here? Why won't I appreciate the truth in this world too?

"And what's all this about a mission he's fulfilling?" She continued to flood Shimon with questions. "How are his *tefillos* different? What kind of path is he on? Shimon, he sounds like he's been nabbed by a cult. I can't see any other reason why he'd express himself so strangely."

Shimon had no answers for her – or even for himself. "I'm going out for a breath of fresh air," he said finally, taking the letter with him. Once outside, he called his old colleague.

"Yochai, we need to talk," he barked into the phone, dispensing with formalities. "No more excuses, my friend. This time, we meet in your office, and I want all the faculty there. I need to know exactly what's going on."

Yochai tried to talk him out of it, but Shimon remained adamant. "And, Yochai, what do you have to say about that little article in the paper about the Jewish and Arab babies that were switched at birth? Why was it published only in *chareidi* newspapers? Why, I'm asking you?" Shimon was uncharacteristically furious, and he was reminded of himself in his former life, as a cold-hearted agent, determined to reach his goal. "I want a meeting with you, and now. You know what? I'm not even setting a time. I'm simply going to barge into your office and wait for you to show up!" With that, he ended the call, and with the letter firmly ensconced in his pocket, reentered the house with a feigned expression of serenity.

"Did you read it?" Shuli asked.

"I did. He's a confused teen."

"He's not a teen anymore. He's past twenty."

"You know what they say about this generation: Adolescence extends until the age of thirty. Listen, Shuli, I've got to run. I've got a couple of important meetings to attend."

"You sure?" she asked skeptically.

"Why are you asking?"

"Because you're suddenly reminding me of the kind of work and meetings you had in the past." A chill ran down Shuli's spine. Years ago, when her husband had told her about "important meetings," she had sat at home and trembled, imagining the worst. Who was her husband meeting? What life-threatening mission had he been sent on? What were the risks this time? Back then, she had spent hours pacing the house, having not yet learned the awesome power of prayer, although she did often find herself beseeching the One Above to protect her husband.

There were nights when she awoke from terrifying nightmares, breathing heavily when she realized that it had only been a dream, and that no one had exposed her husband's true identity. Yotam had done his best to allay her fears, but she had learned that the more lighthearted and jovial her husband acted, the more dangerous was the mission ahead.

Now, his words carried the same inflections as in the past.

"Since when do you have meetings at this time of the day?" she vocalized her doubts.

"Since always. I've got to run." With that, Shimon was gone, the letter still in his pocket. He had a half-hour drive ahead, which he intended to use to clear his head and analyze the hard facts. If only his suspicions would be proven false... but the worrying thoughts would not leave him, and suddenly, he shuddered.

"Yotam will be here any minute, and his son is still hanging around. Get rid of him!" Yochai called to one of his aides.

"Where to?"

"Send him off on an assignment."

"In the field?"

"Yes."

"Isn't he a bit too green for that?"

"Doesn't matter. Send him on a false alarm or something. I can't have Yotam meeting his son here."

Yochai frowned and lit another cigarette. How much simpler things had been twenty years earlier, when Yotam had still been in the Service, and his son, just a baby.

The aide nodded before heading down the long corridor to the little office where Gil was supposed to be working. Quietly, he approached the boy. "Hey, Gil, you've got an assignment today!"

Gil, who was half-reclining on a swivel chair, smiled. "What kind of assignment?"

"Post office. They want you to accompany me."

Gil grimaced. "Give me ten minutes."

"They said now."

Gil rose to his feet with a sigh. "All right, 'now' it is, although you'd think the post office was closing for the day. I want more action. This office stuff isn't for me."

The aide stared at Gil in disbelief. He, at twenty-five years old, had already served in one of the elite Air Force units, and yet in the GSS, he was still doing "office stuff" while patiently waiting and watching and learning… and this pipsqueak thought he could jump over all the hurdles without training? If not for Yochai's personal involvement, this ex-religious kid would have been cleaning ashtrays in the basement, and yet, here he was, complaining!

"I need you to join me now," he replied tightly. "This can't be delayed."

They finally left, and Yochai exhaled a sigh of relief, but thirty seconds later, Gil recalled that he had left his cell phone on his desk.

"I can't go without it," he told the impatient aide.

"I'll get it. You stay in the car," the other man replied.

"No, I'll get it," Gil said quickly, and slipped out of the car before his colleague could stop him. The latter ran after him, but it was hopeless. Gil had already raced into the building and disappeared into an elevator, leaving the other man behind.

He quickly dialed Yochai. "The kid ran back inside, and he's heading up to your floor."

"Stop him!" barked Yochai.

The young man froze, knowing it was impossible.

"If you don't stop him, you'll never advance!" Yochai added threateningly. But at that very second, an encounter took place that neither Yochai nor the young agent were there to witness.

The elevator door swished open, and Gil stepped out. Directly across the corridor from him, a man wearing a *kippah* and a serious expression was standing, facing the opposite direction, but as he heard the footfall behind him, he instinctively turned around to see who it was.

Shimon's eyes widened in shock as he recognized his son. Their eyes met, and Shimon felt Mendy's gaze slicing through him like a razor.

"Tatty."

The word escaped Gil's lips almost against his will. He had no intention of injecting any softness into the word or of perpetuating the relationship between them – but a boy has only one father.

One father, who wraps him in a *tallis* at the age of three and carries him lovingly to *cheder*. One father, who lifts him up high over his shoulders on Rosh Hashanah to watch the *baal toke'iah* blow *shofar*. One father, who dances with him on Simchas Torah. One father who learns *Gemara* with him, who dances with him before the Chanukah *licht*…

If Gil had only known of their impending meeting, he would have steeled himself in preparation; as it was, his defenses crumbled in an instant and he felt his heart flood with emotion at the sight of the man who had raised him.

Shimon, however, had undergone years of training that enabled him to control himself even in the face of such a shock – unlike his son, the word "Tatty," uttered so simply, did not dissolve any barriers.

"Mendy." Shimon's voice was as cold as ice. "What are you doing here? Yochai hired you already?"

"Something like that. Since I never served in the army, I'm kind-of on a trial basis here." The young man's face reddened and he lowered his eyes, unable to meet his father's piercing gaze any longer.

"Oh, I see. And *what* exactly are you doing here?"

"Just learning in the meanwhile. I didn't inherit any of your cool assignments yet."

Shimon wasn't amused, and Gil's shoulders sagged somewhat. "Whatever, I've got to go. They're waiting for me."

"Yes, you've got to go," Shimon repeated, and Mendy detected a strange note in his voice. "I know that you told Mommy not to tell me, but she couldn't keep it to herself. Your letters mean the world to her."

"Do they?" Gil's voice cracked.

"Yes. I also look at them once in a while. I hope you don't mind."

"No… I don't mind."

"And if you'd like to know what we talk about after the letters, you don't have to insert bugs in the envelopes. They cost a fortune. Why don't you just come home, and we'll tell you ourselves?"

His father's last sentence caught him so off-guard that Gil merely gaped, before collecting himself somewhat and nodding vaguely in his father's direction as he hurried out of the building.

"Hey, Shimon! What's with all the threatening messages?" A friendly tap on the shoulder revealed Yochai, on his way down the corridor to await his guest.

"What's that supposed to mean? My son is trying to wiretap me, and you think it's nothing to be concerned about?" Shimon retorted furiously.

Yochai frowned. "Come into my office. I need to have a word with you." Shimon followed him inside, and Yochai shut the door behind them.

Taking his regular seat, Yochai lit another cigarette, not bothering to offer one to Shimon and not even looking at him. Shimon felt himself traveling back in time twenty years to the day when they had said their final goodbyes. Yotam and Yochai had been partners as well as good friends, but while one had continued to climb the ranks almost to the very top, the other had decided to part from the dangers.

"I'm scared," Yotam had admitted to his friend back then. "Even though I'm leaving, I'm still scared. I have this fear that they'll come after me one day."

Yochai, sitting behind his desk, his expression one of supreme confidence, had laughed his fears away. "Yotam, you chose for yourself the name Shimon, like Rabbi Shimon bar Yochai. I'm right there in your name. Trust me. You can."

"I trust in the Name – meaning, Hashem!" Yotam had retorted. "The truth is, I spoke to several of my operatives, but I didn't give any of them the final word that I'm leaving, although I hinted strongly at it. One of them replied with a saying in Arabic…"

"What did he say?" Yochai asked curiously.

"That revenge is a dish best eaten cold, and that I should beware."

"Why would he say that?"

"I asked him the same, but he just laughed and said, 'Good luck, *ya-habibi!* And that was the end of that."

Now, twenty years down the road, he was facing Yochai again, who looked somewhat more serious and balanced than in the past; presumably, an accumulation of failures as well as successes had served to temper his arrogance.

"Remember what that Arab agent said back then?" he now reminded him. "That revenge is a dish best eaten cold?"

"I remember," Yochai, who had a phenomenal memory, replied shortly. "You told it to me during our last official meeting. I even remember the man's name, but let's just say that he's not with us anymore. He moved to Holland, but I sent people to find him."

"Why?"

"Because I also took to heart what he said, and it was clear to me that he didn't just say it by chance. He was onto something. Believe me, Yotam, we're still on top of things, even after all this time. You can't help us, though. Please, just go home, and I'll keep you posted."

"I met Mendy," Shimon said suddenly. "I saw him, and it doesn't look good."

"He's here on a trial basis. I want to rehabilitate him. For you, Shimon."

Shimon didn't know what to say. On one hand, Mendy was his eldest son, the apple of his eye – twenty years had bound them together. On the other hand, he felt duty-bound to share his suspicions with Yochai.

"Yochai…" he began hesitantly.

Yochai lifted glinting eyes to him, and Shimon met his gaze, his worry evident on his face. "About the boy… I just wanted to ask if he's really here only on a trial basis? You won't let him into classified departments, will you?"

"We have strict policies here," Yochai replied firmly.

"And if you see that he's worthy of being promoted?"

"Then he'll be promoted."

Shimon knew how strange it would sound for him to interfere with his son's advancement, and suddenly, the thought of the babies who had been switched at birth, which had previously so distressed him, seemed perfectly ludicrous. Of course Mendy was their son! He even resembled them… After twenty years, should he really permit his thoughts to stray in such a direction?. Yes, he had gone astray, but he was still their Mendy, the boy who called him "Tatty" and who was struggling to return home – wasn't he?

Shimon sighed. "Thank you for your patience with my son. I just ask that you make sure that he proceeds slowly. He doesn't trust us, and he's made use of listening devices to bug our home. I imagine that you know that already."

"We know everything," Yochai said quickly.

Shimon nodded and rose. "I'll tell you the truth, I had some thoughts that I wanted to share with you, but now that I'm here, I don't think they're really relevant."

Yochai didn't reply as he escorted his old friend to the elevator.

"Yotam," he said suddenly, "I know that this may sound silly, but I want you to know that I'm doing everything I can for you."

Shimon froze. Yochai's words were an old code that they had developed years ago between them, which meant that "We can't speak about it, but we understand each other." Yochai knew exactly why he had come, and he wasn't negating the possibility. He hadn't told Shimon to stop drifting into a world of fantasy – instead, he was confirming the validity of his suspicions and promising that he was doing everything possible to investigate and hopefully dismiss them.

Could such a far-fetched story really be true?

"Go home, Yotam," Yochai spoke gently, his voice weary and his expression pitying, a rare look for the indomitable Yochai, reserved only for his closest friends and at times when they were in dire situations. "Don't think about it. We're here for you. Let us do the work. You left this job a long time ago, and your wife is probably worried. Go home."

The elevator opened, and Shimon felt a light push inside. A moment later, he found himself back in the parking lot. Only when he was already seated in his car did he realize that there was a letter in his pocket.

Opening the letter, he glanced inside and recognized Yochai's distinct chicken scrawl.

Don't talk or act regarding your suspicions of Mendy's origins. Let us make inquiries first. It's a matter of life and death for your family and for all of us. Yochai.

Shimon's hands began trembling uncontrollably. If Mendy wasn't his son, that meant that he had a different son somewhere in the world, or alternatively, and more probably, he had a son who was no longer among the living. It was then that Shimon grasped how far Mendy had really gone, and he began viewing him not as a son, but as an enemy.

Shuli mistook her husband's calm demeanor for relief. "What did Yochai have to say?" she asked, the moment Shimon walked in the door, making it clear that she hadn't fallen for his story about sudden important meetings at work. "Did he have anything new to report about Mendy?"

Instead of answering, Shimon threw out a question of his own, taking Shuli off guard. "Shuli, what do you think about Mendy?"

"What do I think about him? What's that supposed to mean? He's my son! I love him! He's suffered a crisis, and he's dealing with it in his own way."

"Precisely what kind of crisis are you talking about?" Shimon's voice was dry.

"I don't know," she admitted. "Each person has his own challenges. You know that."

Shimon settled into a kitchen chair. "And what do you think of Mendy as a person?"

"My goodness! You and your questions today!" she exploded. "What on earth is that supposed to mean?"

"As a regular person, what do you think of him?"

"He's not a regular person! He's my son."

"What if he weren't your son?"

Shuli stared at Shimon in confusion. "Where are you heading with all this, Shimon? Mendy is a good boy, with a good heart – why are you trying to put weird ideas into my mind?" As if consciously trying to ignore the hints her husband was dropping, she hurried on, "Mendy is still devoted to us – I can feel it. In fact, that trait is exactly what got him into trouble in the first place. He somehow got too devoted to this Berman guy, and then… well, you know…"

Shuli paused for a moment, before continuing, "Don't you remember when you burned yourself, years ago? Mendy insisted on staying with you in the hospital even when the doctors tried to persuade him to go home. And there are plenty of other similar stories I could tell you. He's a good boy! He's not trying to hurt us. Other people are, though, and they're using him to do it… I don't know… maybe…" Shuli's voice trailed off – she preferred to put a stop to her train of thoughts before the inconsistencies became too glaring to overlook.

Shimon exhaled slowly. "Maybe, but do you remember that period when he was beating up his classmates in school? The rebbi called us, and we didn't know what to do about it. Remember?"

Shuli looked hurt. "That was ages ago. He was a kid. Boys act that way sometimes."

"But the force of those beatings; the anger in his eyes when we tried to talk to him about it…" Shimon didn't know how to continue. "One kid ended up with a fractured jaw."

"Only because he fell afterward! And Mendy himself got hurt in those fights – he even has a scar to prove it. Why are you bringing all this up now?" Shuli protested. "Stop trying to find faults in him. He's our son! Our flesh and blood! Don't turn your back on him now when he needs us most."

"Who's turning his back? Why can't you stop rationalizing everything he does? What are you pitying him for?" Shimon's voice rose as he walked out of the kitchen.

"Where are you going?" Shuli cried, running after him. She reached the door just in time to hear the elevator shut. Then, she ran to the window, from where she could see her husband emerge from the building a moment later. "Shimon, where are you going?" she called out to him, but her husband didn't reply. He slipped into the car and floored the accelerator, turning automatically northbound when he reached the highway, driving recklessly and ignoring passing vehicles that honked at him.

It was a miracle that he somehow stayed on the road, Shimon reflected as he drove. He felt as if his entire world was crashing down on him, and before him he seemed to see Mendy's life playing out, as if in a movie. There was Gil, not yet Mendy, as a tiny baby, smiling his first smile. Gil crawling, and then taking his first steps, his first words almost unintelligible but still music to his ears. Then, Gil became Mendy, the young boy he took to shul with him, learning with him after *davening* and marveling at his progress. Mendy's bar mitzvah, his entry into *yeshivah*, the *nachas* he had brought them…

Shimon suddenly realized where he was – miles from home already. He took the next exit off the highway and pulled to a halt. Simultaneously his thoughts stopped in their tracks. *Mendy is not an enemy! Sure, he's confused, he's possibly with bad people, but at the end of the day, that's all I know. How can I condemn my child like that?*

Shimon glanced at his cell phone and saw that he had twenty-three unanswered calls. His phone had been on vibrate, and he hadn't even felt it. All the calls were from his home; obviously, Shuli was frantic.

But she wasn't even aware of what they really had to fear, the suspicion that their son was not really their own…

Where is your real son, Shuli? What's happening to him? Is he even alive anymore, and if not, where is he buried? Did he suffer?

Where is he? Where is our real child? And how could Mendy have betrayed us like this? How?

Gil was as tense as a coiled spring when he arrived at the meeting, a fact which didn't escape Laser's attention.

"Listen, I think that it's best for all concerned parties if we make an about-face right here, before going any further," Gil said tautly.

"What happened?" Laser sat down on a comfortable chair and stretched his legs. "What went wrong?"

"Nothing. I bumped into my father."

"Shimon," Laser corrected him sharply. "Or, more correctly, Yotam."

"Whatever. I met… him." Gil couldn't bring himself to utter his father's name aloud. There were still certain concepts that he held sacred, and one of them was his relationship with his parents.

"He knows everything. About the letters. The bugs. Point is, he's got a handle on the situation. I think we should shut up shop and go home."

"You want to go back home?" Laser taunted him.

Gil flushed. "I said nothing about going back to them, just that it's time to forget the plan. As far as you guys are concerned, I'm irrelevant."

"Kid, either you're relevant, or you're dead meat. This plan has been in the workings for two decades. You think we'll let you slip away so easily?" Laser laughed dryly, and the sound was like fingernails on a blackboard.

"You want to kill me?"

"What I want is of no importance. I have my orders."

"You said that I'm one of you," Gil protested, trying to keep his tone of voice even.

"Exactly. You're one of us, and bound by the same orders I am. When one of ours disobeys orders, he ends up dead. There is a higher purpose here, and sometimes, people must die along the way in order to advance that goal."

Cold beads of perspiration broke out over Gil's body. Laser saw right through him.

"Okay, so I guess we'll find a way," Gil finally muttered, his fear manifest.

Laser laughed again and rubbed his hands together in satisfaction. "That's the spirit! Now, let's see what we can do about this. You say that Shimon's discovered the bugs. What does that mean? That he now has reason to suspect you, although he still doesn't dream that you aren't his son.

"So, we'll stop hiding the bugs in the envelopes, but you'll continue sending the letters," Laser continued. "He won't forbid your mother to read them."

"What's the point of all this, anyway?" Gil was weary and displaying signs of cracking.

"What's the point?" Laser raised his eyebrows. "First of all, the letters maintain your relationship with her. Besides, in the meantime, we'll step up things with the GSS. You'll receive your orders and act accordingly. I admit that we didn't foresee all these complications, but we'll still squeeze you for all you're worth."

"Excuse me?" Gil's eyes flashed in sudden fury. "What am I? An orange?"

Laser didn't even smile this time. "This is not Israel, boy, and nobody's impressed with your wit. You were lucky; you grew up all comfy with the Israelis, but you could have just as well grown up in the filth and slums of the villages. Take it easy, *ya-habibi*, and feel honored that you were chosen as a messenger of Mohammad. Do what you're told, and you won't regret it."

Gil inhaled sharply. "All right. What now?"

"Push yourself forward until they let you participate in a real mission. I'm not talking about anything big. Even something minor will suffice. Enough to sniff around a bit and send us whatever information you can glean. It's time to start showing results. You're a special project, and it's about time you understood that. If you fail, your life won't be worth pot. Not in Israel, and not among your true nation either." With that, Laser left the room.

For the thousandth time, Gil regretted having ever trusted the man who had accosted him in *yeshivah*. For the thousandth time, he pondered how differently life would have turned out if he had never befriended Berman, the one who had introduced him to his friends and eventually to Laser. Most of all, he wondered what would have been if he had never learned the truth of his origins.

If only he had remained Mendy, he could have gotten engaged, married, and maybe even had a child by now, like many of his *yeshivah* friends. Instead of weeping over her loss, his mother could have been embracing her grandchild, Mendy's firstborn… Why had he thrown it all away? Even if he really was an Arab, neither he nor anyone else would have known the truth. But now it was too late, and the desire for revenge, implanted in him by his new friends, burned a hole in his heart. He felt compelled to avenge the conquests, the terror, the stolen land and property. He couldn't allow himself to forget the goal of vengeance, not for a minute. He was one of them, after all, and ethical considerations obligated him to join his brothers and his people, and to think like them.

But still, a little voice inside his heart cried out: *Says who?*

31

Yochai had already heard from too many people that Meir was stubborn, a frustrating character who asked too many questions, and then refused to accept the answers provided.

"He's threatening to involve all types of organizations, which is the last thing we want. He needs special treatment," Yochai declared to the two agents already involved with the case. "I think it's best that I meet with him in person, to calm him down. I know how to deal with these types. Let me speak to him, and he'll change his mind."

He invited Meir to a meeting, intending that the unfamiliar surroundings should serve to intimidate the young man – and it was immediately obvious from Meir's expression that he had succeeded in that goal.

"You have nothing to worry about," Yochai began abruptly. "Jamil is in good hands. We just prefer that he maintains telephone silence right now. You have to understand that this is a classified case," he added sternly. "By talking too much, or even at all, you could very well be endangering his life. We're doing our best to keep this on a low flame. And I promise you that as soon as the operation is over, Jamil will be free to contact you, if he so wishes. But you have to let things proceed at the pace we dictate. *We* are the experts here, not you."

Meir was still not satisfied, and despite his timidity, he spoke up. "That's what you think – but there's another area in which you are decidedly not expert. What do you understand of the value of every single *mitzvah* and of each minute of a Jew's life?"

Yochai sighed and rolled his eyes. The last thing he wanted was to get involved with fanatical *chareidim*. In his mind's eye he could already envision Meir standing at the head of a half-million *chareidim* all dressed in black and white and waving flags and shouting, "Free Jamil! Free Jamil!" The picture almost made him smile, but Yochai maintained a serious demeanor.

"And you also believe in the concept of *pikuach nefesh*, saving lives," Yochai countered calmly. "The case we are dealing with definitely falls into that category. Jamil's life could be at stake, which is why you can't meet with him for the time being."

Gil barged into the office right then, without even bothering to knock. He seemed electrified.

"Yochai, I need to talk to you!" he blurted out. Meir spun around, and his eyes met Gil's. The latter nodded curtly to Meir and addressed his superior again. "Yochai, I need to speak to you, now."

Yochai glared at him. "Gil, you're going to have to learn to follow standard procedures here. This is not a kindergarten where you need something 'right now.' Go out, and wait until I call you."

Yochai held back a sigh; someone had obviously been pressuring Gil and trying, once again, to manipulate him. Nobody barged into an office like that and demanded a meeting without requesting an appointment, let alone without knocking. What was the young man thinking?

"Hey, are you related to a guy named Mendy Brand? You guys could pass for twins!" Meir exclaimed, *except for the clothing and hairstyle,* he added mentally.

"He's not just related to Mendy Brand. He is Mendy Brand," Yochai decided to kill two birds with one stone. That would effectively get rid of Nudnik #1 and Nudnik #2. *Not bad,* he thought with a combination of pleasure and relief. "How do you know each other?" He rose from his seat and walked toward the door, relieved that his meeting with Meir hadn't taken place in his private office, but rather in an interrogation room that held nothing other than a table and two chairs. There wasn't even a phone connection.

"I learn a bit with some of the guys in his *yeshivah*," Meir stammered in reply.

Gil's face was crimson. "Meir… Your name is Meir, isn't it?"

"What happened?" Meir asked, horrified by the change that had overcome the *bachur* in such a short space of time.

"If you'll excuse me, gentlemen, I have an urgent meeting to attend right now. Feel free to use the office here to catch up." A second later, Yochai was heading down the corridor, inordinately pleased with himself. Gil was decidedly less pleased.

Meanwhile, Meir settled into the seat that Yochai had recently occupied. "Have a seat, Mendy. If you're here, we might as well talk a bit."

Yochai had been right on target. All thoughts of Jamil had promptly flown out of Meir's head, displaced by overwhelming shock and sympathy for Mendy Brand, who had inexplicably fallen so low. Ashamed of himself, Gil actually listened and sat down, and Yochai, hurrying back to his office, quickly flicked on the video cameras hidden in the corners of the room he had just left, and sat down at his desk to watch and listen.

"Mendy… What happened to you? How on earth did you end up here?" Meir's tone of voice clearly conveyed his dismay. He had to repeat himself before Gil finally replied – by then, the boy had recovered his wits and replaced his mask, the one he had carefully cultivated.

"I could ask you what *you're* doing here," Gil sneered. "And, more to the point, if you have any idea who you were talking to just now."

"To be honest, I don't know. I'm dealing with a different situation right now. But it's a good thing that I came, because now I have an even bigger mission."

"Which is?'

"To save you," Meir said determinedly.

"To save me?" Gil leaned back in his chair and laughed mirthlessly. "My friend, I suggest that you first try to save yourself *from* me. And that's coming from someone who wants what's best for you," he added, in sudden gravity.

"I don't care. I want to save you, Mendy. How could you do this to your family, to yourself?" Meir was wielding a sword on the battlefield, but Gil just continued laughing.

"Sorry to burst your bubble, my friend, but you're wasting your breath. Don't waste your energies on me. There are people who could really use you, people more worthy than me."

"Mendy, every Jew has worth, inestimable worth!"

"And what about the others? Aren't they people too? Don't they have any purpose in the scheme of things?"

"What others?"

"The *goyim*. The people *you* call *goyim*."

"Mendy, stop playing games. It won't get you anywhere."

Gil's eyes flashed angrily. "First of all, my name is now Gil, and I expect you to remember that. From now on, you will call me Gil. Second, I have no idea if you work here or not. Maybe you're employed in the *chareidi* branch, but even if that is the case, I still don't have any desire to continue this discussion, even if we do chance to cross paths again in the future."

"So don't talk, Mendy... Gil," Meir replied stubbornly. "As far as I'm concerned, you can remain silent – you don't have to say a word. But I'm not going to give up on you, no matter what."

Gil stared. "You hardly know me. What's this all about?"

Meir grinned. "What's it to you? Just let me hang out with you, and you'll see for yourself." He withdrew a small *sefer* from his jacket pocket. "Now we begin!"

Without a moment's pause, the sweet words of *Gemara* began resonating in a room in GSS Headquarters where the sounds of

Torah had never before penetrated. Meir had deliberately selected a *sugya* that he knew Mendy's *yeshivah* had already covered, and he learned aloud, not asking Mendy to join him, his voice melodious, his expression intent.

Gil's eyes widened, and he tried to get up, but he felt as if he were glued to his seat, unable to break away, almost entranced.

The scene played out for a full thirty minutes. Finally, Meir paused for a break, and Gil got up to leave, clearly confused.

"I'll be back tomorrow," Meir declared.

"This isn't a public park. Yochai will kick you out faster than you can say '*Amar Rava.*'"

"Yochai will do no such thing. Believe me, I'm holding a strong card against him. I'll be back tomorrow, and I want you here too. In fact, you'll be under orders from Yochai to be here."

Meir shook Gil's hand energetically and walked out, thrilled with his accomplishment. An astounded Gil followed him out of the room, shaking his head vigorously as if he'd just woken from a nightmare.

Just then, his cell phone rang. The contact man, the one who always put him through to Laser, was on the other end of the line, sounding exceedingly anxious.

Laser's tone was deadly when Gil arrived. "We've invested a lot in you, and you're mocking us."

Gil didn't reply.

"What are you thinking, boy? This plan has been in the making for twenty years! How dare you repay us like this? We gave you a golden opportunity, to play a starring role, and you're kicking us in the face!"

Still Gil didn't utter a word.

"They suspect you. Get it? They're onto you. This game of Yochai's doesn't appeal to me at all. Your father is retreating. We've bugged their phone line. He said that he doesn't care about you anymore. Can you guess why?"

"No, I can't, and I also don't believe that he doesn't care about me."

"You don't believe because you don't have a brain in that fat head of yours!" Laser stood up and made a cutting motion against his throat. "We need you to be smarter and act smarter."

Gil maintained an indifferent expression. "What do you want me to do that I haven't yet done? I'm waiting to hear."

"*Ya-habibi,* stop acting like a Jew. You're not impressing me with your antics." Laser looked like he was on the verge of exploding. "Start acting serious. Stick to Yochai. Nudge him. Tell him that you want to learn to play in the big leagues. That you didn't leave everything behind in order to become an office clerk. You want to work. You want action in the security department. Start doing your part!"

"It's you who pushed me in there without any skills or background."

"We thought that your father's reputation would help out. All you managed to do instead was get into trouble with him."

"What were you expecting? That I'd drop out of *yeshivah* and run away from home, and that my father would still be proud of me?" The Mendy inside Gil rose angrily to the surface, despising the Arab in front of him. Yet the deadly glares directed at him in response caused his confidence to falter.

"Okay, so tell me exactly what you want me to do," he muttered in surrender.

"You need to get the Israelis to trust you. We've prepared a clear outline and plan for you. We need you to advance the mission."

"Maybe you'd like to be more specific?" Gil suggested with feigned equanimity, though a turbulent storm raged within.

"No, not yet," Laser replied bluntly. "We're in the process of establishing ties with the family and certain agents. Also with your old world. They can't suspect that you know about us. Don't embarrass your family; your parents await your success."

"Which parents?"

Laser looked disgusted. "Your *real* parents. The ones who sacrificed you for the mission."

Gil froze, while his heart overflowed like a volcano. He didn't know what to think or feel. He felt constantly for those he still considered his real parents, the Jewish parents who had raised him. Yet he had another set of parents in the world, his biological parents. Perhaps the time had come to meet them? To lay eyes on his real father and mother, to try to bridge the gap of twenty years?

"Can I meet them?" he asked, surprising even himself by his request.

Laser stared at the boy. "And why would they want to meet

you?" he replied with a question of his own. "They lost you before they ever knew you. Why would they want to lose you again?"

Gil suddenly felt weak-kneed, and a wave of dizziness passed over him. What was Laser saying? That he would be a *shahid**? Gil had never agreed to that! Let Laser sacrifice himself in a ball of fire before sending others to complete the mission for him! Did he really think that Gil would give his life for their goals?

Laser immediately grasped his error and hurried to soothe the furious, rebellious sentiments burning in Gil's heart.

"My son, of course you can meet them if that's what you really want. All I meant is that now, or rather, for the next two years, you're going to be very, very busy. By the time you meet them, they'll be forced to say goodbye for another two years, which will be extremely difficult and painful for them. Why play with their emotions? My suggestion is that you wait, and meet them only after the mission is complete.

Gil shook his head stubbornly. "I want to meet them first." Suddenly, he was overwhelmed by a desire to encounter his parents and discover why they had chosen him from among all his brothers for this mission. Why had they destined him for such a bizarre – even terrifying – fate?

"Listen," he continued tautly, "the more you try to put me off, the more I'm going to insist that I won't take another step before I meet my parents. I want to get to know them."

"*You* want," Laser sneered. "And who are you, anyway?"

"I demand the right to meet them!" Gil spontaneously changed his approach and rose sharply from his seat. For the first time, he had the upper hand, and he knew it. "Either you introduce me to the man who should have been my father, or," he added sweetly, "your little plan, which you worked so hard to perfect for twenty years, will go down the tubes. Make a choice."

---

* Martyr (in other words, a suicide bomber)

"Make a choice?" Laser repeated dangerously, opening his mouth to reveal beast-like jagged teeth. "You'll make the choice if you want to live or die!"

Gil sat back down, but his eyes were serious as he spoke his mind. "Listen to me, man. After all you've done to me, I'm not sure my life is worth living. I feel like a Jew, and I'm not. I'm an Arab, but I don't feel like one at all, even though I sympathize with the plight of the Arab nation, and I'm beginning to grasp the personal holocaust that they endured, the pain and suffering of being banished from their homes. But I grew up elsewhere, with a different mindset, and I also sympathize with the Jewish holocaust. I'm not taking any position here, but I am willing to take responsibility for my own actions. Right now I have no place – not with you, and not with them. If they knew what I was..." He choked on the words, but swiftly pulled himself together again. "I have no home. Get it? You took me from my home and family and showed me that I have nothing and nowhere in this world. In fact, after everything that's happened over the past few months, I really don't have much to lose if you just shoot me here and now.

"So that's why I'm telling you this: Either let me meet my real family, or I bow out."

Silence followed, and Laser swallowed visibly.

"All right," he said finally. "You'll receive a round-trip ticket to France, and you may remain there for twenty-four hours. Then, you'll return to carry out the mission. We'll take care of the details, as long as you promise to stay calm."

Gil nodded brusquely, a wisp of a smile on his lips. And yet, within him, his emotions churned in a violent storm. Now it was clear that Laser was not bluffing. He really did have an Arab family somewhere out there. A father, a mother, probably siblings too. Until that moment, he had still nurtured the hope that the entire story had been fabricated, but now the truth was clear. He was an Arab baby, stolen at birth from not only his family, but his heritage. The life he had lived from that point onward was false, but the way back to the truth was far from clear. Would he ever reach his goal?

Yochai laughed out loud, as if he had just heard a good joke.

"Meir, you're undertaking way too many projects these days. What's the matter? You're bored or something?"

"Not at all, but my heart breaks at seeing the boy the way he is. I'd like to take responsibility for him, and I'd even dare to wager that within a month, he'll be back on track, a genuine *baal teshuvah*."

Yochai's laughter filled the room. "One month, you say? Well, we'll see."

"Good. So tell him goodbye, and don't burden him with assignments. In fact, don't assume he'll be here too much longer."

"Whatever you say," Yochai said, still amused.

"Yochai, I'm not joking. I'm perfectly serious. You have no idea how serious I am. I'll be back tomorrow, and I would like you to make a room available for me, one that I can use every day. In any case, you really don't need that kid wandering around here now, do you?"

Yochai glared. "Don't tell me what I do or don't need." Then, he paused. "I'm giving you full authorization to befriend him, as long as he's happy with the arrangement. Okay?"

"I'll keep his parents informed as well. I'm sure they'll be glad to hear that someone is taking care of him," Meir added earnestly.

"No, you won't do that." Yochai's expression turned instantly grave.

"Why not?"

"Just don't. They won't be happy to hear that at all. As it is, they're already having a very hard time dealing with the fact that their son went off. Leave them out of it. They're going through a lot. They don't need this on top of everything else."

Meir looked surprised. "With all due respect, Yochai, and I actually have a great deal of respect for you because you're working to protect our nation, you need to understand that there are things that only we, as Torah-observant Jews, understand. Trust me: His parents will be thrilled to hear that I'm involved. It will give them some hope, and that's worth a lot."

"No, Meir, I didn't ask for your opinion," Yochai replied sharply. "You will not tell his parents, and that's an order. I'm willing to let you hang around with the boy, but I have conditions as well, and that's one of them. Another condition is that you wear a recording device and activate it whenever you're in the boy's vicinity. He won't know a thing, and the device is simple to operate. The third condition is that he knows nothing of my consent to your daily meetings. The final condition, for now, is that if you ever leave Tel Aviv with him, you tell me about it in advance, and afterward, you deliver an immediate report to me. You have no permission to meet him outside of the offices here without my direct authorization. Is that clear?"

Meir stared. "I'm not working for you," he replied, confused. "I don't get this."

"As of this moment, you are indeed working for me," Yochai said. "And this is how it's going to work."

"Let me think about it."

"You've got nothing to think about. All you've got to do is listen, and follow orders."

Meir shook his head in disbelief, and remained silent.

"Furthermore, I want you to try to persuade him to make contact with his parents, without his parents knowing that it's coming from you. Don't limit all your discussions to Judaism. You can talk about all kinds of things – in fact, it's better that way. You can even invite him for Shabbat, if you want. But he has to think that it's coming all from you.'

"It is."

"Good. I also want him to be *chozer b'teshuvah*," Yochai surprised Meir with the statement and gazed penetratingly into Meir's eyes. "Look, I have no real connection to my religious roots, and no great love of faith, but the boy's father is a good friend of mine, and I know how important this is to him. What's happened with Gil – Mendy – is a terrible tragedy, in many ways, and I want to help him if I can. I only accepted Gil into our ranks because of his father, and that's also the only reason why I'm letting you get involved. But you have to play by my rules. Understood?"

Meir fidgeted. "Yes… but obviously, I'm not going to do anything contrary to Torah—"

"No, no, of course not." Yochai's expression was already showing his impatience.

Meir inclined his head in reluctant agreement. "What about Jamil?" he recalled suddenly.

"Jamil? Finish up this assignment first, and then you'll deal with Jamil. Are you planning on demanding a salary from the GSS too?"

"Not at all. I'm working under my own initiative."

"Not anymore," Yochai said warningly.

Meir rose from his seat, his shoulders slightly stooped as if carrying a heavy burden. He could already imagine Naomi's tirade when she heard what had happened that day.

"What are you thinking, Meir? That you can play with matches in the forest and not start a fire? One who sleeps with dogs awakens with fleas. One who sleeps in the sand, shouldn't—"

"Be surprised when he wakes up sandy," he would finish off for her.

But the truth was, that he himself had no idea what he had just gotten himself into.

33

Gil gazed out of the window in excitement as the plane lifted off the tarmac and soared into the crimson and purple heavens of a dazzling Israeli sunset. The feeling of freedom, however short-lived it would turn out to be, was exhilarating. Even more, it was surreal. Was he really sitting there, in an airplane, headed, for the first time in his life, out of the country? Maybe this was all just a dream – ahh, if only…

If only I could wake up, and find myself back in yeshivah, and that Berman was just some character in a nightmare. If only I could go back to my humdrum existence…

From one row behind him, a sharp knock on the back of his seat brought him back to his senses, a crude message from one of the two escorts Laser had sent with him, that they were there, that they were monitoring all his actions.

Had Yochai also seen fit to send his own escorts along? He hadn't mentioned anything of the kind, but that didn't mean a thing.

"Paris?" Yochai had quizzed him, when he asked for a few days' leave. "What on earth for?"

"Shopping, and stuff," Gil had responded shortly, resenting that he needed to answer to a boss.

Yochai's eyebrows rose even higher. "Since when is a *yeshivah bachur* into shopping?"

"Since he left *yeshivah*," Gil retorted.

“All right.” Yochai stretched his arms and legs and then, with surprising agility, swung back into place and folded his arms on his desk as he leaned forward. “Where did you get the money for a ticket?” he interrogated him.

“I gave the bank proof that I have a decent job and secured a loan. I got a good deal, so it wasn’t that expensive,” Gil said, as casually as he could.

“Okay… You’ve got twenty-four hours, and a few more on either side. Make sure you bring me back a souvenir! Don’t come back empty-handed!” Yochai’s grin was unsettling. Did he know something? Did he suspect him?

No, it couldn’t be; they were too careful, and they didn’t even risk speaking on the phone.

So why did Yochai look so confident?

“I guess I’m not so important around here if you can let me off so easily,” Gil remarked, carefully watching the older man’s face for any change in expression.

“Of course you’re not important. The GSS is a massive operation. You aren’t even a small screw in it yet…” Yochai was so pleased with himself that he failed to notice the look of anger cross Gil’s face. “But you’ll still make it, kid, eventually. Have no fear. It takes time to advance through the ranks. You have to work hard, and you don’t get bonus points for taking vacations. But it’s okay, just this once. Everyone deserves a break once in a while.”

With that, Gil received the authorization he needed.

And now he was on the way to meet his parents, his real parents. What kind of people would they turn out to be? More importantly, how would they react to the sight of him?

Landing in Paris, Gil was engulfed by a sudden wave of nausea, but he ignored it. He was met in the airport by an anonymous dark-skinned driver who led him to a car with tinted windows, as had been prearranged. Gil slipped inside soundlessly. Another dark-skinned man sat in the passenger seat, but neither one exchanged a word with him during the course of the hour-long drive. Gil hoped they would pause at a rest stop so he could freshen up a little, but his hopes were in vain; the men didn't even offer him a drink.

Finally, they entered an upper-class neighborhood featuring private villas and well-tended lawns, and the driver pulled to a stop in front of a house with a simple, but elegant façade. For the first time since he had entered the car, the man in the passenger seat turned around and addressed him in broken Hebrew.

"Don't talk too much or ask too many questions. We'll be back in ten hours to pick you up. And, don't even think of playing any tricks on us – we have you covered."

In his worst nightmares, Gil could never have imagined his family looking as they did. He knocked on the door, and two teenage boys opened, their eyes glinting with brazenness. From behind them, two little girls wearing head-coverings peered at their guest. All the children were painfully thin and unkempt.

He was invited to enter, and Gil was shocked at the disparity between the pleasant exterior of the house and the decrepit interior. The door squealed gratingly as it opened, and Gil had to swallow another rising wave of awful nausea that threatened to overcome him.

He looked up, and his eyes met those of an older man with a graying beard and broken yellow teeth that gave him the look of a wolf. *My father.*

"*Ya abni,*"* he greeted him and opened his arms wide. Instinctively, Gil retreated.

A shrill cry suddenly rent the air, and from somewhere inside the house, a heavy-set woman with small round eyes came running toward him. "*Ya abni! Ya abni!* How did they take you from

---

* My son

me, *ya abni!*" she cried, banging her head against the wall. It was one of the most frightening sights he had ever witnessed, and Gil took another step back, just to ensure that he was safe.

"Quiet, woman! You're frightening the boy!" the man shouted at her. Yet the woman, *his mother,* continued screaming and hitting her head against the wall until the husband waved his fist threateningly at her and she quieted instantly as if the loudspeaker inside her had suddenly been switched off. They gestured for him to join them in the living room, and Gil trailed after them fearfully.

The house screamed of poverty, but at least it was relatively clean and tidy.

"They stole you from us, *ya-abni!* I always felt that the child I held in my arms wasn't really mine," the woman began to speak, describing her strong feeling hours after the birth when she had first noticed the glaring dissimilarity between the infant she cradled and the one she had borne mere hours previously. "I always felt it. I swear in the name of the prophet Mohammad that I always knew that Jamil was not my son. He was different than the rest, and I mourned him. Your father despised him."

Gil did not say a word and merely listened. For some reason, her final remark piqued his interest, and he found himself appalled by the difference between the mother who had raised him – the sweet, refined Shuli – and this coarse village woman. The latter repelled him, and he automatically related to her words with blatant apathy, yet the thought that his biological father had detested the Jewish child entrusted to him stirred his curiosity.

"How so?" he asked quietly.

"He beat him mercilessly," the woman replied indifferently. "I would ask him, 'Don't you have pity on your son?' but he always brushed me off and continue beating him. That Jamil, or whatever his name was, was a total idiot without a head on his shoulders."

Gil tried to get comfortable on his rickety chair. His mother stood over him, ready to serve him, and now his father beamed with pride.

"You were destined to serve our nation, more so than any of your brothers. I'm proud of you, son," he expressed emotionally. "You will bring us great honor and joy. Great, great honor."

Samira placed a dish in front of him, yet Gil couldn't bring himself to eat. Each successive item of food placed on the table only increased his feelings of nausea. He agreed to take a cup of water, but he measured his sips.

"Tell me," he turned to the man, unable to address him by any title. "Do you know what my mission is?"

"Sort of, not completely. They didn't ask us for permission; we had no choice." His tone was remorseful, and he dropped his eyes to the ground; his was the fate of the downtrodden Arab sworn to sacrifice for the sake of redeeming Palestine.

"If they would have asked you?"

"I don't want to go there." The words were cold and succinct.

"Do you know what they will do with me once I fulfill their mission?"

"I understand that the mission itself poses a risk to your life."

"So there is a good chance that we shall never meet again."

The woman had disappeared momentarily into the kitchen, but she returned in time to hear Gil's final remark. "Do not fear, my son. We have sweets in the pantry, and we will erect a mourner's tent as soon as we receive the news."

Gil stared at her with loathing and repugnance. *What kind of mother is she? What kind of father would send his son to his death without giving him a choice, without even asking him? Accursed Arabs! What other people would eagerly anticipate the death of their sons, even via martyrdom?*

Rashid exited the room just then, and only the woman remained, pleading with Gil in a tearful voice. "Avenge the blood of my brothers! They murdered them! They slaughtered them like sheep! Avenge the blood and land of your grandparents, who fled their home in Haifa and left their houses and property to be occupied by those filthy Jews who plundered everything! Avenge their shame and never forget! You are our greatest hope, and you will restore our lost honor!" The faces of her brothers and uncles rose to her mind, and she began wailing pitifully.

Knocks sounded on the front door, and then, without warning, a wave of people began to stream inside. Brothers, older and younger, uncles, cousins, friends of the family. They all gazed at him with awe, although Gil had a feeling that no one really knew the details of his background or his destined fate. All they knew was that he was a representative of the resistance, an instrument to be used to free Palestine, and they revered and even envied him for his role.

The first two hours of his visit passed quickly.

"Now go and rest, my son. Then we will speak again. There is much I must tell you," the man who professed to be his father told him. Gil was directed to a small bedroom where a low bed had been made for him. It really had been a long day, and he lay down on the bed and tried to sleep, but found he could not. His head was pounding, and his nostrils were assailed by an array of foreign, unpleasant odors.

This is your family, he repeated to himself. *Your family. If Tatty and Mommy – Shimon and Shuli – knew the truth, they would throw you out of the house like a street rat. This is your place. Here, they accept you with open arms and with love.*

But the word "love" was so far removed from what he felt emanating from these people, especially ever since encountering the concepts of Arab pride and martyrdom. He replayed the events of the past hours in his mind, and shuddered again as he recalled the light shining from the eyes of the Arab woman and the hatred that had disfigured her face upon mentioning Jamil.

He couldn't help but wonder what would fill his Jewish mother's eyes when she learned the truth. Would they fill with that same loathing and hatred radiated by Samira? Could Shuli ever hate her son, her Mendy?

34

Precisely ten hours later, the two men who had escorted Gil on his flight to Paris entered the house, prompting a hysterical outburst by the collective family *chamula.** The women especially – his mother, sisters, cousins, and their friends – began shrieking, and even the men cowered in fear.

"Quiet, here!" one of the men roared, and the women immediately fell silent. "Come," he ordered Gil.

Gil glanced behind him one more time, and his eyes fell on his father. Something in his heart whispered that this man had a heart, and that if it had only been possible, he would have thrown those men out of his house and asked Gil to stay. The thought comforted him slightly and evoked a glimmering of feeling in him – until he suddenly recalled the Arab woman's description of the beatings the Jewish boy had endured under his adoptive father's hand, and the warmth was promptly replaced by disgust. Gil's eyes flickered with these warring emotions, but he uttered not a word.

"Let me bless you, *ya-abni*!" the Arab woman exclaimed as she rushed toward him, but Gil purposely took another step toward the door. He simply could not bear the thought of this woman being his mother – how could it be true?

Samira sensed his revulsion, and her shoulders sank. "You're our son! Do not reject us! You will avenge our lost family and

---

* clan

land. You will avenge our honor!"

With that, everyone escorted him to the waiting car in an awful ruckus of cheering mingled with wailing. One cousin's eyes lit up with exhilaration, and he lifted a long-barreled gun toward the skies. Gil's escorts reacted quickly.

"No celebratory shooting!" they ordered sharply. "The last thing we need is half the Paris police force over here. *Yallah!* The party's over. Everyone home!" When everyone remained rooted in place, the escorts shouted again, "*Yallah! Yallah!* MOVE!" The bigger of the two men then stepped forward, and gave Gil's father, who stared rebelliously at them as he watched his son leave to his death, a solid shove.

Once in the car, Gil leaned his head back against the upholstery, trying to regain his composure. The word *revenge* kept swirling in his mind, echoing in his ears and heart.

R-E-V-E-N-G-E!

In his mind's eye, he envisioned his parents' elderly neighbor, Rav Yisrael Reichman, a Holocaust survivor. Whenever Rav Reichman spoke of avenging the blood of his family and that of almost his entire village, his eyes shone with fervor and fire. "My grandchildren and great-grandchildren are my greatest revenge. Look, Mendy. Look at these *zisse kinderlach* with their *peyos* and *tzitzis!* They're my revenge against Hitler, *yimach shemo,* who killed my whole family – my first wife, and my five precious *yingelach*. But today, I've got fifty-four *einiklach* who avenge their deaths in the gas chambers, who every morning and night shout *'Shema Yisrael!'* This is our *Yiddishe* revenge!"

The Arab woman with the flashing, hatred-filled eyes, was also spouting talk of revenge – it was, it seemed, her highest ideal. But what kind of revenge did she envision? The murder of innocent people. Not those people who stole her parents' wealth, nor even the soldiers who had banished her, or, most probably, her parents, from their home. All she aspired to was the death of innocent civilians, of men, women, and children who had never harmed a soul.

Could that truly be called revenge?

The car continued to speed toward the airport. So lost was he in his reveries that Gil hardly noticed that one of his escort's cell phones was ringing until the man stuck it under his nose.

"It's for you," he said.

Laser was on the line, and he sounded as irritable as ever. "They don't trust you at the GSS. Our sources say they're getting suspicious. Now that you got what you wanted, I expect good results from you. Tomorrow you're back to work; no more vacation for you, boy."

Gil narrowed his eyes, concentrating hard. Whenever he was far removed from Laser's presence, everything seemed different, and so much clearer. "What if I refuse?"

"Then we'll kill you."

"So what? You'll kill me even if I do carry out the mission. You don't trust me. I grew up with the enemy."

There was no reply, and Gil continued blasting the man whom he had come to loathe. Everything was perfectly clear now, as if he had suddenly located the path through the dense forest and was on his way out. The Arab woman's words still resonated in his mind, along with the apologetic look in her husband's eyes, along with his powerlessness to beg his forgiveness.

"In fact, it doesn't make a difference whether I carry out the mission or not. I'll die in any case. You've turned me into a *shahid*, but you never gave me a choice. You know what? Just kill me now, and get it over with."

Laser was still quiet, and Gil forged ahead, drunk with victory. "I'm not even convinced that the Jews aren't right. You started a war. They won, and you lost. That's the way it goes. It could have been the opposite, too, and then the Arabs would have been the oppressors and conquerors, and I doubt they would have shown more pity than the Jews had on them."

Laser cut him off, his tone grave. "You're right. You'll die in any case."

Gil's heart froze; it was one thing to know it, but something else entirely to hear it stated aloud. He had still entertained vague hopes that Laser would deny his conjecture, that all these Arabs actually cared about him and felt sentiments of brotherhood toward him. But he was swiftly discovering that brotherhood, to Arabs, meant something entirely different to how the Jews interpreted the word.

"The question is, with whom would you like to die?" Laser continued, his tone suave. "You can perish as a hero and a *shahid,* or you can die now, before the mission, along with the Jewish family that raised you. You can choose how to die, boy. So, let's hear: What's your choice?"

Gil began to tremble as a thousand terrifying thoughts raced through his mind. If this conversation had been taking place just a few months previously, then he would have certainly reacted out of instinctual fear, but twelve weeks of intensive training under the auspices of the GSS had made their mark, and his nerves were strong enough to enable him to think one step ahead.

"You're making a mistake," he replied coldly, his voice betraying not a tremor. "My Jewish family doesn't concern me any longer. On the contrary, I despise them. You can kill them today already, for all I care, along with their neighbors. Destroy their house too while you're at it. They're zero. Your threats are worthless. Nonetheless, I'll agree to cooperate with you on one condition."

Laser was visibly taken aback by Gil's declaration. "And what's that?"

"I'll help you carry out the mission, but not as a *shahid*. Plus, you'll pay me for the job, enough to enable me to start life over someplace else. And, I want a guarantee that you'll keep your word."

"How can I possibly give you that?"

"I don't know yet. I'll have to think about it. But until I do get a guarantee, don't bother trying to threaten me again. And, I think it would be that much the better for both of us if you, instead, tried to prove to me that we really are brothers." He ended the call on that poetic note, ignoring the hatred emanating from the men in front of him and exhaling a sigh of relief, nearly drunk with victory.

The rest of the ride was spent staring out of the window, gazing unseeingly at Paris's world-famous architecture. Gil felt as if someone had just taken his arm and attached an IV line that infused a new, bold spirit into his heart. No longer was this just a fight for survival. Now it was a fight for independence. Never again would he submit to the dictates of another – from now on, he, and only he, would be master of his destiny.

It was mid-morning, and Shimon called his wife on her cell phone, and was astonished to hear her mumble something sleepily in response. "Shuli? You're still asleep? Why haven't you gone to work?"

"Why? I took an extended leave of absence," she dropped the bombshell.

"What? *When*?"

"When? From yesterday. From today. I'm home now, in any case. I'm waiting for him. I know I went back to work for a few days, but I can't play the game any longer. I can't go on like this, waiting and hoping the whole time!"

"For who?"

"What do you mean? For Mendy, of course!"

"Of course?!" Shimon suppressed his urge to ram his head into the nearest wall. Why was Shuli continuing to delude herself like this? Why was she so determined to ignore the hints he kept dropping? In fact, several comments she had made over the past few days had suggested to him that she was beginning to share his suspicions, but now it seemed that she was deliberately burying her head in the sand once again, despite the pain and disappointment that this would ultimately lead to.

"Shuli, you can't do this," he struggled to maintain a semblance of patience. "You simply have to try to adjust to a new reality. Listen, I'm at work now, so I can't talk for long, but, Shuli, you have to be strong and get over this somehow. Stop talking about Mendy! Just drop it!"

Shimon practically dropped the phone upon hearing his wife's livid reaction. "DON'T TELL ME NOT TO TALK ABOUT MENDY!" she yelled furiously at her husband. "Mendy's my son! He's my baby! I want him back!" Frantic knocks sounded at the door, and Shuli suddenly realized that she was screaming. "Someone's at the door, Shimon. We'll talk later."

She jumped out of bed, pulled on a robe, and straightened her snood. Mrs. Lipsky, a neighbor, was at the door.

"Shuli, I thought I heard loud voices from your apartment. Is everything okay?" she asked cautiously.

"I'm fine. Thanks."

The older woman opened her arms. "Shuli, we're all with you in this. We all share your pain," she said, her tone heartfelt. "Mendy will come back, I'm sure of it! We're all *davening* for him. He was always such a sweet boy, and such a special *bachur*! Always so helpful and obliging, with a heart of gold. Shuli, I'm sure he'll be back."

With her defenses already down, Shuli crumbled and fell into the older woman's arms, burying her face in her shoulder. "My Mendy!" she wept. "I never thought… my baby…"

"He'll be back," old Mrs. Lipsky whispered soothingly. "He's gold, that son of yours, and he'll be back. *Hashem yishmor!* I don't believe it!" she suddenly cried. "Shuli, open your eyes. Look who's here! It's like he fell from *Shamayim*! I knew he'd come, and… would you believe it? Right after you cried and *davened*! Look, Shuli!"

Shuli lifted her head and gazed at the young man standing at the door, his pose one of quiet confidence.

Mendy.

"Mommy, it's good to see you. Is everything all right?" he asked in concern. "Where's Tatty? Did something happen? Does Tatty know that you're crying? Why are you crying?"

He strode into the house, leaving the door open.

Shuli latched fearfully onto her elderly neighbor's arms. "Don't go, Toiby. Stay with me. Don't go anywhere yet, okay?"

Toiby followed her neighbor into her apartment, supporting her gently by the arm.

"Have a seat, Shuli. Calm down. Mendy, bring your mother a drink!" she told the boy, talking to him as though he was the little boy she remembered from years past, not the intimidating young man who now stood before her.

"Did something happen?" Gil asked again, in rising concern.

"No, or rather, yes. Your mother was crying about you, Mendy dear. What are you waiting for? A bit of *kibbud horim* wouldn't hurt. You're still going to give your parents a lot of *nachas*, Mendy. Mark my words!" Gil allowed himself a small, sardonic smile, before heading to the kitchen to get his mother a cold drink.

"Here, Mommy. Drink it slowly," he instructed her authoritatively.

Shuli, however, trembled violently. *What did Mendy want from her? Why was he here now? Should she call Shimon to update him and tell him to come home?* The doubts stormed within her. Was this really her Mendy? The boy she had raised for twenty years?

Gil settled down across from her. "It's okay, Mrs. Lipsky. You can go now. I'm here now with my mother."

"Don't go!" Shuli choked, unable to even sip from the water.

"Go, go. Everything will be okay." Gil rose again, straightening up to his full height, and something about his presence seemed threatening. Toiby rose, as well.

"Should I go?" she murmured uncomfortably. Gil opened the door for her, his intentions clear, and she took meek steps toward the entrance, but not before laying a comforting hand on Shuli's shoulder. "It's all right, my dear. You can calm down. He's your son, and he wants to tell you how much he still cares about you. If you need me, call me back right away."

"Please go," Gil repeated, with more than a trace of impatience.

Toiby disappeared, and Gil closed the door behind her. He was about to lock it, but sensing his mother's fear, chose otherwise. He glanced at Shuli for a moment, hesitated, and then opened the door again, leaving it slightly ajar. "That way, she can come back if she wants," he explained, almost apologetically. "Mommy, why were you crying about me?"

Shuli sighed, feeling safer with the door open. "Mendy, it's very hard for me. I don't sleep well at night, and… and that's where things are holding. I have no peace of mind, and I have no idea where this is going to end."

Gil's eyes narrowed. "What would give you back your peace of mind?" he asked, his tone rough.

A flood of tears poured from Shuli's eyes. "My son, Mendy. My son! Only he can bring it back. My baby Mendy."

"I'm still a baby?" Gil looked semi-amused, but very alert.

Shuli tried to regain her bearings, and she immediately discerned the warning glare in Gil's eyes. "I'm just remembering you as a baby now," she stammered.

Gil's expression was serious. "What did you see in me as a baby?"

Was he here to take revenge? Was he collaborating with the enemy? Why had he come?

"Mendy, what brings you here now, all of a sudden?" she spontaneously changed the subject. "You said you were cutting off contact." She had her other children to protect, and they would be home from school within the hour. She needed to get him out of the house before they laid eyes on their brother.

"Are you disappointed that I came?" he asked slowly, looking sporadically around the room.

"Chas v'shalom!" she exclaimed. "Just… a bit surprised. What made you come?"

"I wanted to know what you think about me. And, what you thought about me as a child. Also, what you think of the steps I've recently taken in life."

Shuli took her time before answering, pausing the conversation to make coffee. Mendy, as she called him, although he might have been an Ahmad or a Muhammad, trailed after her like a stray cat.

"What's the question? What's the difference? Does it matter what I thought then? What matters is what I think now. You know I'm disappointed," her tone quivered as she boiled water in the electric kettle.

"I can make the coffee," he offered.

"I don't want you to make it."

"Why not? It's *kibbud av va'eim.*" His words were spoken so smoothly, so naturally.

His reply grated on her nerves. "Why is that the only *mitzvah* that concerns you?" she asked coldly.

"Mommy…" Suddenly, his tone was completely different, and she instinctively spun around. His black eyes were large and pleading, and once again, she saw the little boy she had always known and loved.

"Mommy…" His lips trembled violently, and a thin glassy film misted over his eyes. "Please, don't be so cold. Sometimes, I wonder what I have to live for, and then I think that the only reason is because of you."

Shuli had always heard that Arabs were cunning and sly, and she was beginning to perceive the same in her son, even though his words pulled her into an emotional whirlwind in which she was finding it hard to keep her bearings.

The water boiled, and as she slowly poured it over the coffee, a heady aroma filled the room.

Gil sat down at the kitchen table beside her. She deliberately moved her chair to the side, but her son seemed to be begging for closeness.

"You know, Mommy," he tried again, pronouncing the word "Mommy" so yearningly that Shuli's heart broke in two, "seeing you now is bringing back so many happy memories. Remember the time when we travelled to the Golan, and a cat managed to get into our bungalow? I was the only one who dared to get rid of it! Everyone was screaming, and you told me that I was brave and also good because I didn't hurt the cat and I was *mekayem kibbud av va'eim*. Remember?" For a moment, he seemed to soften as he let his mind wander back into the past.

"And remember when I bought you a birthday present with all my money? I bought you a fake diamond ring. It cost three shekels, but it was all I had. I was… how old at the time?"

"Five," Shuli supplied.

"Right, five. Remember how happy you were that I thought of you? Tatty said that it was such a good present, but I was so upset when he saw the ring and laughed… Remember?" He didn't even await her reply. "And remember that time when we sifted flour together, and you dropped the whole thing on me because you thought you saw a bug inside? I looked like a ghost, and then Mrs. Lipsky walked in, and—"

"And had the fright of her life, and we all laughed and laughed," Shuli filled in, carried away as well. Both of them laughed at the memory, and then, their eyes met, and they both remembered… something else. She remembered her suspicions, and he, the truth; and the laughter immediately died on their lips.

"Mommy," Gil tried to recapture the moment, "nobody can take away those memories. Right?" Was he pleading with her?

"But what's going to be?" she challenged him, hoping that the Arab inside him would remain dormant.

"I don't know," he replied honestly, and then immediately asked, "Where's Tatty?"

"At work. It's the middle of the day," she replied, surprised as the answer should have been obvious. It suddenly occurred to her that Mendy must be plotting something, and fear clutched at her heart.

Gil nodded. "Of course. What a silly question. The truth is that I only came by to collect a few things of mine. If you don't mind, I'll go to my room now and take them. I also need some of my personal documents that are stored in the safe."

"Tatty changed the code, and I don't know it anymore," she said quickly.

Gil's expression darkened. "But they're mine, and I need them."

"What's yours?"

"Documents. I'm sure Tatty knows what I need. Can you call him and ask him for the code?"

"He's at work now. You know I never disturb him at work. Why don't you come back tomorrow, and I'll tell Tatty to leave your things for you on the desk?"

Gil had the distinct feeling that she was trying to get rid of him. Quickly.

"I need them now, Mommy."

Careful, Shuli. You don't know what he's capable of. Something has happened, maybe even… what you most fear, and anything is possible now. Who knows what kind of blood is flowing through his veins? He's your son, but he could be either friend or foe…

"So call Tatty yourself, if you want."

"I think it's best that he doesn't know that I'm here." Shuli wondered if he was deliberately avoiding use of the word "Tatty," but there was no question that his eyes had turned cold and that his entire being now radiated hostility and even danger.

"Mendy, if you want the code, I'll have to tell Tatty that you're here," she replied, trying valiantly to keep her voice steady.

"You know the code, Mommy. Just remember it, please, and quickly, for both our sakes." He would never draw his gun, but he was sorely tempted to at that moment. Simultaneously, he felt sick. How could he rob his own mother?

It wasn't her fault. She had no way of knowing that he needed the money to protect them both; he needed his independence if he wanted to save his family. And the only way he could manage that was if he could prove to them that he had money, and that if he died, there would be someone to answer to.

But Shuli was terrified, and he couldn't handle that. He couldn't take frightening the woman who had loved him and raised him for twenty years; and now she quivered in fear.

"Are you giving it to me, or not?" He took a menacing step toward her.

"No, she's not!"

Gil and Shuli spun around in shock to face Shimon. The voice was Shimon's, but not the hands. These hands were those of a trained GSS officer, and now they held a gun that was pointed at his son.

"Step aside, Mendy."

"But—"

"Move!"

Gil retreated, and accidentally dropped his coffee cup. As he rose to pick it up, he found himself reacting by drawing his own gun and aiming it at his father.

Shuli was the first to react.

"Put them down! Drop those guns this instant! What's wrong with the two of you! Put them down, or I'm calling the police!"

"Why are you protecting him?" Shimon asked in a hard voice, his finger still on the trigger.

Shuli turned to look at Mendy, whose face was pale. Shimon took a step forward. "You won't make a good GSS agent," he said with a triumphant smile. In a flash, he twisted Gil's arm backward and pried the gun out of his hand before it landed on the floor.

By then, Shuli was hysterical. "Shimon, you're doing something we're both going to regret! Mendy is our son!"

"I know very well who he is."

"This is the son that I raised!" She turned to Gil, whose dark eyes were glittering. A man of twenty didn't cry, but he was tearing. Why? What had inspired his emotional reaction.

"There's no sign of appreciation," Shimon said cynically.

"He still holds the values that we instilled in him. Don't you, Mendy?" she turned pleadingly to her son. Gil blinked back his tears, trying to feign indifference.

"Right now, you're stronger than me, Tatty, but I'll learn; and one day, we'll settle the score."

"Don't you call me..." Shimon's body trembled in fury. "You hear me? Don't call me... You..." The images flooded him with almost physical force. Shabbos afternoon. Mendy learning *Gemara* with him, asking an excellent *kushya* that would make any father proud. Walking together to shul. Dancing together at a *chasunah.* Mendy at his bedside the time he'd been sick. Mendy. The son who should have brought him so much joy…

"Why shouldn't I call you Tatty?" Gil seemed to be enjoying taunting him.

Suddenly, Shimon dropped both guns on the table and clutched at his heart.

"Shimon! *Shimon!*" Shuli began to scream. "Mendy, call Hatzolah! Help! Call an ambulance! Shimon! *Shimon!*"

Gil raced for the phone and dialed Hatzolah. When Shimon crumpled to the floor, Gil kneeled down beside him and held his hand. "Tatty!" he said urgently. "Tatty, look at me! Tatty, I promise everything will be okay," he pleaded. "Take a deep breath and try to calm down. Nothing happened!"

"It *is* happening," Shimon barely managed to mumble, and his eyes narrowed as he moaned in pain.

"No, nothing happened. Tatty, you're okay! It's just the tension between us. You'll be all right." Tears began to run down Gil's cheeks.

"No, it won't. They killed my son…"

"Who?"

"My Mendy…" Shimon gasped. "My real son…"

Gil remained rooted to his spot in a kneeling position, unable to respond to his father's words. Not for a moment had he considered the other side of the story, his parents' tragedy. He had lost them, but they had lost a child. He had never felt so confused in his life.

"I've lost my son," Shimon began to weep without tears, the sobs of an old man. "My child was taken, twenty years ago…"

Gil squeezed his hand. "Tatty, I'll find out. I'll find out where he is," he promised the impossible.

"I don't even know who you are."

"I'm Mendy," he choked out.

"Who are you?"

"Mendy. Your Mendy."

"Mendy… My son…" Shimon lifted his arm, which had once been so strong and was now so terribly frail and powerless. With great effort, he stroked Mendy's cheek. "You're a good boy. You always were…" Shimon's voice was becoming weaker and his words more difficult to understand. "You always gave me so much joy, until this past year. You're still a good boy." His hand froze and then fell limply to his side as his eyes closed.

Shuli and Gil both let out screams at the very second that three men dressed in orange Hatzolah vests came hurtling into the house, pushing the wife and son aside. Within seconds, the house filled with neighbors, and inexplicably, even Yochai was there. He didn't say a word, chewing his fingernails as he watched the paramedics attempt CPR.

After five minutes of failed attempts, they announced that they were taking him to the hospital. "It doesn't look so encouraging," they said gently. "We're taking him in, but we can't promise anything. Even if he survives, it's not clear what condition he'll be in."

Shuli trembled and practically fainted, but Gil supported her. They watched in tears as Shimon was carried out on a stretcher, and then Gil loudly asked everyone to leave. Shuli was too shaken to join her husband in the ambulance, and after a moment's hesitation, Gil decided that his mother needed him more than his father did right then.

Shuli looked like a worn-out ragdoll. "He'll die, and I'll have nothing left to live for!" she wailed.

"Mommy," Gil said firmly, trying to restore her equilibrium, "when are Suri and Nachum coming home?"

His words had the intended effect. "*Hashem yerachem!* I don't know. What time is it? Um… In about half an hour. Who…

Who...Where..." She couldn't focus enough to think straight.

"Mommy, I'll talk to Mrs. Lipsky and ask her to watch them. I'm driving you to the hospital now. Don't worry. Everything will be okay."

"How can you know?" she asked him.

"I feel it," he said strongly, and his words sounded like a promise.

Shuli gazed at her son through her tears. Mendy was back. Her son, the child she had raised and loved, the son who loved to help everyone. In an instant, all the horrible doubts vanished from her mind.

"It's all my fault. I wish I hadn't come," he said suddenly.

"No! I'm happy you're here."

"But this wouldn't have happened if I hadn't come," he repeated guiltily. "Seeing me with a gun was too much for him."

"A gun isn't enough to frighten Tatty. It was just a spontaneous heart attack, and not his first one. Nothing happened between you. A father and son don't shoot each other."

"A father and son..." he echoed dully.

Shuli treated her son to a hard look. "Mendy, please – don't start with that now. Yes, a father and son! You are our son, no matter what. Tatty is your father, and you're our son."

She stood at the threshold, but was too frightened to venture further alone.

"We should go, Mommy," he said gently. "They said that it's not good. I hope that it's not so bad though, and that he'll be conscious by the time we reach the hospital."

Shuli tried hard to believe him.

Too distraught to drive, Gil flagged a taxi. "Sheba Hospital," he instructed the cabbie tonelessly. At the emergency room, they discovered that Shimon had been wheeled directly into surgery for a triple bypass operation. Mother and son waited anxiously outside the operating theater, with the occasional entering or exiting doctor or nurse giving them pitying looks.

Within just twenty minutes, a group of men had assembled outside the operating room together with them. Yochai was there, along with other members of the department, two of Shimon's closest friends, and three men from his evening *kollel*. There was something stirring about the moment when all twelve of them – black-hatters, knitted *kippot*, and bareheaded alike – joined together to recite *Tehillim*, a rare scene indeed.

It suddenly occurred to Gil that even Yochai had donned a tiny green knitted *kippah*, and this elicited a small smile from his lips, one that faded away almost as quickly as it had appeared.

An hour later, his cell phone shrilled in his pocket. Laser's voice sliced through the line, sending chills up Gil's spine. "Don't go anywhere," he ordered him quietly. "Stick to your Jewish family now, and try to squeeze whatever you can out of Yochai. This is an opportunity for you to see a bunch of the top brass. Don't go anywhere." With that, the line went dead.

"Who was that?" Shuli asked.

"A friend," Gil replied, still pale.

A quarter of an hour later, a doctor exited the operating theater wearing a grave expression. His eyes roved the crowded room in surprise, and he motioned for Shuli to join him. They started down the hall along with two nurses, and Gil automatically followed.

"Who are you?" the doctor stopped him.

"A son," Gil replied automatically, momentarily forgetting that his appearance would raise suspicion. The doctor cast a quizzical gaze at Shuli, who nodded.

"He's my son," she confirmed. "I want him with us now."

Nodding wordlessly, the doctor ushered them into an empty office. Gil stiffened as he noticed a nurse pouring a glass of water into a cup and dropping some substance inside.

"Drink this. It'll make you feel better," she crooned to Shuli. "It'll give you strength."

Gil's heart constricted as he realized that his mother was being given a tranquilizer in preparation for the trauma. Perspiration broke out all over his body, and he could hardly breathe. In a daze, he heard the doctor's voice…

"…we did all we could. Everything humanly possible. Please believe me. I know this is difficult to hear, but you're religious people who believe in G-d and in His *hashgachah*. A person has his allotted days of life, and your husband fought for his life until the final moment when… Mrs. Brand, do you understand what I'm telling you?"

Shuli stared at him through glassy eyes.

"Mr. Brand, if you'll accompany me," the doctor turned sympathetically to Gil. "The nurse will care for your mother now. She's still in shock."

"NO!!!!!!!!!!!!!!!!!" Gil suddenly released the cry of a wounded animal, the shocked plea of an orphaned child. "NO!!! It's not true! It can't be! You're lying! *TATTY!*"

He fled from the room, but was stopped by his father's *chavrusa* who caught the weeping son in his strong embrace and held him in his arms in a vain attempt to soothe the impossible pain.

Four days later, at noon, Toiby Lipsky closed the door to the house firmly.

"Shuli, dear, you need a break. You need to lie down. I'm putting a stop to this. People can't just come and go as they please. You need to rest."

Shuli nodded dully and walked obediently to her bed.

At a quarter to four, her neighbor roused her gently. "Shuli, I'm sorry, dear, but it's time to get up. People will be coming again soon. You should eat and drink something before then." Shuli rose, ate and drank like a robot, and returned to sit in the low chair.

Her expression was blank and frozen, and her motions were mechanical. Despite her protests, both Nachum and Suri were staying with one of Shuli's closest friends. Nachum came once a day to visit his mother, but he spoke little. He was just as much in shock as the rest of them, and Shuli kept wondering if it wasn't better for him to be at home with her during the *shivah*. He was already ten, after all, and mature for his years, but in her state of emotional exhaustion, Shuli ended up capitulating to whatever people told her was best to do.

The kitchen table overflowed with cooked food, cakes, and drinks, as if Shuli was even vaguely interested in eating – and, in any case, she certainly had no need for such quantities. She was the sole mourner, living in a haze, doing as she was told, answering questions and relating events, but feeling nothing.

"Cry, *neshomale*," Mrs. Lipsky crooned compassionately. "It's good for you. Crying releases the pain; it's healthy." But Shuli couldn't cry. She hadn't cried at the *levayah* either, even when she stared in shock at her husband's form covered in a *tallis,* nor had she cried when they returned home, although she did occasionally mutter, "I can't believe it. It can't be."

Old Mrs. Lipsky, who had endured her own share of suffering during her time, took the younger woman under her wing. She was consumed with guilt. She had been the one to call her husband and have him summon Shimon home when Gil had arrived on that fateful day, and although nobody could have anticipated the ramifications, still she blamed herself for what had happened. If only she hadn't called him! If only she hadn't been the one to prompt that critical clash between father and son… then perhaps Shimon would still be alive, and poor Shuli wouldn't be an *almanah…*

On the second night of the *shivah*, when the house which had been bursting at the seams with friends who had come to comfort Shuli finally emptied out, she volunteered to spend the night with her young neighbor, so that she wouldn't have to sleep alone.

The apartment was silent and cold, lacking the warmth and vibrancy once so characteristic of the Brand family.

At midnight, Shuli rose from her bed, unable to sleep and feeling suddenly starved. Although she tried not to make noise, Mrs. Lipsky, who had always been something of an insomniac, heard her and followed her into the kitchen.

Shuli sank onto a kitchen chair and listlessly cut herself a piece of caramel-topped cheesecake. It was delicious, but she tasted nothing.

"I feel like I'm choking," she spoke suddenly to her elderly neighbor.

Toiby Lipsky nodded her head understandingly. Unfortunately, she had already sat *shivah* for both her parents, three siblings, and even a child, and well did she know the feeling. Mourning could be choking, painful, threatening; every person dealt with it differently.

"I can't anymore," Shuli whispered, her expression so tired and worn out.

"You can. You must," Mrs. Lipsky clasped Shuli's hand in her wizened one.

"No, I can't. I really can't."

"Of course you can. Just as we carried on after the wars," Toiby insisted, smiling encouragingly at the desperate younger woman. She was about to remind her that she still had her children to care for, children who needed her.

"Maybe with a glass of water," Shuli finally sighed in compromise.

Toiby stared at her in concern. Was Shuli cracking?

"I can't finish the cake. It's so dry. Maybe a glass of water will help," Shuli explained.

"You were talking about the cake?" Toiby gaped.

"Of course. What else?"

Toiby's mouth stayed open, and she squeezed Shuli's hand again. "You can cry, my dear. It's allowed, and it's good." Her voice contained so much compassion. "Cry. It's not good to bottle up the pain for so long."

Shuli answered her severely. "Everyone deals with pain in their own way, Toiby. Please understand me. When I'm ready to release my pain, I will."

"Maybe you should speak to someone?" the woman tried delicately.

"I'm speaking to way too many people. I need some peace and quiet," Shuli sighed.

"Are you thinking of Mendy, who isn't here now?" the old woman tried again.

Enough! Shuli wanted to scream, restraining herself only out of respect for the old woman's own suffering in life. *She wants to help, but I can't anymore! It's enough that women talk behind my back all day long, about Mendy and about Shimon and all they think and suspect! Stop treading on my open wounds!*

"Please, Toiby. I really need to be alone now," she said firmly, and practically pulled the old woman to the door.

As soon as she shut the door behind her, Shuli sagged against the wall and released torrents of hot tears.

Meir ambushed Gil right outside the entrance. He had already heard the news from Yochai and had headed straight to the *shivah* house, only to learn that Nachum was the only male there, and only for one hour a day. He immediately called Yochai, who casually replied that Gil had announced that he preferred to go to work.

"What's the matter with him? Who ever heard of a Jewish boy refusing to sit *shivah* for his father?" he pounced on him accusingly.

Yochai had been quiet for a moment, finally replying in a weary tone laced with scorn. "What do you want from me, Meir?"

"I want to meet him. Right now."

"Listen, I'm not authorized to give you his cell number, but why don't you wait for him outside the building tomorrow morning? I imagine he'll be there, right on time."

Meir couldn't end the call without releasing his frustration on the hard-hearted agent. "You should be ashamed of yourself, Yochai. You're a Jew, after all. Where's your heart? You should *order* him to sit *shivah* for his father!" Yochai didn't deign to reply and merely ended the call.

Naomi couldn't understand his distress. "Meir, why don't you just let it all alone? When are you going to give up? First, it was that Jamil. Now it's this Mendy of yours. What's gotten into you?"

"Naomi, there are many people in the world who need help, but Hashem put me in a position to help these two specific people. I was the first one to meet Jamil and discover that he's a Yid. Then I came across Mendy, who was once a fantastic *bachur* and suddenly, almost out of the blue, went off the *derech* to the point that he won't even sit *shivah* for his father! Do you really think I should just ignore the fact that our paths crossed?"

"No, not ignore it, but just the same, this is turning into an obsession!" Naomi knew that her words were falling upon deaf ears, and with that, she surrendered. For all his failings, her husband was a *yarei Shamayim* with a heart of gold, and nothing would stop him from doing what he felt was right.

The next morning, Meir got up earlier than usual, in order to *daven netz* and arrive at Headquarters before eight. The guard treated him to a stern gaze.

"Your identification," he barked.

Meir withdrew his identity card.

"State your occupation and your purpose for being here."

Meir frowned in annoyance. "You can ask Yochai about that!" His words had the desired impact.

"Yochai?" the guard reacted in surprise.

"Yes. Ask Yochai."

"You two are friends?"

"Something like that."

"He's got *chareidi* friends?"

"Stranger things have happened."

The guard's curiosity was piqued. "Don't tell me that he's being *chozer b'teshuvah!*"

"Why don't we start with you?" Meir kidded.

The guard radioed someone and nodded at Meir to enter. The latter took his seat in the lobby, but it was a long wait until nine-thirty, when Gil finally entered the building wearing a baseball cap and a serious expression.

"Mendy!" he cried, and leaped off his chair.

Gil seemed surprised at the greeting as he glanced around to see who was looking for him. Something in his eyes was almost hopeful. "Oh, it's you," he said, when he noticed Meir, his disappointment evident in his eyes. "What do you want?"

"Mendy, you must be feeling terrible. And this is your last chance to honor your father! Is this really the way you want to end your relationship with him?" Meir challenged.

Gil tipped his cap backward, and played with the lock of hair that grew brazenly across his forehead. "Listen, Meir, you're a nice guy, but you're starting to get on my nerves," he replied.

"Why? Because I'm reminding you to sit *shivah* for your father?'

Gil's eyes narrowed. "Now you've really gone too far. Just leave me alone, okay? I don't want to talk about it, and definitely not to you."

"Can't you do *anything* to honor your father? One last *chessed l'ilui nishmaso*?"

"What kind of *chessed*?" Gil asked impatiently.

"You know what? Don't sit *shivah*! But at least let's learn one *daf Gemara l'ilui nishmas* your father. One *daf*, that's all."

Gil released an empty laugh. "You're one bored soul, Meir." But the smile froze on his lips as he suddenly lapsed into thought. Meir continued staring unflinchingly into his eyes.

"You know what?" Gil said spontaneously. "You got yourself a deal. One *daf Gemara.* It doesn't sound too bad. We'll learn *b'chavrusa*."

"*B'chavrusa*," Meir nodded in agreement, trying to conceal his excitement.

"You know that shul down the block?"

"On the left?"

"Yeah."

"Good. I'll meet you there at eight tonight."

Gil disappeared into the elevator, and Meir practically danced his way home. Who would have believed that Mendy would melt like butter upon hearing the words "*daf Gemara*"? So he wouldn't sit *shivah*, but at least he'd learn something for his father.

It wasn't ideal, but it was something.

From his office on the sixth floor, Yochai watched the exchange on a close-circuit camera, listening to every word; and his expression dulled. Who knew where all this would lead? Meir was doing his best, but he was hardly a professional.

He rose from his seat and sighed, somewhat satisfied by Meir's persistence but still anxious. He stole a glance at his watch; he really owed Shuli a *shivah* call, and he cringed at the thought. There was really no choice, and he would have to play the part. He and Shimon had been friends for decades, and he owed Shimon's wife that much.

Fishing through the drawers in his desk, he found a white *kippah* and stuffed it into his pocket. He'd put it on in the car. He was best off going in the morning, rather in the evening hours when most people came. He wouldn't stay long – just long enough to murmur a few words of consolation. A few words that would achieve absolutely nothing, to his mind.

When Meir saw him approaching the shul with the visor of his baseball cap pulled down low over his face and his hands stuck deep into his pockets, he practically jumped for joy. Quickly suppressing his outward excitement, he scurried away from the window and took a seat, rising in feigned surprise when Gil entered.

"I'm glad you came," he greeted him pleasantly.

Gil merely shrugged in reply. "Shall we start?"

"Right, let's get started," Meir agreed, and the two opened matching volumes of *Gemara Pesachim* without another word.

It was incredible, but in no time at all, Gil demonstrated his excellence in learning, his sharp mind and quick grasp surpassing Meir's, who found himself struggling to keep pace. They learned without a break for a full hour, and it seemed that Gil had no intention of stopping. He continued plowing ahead, another line, another *mishnah*, another *peirush*, with his finger pressed tightly against the page. For a moment, he looked so young and innocent, his face without a trace of the angst previously so visible on his countenance.

Two hours passed, and Meir felt himself growing hoarse. He needed a drink, and was finding the effort intense. As a tutor, he was usually the one urging his *chavrusa* along, but this time, the roles were reversed, and he found that he needed to use his full powers of concentration just to listen, follow, and keep pace with this brilliant young man.

After another half-hour, Meir rose, and to his chagrin, Gil followed suit.

"Wait a second. I'm just getting myself a tea. Should I get you one too?"

Gil looked confused. "No... no, it's really getting late, and we spent too long on this. I've really got to go now." Meir's thirst vanished immediately, and he longed to say something to the boy before he risked losing him forever.

"Mendy... It's your father's *shivah*. Your father was *niftar*! There's only one week of *shivah* – that's all the chance you get. Let's say you don't sit *shivah* — that's your choice and I won't interfere. But what about your mother? She's still alive, and she's grieving alone! Have you at least been *menachem avel*?"

Gil lowered his eyes, and his reply surprised the *avreich*. "How can I comfort her looking the way I do? What kind of comfort is that? What can I possibly tell her?"

"You don't have to say anything, Mendy. You're her oldest son, and your presence itself is comforting. She needs you now more than ever."

"It won't help," Mendy replied in a cold, metallic tone.

Meir exhaled a long, heavy sigh. "Listen, Mendy. Why don't the two of us go together now to your mother? You'll be *menachem avel*, even if you just say the *passuk*. It's only right. You can't turn your back on everyone including your mother! She's an *almanah* now! Even if you don't do it for your father or yourself, do it for her! Think of her pain for just one minute!"

Gil nodded slowly, and without another word, started to trail after Meir like a puppy on a leash. He didn't have it inside him to protest anymore. They entered Gil's car, and began to drive to Bnei Brak.

Half an hour later, he pulled to a stop in front of the building. "Let's go inside," Meir said encouragingly.

Gil shook his head. "There are probably women there now."

"I doubt it. It's past eleven."

"She'll be angry. I'm not sitting *shivah* myself. What am I doing here?" His was the voice of a small, frightened child.

"She won't be angry. She loves you. She'll understand."

"Yes, she will understand," Gil murmured aloud. "You have a point."

"What point?"

"Nothing. Forget it."

Meir gazed helplessly at the younger man. "Come on, Mendy. Let's go inside. We'll spend a few minutes with your mother. She's alone now. She's sitting *shivah* alone. Your siblings are with friends. She needs company. *Your* company. Tell her that your learned a *daf Gemara l'ilui nishmas* your father. Just sit with her and hold her hand. Sit for yourself too. You can't be so angry or hate your father so much that you won't allow yourself to mourn." He couldn't fathom the mocking smile that flitted briefly across Gil's face.

Slowly, they ascended the staircase, Meir confidently, Gil far less so. Meir knocked gently and opened the door, gently pushing Gil ahead of him.

As Meir had predicted, the house was empty, and Meir, who remained outside, closed the door behind Gil's back. Spontaneously, Gil opened the door a crack, for his mother's sake, for the sake of the *chinuch* that his parents had instilled in him.

Meir didn't notice, as he had already turned around and headed back downstairs to wait for him, affording Gil his privacy.

"Mommy?" Gil called softly into the house.

"Who's there?" Shuli's voice sounded back fearfully. "Who's there?"

"It's just me," he called back soothingly.

"Who?"

"Mendy."

Suddenly, she appeared in front of him, her eyes red-rimmed from weeping, her face pale.

"Mommy!"

"Mendy. What are you doing here?" Her voice was neither happy nor sad, neither frightened nor excited. Her words lacked any expression at all.

"I came to see you… to see how you are."

"Not to sit *shivah*?" she asked directly.

He looked into her eyes. *Did she know? What would she think of him if she really knew the truth, with one hundred percent certainty?*

"Mommy, I don't need to sit *shivah*," he said quietly.

"Why not? What son doesn't sit *shivah* for his father? For the father that raised him and loved him and gave to him every day of his life?"

"You're right, Mommy. He was the father who raised me, and… It's my fault… I'm guilty for…" He choked over the words.

Shuli's eyes caressed him with her motherly gaze. "No, Mendy. It's *not* your fault at all. You have nothing to feel guilty about. You did not kill Tatty. *Hakadosh Baruch Hu* sends every person into this world for a predetermined number of days, and when he reaches the end of his time, he returns his *neshamah* to the *Kisei Hakavod*. It makes no difference how it happens; you are not responsible for Tatty's *petirah*, Mendy." Her voice overflowed with compassion and love, and Mendy closed his eyes, melting in the sweetness of that love.

Accursed Hamas that had done this to him, that had designated him for such a cruel fate when they decided to switch him for a Jewish baby! Cursed be that moment when he had reached the loving arms of these wonderful Jewish parents… And cursed be this moment when he could hardly stand beneath the weight of his mother's overpowering love for him.

"Do you understand why I can't sit *shivah*?" he tried again.

"No, I don't," she replied. The emotion in their voices had dissipated, and now they spoke like two foreigners trying to understand each other.

"I heard that you were here on your own, and I wanted to come to comfort you. Can I?"

"Go ahead."

"Please sit down, Mommy, and we'll talk. It's important to me that you know that whenever I think of Tatty, I… I think only of the good that he showered on me, of the light in his eyes, of all he invested in me, and the time we spent together learning, talking. He was the best father in the world… And I want to help you with the little ones… But I know that he wouldn't want me to do that now."

"You're right.'

"So you're not angry at me?"

Shuli sagged in her chair. "Angry? No, Mendy. I'm not angry at you. I pity you deeply. Whatever happens, you'll always be my son. The son that I raised, loved, and still love. And I pity you so much. I feel sorry for myself, but I feel even more worry and anguish for you."

"Because… I'm confused?"

"Because you're in trouble," she answered truthfully.

For a moment, he felt cold fear swathe him, and the blood drained from his face. Did she know the truth? Did she suspect that he wasn't really her son? She was purposely being ambiguous, but why? Why wasn't she angry that he refused to sit *shivah*?"

To both of their surprise, Gil buried his face in his hands. "I really am in trouble."

"You are, and so am I. But for the kids, I have to be strong. Mendy, I have one important request for you, and I'm begging you to honor it."

He gazed questioningly at her. "You can ask, but I can't promise."

"Even just one thing you won't promise me?" Shuli asked pleadingly, her eyes filling with tears. "I raised you for twenty years, Mendy. You can't promise me even one thing?"

"What is it?"

Shuli sat up straight in her chair and stared hard at her eldest son. "Don't come here, Mendy. My heart can't take it anymore. Every time I look at you, my heart breaks in two. Please, go away and don't come back. Don't call. Don't speak to your brother or sister. Disappear, and don't make things harder for us. Okay?"

Gil's eyes widened, the shock more than he could bear. His insides seemed to be writhing in agony, and he gazed into his mother's eyes with anguish pouring from his. "Mommy, is that really you talking? How can you throw me out? This is the only home I have! The only family I've got! Mommy, you don't understand..."

But Shuli's eyes were cold, and she resembled a lioness determined to protect her cubs from attack.

"You're right, Mendy. I really don't understand. But I do know that this whole house was turned upside down because of you. I gave you all I had. Now, please go, Mendy. Do you understand *me*?"

"Mommy, do you know that..." he began, but didn't finish. For a moment, a flash of understanding glimmered in her eyes, and he realized that she did know. It was too late; she had discovered the truth. She saw him as the Arab that he was. *Mommy thinks of me as a cursed Arab. Mommy, who wept for me when she bentched licht, now despises me as a goy, and not just a goy, but an Arab... Oh, Mommy, don't reject me!*

"I know nothing, Mendy," she said through clenched teeth, trying to still the trembling of her lips and swallow her tears. "But I do know that you tore our family apart, and if you want us to recover, you'll understand that it's best for you to stay away from us. Okay?"

Surrendering to her pleas, he walked brokenly to the door.

"I thought you'd ask me to sit *shivah* for Tatty," he tried one last time as he grasped the door knob with a shaking hand.

"Do what you think is right," she replied.

"I thought you'd want us to draw strength from one another, and that you'd understand that I didn't want this to happen! You know, it wasn't easy for me to—"

"I know, Mendy."

He turned around, facing her with pleading eyes. "Mommy, will you still *daven* for me?"

The question hit her almost with physical force. Everything was spelled out, and they understood each other perfectly. There was no more secrecy, just pure, unadulterated pain at the harsh fate.

The eyes were Mendy's, her frightened, lonely son. But in her heart, she was a mother and wife grieving her lost son and husband. Yet Shuli still could not bring herself to reject the child she had raised and loved, no matter what his origins.

"I'll *daven* that you should be a good person and find happiness," she whispered her promise. All curtains of obscurity melted away to be replaced with clarity and sadness. They stood there, their gazes locked for a long moment, until Mendy dejectedly dragged his feet away from the house where he had been raised.

As he tread sadly down the steps, he heard his mother call to him one last time, her tone unyielding. How her heart withstood the agony, Gil couldn't fathom.

"Mendy!"

"Yes, Mommy?" His expression was filled with such yearning, and tears scorched his eyes. This was goodbye – he knew it.

"Goodbye, Mendy. Please don't come back. I'm asking you one last time, my son. Don't come back."

"You can't keep me here!" Jamil shouted in frustration. He stared out of the window at the Tel Aviv skyline and the blue sky beyond. "You said you wanted to question me. You did that already. Now what? How long am I going to be stuck here?"

The agent in charge of him smiled mockingly. "As long as we want you to be, Jamil."

"I'm not in jail!"

"Not officially, but essentially, that's what it is."

"Let me out! I didn't do anything wrong!"

The bored agent faced him sternly. "Listen, Jamil, I've received orders to stick with you until you're let out, which means I'm also being punished, don't you think?"

"Not at all. You come at eight and leave at four. You've got working shifts and breaks. I can't come and go as I please. You've got to let me out a bit or I'll go crazy!"

Another agent walked in just in time to catch Jamil's final sentence. "The kid has a point," he commented. "What was Yochai thinking exactly?"

"Keep your voice down, or you'll be in for it."

"It makes no difference if he hears or not. What Yochai says, goes," the agent replied with a sour expression.

Jamil brightened at the other agent's words. "I want to speak to Yochai. I want to know what's happening and when you guys are finally going to make some progress. I want to know if they've located my Jewish family yet, and I want to find a job and a way to support myself. You guys have no excuse for keeping me locked up in here, and I want out."

"We'll speak to Yochai," the first agent replied soothingly.

"No. No more speaking to Yochai. *I* want to speak to Yochai, and now!" Jamil insisted.

What prompted the junior agent to relay his complaints to Yochai Jamil would never know, but he was duly astonished when, just fifteen minutes later, the Big Boss himself appeared in his room.

"Jamil, we don't intend to hold you against your will," Yochai surprised Jamil with his announcement. "It's just that we're slowly starting to grasp how valuable you are to some people – dead more than alive. There are a good number of people out there who want you out of the picture, and if you walk free, we can't take responsibility for your safety. You yourself claimed that they tried to get you more than once."

Jamil paused carefully before replying. "Yes, they tried, but I prefer being hunted than to living like a caged animal for the rest of my life with no company but bored agents. At least I could learn something, do something, make something of myself..."

This time, it was Yochai's turn to listen silently. He couldn't deny the truth in Jamil's words; true, they were protecting him, but simultaneously, they had turned him into their prisoner.

"You know, I've got an idea, and if it appeals to you, I can bring in someone who will gladly teach you about Judaism. You mentioned that you wanted to learn a bit about religion, didn't you?" he recalled a prior statement of Jamil's.

"Yes, that's right." Jamil's expression brightened.

Yochai grinned, gratified with his brainstorm. "So, look, remember your friend Meir, the guy who brought you here? He'll gladly teach you about Judaism and related stuff and prepare you to live a Jewish life. How does that sound?"

Jamil wasn't so quick to reply. "Plus I want out of here for four hours a day."

"Two hours," Yochai corrected.

"Three." Suddenly, they resembled two seasoned businessmen.

"With bodyguards."

"Agreed. With bodyguards. Plus, I need money."

"Why?"

"So I can be free and do what I want."

Yochai laughed mirthlessly. "We'll give you whatever you need."

"And I want to know who my family is."

"That will take time."

Jamil rose defiantly. "You know who my family is, don't you? If you didn't, you wouldn't be protecting me. If I didn't come from a high-profile family, no one would be out to kill me."

"I can't volunteer any information on that subject at the present moment," Yochai replied smoothly, but unyieldingly. "All that we've agreed will begin as of tomorrow morning. You'll be free to leave the premises for an hour-and-a-half in the morning, and an hour-and-a-half in the evening. In the afternoon, Meir Landsman will visit you. That sums up the plan for the next month or so."

Jamil had no choice but to content himself with that. He desperately awaited the opportunity to restart his life, reunite with his family, and acquaint himself with a whole new world. Even the few weeks he had spent working in stores alongside Jews had broadened his horizons and given him a different perspective on life, and for the first time ever, he viewed the future through hopeful eyes.

Gil met Laser inside a dingy coffee shop to provide him with his latest update.

"What's your goal?" Gil ordered a bottle of mineral water while Laser sipped thick, sweet Turkish coffee.

"Our goal, not just mine," Laser rejoined sharply. "You're raising too many suspicions with all your activities with the Jews, and I haven't seen you advancing much so far."

"It doesn't work like that. First they send you for training. You don't just walk into the GSS and secure a top position that grants you access to classified information."

"So work your way up there, and quickly," Laser shot back.

"It will be years before they decide to use me in any operation that entails sharing classified information. If you're looking for immediate results, you won't find them in the GSS."

"Quiet!"

Gil hid a grin.

"They suspect you," Laser sneered at him. "I'm telling you this from information secured by real agents of ours, not dumb, lazy ones like you. We need to carry out the mission now – we can't wait much longer."

"What mission?"

"The GSS is involved whenever there's a major public gathering or event. I'm waiting to hear about some major gathering that's supposed to take place in the near future, which will be loaded with VIPs, like the Prime Minister for one. I want you to be working as one of the security guards."

"It doesn't work like that! I can't just get myself transferred wherever I choose."

Laser crashed his fist down on the table. "You'll find a way to make it happen! You have access to Yochai, which is more than most other people have, and you have to start making good use of it. So, I'm going to be needing real-time information from you regarding any major gatherings in the future. And one more thing: Jamil. The GSS is going to be investigating his story in minute detail – in fact, we've heard that they already are. That's why I want you to keep a low profile, but stay in touch with the widow nonetheless."

"She refuses contact with me."

"No such thing. Buy her with gifts. Send her money; she'll probably need extra support now."

Gil's patience was reaching its limit. "How am I supposed to support her when you barely give me enough to buy groceries for myself?!"

"Greedy one, like all the Jewish bloodsuckers..." Laser cursed quietly but withdrew a wad of bills from his pocket. "Take this, and give it to her. Tell her that as the eldest son, it's your responsibility now to support the family. You need to allay any possible suspicion from them, at least until the event."

Gil nodded. "Okay. And what happens at this event, whatever it is? Suppose I manage to shove my way in as a guard, then what?"

"Then you carry out your mission. I'm waiting for an event that will eliminate all the VIPs in the Zionist state in one fell swoop, and you'll have a part in it! We've been developing this plan for the past twenty years. Now is the time to reap the fruits of our labor!" Laser banged his empty coffee cup on the table for emphasis. "Do you realized how many hopes are being pinned on you right now?"

"So you'll send off some *shahid*, and I'll help him get past?" Gil was still trying to make sense of the vaguely-expressed plans.

"No, we won't send a *shahid*. We already have one."

"What are you saying?" Gil narrowed his eyes suspiciously.

"I'm saying that even before your birth, you were destined to sacrifice yourself for the sake of Islam. You are the chosen one. And this is why you are being sent to carry out this mission.

Gil maintained a cool façade, but his innards were broiling.

"You remember our agreement, don't you?" Laser's voice was mocking. "If you give yourself as a *shahid*, then your Jewish family lives; if you don't, then perhaps your own life will be spared, but theirs certainly won't. You try to deny it, but we know that those Jews who brought you up are still important to you, and you wouldn't want to see them suffer. Ultimately, you remain faithful to them. We have people watching the house constantly, and they'll have no trouble shooting them all dead in their beds. And, when they die, you won't even have anywhere left to turn. Perhaps to Yochai, but by then, he'll know that you betrayed your own people…" He spoke quickly and unfeelingly, his words laced with scorn. "We gave you the opportunity to meet your biological parents. You saw how much it means to them for you to carry out your mission in life. Don't let them down."

"I wouldn't dream of it," Gil stated dryly, his mind still frozen as he tried to figure out what his remaining options were.

"I trust that you'll do a good job. Keep fighting for field assignments. We're nearing our goal."

The men shook hands and rose. Laser paid both bills, adding over his shoulder, "Your Jewish friends wouldn't dream that you're here right now; this joint is frequented only by Arabs. But that doesn't mean that they don't have their eyes on you and aren't following you. Keep this in mind."

Gil didn't reply. He watched Laser climb into his luxury car, and his heart sank with the knowledge that he was caught between two enemy foes. The first was the Arab enemy who saw him as a *shahid* – the second was the Israeli enemy who most likely wouldn't hesitate to kill him once they discovered that he was collaborating with the other side.

How had he become caught in the crossfire?

Gil closed his eyes, trying to figure out how he had sunk so low. Just one short year ago, he had been happily learning *Gemara*, his life so simple, so tranquil. Even Yehuda Berman hadn't dreamed that they were both being used by the enemy; had either of them known, they would have both run for their lives as fast as they could.

Dejectedly, he got into his car and drove it out of the derelict neighborhood toward his rented apartment, a dank studio where loneliness was his only companion. Sinking onto the bed, he asked himself, *What now?*

One thing was certain: He would never agree to die as a *shahid*. However, what was even clearer was that he couldn't allow them to harm his widowed mother and orphaned siblings. Tatty had died because of him, and he would fight to protect what was left of his family, if it was the last thing he managed to do. Therefore, it was now imperative to come up with a plan to safeguard his family. Laser was no fool; he wouldn't allow Gil to slip between his fingers, and if he failed, the ones to pay the price would be those he loved most.

Toiby knocked gently at the door. "Shuli, dear, it's me. Open up. I've brought you lunch. You need to eat to keep up your strength."

Just to spare herself additional knocking and intervention from other neighbors, Shuli opened the door and ushered the older woman inside. "Shh… Toiby, it's okay, you don't have to shout. I hear you, and I really appreciate all that you're doing for me."

"It's like this after *shivah*," Toiby sighed as she placed the tray down on the kitchen table, glancing around the tidy, empty house. "People forget, or they assume you can just jump back into life as if nothing happened. But I've been there, and I know that it's never so simple. When are your children coming back home?"

"This evening."

"Good. So let's gather strength and infuse some life into this house. Things will never be the same again, but that doesn't mean that they will stay like they are now, forever. Come, dear, let's wash and eat something together."

"Don't your grandchildren come to you today?" Shuli recalled, grateful for the chance to escape. "You usually give them lunch and watch them on Tuesdays, don't you?" she dropped an obvious hint.

"Right – usually I do, but not today. I told them that Bubby is busy today. I made them lunch, but they're eating on their own and they'll wait for me nice and patiently until I get back."

Trying to hide her sigh, Shuli washed, sat down, and bit into a fresh home-baked roll. Toiby sat down across from her, and they ate in silent companionship for a while until Shuli proclaimed aloud without forewarning:

"Toiby, I've thought about this long and hard, and I want you to be one of the first to know that I'm planning to move soon."

"WHAT?" Toiby yelped. "Shuli, my dear, don't make such a drastic decision so hastily. You need time, time to mourn, and time to recover. Your children need it too, and they also need the comfort and familiarity of friends, teachers, and neighbors to help them get through this. After everything that's happened, this is the worst possible thing you could do right now!"

"We're moving to a small place up north, somewhere in the Golan," Shuli continued, as if she hadn't heard a word of her neighbor's protests. "Somewhere with pretty scenery, grass, maybe with a view of the Kinneret... It's always been my dream."

"*Your* dream? What about the children? Where will you send them to school?" Toiby was aghast.

"There are excellent schools in Tzefas. They'll bus in or carpool. It's not far, and a fresh start will be good for all of us."

"But... but who will help you out over there? Who'll take care of you? Shuli, here you have friends, neighbors, me... People who care about you and want to help!" Toiby stared at her with pitying eyes. "Listen to what you're saying, and you'll see that it makes no sense, none at all. You don't know anyone up there! Yes, you'll have quiet, and beauty too, but who will look out for you?"

"Don't worry, Toiby. You're wonderful, the best neighbor I could have asked for, which is why I'm telling you. I'm not even telling most other people, and I don't want it to become common knowledge either. Just tell anyone who asks that I took the kids away for a while to escape all the sympathy and try to get back to ourselves. I can't take the pitying looks anymore."

Toiby rose, clearly distraught. "Shuli, my dear, don't you dare try escaping the pity. It's not just pity, but also love and compassion that you deserve. Everyone has their *peckel* of challenges, and Hashem just gave you one that's much harder to bear than most. Everyone pities everyone for what needs to be pitied… Shuli, you can't just up and leave like that!" she exclaimed, almost as if she was willing to fight tooth and nail to hold onto the *chessed* case that had fallen into her lap.

Shuli smiled gently. "I understand that it will be hard for you without me, Toiby. We've been close for years, but I've made my decision, and I ask you to respect it. The kids are coming home tonight, and I've already started packing. I'd actually appreciate it if you could help me a bit – we could even start now. I ordered a bunch of boxes from a moving company, and I packed up a few already. It would be a great help if you could lend me a hand."

Toiby shook her head in disbelief, but approached the boxes, staring at them through eyes veiled with tears. "Shuli, this isn't good," she shook her head again. "It's unhealthy and wrong to do this to your children." As she spoke, she opened one box and let out a yelp.

"*Oy vey, oy vey,* Shuli, what's all this? Why are you taking these with you? Why, Shuli? You said you're going in order to escape the pain and memories, so why bring these with you?" She lifted a pile of Shimon's ironed shirts from the box. "*Oy,* Shuli, you're burying yourself in anguish. Don't take this with you. It's the last thing you need. Leave it here, and I'll deal with it. I'll send the good stuff to a *gemach*, and dispose of the rest of it."

Shuli rose fiercely, like a lioness guarding her cubs. Her face turned crimson and then white. "Leave it alone, Toiby. I can't bring myself to throw out his stuff yet. I'll part from it when I'm ready to."

"Shuli, I won't let you torture yourself with all these things! You'll just wallow in your painful memories. Shuli, my dear, really, why do you need his belt, his slippers, every shirt and other item? Take just a few select items, or even just one would be best. Why take all of it?"

Instead of replying, Shuli spontaneously burst into tears. "You don't understand," she sobbed. "I need these things. Please, Toiby, let me be now. I'll manage to pack on my own."

"No, my dear, you need someone to help you," Toiby argued. "I'll help you pack, and I won't say another word. I promise."

"Okay," Shuli agreed reluctantly, knowing that the job really was too big for one person to complete on his own.

"Did you finish packing your bedroom?" Toiby asked gently.

"Almost. There are only a few more things left there to pack." The few things turned out to be several boxes worth, and they included many of Shimon's belongings, including his watch, phone book, and so many other mementos that Toiby couldn't restrain a sigh.

"You're making it so much more difficult for yourself," she tried again, but seeing Shuli's warning glare, changed the subject. "What does your new house look like? How did you manage to find a rental so quickly? Who's going to help you unpack if the children start straight away at their new school? You know what, Shuli? I have a great idea. I think I'll come with you, to help you settle in. I'll take a vacation from work and join you for a few days until you're all sorted."

Shuli wrinkled her brow in confusion. "What vacation from work?"

Toiby chuckled. "Well, I don't have an actual job, but that doesn't mean that I'm not a busy woman! As you know, I watch Miriam's kids twice a week, and I host them all frequently for Shabbos, which is a project that starts on Wednesday and continues until Monday morning... So I'm not bored, my dear. But a change of scenery would be good for me too, and that way I can help you out."

"No!" Shuli replied suddenly. "I don't want anyone to know exactly where I'm moving to, not even you. It's nothing personal, but

I need my time and space now. I don't want any visitors. I just want quiet after all that I've been through. I need to get away from it all."

"How long will you go for?"

"How long? Who knows? A few months, maybe a few years… We'll see how it works out. I'm not selling the house here, so we can come back whenever we want. But now we need to be alone. Alone by ourselves," she emphasized.

"What about Mendy? Did you tell him? Will he know where to find you?"

"No, and I don't intend to tell him just yet. I need a break from him too. If he really wants, he'll manage to find me," she added ambiguously.

Toiby's eyes widened in panic as she began to wonder if her neighbor was suffering a breakdown. "Shuli, my dear, I'm really very concerned about you. You can't give up on your son like that! He'll be back! He'll do *teshuvah*, and you'll get over this together. How can you speak like that?"

How could she speak like that? How dare Toiby, for all her age and wisdom, interfere right now or tell her what to do?! Shuli was tempted to shake the old woman off and even add that the path to *Gehinnom* is paved with good intentions. In fact, the expression definitely seemed to fit right then. Toiby had been with her when Mendy had arrived unexpectedly, and she had been the one to notify Shimon of his arrival. That was why Shimon had hurried home, suffered his heart attack and then…

Shuli took a deep breath, trying to still her racing thoughts. "Toiby, thank you for your help and advice, but I'm very tired now and I need to lie down. I feel a headache coming on, and I need to rest."

"I think I should stay with you," the older woman insisted.

"I'd rather not. I need to be alone right now."

"Shuli, you can't run away from problems! Problems are meant to be confronted and dealt with, not avoided."

"Thank you for your wise words, but now I really need to rest." There was no mistaking Shuli's intent.

Toiby grimaced, but headed to the door, her expression deeply wounded. "I'm not allowing myself to feel insulted by this treatment, Shuli, because I know that you're going through a difficult time right now."

"I appreciate that," Shuli replied tightly.

Toiby left the apartment, closing the door behind her just a bit too hard. From the hall, Shuli thought she heard her neighbor muttering, "Doesn't want help? That's just fine."

As soon as she heard the door close across the hall, Shuli sprang back into action, opening closet doors and dumping all the contents into boxes in complete disarray. She worked steadily for two hours, until all the closets, cabinets, and shelves were empty. Shimon's belongings were stored meticulously in separate boxes, each of which she marked with a white sticker and a small black letter "S."

All that remained now was the kitchen, and she attacked it feverishly, knowing how big a job it was, and how little time was left.

The children arrived home just three hours later in a flurry of hugs and kisses. Shuli had already informed them that they were leaving the next day, and she fed them pizza on paper plates. She had left only pajamas, linens, one change of clothes, and necessary toiletries out for the three of them, and even after the kids fell asleep, Shuli worked late into the night, finishing all the last-minute packing and falling asleep, fully-clothed, shortly before dawn.

The movers arrived at six the next morning and carried everything out of the house without a word. Shuli had obviously hired a cheap company, because the movers were clearly untrained. Neighbors peered in shock from the windows, but Shuli maintained an air of indifference, ignoring their looks and whispers.

Toiby wept in the stairwell. "I told her to stay. I promised to help her! But she's depressed. What can I do? The woman is simply depressed, and I'm afraid she's going mad! Oy, Shimon, *daven* for her and the children from *Shamayim*. Oy, the poor *kinderlach*..."

As a desperate last resort, she tried calling to the children, but they were already safely ensconced in the cab of the truck, enjoying a spirited conversation with the driver. Despite their clumsiness, the movers worked with surprising alacrity; by eight-thirty they had finished loading everything onto the truck. Shuli cast one final loving look around her empty apartment and wiped away a tear, trying to swallow the cry that threatened to emerge from her throat. Then, she quietly exited and locked the door behind her. Before descending the steps, she looked toward the apartment across the hall, to Toiby, her longtime elderly neighbor who had been almost as much a mother as a friend. But Toiby's door was closed in an act of protest at Shuli's decision.

Shuli walked sadly down the steps and out of the building, wishing a silent and final farewell to the place where she had lived and raised her children for sixteen years. Curious eyes peered at her from every apartment in the building and the neighboring ones, as well, each one pondering her tragedy and analyzing her choice.

She took another deep breath and climbed into the backseat of the truck. The movers leaped into the back, and the driver let out a warning honk to alert pedestrians and drivers that he was pulling out of the parking lot.

"Wait! Wait!" came a cry. It was Toiby, who now burst into the street, blocking the truck from moving and waving a handkerchief toward the driver to force him to stop. The truck pulled to a halt, and the driver opened the door in surprise. "Shuli, I can't let you go without saying goodbye!" the old lady cried, leaping into the cab with the agility of a much younger woman. "Oh, Shuli, I'll never see you again!" she sobbed, tears streaming from her eyes. "How everything fell apart so quickly, I'll never understand, but... *gam zu l'tovah*. My dear, I'll always remember you and I'll be *davening* for you and the children every day."

Toiby sobbed loudly, which was just as well as it allowed Shuli to shed her own tears quietly. "First Mendy, then Shimon, and now the rest of you… Take care of yourself, Shuli. Promise me that you will! I know you're upset at me for sticking my nose where it didn't belong, and rightly so, but I only did it because I care so much about you and the *kinderlach*! Goodbye, *kinderlach*! Give Bubby Toiby a kiss! You will take care of yourself, Shuli, won't you?"

Shuli was tempted to bury herself in the goodhearted older woman's arms and release all her pain and suffering like a baby, but there was no time for such luxuries. Toiby smothered Shuli and Suri with hugs and kisses, repeating her words of support and encouragement until the driver grew annoyed.

"Listen, Grandma, it's getting late. It's time to go now. You climbed aboard without permission, and now I'm asking you to get off so we can get going."

"I'm going, don't worry. Patience, young man!"

"Now!" he repeated firmly.

Toiby surrendered, and with a final round of hugs and kisses, was gone. The truck rumbled heavily down the street, turned right, and several minutes later, was speeding along the highway northbound.

It was pouring rain, and in all that dark night, it felt like he was the only one out on the streets, walking fast, engrossed in his thoughts and almost oblivious to the elements.

For the last three hours, he had been trying to contact his mother, to try to convince her to reconsider her decision to cut off all contact with him. He was going to tell her that he was willing to do *teshuvah*, or, more precisely, to convert. She, more than anyone else, appreciated that he couldn't continue living this life. He wasn't to blame for being born a gentile, but he didn't want to continue living as one. He had other aspirations, higher goals in life.

He called and called again, but no one answered. He tried the house, his mother's cell phone, and even the spare cell phone that Shuli sometimes gave the kids when they went to the grocery store, but to no avail. Finally, he decided to risk it and pay them a visit; that way, at least he could tell Laser that he was doing all he could to restore contact with his family.

He parked his car on a nearby street, deciding to walk the rest of the way, which was how he found himself walking in the rain and getting drenched to the bone. He strode quickly into the building, shaking drops of rain off his jacket, and took the steps two at a time. He knocked loudly on the door, but there was no answer. Peering into the peephole, it seemed as if the house was dark.

How strange, he thought. *Where would they have gone in this weather? It's ten at night – why isn't Mommy opening?*

Because she's not your mother, came another taunting voice from inside. *She's not your mother, and she owes you nothing. So she's locking you out in the cold and rain.*

He continued knocking, hardly realizing that his knocks were becoming louder and more desperate, yet the only reply was silence.

Finally, the door across the hall opened, and old Mrs. Lipsky stared at him in surprise. Gil had fond memories of the old woman, even if she was a bit crabby and extremely nosy.

"Why are you knocking?" she asked him bluntly.

"What do you mean? I came to visit. I want to speak to my mother."

"You should have called first." Was there a triumphant note in her voice?

"Why?"

"Because your mother took the kids and moved up north. She didn't even say where to."

"WHAT?" Gil spun around and gaped disbelievingly at the old woman.

"Yes, they moved away."

"So who *does* know where she went?"

"Nobody, except the movers. She refused to tell me, or anyone else. I imagine she'll call you once her emotions settle down. You were always the apple of her eye, until… Well… What happened, happened, but you caused her a lot of anguish, Mendy." There was blatant reproof in her tone of voice.

"Does she at least take her cell phone with her?"

"I don't see why she shouldn't have done. Did you try calling it?"

"Yes, but she's not answering."

"Listen, Mendy, keep on calling. Even if she doesn't answer, she'll see that you called, which is something. She's called me back many times in the past."

Murmuring a muted "thank you," Gil turned away and headed back down the stairs and out of the building. He was in shock. Where had his mother moved to, and why? Was it because of him? Had her suspicions of him been confirmed by something or someone? Would he manage to track her down?

Does she fear you so much that she felt it was necessary to disappear, Mendy? he asked himself and then laughed aloud. *Mendy? You should call yourself Jamil. You're not even Gil anymore. You're Jamil now. Jamil the nobody.*

He sprinted back to his car, tore open the door and leaped inside, soaked to the skin. Then he pulled his cell phone out of his pocket and pressed 'redial' to call his mother once again, but as expected, the call went immediately to the voice mail.

But this time, Gil left a message. "Hi, Mommy, it's me. Mendy. You told me not to call, but I can't not. You're my mother, and if I don't call you, who can I call? How could you just leave like that without telling me? After everything that happened, I also need a home to return to. Please call me back, and we'll see what we can do to iron things out. I know that you don't want to have anything to do with me, but I can't live like this! I need a family. I need to have some kind of connection with you. Otherwise," his voice betrayed him, and he choked, "otherwise, I'll really have nothing to live for." Tears overflowed from his eyes, as he wondered if his mother would mourn him if he died. Would she miss him?

The inspiration came suddenly, and he realized that the only one left to whom he could turn was Yochai. It was no secret that the Big Boss was in his office at all hours of the day and night.

He drove carefully, mindful of the hazards of driving in such weather, and it took him nearly an hour to reach Headquarters. His boss was duly surprised to see him at the late hour.

"Gil? What are you doing here? I never got the impression that you were such a devoted worker that you work nights too," Yochai greeted him cynically.

"Very funny," Gil retorted. "I just went to visit my family, and they've disappeared."

Yochai didn't look very surprised. "So?"

"*So?*" Gil cried. "Yochai, I need to find them! I'm starting to recall now that my mother actually hinted at her intentions in the past, but she didn't pick up on the fact that I..."

"That you're what?" Yochai never missed a beat.

"That... that I need family too. It's not just about me. I just lost my father! I changed my whole direction in life, but I still need them."

"Would you like me to remind you what caused your father's heart attack?"

Gil reacted by leaping at Yochai and grabbing him by the shoulders. To his credit, Yochai didn't respond with a simple maneuver that could have left the kid crumpled and gasping on the floor.

"Don't you dare accuse me of killing my father! It wasn't me! It wasn't my fault! It happened because Hashem ordained it. Even my mother said so! You can't blame me for what happened. I came peacefully; it was he who drew the gun first."

A heavy silence filled the room as Gil gasped for breath and Yochai shrugged off the boy's tight grasp.

"You say you came in peace, but your mother didn't think so. In any case, what do you want now?"

"For you to help me find them."

"I'm sorry, but I can't do that, Gil."

"Why not? You actually want my family to reject me?"

Yochai frowned. "Kid, I'm not involved in your personal life, not in the least, I'm not authorized to assign agents for personal reasons, and this definitely constitutes a personal reason."

A strange thought flitted momentarily through Gil's mind. If his mother knew that he was an Arab, then ostensibly Yochai knew too. And if Yochai knew that much, then he had obviously accepted Gil into the ranks of the GSS with a specific purpose in mind. Or, it could just as well be the opposite. It could all be a figment of his too-lively imagination. It was distinctly possible that his mother was still in some doubt regarding his true origins, and that Yochai had never been apprised of her suspicions.

"Listen, Yochai. You don't have to help me. Most probably I'll be able to figure it out on my own."

"How?"

"I'll hire a private investigator," he replied nonchalantly.

Yochai laughed caustically. "Gil, you can hire a thousand PIs, and I wish you great success, but I'm warning you not to lay a finger on any GSS resources. I won't have a rookie officer exploiting our resources for his personal benefit. Is that clear?"

"Perfectly," Gil said coldly and turned to leave, but Yochai stopped him.

"Gil, you clearly haven't given this much thought, but maybe you should. If your mother disappeared without leaving you any way to contact her, what does that mean?"

"That she doesn't want contact with me. But she's my mother! She must realize that I need her."

"But maybe she doesn't need *you*. And maybe what *she* needs now is to be away from you. She's only recently lost her husband, and she still hasn't gotten over your… defection, shall we call it. Try to think about her and her needs for a moment. Maybe she needs some time to recover and sort through her feelings and emotions. Look beyond yourself for a moment to think about her and what she wants."

Gil fidgeted uncomfortably. "Are you saying this from knowledge?"

"Look, I spoke a lot to your father after you left home. Despite the fact that I'm unaffiliated, and he was religious, we remained in touch, and I think we understood each other. I may not be observant, but I respect faith and believe in G-d, which is one reason that your father and I never broke off contact completely. He was heartbroken when you 'left the fold,' as he put it. There were months when your parents did nothing but think about you and try to devise ways to bring you back home. You weren't available for them back then. Don't you think your mother deserves a little peace and tranquility now, Gil?"

Gil fell silent for a moment, his eyes drifted out of focus as he tried to make sense of his thoughts and feelings. Finally, he nodded in acceptance. "I hear what you're saying. You do have a point," he admitted slowly.

"So my suggestion is, give her time. She's your mother, and in the end, I'm sure she'll want you back. I have no doubt about it. She loves you very much."

"I know," Gil whispered, his eyes downcast. "I know."

He felt slightly better when he exited the building and slipped back into his car. As he turned out of the parking lot, he felt a dull thud and winced; he'd hit a car on the side, and to compound his bad luck, someone was sitting inside.

The driver immediately leaped out of the other car and peered inside Gil's window.

"I want your insurance details."

It was cold outside, and Gil didn't have the energy to argue with the irate driver. "All right. Come inside for a minute." The man opened the door and entered the car.

"Mendy-what? What's your last name?" he queried.

Gil whipped around in surprise. "How do you know my name is Mendy?" he demanded suspiciously.

The guy, who looked even younger than Gil, paled slightly, and it was then that Gil noticed his Arab features.

"What do you want? Who sent you?" Gil asked harshly, his fingers automatically reaching for his gun.

"Okay. You got me," the boy admitted. "Don't start yelling. They told me to tell you that they're tracking you wherever you go.

They wanted me to give this to you too." He handed him a cutout from a newspaper, which Gil perused quickly in astonishment. A small headline proclaimed, "Infants Switched at Birth in Russian Hospital."

The article told the story of two girls switched at birth, who discovered the truth only twelve years later. The biological mothers both demanded their real daughters back, while the girls were protesting that they wanted to remain with the families that had raised them.

This doesn't sound like one of Laser's tricks. What does he want from me?

"You're looking for your family, but keep away from them," the boy told him coldly. "They won't protect you in the moment of truth and will sacrifice nothing to save you. You're the only one interested in a relationship. Laser wants you to know that we've been following the family and know exactly where they are. You need to carry out your mission without falling prey to your emotions. Feelings will get you nowhere. Is that clear?"

Gil lowered his head as the cold, cruel reality stared him in the face.

Yes, it was patently clear. Since learning that he was not really their son, they had lost all interest in him, a lowly goy, even though he still craved their closeness. His mother would do anything to find her lost son, but she had rejected him.

The Arab youth continued speaking. "Focus on your mission. Forget everything else. Remember, you have nothing to live for without us."

For the first time, Gil had to agree with the Arab point of view. He was historically and eternally linked to them, to this terrorist organization, to his Arab brothers, to the mission that G-d or Allah had destined him to carry out. This was his purpose in life; why was he continuing to deny it and clutch to an empty past? He was an outcast, rejected by his family and even his mother…

He nodded with steely determination. “I understand your message. Now get out of my car,” he ordered the boy.

His eyes lacked all expression, and even the brutal cold didn’t bother him anymore. He had just encountered his destiny, and now he was headed toward his future.

Gil felt no anxiety as he drove into the quiet Arab village nestled at the foot of the mountain range. He had a meeting scheduled with Hussein al-Abdul, an old Arab historian, to whom he had introduced himself as a journalist investigating the truth of Islam and the legacy of the Palestinians. Al-Abdul had been only too happy to oblige and promised to procure whatever reading material Gil requested of him.

The older man welcomed him warmly into his expansive villa, a sprawling house which was a bizarre contrast of splendor and neglect. Glistening crystal chandeliers were suspended from the cracked ceilings and paintings in gilded frames hung on dingy gray walls. The floors were covered with heavy Persian carpets, but dirty and cracked floor tiles peeked out from beneath them. Old Hussein invited him to be seated on a velvet-upholstered couch.

"Please, make yourself comfortably, *ya-ahi.** What brought you to investigate Islam?"

Gil was silent for a moment. Briefly, he was tempted to share something about his past, but then he changed his mind. "I've been commissioned to write a comprehensive series of articles, and I need eyewitness testimonials about the Zionist conquest."

"That I'll gladly give you," al-Abdul declared festively. "The story is that you folks, the Jews, exploited the excuse of the Jewish

---

* My brother

Holocaust to seize our land, thus triggering an even greater Holocaust among the Palestinians, the rightful owners of the land. As soon as the British left, the battles began. The country was flooded with newly-arrived Holocaust survivors, and the Zionists shoved weapons in their hands and told them to fight. They were fighting for their lives, I suppose, just as we were fighting for ours.

"And the bitter end is known to all. We were forced to flee – men, women, and children – while the Zionist army fired mercilessly upon us, killing thousands of innocent civilians—"

"One moment," Gil interrupted. "Let's get some hard facts here. You're getting carried away with emotion."

"We were forced to leave everything behind," the old Arab continued, ignoring the interruption. "Our pots and pans, our cribs, even our clothing. They plundered it all, taking everything for themselves, occupying our homes and sleeping in our beds. Whatever they didn't have a use for, they destroyed. They didn't even leave us with our memories."

Gil stretched his legs. "Hussein, I'd like to ask you: If the situation had been reversed, would you have allowed the Jews to flee, or would you have killed them?"

"Ah, but I thought you wanted to stick to hard facts," the Arab retorted, his eyes flashing with fire.

"Okay," Gil conceded. "Go on."

"Our refugees were wretched souls, and many weren't welcomed by the neighboring Arab lands. The Palestinian nation—"

"One moment, please. The Palestinian 'nation' – does it really exist? Not so long ago, you were just a bunch of tribes which had settled in scattered areas throughout the country. How did you suddenly become a nation?" Gil asked pointedly.

"Young man, are you here to ask questions or receive answers?" Hussein glared at him with narrowed eyes. "Look at what happened to the land that we tilled and cultivated – for generations! And now, you are the rulers, and we are the oppressed. You stole our homeland from us; you caused us to abandon our culture. Today, the greatest dream of our youth is to assimilate into the Western world. We were robbed!"

Gil lit a cigarette, a recent habit that he privately admitted he loathed – but it was necessary for his image.

"Why are you willing to die for this land?" he asked seriously.

"Because it is holy to us. It is our history, the land of our forefathers."

"Is the same not true for the Jews?"

"Perhaps it is. But we were here first. You want to live together with us in peace, be my guests. But please respect our culture and customs."

This time, Gil couldn't contain his amusement. "What customs, Hussein? Look at what's going on in Lod, for example. Every week there's another shooting or bombing, deaths and casualties. What are you referring to?"

"Every nation has its way."

A long silence passed, and Gil nodded slowly. "That's certainly true, Hussein. Every nation has its way."

Hussein continued wistfully: "The day will come when we will slaughter them all, one by one. We'll enter their houses, and we'll take them for ourselves. Our sons and daughters will have what we never had. I myself built Jewish homes with these two calloused hands. They told me where to lay the cinderblock, where to paint; and I promised myself that the day would come when I would personally slaughter those Jews, and their houses would become mine. Only then will I restore my pride and the lost pride of my nation. Much blood will yet be spilled. Yes, young man, write that down! Much blood will yet be spilled…"

What most astonished Gil at that moment was that Hussein spoke so confidently, convinced that his provocative statements would be included in the leftist article, if slightly modified by the journalist or editor who would make his views somewhat more palatable to the Jewish reader. Was the left wing of Israeli politics really so hand-in-glove with the Arabs that they had virtually adopted Hussein's way of thinking as their own?

Gil summed up the interview with several additional, more theoretical, questions and then rose to take his leave. "I think I've got it all down now," he concluded with a firm handshake. "I appreciate your time and input."

"You will remember to include the part about my eldest child who died in the intifada, won't you?" Hussein pressed him. "Those terrorist soldiers thought that he was holding a gun when all he was doing was lifting his arms in surrender, and they riddled his innocent body with bullets. You got that down, didn't you?"

"I did, I did," Gil assured him. Despite the violence of his narrative, Hussein's story had touched a chord in his heart, and now that he had heard the story as told by the other side, it was no longer as difficult to relate to them as it had been previously. He had come with many questions and some of those answers allowed him to better identify with his brothers, those of the Arab nation.

Laser spread out the map on the table and peered closely at it, speaking thoughtfully.

"What we're looking for is somewhere closed off, but large. Somewhere that can accommodate a huge number of people, but that won't be overly secure… Recently, I was told of an event that's scheduled to take place in two months, something that might be exactly what we're after. It's a *hachnassat sefer Torah*, they call it, and it's going to be held somewhere in Yerushalayim, in a large synagogue, but the crowds will probably spill over to the surrounding streets. These sorts of events, apparently, attract all sorts of people, not just from the synagogue where it's taking place, but from the surrounding area too." Laser frowned, his devious mind already starting to analyze the challenges inherent in planning such an operation.

"One point in favor of choosing this particular event is that because it's religious, the security won't be as tight as with the political stuff," Laser continued. "It will be much easier for Gil to get in, and that's becoming a major concern. I'm almost certain that the scum at the GSS are already aware that he's connected to us and is up to something. So we have to be doubly careful. We'll supply him with all the necessary ingredients without him having to go anywhere to get them, and then we'll send in Marwan to put everything together and arrange his transportation."

"They'll be following him," one of the five men present declared in a tone that boded no good.

"It's a religious affair, so they won't be watching him so carefully. In fact, I doubt they'll pay much attention at all. My hope is that they'll simply chalk up his attendance to nostalgia."

"Why do you think they were willing to accept him into their ranks?" the same one asked.

Laser hesitated. "My best guess is that they plan to persuade him to work for their side. When the story explodes, and the newspapers start featuring articles about the babies that were switched at birth, then, they'll act, trying to win him over. Obviously, they're not dumb enough to imagine that we won't make a similar attempt, but what they don't realize is that we would never trust him as an agent. No, we have an entirely different plan for him." Laser chuckled, an evil glint in his eyes. "That's also the reason why I never let anyone kill the Jew, even though that idiot Rashid ran out of patience years ago. The whole story looks much more innocent that way – an accidental switch that somehow occurred, already twenty years ago. There's not even anyone to blame by now; the nurse is long since senile."

The others nodded grimly, well aware that the nurse's senility had been induced by heavy doses of medication. The best minds of their organization had been invested in this plot, and they weren't about to let it fail.

Laser continued, keenly aware that he was starring in a one-man show. "They slaughtered us in Gaza, and murdered our women and children. Now we'll show them that we don't need war to kill an equal number of people."

"You think they'll have a thousand people there?" the one who couldn't keep his mouth shut couldn't resist asking.

"They'll have no less than five thousand, if not close to seven or eight," Laser replied with satisfaction. "Many will come with their whole families. I've done my research, and my patience has paid off. There's only one problem, and that's the boy himself." He lowered his voice slightly. "He's still not completely convinced. He's wavering. We need to keep the rope taut until the event. He's still foolish enough to believe that, once this is over, we're going to use him as an intelligence agent; he doesn't really believe in his destiny as a *shahid*. I see it in his eyes. He doesn't understand why we aren't exploiting him as a golden key to the GSS. He's so stupid and naïve that he doesn't even realize why the GSS accepted him in the first place. It hasn't even begun to occur to him that all the duties assigned to him so far have been fake, and that he himself is being closely watched by five of them."

Laser's tone suddenly turned anxious. "My fear is that at the moment of truth, the kid is going to get cold feet and run away. He wasn't brought up with the aspiration to sacrifice his life for a higher goal. And that's why the four of you are here with me now."

What followed was an expectant silence, as they waited with bated breath to hear Laser's next revelation.

"For some reason, his adoptive family has decided to cut off all contact with him. He has a mother and two siblings, and I want him to renew contact with them. My intention is that in that moment of truth, when he has to decide, we will be able to use them for our own purposes. He'll have to choose between his life and theirs, and I believe that his family will come first."

"Why do you think so?"

"Because Jews are soft, and he grew up with them. From what I've heard, it appears that his family has rejected him because he abandoned their ways and religious observance. The woman knows nothing of the switch; of that I'm convinced. Nonetheless, she decided to break off contact with him. Your job is to discover where they've disappeared to and where exactly they're living. Our sources say that they're hiding somewhere in the Galilee or Golan.

"Our job now is to bring our young friend back to his family, and he will be eternally grateful to us for it!" Laser mocked, his lips upturned in a smile although his eyes were frigid. "What he won't know is that, simultaneously, we will be digging four graves: his, the mother's, and those of his two siblings."

Not knowing where else to turn, Gil decided to try Toiby Lipsky once again. Laser had been pestering him non-stop to renew contact with the family, not that Gil needed so much convincing. He was desperate to see his mother again, to feel a sense of belonging, warmth, and love – and he was convinced that despite her plea to him not to return, Shuli would still welcome him back with open arms.

To his chagrin, Toiby was as unhelpful as she had been previously. "Mendy, I wish I could tell you otherwise, but your mother and siblings seem to have disappeared off the face of the earth. I've been saying the whole *Tehillim* every day and giving money to *tzedakah* asking that Hashem should watch over them, but I have no idea where they are or how they're faring. Your mother disconnected her phone, and after all I did for her, I didn't think this was the way she would repay me," she concluded.

Gil decided to try Yochai again.

"Yochai, I need to speak to my mother. It's very important," he explained urgently.

"I thought we decided that you were going to give her a break," Yochai reminded him pointedly. Yochai never consciously forced his opinions on anyone, but he expressed his views in such a manner that others generally did end up going along with him.

Gil nodded impatiently. "Yes, fine, but please bear in mind that *we* didn't decide anything. *You* made that decision. Second, my mother and I left several matters unresolved, and I need to settle them. Every day takes me farther away from them, and it hurts, Yochai. At the end of the day, I just lost my father," he added, trying to arouse the man's sympathy. "Can't you just do a bit of research to find out where they are?"

Yochai shrugged and turned in disinterest back to his computer screen. "How should I know where they went? I was in touch with your father, but now that he's gone, I have no reason to maintain any connection with your mother."

"Oh, come on, Yochai, give me a break. If you really want to, you can find out where she is. Her neighbor said something about them heading up north, to some anonymous moshav. Maybe you have some kind of idea which one it could be, based on something you might remember about my parents from the past?"

Yochai looked bored. "Listen, Gil. I've got a ton of things to worry about right now, and this isn't one of them."

"Okay, so I'm taking a day off."

"What for?"

"To find them," Gil answered, his tone matter-of-fact.

Yochai looked annoyed. "Don't be stupid, kid. You'll never find your mother in one day. Have you ever counted how many settlements there are up north? You're being ridiculous. Stay here and get on with your job."

Gil's eyes narrowed. "Yochai, you know as well as I do that what I do here makes no difference to anyone. Send me for a training course at least – then I'd be doing something useful. To be honest, I'm bored here. Besides, to answer your question, no, I've never counted how many settlements there are up north, but I do have a certain idea, and I think I might find my mother rather quickly."

"Oh yes?" A slight note of tension sounded in Yochai's voice. His fingers continued tapping at the keyboard, but his eyelids fluttered quicker than usual.

"I have an idea, and I'll keep it to myself for now. When I find them, Yochai, you'll be proud of your brilliant agent!" He concluded on a humorous note, never dreaming that his words would stimulate such a violent outburst.

"You're out of line!" Yochai shouted furiously. "What do you think? That this place is a playground, and you can do whatever you please? This isn't child's play, Gil, and you'll do exactly as you're ordered. Now, back to your post!"

Gil's eyes widened in shock as he realized that he'd crossed a red line. Swallowing an equally angry response, he spun around and exited Yochai's office with a bitter smile on his face. He was determined to find his mother, to speak to her, and maybe even to tell her what was really going on and discover how she felt toward him. Was he still her Mendy, or was he a stranger, a *goy*? The more he reflected upon the dilemma, the less certain he felt about how she perceived him. Did she view him through the prism of the twenty years of their shared history, or did a few moments of cold, hard truth have the power to dissolve hours of love and devotion?

The pain that sliced through his heart as he pondered that question was almost too much to bear, and Gil forcefully diverted his thoughts to another direction. Sitting down at his desk, he started to scan the online telephone registry for a list of all the religious schools in the north of the country, correctly surmising that there were few institutions that would meet his mother's exacting standards. His fingers flew over the keyboard as he scanned the list and quickly eliminated one option after another. From his office, Yochai dogged his activities with anxious eyes with the help of the cameras positioned in every cubicle in the building.

He lifted his desk phone and dialed an internal number. "Alon, I need your help. First of all, knock off Gil Brand's computer connection right now. The next thing we'll have to do is assign him some bogus mission in the field. The kid is a lot brighter than I anticipated, and we have to work quickly."

"Yes, sir," Alon replied. A second later, a cry of delight emerged from Gil's tiny cubicle as he located the *cheder* he was sure that his mother would choose for Nachum, but his excitement was immediately doused when, a moment later, his screen went black as the whole department suffered a sudden power cut. The lights flickered back on a few seconds later, but when Gil tried to reboot, he discovered that his computer was dead.

"Hey, Gil. I need you with me now," Alon poked his head urgently into his cubicle. Gil hardly heard him, so busy he was trying to bring his computer back to life. "Gil!" Alon laid a heavy hand on his shoulder. "You're coming with me. Let's go."

Gil got the hint and silently cursed his bad luck. *You won this round, Yochai. But as soon as I get home, the information is all mine.*

With Gil safely ensconced in the vehicle, on his way to do absolutely nothing, Yochai called a number on a secure line. The phone rang several times until it was answered by a woman who spoke in a measured tone of voice.

"It's Yochai. What's doing? How are you folks settling in?" the agent began without preamble.

"*Baruch Hashem*, it's going well," Shuli replied, sounding relaxed.

"Good. But now, listen. There's been a change of plans. We're on our way as I speak to pick you guys up and take you down to Eilat. From there, you're flying to Turkey, and then on to London," Yochai dropped his bombshell.

Shuli didn't reply at first, but even her silence expressed her objections. "What's going on, Yochai? We can't just jump up and leave again. And what's more, I don't want to leave the country."

"If you don't, you'll be endangering your children," Yochai touched on her rawest nerve.

"*I'll* be endangering the children?" Shuli's voice rose defiantly. "What about you, Yochai? How do you know that *you're* not endangering my children, physically and emotionally? You're playing games, experimenting on real people! Why don't we just surrender and put an end to all this? How many more times can we run away?" Uncharacteristically, Shuli burst into tears.

"Yochai, how much longer? How much more can I suffer? Didn't Shimon give his all to the country? Can't you do anything to help us now? Just make sure that he keeps away, from me and from the kids. That's all I ask."

"It may well be all you ask, but it's much harder than you think to make it happen. He lives in Tel Aviv, and it's not exactly too complicated for him to find out what's going on just two hours away, especially in your tight-knit religious circles," Yochai sounded genuinely apologetic. "Believe, me, the last thing I want to do is mess with your lives right now, especially given all you've just been through, but I really believe that your lives are in danger if you choose to stay."

"So what should I do?" Shuli sounded on the verge of despair.

"Don't even bother packing. Take whatever you need for a day or two and prepare the kids for a long-term vacation. I'll have people on their way to you within the next half hour."

A long silence was finally broken by Shuli's tearful voice, "Are you sure about this? I know Mendy, and he would never harm us, and certainly not the kids. I know we have to take precautions, but this seems so excessive."

Yochai had no choice but to lay down all his cards. "Shuli, Mendy isn't even a tiny screw in this whole operation. There are no less than twenty pairs of eyes watching his every move, and each one of those people is trained and dangerous. Mendy is so innocent that he doesn't even realize what a gold mine is he to them. They're following him everywhere, and he's committed to finding you, not realizing that he'll be leading all those beasts right to your front door."

Soft weeping sounded from the other end of the line, tugging at Yochai's heartstrings. "Can you be ready to leave within the hour?" he asked gently. Shuli murmured something indistinct, which Yochai chose to interpret as a positive reply, and he ended the call and immediately pressed another button.

"Nir, I need at least five of your boys to help me with the next operation. It has to be carried out clean and quick. I need guys we can trust, got it?"

"Will do, sir."

Yochai exhaled a sigh of relief and got back to work. In a few hours, the family would be safely on their way out of the country, and Gil would be clueless regarding how they had managed to elude him. He would never discover how they had escaped or where they were headed to. Yochai wasn't oblivious to the other reason why Shuli was so reluctant to leave the country, and he sympathized with her. Shuli couldn't bring herself to part once and for all from her eldest child – but she had to understand that the true threat wasn't from Mendy, but rather from the evil-minded people manipulating him.

He was looking forward to hearing that the family had landed safely in England. Only then would he allow himself to exhale a final sigh of relief and proceed to the next task: taking care of Gil and Jamil, the boys switched at birth. If only simply switching them back was the answer…

Laser was furious. "They think they're so smart, huh? Yochai thinks that he can spirit them off to England and save them? What a fool!"

Gil stood among the group of hard-hearted terrorists, like a chick in the middle of a pack of lions whose teeth dripped with the blood of their prey.

"What do you want from me? You told me to find my mother. I did my best, and it didn't work." Gil tried to weasel out of his failure, which only further fanned Laser's fury.

"Shut your mouth, kid! You understand nothing!"

Gil promptly fell silent.

Laser paced back and forth restlessly. "Yochai won't release the Jewish kid; he won't let him out. So it's one against one. You hear me, kid? One against one."

Gil paled. "What are you talking about?"

"We have your family. I know you think only of your Jewish family, which is why I'm telling you that. Either you play by our rules, or we eliminate them one by one. Shimon is gone. Next, we'll kill the boy, the one we switched for you. When your mother goes to attend the funeral of the son she never knew, we'll kill her."

Gil couldn't quell the trembling of his lips, no matter how hard he tried. "I already told you: That family doesn't interest me anymore, and I don't know why you think that killing them will get you anywhere." He managed to maintain an indifferent tone, but Laser wasn't fooled.

"You're one of us, but you're still one of them, too. When we hurt them, we hurt you. You're dismissed."

Gil was led out of the room, where the meeting continued without him. He knew that he had nothing left to give to them. He would never be one of them – he wasn't born to kill or plunder, and their characters and ways repelled him completely.

At that moment, he realized with perfect clarity that he had never really been one of them, and that he could never identify with them, no matter how much his intellect struggled to comprehend their mindset. They didn't view him as a brother, but rather as a tool to be used and then discarded. And he… he wanted nothing more than to disappear forever, never to see them again, never to be found… He was tempted to rush over to Yochai, admit the truth, and beg to join the other side, but he swallowed his instincts and returned to his dingy studio where he forced himself to analyze his reality with a clear and unbiased mind.

Am I a Jew? No. My name is not Gil or Mendy; it's Jamil. I'm an Arab, a son of the Arab nation, a nation that lives by its sword, he recalled the words of the Torah. Unexpectedly, hot tears rose in his eyes, and Mendy-Gil-Jamil lowered his head and allowed them to fall. For a long hour, he wept over his life, his loss, his loneliness. He was neither a Jew nor an Arab; he was nothing, loved by no one in the world.

Who cared about him? The Arabs who pulled at his strings as if he were a puppet, playing with his life and feelings and desiring only blood and money? His poverty-stricken Arab parents who had received paltry remuneration for their enormous sacrifice? His dear mother who had raised him throughout his life and now believed him to be pursuing her with the intention of harming her and her children?

Did anyone even spare a thought for him? Did anyone even care if he lived or died? He stared out of the window with unseeing eyes, and felt the cold reality sink in. He was alone – it might just as well have been just him in the whole world, under the huge blue sky. Inexplicably, the thought was somehow comforting; it reminded him that he, too, was one of G-d's creations, and his eyes filled with tears.

I may not be a Jew, but I was still fashioned by the hands of Hakadosh Baruch Hu, Who hears the cry of Jew and gentile alike. He made me, and although I am not a member of the Chosen Nation, I am still His child, His creation.

With that, the sweet words of *Tehillim,* indelibly imprinted upon his mind, began to pour from his lips, and as he spoke them, he wept over his past, his present, and his unknown and perhaps nonexistent future. For a split second, he wondered if he was even allowed to recite those sacred words, but then he reminded himself that Dovid Hamelech had been a descendant of Rus, a Moabite, and that surely the words belonged to him, just as they had belonged to all other broken and downtrodden people throughout the ages.

A steely determination filled him, and Gil decided that the time had come to approach a rav and request a conversion. It had taken time to appreciate the truth, but with sudden clarity, he realized that he abhorred all that his life had become ever since he had abandoned the world of Torah. He longed to reconnect to what he had lost, to the People he had turned his back on. Above all, he yearned to *daven* again and feel close to his Creator. And, he couldn't wait for the moment when he would once again see his mother – Shuli – and tell her that now he was truly a Jew.

With this resolution firmly entrenched in his heart, he wiped away the final tears. Once again, his future seemed secure. Laser and his cohorts, along with their ruthless plans, were suddenly meaningless. *B'chol dor v'dor omdim aleinu l'chaloseinu*, he whispered. In every generation, they rise up against us, attempting to destroy us, but *Hakadosh Baruch Hu* would save him, in the merit of his attachment to the Jewish People. Of that he had no doubt.

Glancing at his watch, he realized it wasn't even so late. If he hurried, maybe he could still make an appointment to see a rav that night. He was certain that once he was a Jew, everything would become clear.

It was one of the most difficult conversations that Yochai had ever held. What began as a casual phone call, just to see how things were going, swiftly revealed the frightening truth.

"Yochai, you asked us to move to England, and we did, even though I didn't want to leave Eretz Yisrael. We did everything exactly as you said," Shuli reminded him.

"We did it in order to protect you," Yochai reminded her.

A short silence was followed by Shuli's protest. "I don't know. Maybe you just wanted us out of the way. Maybe you were afraid that the story would break and you thought that in England, I wouldn't hear about it. But it's too late for that. I already know, and I'm not about to ignore the facts just because they happen to be inconvenient for you."

"So, what do you want – compensation?" Yochai demanded.

"Me? *Compensation?* Have you lost your mind? What kind of mother would accept money in place of her child? Do you really think so poorly of me, Yochai?"

Yochai was chastised into silence. "So what do you want?" he finally asked.

"I know that you're holding my son."

"Mendy is free to come and go as he pleases," Yochai tried to postpone the inevitable.

Shuli replied icily, "I'm not talking about Mendy, or at least not the Mendy that you're talking about. Yochai, I want *my* Mendy. The real Mendy. My Jewish son. The son that I *davened* for all the years but didn't even know existed. Never did I dream that the child I was *davening* for wasn't the one I was raising. I'd actually like to know at what point you discovered the truth, but I doubt you'll deign to tell me."

Yochai let out a frustrated sigh.

"I don't have the slightest idea what you're talking about," he told her.

"Yochai, stop it! Stop playing games! We're talking on a secure line – nobody's listening in. I want you to talk straight, just like I am. You know exactly what and who I'm talking about!" Shuli hesitated a moment, and then added, "I want to meet Mendy, or, rather, the boy you call Jamil."

Yochai slammed his fist angrily on the table, and then winced and rubbed it to alleviate the pain.

"How do you know his name?" he roared.

Shuli didn't reply.

"Who told you his name?!"

"Please don't ask," Shuli finally whispered. "But I know."

"I need to know who told you! It's critical. What's going on here?" he cried in angst.

"It doesn't matter. All that matters is the fact that I want to meet my son."

"It does matter. It matters very much. And besides, he's in Israel, and he can't leave the country."

"Okay, so I'll get on a plane and come back to Israel to meet with him."

"You're out of your mind, Shuli. You'll endanger yourself and everything we've done to protect you."

"I'm also in danger if I never lay eyes on my own child. I have to see him, and this is not up for debate."

Yochai struggled to maintain his equilibrium; this was the last twist he had anticipated. "Okay, you know what? Have it your way. We'll fly him out to meet you. You'll see him for one day. Good?"

"A week."

"Two days."

"Two weeks."

"Three days, and that's final."

Shuli fell silent, knowing she had pulled the rope as far as she could.

"And don't think that I won't have to recruit some of my top boys to keep the two of you safe," Yochai added warningly. "Shuli, this is not a game, and I don't know how much longer I can keep this up." Yochai ended the call and rubbed his eyes in exhaustion, feeling the impossible weight of the burden on his shoulders. He had his men tracking Gil, and he was fully apprised of Laser's plans, but he had a strange feeling that the story had just grown much more complicated.

Too many people now knew of the babies that had been switched at birth. The last thing he needed was Jamil reaching the press and announcing his initiative to reunite with his birth parents.

Taking a deep breath, Yochai proceeded to call several colleagues before flicking the 'on' button attached to the bug planted in Jamil's room, just in time to hear the young man exclaim in delight upon receiving the news of his upcoming trip to England. Somehow, it didn't surprise him that Jamil was more excited about the opportunity to visit a new country than to meet his birth family, and Yochai reflected briefly on the thought that despite all the revelations, Jamil had remained Jamil, an ignorant and hopelessly naïve village boy – an Arab.

"Which city in England?" Jamil was asking his guard. "When are we leaving? I can't wait to get out of here!" It took a while for him to remember the true purpose of the trip, and then another thought occurred to him. "I want to buy them a gift. What do you suggest?" he asked the agent with him suddenly.

"A gift? Why?"

"They're my family, after all."

"But you don't even know them."

"But I will. And I also want to get out of here!"

Yochai sighed and pushed the button again, silencing the device. His office was now quiet, allowing him to think and plan. Apparently, it was now time to start worrying about the day when Jamil would go free and tell everyone in sight about the months he had spent in the basement of GSS Headquarters. Initially, Jamil had seemed grateful for the protection and haven they were offering him, but over time, that gratitude had turned to resentment and suppressed anger for holding him for so long; and Yochai wondered where those roiling emotions would lead him.

The very next morning, Jamil was driven to a small air base and flown on a private plane to a small airport somewhere near the Scottish border.

"I'd much rather fly on a regular passenger plane," Jamil grumbled to Segev, a tall, handsome, and disconcertingly quiet young man who stuck to him like a shadow. As usual, Segev's reply was silence.

Although there was little to see from the airplane's window save for blue sky and white clouds, Jamil kept his face pressed against the windowpane throughout the duration of the flight.

"Even now, I'm still a prisoner," he complained again to Segev, who had long grown accustomed to Jamil's seemingly endless litany of negative comments. "I know I wanted protection, but I didn't expect to be locked up. Okay, it's a comfortable prison, at least compared to what I've heard of Israeli prisons, but I didn't do anything wrong! They could at least give me some freedom."

Segev hid a smirk, and remained silent.

They landed in a private airfield where they were met by two broad-shouldered men who were even taller and showed even less expression than Segev. They quickly ushered the two arrivals into a nondescript vehicle and then set out on the half-hour drive to Gateshead.

Once again, however, Jamil found reason to complain.

"I was cooped up in the plane for hours, and I need to stretch my legs a bit. Some fresh air would also be nice once in a while."

Segev exchanged glances with his two escorts, who murmured something to him. Segev nodded.

"We'll stop at the next gas station – we need to fill up, in any case – and you can get out for five minutes."

Jamil opened his mouth to protest at the ridiculously short amount of time being allotted him, but shut it again when he saw the warning glare in Segev's eyes.

Ten minutes later, the car pulled into a gas station and Jamil jumped right out, closely followed by Segev. The two of them strolled over to the grassy expanse at the side of the road, and Jamil tried to start up a conversation.

"You know what I've been thinking?" he mused aloud, automatically replying without awaiting the other's reply. "I've been wondering what's going to happen when I meet my family. Will I somehow manage to fit in? Will I be able to live with them? Will they accept me? Or will I spend the rest of my life in hiding?"

As usual, Segev's reply was an expressionless silence.

Jamil looked annoyed. "Are you not answering because you don't know or because you don't want to answer?" he demanded.

"Don't know." The reply was as concise as possible. Jamil grimaced.

"It's been ages since I've spent time with normal people," he tried again. Segev listened, but as was usual for him, didn't respond. "If you guys would let me, I'd stand here for hours on end, just watching the people go by," he added longingly.

The gas tank was full by then, and Segev politely asked Jamil to step back into the car.

"No, not yet. Give me another few minutes," Jamil replied defiantly.

"Come on, Jamil. It's time to go. We don't have time to spare."

"Soon."

This time, it was Segev's turn to look irritated, and he turned around to consult with the driver, who, together with the other agent, was already back in the car. Just twenty seconds later, Segev turned back to Jamil to tell him what the three agents had decided – and his heart skipped a beat.

The spot where Jamil had been standing just a moment ago was empty.

"Jamil?" he called aloud, scanning the area with trained eyes, but there was no reply. Segev broke into a run, racing toward the mini-strip mall nearby. Could Jamil have stepped inside a store for a minute to buy himself something? It was more than a minute's walk away, he estimated, but maybe Jamil had covered the distance at a run? He had some money of his own, after all, and he had been so desperate to break free of his escorts and spread his wings a little.

And he, Segev, had been responsible to keep his eyes on the kid… Now what? How had Jamil managed to disappear so quickly? And how on earth did he think he would manage on his own in England when he didn't speak a word of the language? Or – and the thought caused Segev to break out in a cold sweat – had somebody nabbed him?

Alerted by Segev, the other two agents jumped out of the car and joined the search, but when thirty minutes passed with no sign of the boy, they reluctantly admitted that Jamil had successfully eluded their grasp.

"The only question remaining now is if he left of his own accord or if he was 'assisted' by someone," one of the agents added gravely.

Praying that the phone call wouldn't mark the end of his career, Segev took a deep breath and called Yochai at Headquarters. Uncharacteristically, Yochai sounded extremely unsettled himself. "You arrived? I thought I'd hear from you sooner. What's going on?"

"He's gone," Segev reported tonelessly.

"GONE??? WHAT DO YOU MEAN, HE'S GONE?" In fifteen years of working for the GSS, Segev had never heard his boss lose control like that.

"I mean, he's gone."

"He ran off, or he was kidnapped?"

"We don't know," Segev admitted wearily. "I turned my head for less than thirty seconds, and when I turned back, he had disappeared. This kid can't be left alone for a second! He was right there, and then he was gone…" Segev was mortified, and he couldn't even manage to sound coherent in his effort to explain how such a thing could have occurred.

"I told you not to leave him alone for even a minute," Yochai raged.

"You did, sir. And this was significantly less than a minute. It's unbelievable, sir."

Yochai didn't reply, and his silence spoke volumes.

"Listen, don't continue on to the family. I'll call them, and tell them that there's been a delay. In the meantime, keep searching for him. Don't leave any stone unturned. Is there public transportation in the area?"

"There is, sir."

"But in any case, the kid had no money on him, right? Unless you were dumb enough to provide him with it?"

"No! Absolutely not!" Segev hoped he sounded sufficiently genuine.

"In which case, the second option is the more likely of the two, and if he has indeed been captured, then I very much doubt that you'll succeed in finding him." Yochai slammed the receiver down in frustration, knowing that it was pointless to reprimand Segev, a talented officer who was just as devastated as he was at his failure.

Knowing that it would be a difficult conversation, he sighed before reluctantly dialing Shuli's secure line.

"Shuli? It's Yochai. I'm really sorry, but there's been an unexpected delay. They won't be arriving for another few hours."

Shuli was furious. "How can you do this to us? How much longer are you going to play with my feelings like this? I'm a person, Yochai, a human being, and I don't deserve this… None of us do…" She burst into tears of pain, frustration, and anger.

Yochai feigned coldness. "Shuli, do you want to see your child deal or alive? You have no idea what's going on, but what you have to know is that your son's life is in grave danger. A lot of people are determined to get him out of the picture. I'm not saying that you'll never meet him, just that the meeting is being postponed."

"For how long?"

"An hour, two. Maybe a day or two. It's hard to know exactly."

"So maybe a month or two or a year or two?" she asked sarcastically.

Yochai was aggravatingly calm. "Anything is possible."

"So you're cancelling the meeting totally?" Shuli sounded totally betrayed.

Not knowing how best to reply, Yochai remained silent. There was no sense in confirming her worst fears – and, in any case, maybe they would still manage to find Jamil.

He ended the call apologetically, knowing that he had no words with which to comfort the distraught mother.

Gil was starting to become impatient with his new friend. "Meir, I've been trying to tell you something very important, but you're not listening."

"I *am* listening."

The two were sitting in shul, and Meir treated the younger man to a caring look. "I'm listening to you, and I hear every word. I just pointed out that if your father were alive, he'd be very proud of your *hasmadah*."

"Meir, my father was never proud of me, and definitely not because I was a *masmid*."

"I disagree."

"Meir, I'm trying to tell you something!" Gil practically shouted. "Listen to me! I've been trying to tell you that I'm not really a Jew."

Meir looked scandalized. "Mendy, never say such a thing again! Whatever happens, whatever you do or don't do, your *neshamah* remains intact! Think of all the *mitzvos* you've done in your life, all the Torah you've learned – how can you think of saying such a thing just because of a temporary phase in your life where things aren't going so smoothly? You just have to—"

"Meir, one more word, and I'm going to set this place on fire! I'm trying to tell you something important. Please, just be quiet and *listen!*"

Meir sat up straighter, suddenly grasping that the boy really was trying to tell him something other than what he thought he was hearing. He folded his hands on the table and leaned forward. "I'm sorry, Mendy. You're right – I didn't grasp what you were trying to say. Talk, and I won't say another word until you're done."

Indeed, he didn't utter a word of interruption. For the next half hour, he listened in stunned silence, his expression changing from shock to appall to doubt and finally to amusement. When Gil finished, he shook his head.

"You should write a book, Mendy," he smiled wryly. "If we weren't in shul, I'd give you a standing ovation."

"Whatever you want. But can you come up with any other reason why my family is avoiding me?"

Meir's mouth opened and closed like a fish. "Mendy... Your family isn't necessarily *avoiding* you. As I understand it, they need a bit of quiet. Although your mother denies it, maybe she does subconsciously – or even consciously – blame you, at least partially, for your father's death."

"Since when does somebody die because of this type of thing? Tons of kids go off the *derech*, and their parents invariably wait for them to come back to the fold, however painful it might be, even though it's probably easier to just give up on them. Why should it be any different between me and my father? Something much deeper happened here, and I want you to help me find out what it is."

Meir looked suddenly overwhelmed, and he shifted uncomfortably in his chair. Mendy's story was more than a challenge; it had become downright chilling.

"So you're telling me that… that you're really an Arab?"

"Basically, yes. That's exactly what I'm trying to tell you."

"And they're asking you to…" Meir stared penetratingly at him. "What do they want from you?"

"Whatever. The point isn't what they want. The point is what *I* want. Look at me, Meir. I'm an Arab, a son of Yishmael. My Jewish family ran away from me, and my Arab family couldn't care less about me until I carry out the suicide mission and go to Paradise as a good Arab… Meir, please look at me. I need your help! I may not be a Yid, but… I still really need your help."

Meir paled. "How can I help you?"

"I want to convert."

"Why?"

"Don't hurt me with pointless questions. I know what you're doing, but you won't succeed."

"But, Mendy, even when you thought you were a Yid, you went off the *derech*. So why would you want to be *misgayer* now? You can keep the *sheva mitzvos bnei Noach* and enjoy life as a righteous gentile." With each additional word Meir spoke, the more frightened he appeared. For a moment, his suggestion seemed to amuse Gil, but the feeling was quickly replaced by anger.

"Why are you pushing me away after everything I've been through?" he asked in genuine anguish.

Meir fell silent for a moment. "To tell you the truth, on the assumption that everything you've said is true... I simply think that you'll have an easier time hiding out in the world as a non-Jew. You've got the GSS after you, and the Arabs too... From what you say, it seems like everyone's hot on your tail."

Gil cringed. "It sure seems like it."

"So why take on the added burden of converting?""

Gil didn't reply at first, instead gripping the edge of the table until his knuckles turned white, and his internal struggle showed clearly on his face. Finally, he choked out, "Why? How can I ever explain that to you? Just trust me, please, Meir! You're the only one in the world who knows me and cares enough to help me do this. I have to convert! Please help me!"

46

Yochai was livid. Twenty agents had been recruited to scour a radius of fifty kilometers from where Jamil had disappeared, and reports – all of them negative – were flooding his office by the minute. He listened to each one with a sinking heart, knowing that with every minute that passed, their chances of finding the boy were growing slimmer and slimmer.

With a not inconsiderable degree of anger, Yochai reflected that if Jamil had not been Shimon's son, there was no way that the GSS would have invested such massive resources into locating him. Every agent on the field was knowingly endangering himself with his activities, and though their paychecks were commensurate with the risks, there were some things that went beyond compensation, such as the lives of one's own children. And that, of course, was why they were hunting for Jamil in the first place. Shimon had put his life on the line many times for the Service, and now, they owed him at least that much in return. In fact, Yochai was willing to risk leaking the secret among additional agents, if only it would lead one of them to find Jamil.

The sight of Meir Landsman, hurrying down the corridor toward his office, did nothing to improve his foul mood. "Not now, Meir. Do me a favor, I'm busy, and I can't talk to you right now." Meir immediately noticed that Yochai was acting completely out of character, his eyes burning feverishly as he tried to think of some solution to his dilemma. Nonetheless, and true to form, Meir was stubborn as a mule.

"I see that you're busy," he admitted, before rushing on, "but, Yochai, this is really important. You'll see that for yourself once you hear what I have to say."

"Meir, I'm asking you to leave my office this minute," Yochai told him sternly.

"I'm not going until we discuss this," Meir argued.

"Meir, if you're not out of here in one second, I'm calling security."

"You've got a traitor in your midst!" Meir fired at him, his eyes clear and determined.

"Thanks for the info," Yochai replied sarcastically. How had he managed to hook up with this idiot? How dare this *chareidi* kid, who had never even served in the army and had no skill to speak of other than teaching *Gemara*, prance into his office and waste his time like this? He pressed a concealed button beneath his desk, and, a second later, a giant of a man strode in.

"Is there a problem, sir?"

"Please escort this man out of the building," Yochai ordered succinctly.

The guard grabbed Meir by the arm. Meir had a despairing look, yet he didn't protest, and the two soon exited the room together. A second before he disappeared, Meir somehow managed to poke his head back in and hiss, "He's an Arab! You're paying an Arab. Mendy!"

"WHAT DID YOU SAY?" Yochai roared, catapulting out of his seat. Upon the arranged signal, the guard promptly released Meir's arm, and the young man walked freely back into Yochai's office with a triumphant smile stretched across his face.

"Exactly what you heard."

"Say it again."

"Mendy is an Arab."

"No. No. It can't be that you know that." Perspiration broke out all over Yochai's forehead. "Who told you?"

"I got it straight from the source."

"Meaning?"

"Mendy himself."

"Gil told you?" Yochai looked powerless. "You? *Why you?* That kid is simply desperate," he groaned.

"Yes, he really is."

Meir sat himself down comfortably across from Yochai, allowing himself a quick glance around the room, which was elegantly furnished, if not exactly luxurious.

He found himself recalling his conversation with his wife that morning, and how she had begged him not to go. "Meir, someone's laying a trap for you! You'll end up in jail or who-knows-where! Just stay away from that lion's den!"

"Who's laying a trap for me?" Meir had queried innocently. "Besides, if I ignore what I heard and conceal information like this, I could really end up in jail!"

Poor Naomi had been hysterical. "Meir, what exactly do you think you're doing? How on earth did you manage to get caught up in this? Why can't you just keep away from this Jewish Arab or Arab Jew, or whatever he is! If he wants to be *misgayer*, let him go to a rav! He doesn't need you. You're not a rav. Yet," she added, noting his injured expression.

"You're right about that, but this kid is working for the Israelis. Do you understand what that means?"

Uncharacteristically, Naomi burst into tears. Not only was she by nature intensely suspicious, but she also had extraordinary intuition that, more often than not, proved to be right on target. "Meir, why can't you just drop this? There are enough people involved apart from you! I can just see how this is going to end! It's just like the story with the cow and the donkey."

"What story?"

Naomi took a deep breath and tried to calm herself. "The story… I only wish it didn't fit what's happening so well. Once, a donkey decided that it had had enough of schlepping for its master, so he played sick, dozing the whole day and pretending not to have the strength to work. The owner soon became concerned, and he called a vet to examine the donkey. When the cow saw what was going on, she hurried over to the donkey and said, 'You'd better get off your rump, or the vet will diagnose you as sick, and then, they'll put you to sleep.' But the donkey was stubborn and shut his eyes again, continuing to play sick.

"The vet showed up, examined the donkey, and saw that it was apathetic. He told the owner that he'd be back the next day, and if the donkey seemed better, he'd treat him; but if not, they would put it to sleep.

"The vet left, and the cow hurried back to the donkey to warn him. 'This is your last chance! You'd better show some signs of life, and quick!' But the donkey was stubborn and insisted on continuing with his game.

"The next day, the vet showed up, saw that the donkey was still apathetic, and said that they had no choice but to put the donkey to sleep for good because it was obviously very ill. When he went out to his car to get the drugs to inject, the cow ran back over to the donkey and said, 'I'm begging you! Once the vet injects the drug into your rump, it's all over, and you'll never be able to get up again!

"Hearing this, the donkey started to panic, and when he saw the vet approaching from the distance holding the drugs, he immediately jumped to his feet, braying loudly. The owner was delighted, thanked the veterinarian from the bottom of its heart and said, 'Thank you so much for saving my donkey! I'd like to host you for a special dinner, in honor of which we'll roast the meat of this delicious old cow!" Naomi stopped and made a face that was somewhere between a smile and a grimace. "Do you get the point?"

"You think I'm being the cow?" Meir asked thoughtfully.

"No!" Naomi seemed aghast at the idea.

"So, I'm the donkey?" Meir looked so mournful that they both burst out laughing.

"Definitely not. You're an incredible husband, father, and person, but you have to learn to keep out of things! Ultimately, you'll be the one to pay for it! This Yochai's got dozens of men keeping him safe. Mendy has his Arab friends or enemies or whoever. But if *you* get into trouble, who's going to watch over *you*?"

Meir listened quietly and then nodded. "Naomi, the truth is that I'm not sure what to answer you on that, but what I can do is stop following my instincts and act only *al pi daas Torah.* I'll go speak to Rav Greenstein now. Is that fair?"

"Very. Thank you."

"And, the only other comment I have on your *mashal,* besides for the fact that it was humorous, is that it doesn't really make any allowance for the *chovah* of every Yid to help his friend."

"But it does allow for you taking care of yourself and being responsible!"

"Somehow you seem to track down every single rule, *mashal,* or story that emphasizes being careful," Meir laughed as he donned his hat and jacket and turned to leave.

He spent the next hour closeted in the study of his rav, who, after hearing the story, fully agreed with Meir's opinion that he was obligated to share the information with Yochai, given the potential risks involved.

And yet, now that he was actually facing Yochai, who stared at him tautly, Meir was beginning to have second thoughts. Maybe, just maybe, Naomi had been right this time? Aside from the tension, there was blatant hostility in Yochai's eyes, and Meir suddenly grasped that he viewed him as the enemy.

"What in the world impelled Gil to tell you all this? Since when are the two of you so close? I was under the impression that you two are *chavrutas,* but nothing beyond that." His pronunciation of the word was so strange that Meir had to restrain himself from laughing out loud.

"First of all, the word *chavruta* translates as 'friend.' Second, the hours spent together in learning automatically engender closeness, and Mendy told me this after our learning session. When I heard his story, I felt obligated to share it with you."

"You'd better not breathe a word of this to anyone," Yochai warned.

"Understood."

"And as of today, you're being watched."

"*Me?* But why?" An image of Naomi's cow suddenly came to his mind and Meir winced.

"Why? Because you're sticking your nose into places you don't belong in! Why did you have to go and become friends with him?" Yochai seemed to be lamenting the fact more than expecting an answer to his question. "What else did he tell you?"

"That he wants to convert."

"You're kidding."

"Not at all."

"Like, all the way?"

"Obviously. You can't just convert part of the way. Conversion is an all-or-nothing deal, and Mendy knows that."

Yochai didn't seem impressed. "Did he say anything else?"

"That I should direct him to a rav who will understand him. He said he feels like he's all alone in the world, and that no one cares whether he lives or dies – not the Jews or the Arabs. He seemed really depressed, in fact."

"Spare me your psychological opinions," Yochai snapped, studying him carefully. "You know what? It's possible that this could actually work out to our benefit. We'll attach a bug to you, and from now on, I want you recording every conversation with him."

"Why?"

"Because it's important to us."

Meir's lips went dry. "I'm not sure about that. I'll have to consult with my wife."

"You'll have to consult with your *wife*?" This time, it was Yochai's turn to laugh, although he was not at all amused. Jamil had disappeared without a trace, and now Mendy-Gil was telling his story to anyone who would listen. It was too unlikely a string of coincidences to be anything but clearly plotted by Gil's superiors. The more Yochai evaluated the situation from an objective standpoint, the more he grew convinced that Gil was cooperating with his Arab handlers. Mendy wasn't stupid; he knew that even if he did convert, after everything that had happened it was far from clear that his adoptive family would simply welcome him back without questions. From Yochai's secular standpoint, he failed to understand the attraction of being obligated in Torah observance. Why couldn't Gil just do as he pleased and keep those of the commandments he liked, without worrying about a piece of paper from a rabbi? No – it must be that his Arab masters were pulling the puppet strings, aiming to get "their man" better assimilated into Israeli society and the GSS.

"All right, Meir," Yochai emerged from his reverie in a fraction of a moment. "For now, let's just say that we don't have enough information to reach any conclusions at this point. We'll speak again when I know more. In the meantime, please wait outside, and don't go anywhere."

"How long will I have to wait?"

"As long as it takes."

"An hour, two? I have a schedule you know. I can't just hang around here indefinitely."

"No? Really? Well, in that case… You know what, Meir?" Yochai suddenly backtracked. "Don't hang around. Go home, but be prepared to show up whenever you're summoned. And remember: You don't open your mouth to anyone about this. And most certainly not to Mendy. Got it?"

Meir left Headquarters with sagging shoulders, feeling as if he had just sold himself as a captive. He didn't glance in the mirror, but he had no doubt that Naomi would immediately recognize the signs of the condemned cow on his face.

"Segev, please explain to me how it can be that you still haven't found the kid."

"He simply disappeared into thin air," Segev replied glumly, well aware of the gravity of his failure.

"Oh, he *disappeared*, you say. How exactly? This is Jamil we're dealing with, please recall. And he didn't even have any money on him." Yochai exhaled slowly. "Okay, gather the guys and go back to searching the immediate area where he disappeared."

"We shouldn't expand the search to the 100 kilometer radius?"

"No."

"Are you sure, sir?"

"Yes. Those are your orders. If you'd listened to me and kept your eye on him…" Yochai stopped short. True, he was Segev's superior, but he always made a point of speaking respectfully to his agents, and he knew that there was no point in haranguing the man. Segev already knew what was in store for him; in years to come, he would pay a high price for his negligence, and would almost certainly be excluded from any other significant operation indefinitely, unless he somehow managed to salvage his reputation. It would take him a long time to regain the trust of his superiors.

"Yes, sir," Segev mumbled and hurried to carry out the order. Within half an hour the entire group had converged in the gas station only to fan out once again to scour the shops and eateries in the strip mall. Segev, for his part, headed for a cheap store to purchase a few bottles of Coke and beer for the guys. He was doomed, but at least the others could still enjoy life.

He entered the store, and as he did, he brushed by someone who seemed familiar. Segev almost walked right past him, but suddenly, he spun around and shouted, "JAMIL!"

The kid blushed and dropped his eyes. Restraining his fury, Segev dropped his arm casually around the boy's shoulders and repeated, "Hey, Jamil! Long time no see," for the benefit of any curious observers. Then, he steered him roughly toward the vehicle parked outside, despite the boy's obvious reluctance.

"Come off it. Leave me alone," Jamil whined. "Why did you come back looking for me? I thought you'd given up and gone!" He began cursing quietly in Arabic. "You Jews thought you could buy me. You never planned to introduce me to my family, only to throw me into some filthy pit that I'll never escape from. You thought I wouldn't figure it out, huh?"

He continued ranting away in Arabic, which Segev spoke fluently, but the latter didn't deign to reply. The other operatives nodded in relief when informed that the mission had been accomplished, and Segev quickly gave the order to disperse. The guys scattered quickly, each one going his separate way at a different pace in order to conceal the connection between them.

Segev lost no time in securing Jamil in the vehicle and then calling Yochai with the update. His superior received the announcement with mixed feelings. He had wasted far too many dormant agents on this operation, and now he wouldn't be able to call any of them into action for another few months at least, in order to maintain their low profile. Nonetheless, Segev was disappointed by Yochai's reserved response.

"All right. Take him to his family now. We'll allow him a five-hour meeting, after which he's coming right back on a plane to Israel. I've had enough of this three-ring circus."

"When will you tell the family that we're on our way? We should be there within the next hour, maybe less."

"I'll call them right now," Yochai replied. "Let's get this over with and bring him back to Israel. We can't let this continue; the kid has no clue what he's involved in."

Shuli stood outside her house alone, her eyes fixed on the winding street as it stretched out into the distance. The GSS had arranged the rental of a small cottage in a rural town just north of Gateshead that boasted a handful of frum families whose fathers primarily worked in *shechitah* and dairy production. Her children commuted daily along with the other frum children in town to Gateshead, leaving early in the morning and returning home late in the afternoon. It was a high price to pay, but well worth the knowledge that she was protecting them. As long as Nachum and Suri were safe, she felt she could deal with anything.

Now she stood on her doorstep, gazing expectantly down the street and waiting for the car to arrive. Yochai had called her to tell her that his men would be arriving with her son in less than an hour, without even bothering to explain what had caused the initial delay.

For some reason, the news that her son was finally on his way only served to anger her. "What's wrong with you people? Can't you keep to a schedule?" she cried. "You just told me the visit was pushed off indefinitely, and now, once again, everything's changed."

"Sorry, but that's the way it works over here," Yochai replied, his tone at least somewhat apologetic.

"Don't be sorry. Improve your system," she retorted.

"Will do," he murmured, with such equanimity that Shuli was tempted to scream. He was making fun of her, but at least now she could wait for her son.

She spied the car from afar and, somehow, she knew it was them. In any case, very few cars passed through this rural town at any hour of the day, and any unfamiliar car drew attention. Her son was sitting inside, a son she hadn't laid eyes upon in twenty years, since mere minutes after he was born. Now, they were about to face each other again. How would she feel when it finally happened?

A minute later, the car pulled to a stop outside her house, and Shuli approached. Segev exited first, smiling perfunctorily. "We're here!" he announced with feigned enthusiasm. Shuli wondered at his cheerful façade – after all, the GSS was not exactly renowned for its benevolent nature.

"Nice to meet you, Mrs. Brand," Segev continued. "We've brought your son here for the next five hours."

Shuli didn't reply, even though Yochai had promised her three days. Now, the argument seemed trite, and in fact, her mind had gone completely blank. The tears, the pounding of her heart that she had imagined time and again, weren't there at all. Instead, a deep, overwhelming sadness enveloped her, and all she could think of was that her husband should have been at her side.

A young man followed Segev out of the car, and Shuli immediately identified him as her son because of his startling resemblance to Suri, except for the tall, broad build. She knew he would be bare-headed, but what caught her most off guard were his confused eyes. She clasped her hands together emotionally, unsure what to say.

What emerged from her lips was a banal, "Hello."

The boy returned an angry, defiant look, and Shuli suddenly remembered that despite the physical similarity he had to Suri, his demeanor and expression were thoroughly Arab. The realization caused her to automatically retreat a step.

"Hello," she repeated, forcing herself to take the lead, regardless. "My name is Shuli Brand." Segev and his two colleagues watched the drama unfold with incredulous eyes. This was not the melodramatic reunion of a mother and son, but rather the playing out of a terrible tragedy that was literally painful to watch.

"I'm Jamil. They tell me you're my mother," he replied, his tone mocking.

"That's what they told me too. That you're my son," she confirmed. "Would you like to come in? Please, you're all welcome," she gestured graciously to the others. Wordlessly, they followed her inside.

Shuli led them to the living room and then rushed to the kitchen to bring the tray of drinks and cake she had prepared. The boy scared her, but what scared her even more was the thought that she was his mother.

She placed two pitchers, one with juice and another with water, on the table, along with glasses. Jamil reached to pour himself a glass of juice, but Shuli stopped him.

"You know that you're a Jew?"

"Yeah. Tell me about it."

"Jews recite a blessing on food or drink before we eat. We thank G-d for creating the world and granting us sustenance."

Jamil stared at her as if she had fallen from the moon, and then snorted. "I never saw Yochai say a blessing."

"That's right, because there are observant and non-observant Jews, but Jews who live according to their faith recite blessings all the time. Our family is *mitzvah*-observant, meaning we try to fulfill all the commandments in our Torah."

To her surprise, Jamil's scornful gaze softened. "You're nothing like my mother – meaning, the mother who raised me," he said honestly. "What am I supposed to say?"

Shuli pronounced each word, and Jamil repeated after her, clearly making an effort to be polite. Meanwhile, the agents made a graceful exit into the adjacent dining room where they spread a small map out on the table and began a whispered conversation, affording Shuli and Jamil a semblance of privacy.

"I couldn't wait to see you, from the moment I heard about you. I can't believe that the last time I saw you, you were only a few minutes old." Her voice caught in her throat.

"Right. That's what they said." Jamil lowered his eyes. His demeanor stirred a wave of deep pity in Shuli. What had those Arabs done to him that he didn't have the confidence to look her in the eye? Why was he so self-conscious and insecure?

"Was it hard for you there?" she probed gently.

"Where?"

"In the Arab village."

"Rotten."

His one-word reply caused the tears she had kept at bay to spring forth with sudden force, and to her surprise, a film of moisture appeared in his eyes as well.

"Why are you crying?" he asked.

"Because you had it hard, when I always prayed that you should have a good, happy life," she replied truthfully.

"Don't cry. At least I have a better future in store. You're nothing like my mother," he repeated with a mix of innocence and concern, discomfited by her tears.

The agents returned at that point, staring hard at Jamil as if to demand an explanation. Jamil, for his part, returned a helpless gaze. "I didn't do anything. She's just crying."

"She's overcome with emotion," Segev explained. "Your mother is very overwhelmed now, and she's waited a long time to meet you."

The next moments passed in silence, as each struggled to come to terms with the new reality.

"Should I tell you a bit about our lives before you were born and after? What happened to your father, and how we discovered you were missing? Would you like to hear?"

This was the seed of the new relationship that slowly took root between mother and son. Jamil sat and listened, saying little while

Shuli spoke fervently of her prayers for her child. When she described the moment when she learned that her son had been raised for twenty years in an Arab village, Jamil grew visibly emotional.

"I always felt as if Someone was protecting me, and now I understand that it was your prayers all these years. But… would you be willing to accept me as your son, even though I'm an Arab?"

"You're not an Arab; you're my son," she corrected him.

"Yes, that's true," he agreed, glancing suddenly around the house as if having only just noticed his surroundings. "I am your son, which makes this place my home. By the way, do you have other children?"

Shuli had been prepared for the question. "You have a brother and a sister, but they're still young, and I think we should wait a bit before introducing them to you. It's going to be difficult for them to get used to the idea, and, in any case, they're not even home now."

"Hard for them to get used to what?"

"To… I mean… They still don't know anything about… what happened. To be honest, I'm still a bit in shock myself. For them, it could be a major trauma, and we have to plan carefully how to break the news. After all, they are still very attached to… well, you know." Shuli's voice trailed off as she noted the displeasure in the boy's eyes.

"I know… that they think they have a different brother. But I was so looking forward to having a real family after all this time. They hardly let me see anyone when I'm in Israel. It's really lonely."

"I understand," Shuli said, "but just the same, the kids aren't ready to hear this yet. Just imagine if it was you, and suddenly someone dropped such a bombshell. It's really not simple."

Jamil was disappointed, but also suspicious. "You're very protective."

"I wish I could have protected you too. Believe me," she spoke earnestly, but Jamil didn't seem convinced.

She was surprised by how slowly the hands of the clock moved. Five hours had seemed so little at first, but as the minutes barely crept by, Shuli found herself looking forward to the end of the meeting. It was an awful, guilty feeling, but she couldn't help but glance occasionally at her watch, surprised each time anew at how little time had passed. *What did you think?* she reflected accusingly. *That he'd show up, and suddenly, you'd love him and enjoy spending time with him? How long will it take to feel comfortable with him – and, will it ever happen at all?*

"Are you hungry? Would you like something else to eat?" she asked finally, after yet another long pause during which both of them looked distinctly uncomfortable.

"No."

Shuli was beginning to feel helpless. After the initial flow of words, the conversation had become stilted and artificial.

Noting the dejected atmosphere, Segev uncharacteristically spoke up. "Do you have some family pictures?"

"Of course."

"Why don't you look at them together?"

It was the best way to pass the remaining time, of which there was far too much. Shuli got up and went over to the shelf where she had stored the pile of family albums that she had managed to grab before fleeing the country, one of the few mementos that she had refused to leave behind.

Jamil opened the first album and peered in interest at the old photos.

"That's my father?" he pointed to a smiling young man.

"Yes, that's your father."

Jamil gazed curiously at him. "I look a bit like him, don't I?"

"Yes, you do," Shuli replied encouragingly, even as a little voice in her mind piped up: *You do… and you don't. There is definitely a physical resemblance, but the expression in your eyes is so… Arabic.*

Jamil flipped to the next page and froze when he saw the photo of a tiny, probably only days-old baby, nestled in a young Shuli's arms.

"That's him? The other one?" he asked, his voice suspiciously gravelly.

"No, actually that's you. Shimon – your father – took this picture just minutes after you were born, before they transferred you to the nursery."

"So this is really me?"

"Yes. You and me, with the picture taken by your father. See? At least we have one family picture." She smiled warmly, and Jamil smiled back. Another bridge had been built over a twenty-year gorge.

He turned another page. "So I guess that's him?" he pointed to another photo.

"Yes." Shuli gazed sorrowfully at the picture, overwhelmed by an intense longing for her Mendy. The Mendy she had known and loved. His image rose in her mind and brought her to tears. She was still intrinsically connected to Mendy; he would forever be her eldest son, despite everything. Jamil, in contrast, gazed at the baby in the photo as if he were his mortal enemy.

"You know that they tried to kill me. My guess is that he's the one behind it all," he said tonelessly, almost accusingly.

Shuli felt uncomfortable, not knowing whom to favor or defend. "None of us chose this situation," she replied, deliberately omitting mention of Hashem. It would be far too complicated to enter into a theological discussion at this point, and once again she found herself wondering if this boy, her son, would ever really adjust to life as a Jew.

"You loved him, didn't you?" Jamil added, studying the photos one by one. There were pictures documenting virtually every milestone and stage in Mendy's life, from his infancy until young adulthood. There were photos of his first smile, his first tooth, his first step. There he was getting his haircut and going to *cheder*, celebrating his *Siddur* and *Chumash* party, his seventh birthday, his first *siyum Mishnayos*, becoming a big brother, his bar mitzvah… Family pictures on vacations, Yomim Tovim, at the Kosel. All the pictures were filled with smiles, with Mendy often in the middle between his two parents.

Shuli's throat constricted with tears as she caressed the pictures with her gaze. Mendy was her firstborn, the apple of her eye; she had dedicated her heart and soul to raising him. How could he have deserted them like that? How had he come to betray her, to betray his entire nation? Whenever she allowed herself to think of it – which was not often – she still couldn't bring herself to believe it. Something inside persisted in hoping that it was all a mistake, a tall tale invented somewhere in the basements of GSS Headquarters for the purpose of an unknown, top-secret mission.

Externally, she kept up a vivacious front, pointing out certain pictures, describing, explaining, trying to acquaint her son with the family he had never known, to enable him to feel a growing sense of connection to them.

Finally, they reached the last few photos, and Shuli exhaled in relief. The experience of reliving some of the happiest moments in her life had taken a toll on her. The memories were so real, and so painful.

Jamil looked pensive. "You know, when I told my friend about what happened, and how I'm really a Jew, he said that it will probably take years for us to make up for all the lost time. And, most likely, that other person will remain your son forever, and I'll never manage to replace him."

"You don't have to look at it like that. No one is replacing anybody. There's no limit to space in the heart. And don't forget that…" Shuli's voice trailed off as she suddenly noticed Segev's face. His eyes shot sparks of fury, and his lips trembled in rage. He seemed so taut that she almost wondered if he was about to pull a gun on them. His colleagues stood behind him, their expressions as grave as his.

"Who did you tell about your story?" he fired the question at Jamil, who took it in stride, despite the latent threat in the agent's menacing tone.

"Oh, I ran into a friend at the rest stop. What did you think I was doing the whole time I wandered off?" Jamil tried to smile, but Shuli's heart sank as she realized that her cover had been blown.

"Which friend?" Segev practically roared.

"A guy from the village. He's a nice guy. He came here to get a job and earn some money before moving back. I couldn't believe it when I saw him, and he couldn't believe it either. It was such a coincidence. I told him what's been going on, that I was switched at birth and am really Jewish, and that I came here to meet my family. He couldn't get over it."

Segev looked like he was about to suffer a heart attack. "What else did you tell him?"

"Whatever. What's the difference? I'm not under interrogation again, am I?"

Segev didn't deign to reply. Whipping around, he hurried to the kitchen to inform Yochai of the catastrophe.

"You mean they were on to us all this time? They knew of our plans all along?" Yochai was livid, and almost incredulous. "Okay," he continued, struggling to calm himself and keep his voice steady. "Tell the lady to start packing."

"Where's she going?"

"No idea. Germany, France, Belgium, Austria, or maybe Australia. We'll figure it out."

Segev returned to the living room and motioned for Shuli to join him. "Prepare to leave. Anytime in the next four hours. Pack whatever you can; we're getting out of here."

"Who's 'we?'"

"Well, the first to go is going to be Jamil, and then, as soon as we can, we'll send some people to pick you up, as well. You've been exposed."

Overhearing the conversation, Jamil took a step closer to them. "I don't get it. They're also on the run?"

Segev rolled his eyes and didn't reply.

"Hey, talk to me, man. What's going on? Who's chasing us? Don't tell me that it's their son. No son – even if he's only adopted – would hurt his own parents. As bad as they treated me – and they treated me real bad – I still would never be able to hurt my family. My other family, that is," he corrected himself for Shuli's sake.

Segev was already deeply engrossed in a phone call, as were the other two men, each on his own device. Meanwhile, Shuli sprang into action, grabbing several suitcases from a closet and starting to toss basics inside. Feeling redundant, Jamil offered Shuli his assistance.

Shuli was almost tempted to reply that the biggest help would be if he simply disappeared from her life, but she forced herself to smile and thank him for his offer. "That would be a big help. Why don't you empty those drawers over there?"

"I'm sorry. I didn't realize that it would be a mistake to talk. It was so nice to meet an old friend that I couldn't help myself. He offered me a ride to a nearby park, and I agreed. Then, he took me back..."

Twenty minutes later, Segev joined them in Suri's room. "All right. Another few minutes, and we're out of here, Jamil."

"Already?" Jamil asked reluctantly.

"*Already?* It was a mistake to bring you here in the first place," Segev retorted.

"You said at first that I'd be here for three days," Jamil whined.

"Well, things might have turned out different if you hadn't pulled that disappearing act of yours and blabbed. Let's move, kid. Say goodbye to mama. We'll be back for you later," he promised Shuli.

"Where will you take them?" Jamil asked.

Segev looked murderously at him. "You really think I'm going to answer that?"

It was time to say goodbye.

As she watched Jamil enter the car, Shuli knew once and for all that he was her son. It was difficult to part from him, and not knowing what to say to him only made things worse. Finally, she promised that they would meet again, and that one day, Jamil would meet his brother and sister.

"Tell them I was here," Jamil begged, right before he disappeared into the car. "I want them to know that they have a brother..."

Gil blocked his Caller ID when he dialed Meir's cell phone.

"Hey, Meir. I really need to speak to you. When can we meet?"

Landsman sounded frightened. "Why are you coming up as 'unidentified caller?'" he demanded.

"I was afraid that you wouldn't answer me. When can we meet?"

Meir hesitated. "It's pouring rain and freezing cold out. Why don't we talk tomorrow?"

"I'm actually right under your house. Want to come out to my car?"

Meir thought for a moment. Gil was clearly determined, and if he refused to go down to meet him, he would probably just come up to his apartment and knock at the door. Deciding it was better to spare his wife knowledge of his continuing involvement in the story, he made up his mind to meet him.

Glancing at his watch, Meir was relieved to see that it was almost time for *Maariv*. "Naomi, I'm going out to *Maariv* before the rain gets any worse," he told her, and grabbing his hat, a raincoat, and an umbrella, he hurried outside. He would indeed *daven Maariv*, he promised himself, and meet Gil on the way.

Gil's car, as promised, was parked right outside the building, and as soon as he saw Meir emerge he opened the door to the passenger seat. Reluctantly, Meir entered the car.

"Tell me, did you tell anyone about my plans?" he fired his question at the anxious *yungerman*.

"Why would I, and what plans are you talking about?" Meir answered, gracefully avoiding an outright lie.

"Converting."

"Listen, Mendy, it's not such a simple process. Who should I tell?" Meir again dodged the question.

"Good," Gil sighed in relief. "For the time being, I don't want you to tell anyone at all about it, okay? Yesterday, I met with Rav Sheinberger, who runs a *yeshivah* for *baalei teshuvah*. I told him that I just discovered that my mother's conversion wasn't kosher, and that I want to be *misgayer*. I explained that I went through the entire system – *cheder*, *yeshivah*, etcetera. He was surprised and said that it was an unusual situation, but not unheard of. He also told me an interesting story."

Meir tried hard not to tremble. He was sitting in a vehicle together with Arab who had a planned role in a massive bombing that was set to take place in the near future, and however hard he – and especially his wife – tried, he was finding it impossible to extricate himself from this complicated web. And now, to add to the sense of unreality, Mendy wanted to tell him a story!

"What was the story?" Meir replied obligingly, hoping it would be short.

"He said that he once had a *baal teshuvah* in the *yeshivah* whom the entire staff worked hard to be *mekarev*. The kid had grown up unaffiliated, but was drawn to *Yiddishkeit* and was taking things seriously. Five years after he became frum, he decided it was time to think about getting married, and it was only then that his mother revealed that she'd converted 'Reform.' As soon as he heard this, the boy ran to his *rosh yeshivah* and told him the story. They investigated her claim and found out that it was true; she really wasn't Jewish, and neither was he, but he wanted to convert immediately."

"So?"

"The rav said no problem, especially as he already knew all the *halachos* and everything that *Yiddishkeit* entails, but that he should still take a break to think it over and check out the opportunities open to him in the outside world before making his final decision, because a *baal teshuvah* is as obligated as an FFB, but a *goy* has no obligation to convert. And you know what happened? The kid flew back to America, met up with his *goyishe* cousins, aunts, and uncles, and decided to stay there. He came to realize that his main motivation in wanting to convert was the comfort factor – Yiddishkeit was simply what he was used to by then – but that at the end of the day, once he saw that he could make it in the outside world, he made that decision. I guess this story shows that it's a *neshamah* thing – he simply wasn't at Har Sinai."

"And what about you?" Meir pressed.

Gil bit his lip before replying. "Meir, it's different for me. I grew up frum. I went to *yeshivah*, and I loved learning – in fact, I loved almost everything about a frum way of life. You knew me as a *yeshivah bachur*, and you know how much I invested into my learning. I fell in with bad company, and I was lured by the outside world and points of view I'd never heard before. I didn't realize that this guy Berman was really just an ignorant, secular Jew who had been hired to trap me. But that was then. Now, I see things for what they are. I don't want this anymore – I have to get out, fast." Gil sighed. Getting out, either fast or slow, seemed like nothing short of impossible at that point in time.

"All I want is to go back to *yeshivah*," he confessed. "Even though the guys my age are mostly married already. In fact, I told them that, months ago – which was when everything came crashing down on me. That was when they told me the truth – that I'm not even Jewish at all." Gil's eyes narrowed in pain and Meir felt a rush of sympathy for the conflicted young man sitting next to him.

"I refused to believe them at first, and demanded proof. And… they provided it. Apparently, they've been waiting a long time for this, to pounce on me and turn my life upside-down.

Meir, I don't know if I can make things right again, but I'm determined to try."

Meir drew a deep breath. "Why are you telling me all this?"

"Because I'm going to a rav, and I want to be *misgayer*. I want to be a real Yid, even if I don't have much time left in this world. I tried out the other world already. I saw enough – I don't want any more of it! I even travelled to Paris to meet my real family. But I feel no sense of connection to them. And as for what they feel toward me – it revolts me. My place is with the Jewish People, Meir. My *neshamah* – if you can call it that before I convert – is Jewish, and it belongs here."

Tears sprang into Gil's eyes. "I probably don't have much time left. They're following me; everybody is, and I don't even know anymore who's on my side and who's out to get me. So that's why I'm begging you, Meir, please, *please*, help me! Maybe I'll die tomorrow, but at least let me die a Jew!"

Meir panicked. If Mendy was under constant surveillance, that meant there were eyes upon him as they spoke… and that they knew he was meeting with him! Was he in danger? Had he just endangered his entire family?

"What do you want from me?" he managed to squeak out.

"I need you to talk to the rav about me. Tell him what's going on, and vouch for my story, without getting too deeply into the details. Obviously, a lot of what I've told you is supposed to be classified."

Meir looked uncomfortable. "Mendy, how do you know this is the right thing to do? Maybe you need a bit of time to think it over? Why rush into conversion now? Who knows? Maybe you can have a wonderful, fulfilling future as a gentile?"

"Meir, I've got no wonderful future at all, and certainly not as a *goy*. I have no expectations for any future; all I want is the present. In my heart, I know I'm meant to be a Yid. My *neshamah* was there with yours on Har Sinai. I know it."

Whether Meir knew it too, he didn't say. All he knew was that, once again, Naomi had been right.

Nachum waited on the doorstep for his sister, who was expected home any minute. As soon as he saw the car stop and Suri alight, he rushed toward her.

"Suri, don't go inside yet. We need to talk."

"What's up?" His younger sister looked concerned. So many things were happening so suddenly in her home, and the changes had taken a toll on her.

"Listen, I got home fifteen minutes ago, and Mommy is losing it. She's packing again and talking about going on another vacation. What do you think about that?"

"That Mommy needs a break," Suri replied with maturity that surpassed her years.

Nachum shook his head; his little sister was obviously too young to grasp what was going on "I don't think so. It started with vacationing up north in Eretz Yisrael, and then, we came here, with no explanation or even time to prepare. And this time, I don't believe Mommy when she says we're going on vacation. We're leaving the country! Get it?"

The little girl looked frightened. "What am I supposed to get? It doesn't make sense. Why would we move again?" She broke out in a run toward the house, but her brother grabbed her by the arm.

"I'll come with you. Let's hear what Mommy has to say, and then we'll decide what to do," he announced in a mature tone of voice. "I just wanted to let you know first, so you wouldn't be caught off guard."

They whispered together until they reached the house. Hearing them outside, Shuli hurried to open the door.

"Oh, Suri, I'm glad you're home. I'm really under pressure here, and I have to finish packing, because the truck is coming in an hour. We're going on vacation again."

Suri shut her eyes and shook her head, refusing to hear it.

"Where are we going?" she asked in an unnatural voice.

"Um, could be back to Eretz Yisrael. Come, darling, eat a quick supper and help me pack up your stuff."

"Should I pack my school stuff too?" the little girl asked in desperation.

"No. Just take what you need for a short while." Shuli ran frantically through the house, grabbing assorted items and tossing them haphazardly into boxes that were not even completely unpacked from the previous move.

Nachum took a deep breath and drew himself up to his full height. "Mommy, please stop," he said in a controlled voice. "What's going on?"

"I told you. We're going on vacation," Shuli replied anxiously.

"I don't think so," he said respectfully. "Mommy, I'm eleven years old, and Suri isn't a baby either. We're old enough to know the truth. What's going on? Why are we really packing? Why have we moved twice in a month, and now a third time? Where are we going?"

Shuli felt her heart break. "Nachum, Suri, we've all been through a lot these past weeks, but you're going to have to trust me. Please, you have to understand that I can't explain it right now." She paused in the middle of her packing to cast a pleading look into Nachum's eyes. "I promise you. I'm doing all I can to be the best mother I can be. It isn't easy, but when you're older, you'll understand. Now, please, Nachum, let's pack what we can before the moving truck comes."

"When are we coming back?" Suri enjoyed the quiet of the pastoral village, and she knew she would miss the friends she had made.

"I don't know, sweetie."

"A week? A month?" Suri persisted.

"I wish I could tell you," her mother sighed. "But it could be up to a year or two. Who knows?"

Suri returned a shocked gaze. "But you said we're going on vacation! A year isn't a vacation! Who goes on vacation for a year! I'm sick of moving and going on vacation! I want to stay here!"

The telephone rang, interrupting her whining, and Shuli rushed to answer.

"Yes, we're almost ready. Another hour would definitely come in handy though. Impossible? All right, then, whenever you come, we'll be ready to go… Yes, thank you."

Shuli ended the call and fixed a steely gaze on her daughter; despite it all, this was not the time for tears.

"Suri, listen. Whatever you pack, you'll have; and whatever you leave here, stays. I already packed your clothes and shoes, but you have to decide what other stuff you want to take along. We have another ten minutes before the moving truck gets here, and that's it."

Suri chose to throw a tantrum instead of packing, but Nachum rushed to his room and, with practiced hands, quickly packed his things neatly into a box. Next, saving the day, he ran to Suri's room and yanked her favorite items off the shelves and then simply dumped the contents of her drawers into a duffel bag.

Two minutes later, a small truck pulled up outside the house. Three movers leaped out and began loading the truck, amazing all of them with their speed and dexterity.

"Climb into the front," the driver instructed the kids. "We're leaving in three minutes." Nachum's jaw dropped; the man spoke Hebrew with a perfect Israeli accent, which meant that he wasn't even English at all. He stared questioningly at his mother who maintained a poker face, and then curiously back at the movers, who didn't offer any other hints as to their identities.

Shuli and the children climbed into the cab, and the truck backed out of the driveway a minute later. The entire job had taken less than ten minutes, as they had packed only the bare essentials. The moment the truck turned into the street, the driver floored the gas, and they set off at top speed, driving along a bumpy country road that jolted them constantly in their seats. The little town was still visible in the distance, and Suri waved a sad goodbye to the quaint cottage they had occupied for such a short time, watching it recede before her eyes.

"Hey, look!" she cried suddenly, pointing to what resembled a toy car in the distance. "Someone's stopping outside our house!"

What happened next caused the family to scream in terror. A massive blast rocked the entire town and surrounding countryside, causing the truck to shudder violently, and the Brands and their escorts watched in horror as the little white cottage that they had just left behind exploded in a burst of yellow-orange flames.

"YOU KILLED THEM!" Gil screamed, the expression on his face pure torture. "How dare you! You promised!"

Laser was cool as a cucumber. "Take it easy. You'll still get to see them, at their funeral… Or, maybe not, as from what I understood, they're being buried over there."

Gil narrowed his eyes in pain and fury and then turned on his heel and stormed out of the room, his soul torn asunder. He let loose a horrible shriek of agony and then collapsed onto the floor, weeping like a baby. *Dead. They were all dead. First his father. Then his mother and Nachum and Suri. And all because of him. He was the only one left of his family. How could he survive? How could he live without his mother's tefillos? Without those long, deep conversations with Nachum? Without Suri, the sunshine of the family? With all the guilt…*

He heard Laser's rolling laughter spilling out of the room, and he realized that he would have to bite his lip and continue playing the game. Taking a deep breath, he rose to his full height and strode back into the room.

"Finished your sniveling?" Laser shot at him.

"You killed them. Give me one reason why I should continue cooperating with you. I'm through."

"Because if you don't, the next one to die will be you," Laser hissed dangerously. "We're currently working on the final details of the plan, and then you will carry it out to the very best of your ability. If there was anyone who would have been willing to accept you in the Jewish world, it would have been your adoptive family. But, *alas*, they are no longer. Yochai knows the truth about you, and you know the truth about him. Our game is actually quite transparent at this point."

Gil considered Laser's words and actually found his argument to be logical, but logic still did not have the power to overcome his emotions.

"Why did you kill them?" he asked again, and despite his most strenuous efforts, he still couldn't keep the tears at bay. "They did nothing to hurt you! They were totally innocent. I told you that I would cooperate with you. Why did you have to kill them?"

Laser stretched in his armchair. "It was really a very complicated operation, and it's important that you appreciate that. We have invested a great deal in order to make it happen, burning many bridges along the way. They were hiding out in a small, rural village, but we carried it out, and we succeeded, because it's important to us that you know that you have no other options. We want to see you absolutely focused on your goal, to the exclusion of all else. Is that clear?"

"Perfectly," Gil replied, his eyes still red and swollen.

"Okay, *ya-habibi*, don't mourn them too much. After all, nobody will spill any tears over you. On the contrary: If they could, they would sacrifice you at the first opportunity. They're glad you're not one of them anymore. They aren't even worth your tears." Laser's attempts at consolation were poor indeed. "All right, then, back to the plan!" he exclaimed, finally giving up all pretenses. "As I've said many times, this is a very complex operation that we've invested twenty years in the making. You have to understand that Yochai won't trust you ever again; he'll suspect you forever, and with good reason. And the Jews will be glad to be rid of you. As far as they're concerned, you're a tragedy as well as a traitor to your people. All you've managed to do is bring catastrophe upon them. That's why you're working with us. And only us."

"Only for you," Gil echoed.

"Say it proudly! You've been chosen!"

"I was chosen!" he repeated brazenly. The discussion continued for some time until Gil was unceremoniously led out of the room and dismissed.

Gil staggered blindly to his car and drove recklessly toward the beach. It was close to midnight, and the streets were relatively empty, so that his swerves and lurches went largely unnoticed. Finally, he drew to a halt by the boardwalk and leaned over the metal guardrail, staring at the formidable black waves capped with white froth.

"WHY? WHY? *WHYYYYYYYYYY*?" he screamed at the top of his lungs, his anguished cry disappearing into the roaring ocean. Then, he recalled that a Jew never asks 'Why?' but rather, 'For what purpose?' For what purpose had Hashem caused these tragic events in his life to transpire if not in order to serve Him? But how could he dare to serve Hashem now, after all the sins he had committed, after all the evil that had come to pass because of him?

How he wished he could approach his parents and siblings in *Shamayim*, get down on his hands and knees and beg them for forgiveness! If only he hadn't been so stupid, if only he hadn't been so enticed by the outside world, perhaps those murderous Arabs – his blood brothers – would have given up on him. Alas, the ones to pay the price had been his wonderful family, his innocent, perfect Jewish family that had raised him lovingly, devotedly, and selflessly throughout their lives and received only death and destruction in return.

And Gil couldn't even mourn them.

He stood there for hours on end, staring into the blackness of night and sea, the salty spray merging with the tears on his cheeks.

Only when the first streaks of dawn brushed against the sky did he drag his feet back to his car and drive to the dank studio apartment that he refused to call home. He staggered up the dirty steps and fell into bed, fully-clothed, his face still stained with tears.

He hardly slept, but he was up by eight, ready to face the music. His first stop was Yochai's office, and he had no doubt that his superior was already completely apprised of all that had transpired. He was so convinced that Headquarters would be up in arms that his jaw actually dropped when he entered the building and saw it humming busily and cheerfully as usual, with no sign of the tragedy that had just rocked his entire world. Even Yochai was calm and collected as always.

"You look terrible!" he greeted Gil as soon as he laid eyes on him. "Not feeling well, or a hangover?" he chuckled.

Gil gaped at him. "Didn't you hear?"

"Hear what?"

Gil began to stammer. "M-my family... Somebody said... I heard that..."

"What?"

"Were they... killed?" he finally blurted out.

Yochai shrugged expressionlessly. "I didn't think you cared one way or the other. If someone killed them, it was probably you," he added dryly. "But I'll check it out, if you like. Or would you prefer to go over there and check it out for yourself?"

"No. No, I mean, I'll find out, but I don't want to go."

Yochai shrugged again. "Okay. Something else?"

"No."

Gil almost started crying again. He had longed to hear a word of comfort, of consolation, but now he realized that he really was completely on his own. Laser was right. Nobody would ever accept him again. Not Yochai, nor anyone else in the world. Maybe Meir would pity him, but to get help, Gil needed a lot more than pity.

After two hours of shuffling papers around his desk, Gil decided that he couldn't continue sitting there any longer. He needed fresh air. He needed help. He needed pity. He debated if it was fair to turn to Meir and endanger him, but he was so desperate for a word of comfort that he couldn't suppress the urge to speak to him, and he resolved to head to Meir's *kollel* and corner him there.

Shuli couldn't fathom why Yochai seemed so happy.

"Welcome back to the Holy Land!" he greeted her cheerfully.

"Nice to see you too," she replied, her tone wry. "Why the happy face?"

"You're back home. Isn't that a good enough reason?" Yochai said, his expression as impassive as ever.

Shuli returned a frosty gaze. "Not quite. We almost got back here in a coffin. What kind of security detail was that? This is the world-famous GSS intelligence? A five-minute delay, and we would have all been ashes right now."

"Please calm down, Mrs. Brand. We know exactly what we're doing. In any case, you spent two months in England, and now you're back home in Eretz Yisrael. What could be better than that?"

"Maybe getting here without the dramatics!" she suggested, unable to fathom Yochai's obvious satisfaction.

Yochai leaned back, completely at ease. "Listen to me, Shuli. That bombing was the best thing that could have happened. Don't you get it? Those guys sent people in to kill you. And now they think you're dead. They haven't even bothered to verify it, as far as we can tell."

"What about bodies? Didn't they wait to hear about the bodies?"

"We've got connections in England, and we made sure that the police 'located' three bodies and even made arrangements for burial in a Jewish cemetery. It was all over the papers, even though you kept a low profile, and nobody really knew you in the village. It seems that the kids had more friends than you did."

"So, in other words, I'm dead."

"Right. On paper," Yochai added.

It was almost funny, but Shuli wasn't even slightly amused. "Yochai, I can't do this anymore. First it was that settlement up north. Then England. Now we're back in Eretz Yisrael, and we're all considered dead. How's this going to end? When are you going to get things right finally?"

Yochai sat up in his chair and narrowed his eyes. "Shuli, you were minutes away from being blown to bits. We're doing everything in our power to protect you, and I expect a bit of gratitude."

Shuli rose stiffly. "So where are we headed now?"

"To the south."

"And who knows that we're here?"

"Nobody, and nobody must find out! I doubt that they will work too hard to confirm your deaths, but we'll still be taking every precaution to guarantee your safety."

51

Meir returned home from *Shacharis*, removing the paper from his mailbox on his way up the stairs. Uncharacteristically, his wife did not have breakfast ready on the table, and the remains of yesterday's conversation still lingered heavily in the air. Poor Naomi looked exhausted, and Meir knew that it wasn't just because Akiva, who was teething again, had screeched all night long.

His wife picked up exactly where she had left off the night before. "Meir, why? What do we need it for?"

"Yochai claims that he'll pay, and pay well." Meir pulled out his winning card, the one he had saved for the morning, when Naomi would be more alert and receptive to the idea of earning a decent wage. Finances were always tight for the Landsmans, and ways of earning money were in short supply.

"Money? Who needs money?" she retorted, much to Meir's chagrin. "*Marbeh nechasim, marbeh da'agah. Normal* people are willing to pay a fortune to live a tranquil life. The last thing I need is money, especially if it's going to cause more trouble than it's worth," she said dismissively.

"It'll be my trouble, not ours," he promised.

"No such thing! It's about the safety of our family, and you know that very well." Naomi began to pace back and forth in agitation. "Meir, you've hooked up with a kid who was once frum but is really an Arab! We don't know what his goals really are or what he wants. It's been nearly a year since he went off the *derech*, and suddenly, *supposedly*, he's seeking to come back. Right?"

"Right." He didn't have to say any more, understanding that his wife was talking more to herself than to him.

Naomi started to rock the baby's crib, even though Akiva was sleeping, while Meir searched frantically for something to answer his wife. The truth was that he agreed with everything she was saying, but he had never imagined that things would spiral so quickly out of control to the point that Yochai would refuse to let him abandon the mission.

"So he wants to convert, and he's also part of some kind of terrorist plot."

"Something like that."

"And then there's you, nice Meir Landsman, a frum Yid whom they found to do the dirty work. How much did you say they're willing to pay?" she asked scornfully.

"I didn't say, but I think you'll be pleasantly surprised."

"Nothing will surprise me at this point."

With a flourish, he presented her with the signed check. Naomi's eyes widened when she saw the amount written on it, equal to over six months of *kollel* pay, and she nodded darkly.

"You know what that means, don't you?"

"What?"

"That they're willing to do a lot to keep you on board. Which means that it's a dangerous mission. If something happens, they'll say that they paid you well for the job, and that you knew the dangers involved."

"What makes you think so?" Meir shot back. "I don't think the Israelis sacrifice their people so easily."

"No? Ever heard of Jonathan Pollard? Was he ever rewarded for his dedication? And how much effort do you think was invested to get him out of jail?" Naomi fired her questions like bullets, without giving her husband a chance to reply. "We don't need the money or the troubles, Meir! We don't need the GSS. If Hashem wants us to be rich, He has other ways of sending us money. Go back to that Yochai and tell him there's nothing doing."

"I already told Yochai that I couldn't undertake the job without your consent, but he said that it's too late. I'm already in too deep," Meir muttered uncomfortably.

The wheels in Naomi's head spun rapidly. "So tell him that you're *chareidi*, and that you don't do anything without authorization from your rav. That'll get him good! He'll get rid of you faster than you can say 'cholent.'"

Meir closed his eyes, willing himself to stay patient. "Naomi, there are things that I can't tell a rav, things that you don't know either. Classified information and stuff."

"Meir, you're already talking like a GSS agent! 'Classified information' and all," she mimicked him derisively, but then her shoulders sank in surrender when she realized that she had nothing left to say.

Meir took advantage of the lull to continue. "I also want you to know that Yochai promised to attach a security detail. He said that we have nothing to worry about, and that we're protected." He stopped short, realizing that his words were only exacerbating the tension in the room.

Naomi collapsed onto the faded sofa. "All right. I give up. Do whatever you think is right," she said dully. She let go of the crib and picked up the paper that Meir had just dropped on the coffee table. "Not that I can read when I'm like this…" she added, but then began to scream.

"MEIR! Oh, my G-d! *Meir, did you see the headlines?*"

"No. What happened? I just brought it upstairs, and—"

"They're dead! Oh, my G-d! They died! They must have killed them!" she pointed in horror at the blaring headline. Meir grabbed the paper out of his wife's hands and scanned the front page, his face paling as he read on.

"A Jewish family, a mother and two children, perished in a house fire in a village outside of Gateshead. Arson suspected with anti-Semitic motives. Local police are actively trying to locate the perpetrators." The article went on to mention the names of the victims, Shulamit Brand and her two children, Nachum and Sara.

"It's Mendy's family! They're all dead! See, Meir? They went after them, even abroad, and they got them! Meir, I don't want to die! Look what happened!" Naomi burst into tears. "Get out, Meir! Quit this crazy job before it's too late. I won't hear another word about it. Tell Yochai that you can't. Tell him that *I* can't, or I'll end up in an asylum. You're not cut out for these kind of jobs. Tell him you're petrified that you'll suffer from a nervous breakdown… I don't know, just tell him whatever so you can get out of this!"

After his wife's outburst, even Meir found it difficult to breathe. "I need fresh air," he muttered apologetically and then staggered to the tiny porch off their living room. He leaned over the railing, spying a street cleaner whom he had noticed earlier, as well. Something about the man's motions didn't strike him as natural, instantly activating Meir's imagination. Was he one of the security men whom Yochai had stationed to protect him and his family?

And then, to his utter shock, a black car stopped right in front of him, and the driver leaned over to open the passenger door. It was Mendy.

"Get down here now," he ordered him impatiently. "I'm blocking the traffic. I need to speak to you. I'm desperate."

Nachum and Suri unpacked boxes listlessly while Shuli placed the items neatly in drawers and on shelves. The children were being extremely quiet, and Shuli thought her heart would break as she gazed into their eyes.

"It's so hard for you," she whispered, tears rising in her own eyes.

Nachum didn't reply, but Suri shrugged complacently. "We've gotten used to it. Even though it's so annoying! By the time I finally made friends and started perfecting my English, we had to move again and start all over. And we can't even use our real names now. What's going on? Why, Mommy?"

Shuli remained silent. How she longed to tell them how hard it was for her too, that she couldn't keep up with all the changes in their lives. She longed to break down and cry, and hug them, and have them hug her back. But she couldn't. She needed to continue being the strong one. She was the only one left who could protect them and keep them safe.

Or so she had thought. But she had failed. They weren't protected; they weren't safe. They were terribly alone and abandoned, and she could make no promises regarding their future.

"I'm glad we moved back to Eretz Yisrael," Nachum spoke up suddenly. "But there are a lot of things that bother me. Like, why did the paper say that—"

Shuli dropped the glass Suri had just passed her, and it shattered all over the floor. She cast a desperate look at her son, glancing beseechingly in Suri's direction, and Nachum immediately got the hint. Luckily, Suri was too distracted by the shattered glass to notice that her brother had stopped short.

Shuli scurried off to the laundry room to get a broom and shovel, and Nachum followed her. When they were alone in the small room, he faced her with his hands on his hips. "Why does it say that I'm dead?"

"Who told you that?"

"I'm not dumb. I know how to read. It's all over the paper."

"Nachum… because… because it's better that way. If people think we're dead, they won't look for us anymore." Nachum was too old for her to hide the truth any longer. She knew that he had already suspected it long ago.

"Are we still in danger?"

"Hopefully, not anymore."

He had indeed known it before, but he still looked a little shocked to hear it confirmed aloud by his mother. "Mommy, you know… I don't know how you feel about it, but I feel kind of funny that people… think I'm dead. It's like, you know…"

"Don't think about it, *zeeskeit*. Just try not to think about it. The people who need to know that we're alive know, and that's what counts. Believe me, we have to thank Hashem every minute of the day. It's a miracle that we're alive."

"Why is this happening to us? Why can't we just lead a normal life?" he protested.

"This is what Hashem wants."

Nachum sagged. "Do you think that Mendy thinks that… we're…"

"Probably."

"Do you think he's sad?"

"I'm sure of it."

"Don't you feel bad for him?"

"I…" Shuli didn't know what to say, and the tears sprang forth, uninvited.

"One day, we're going to meet up with him and tell him that we really are alive. Poor guy, he thinks his whole family is gone, and he probably wants to come back and doesn't even know where to go," Nachum said sadly.

"We don't know that," Shuli replied tightly.

"I think I'll call him!" the boy said suddenly.

"NO!" Shuli shouted in terror. "Nachum, don't you ever even think of doing such a thing! Don't you dare! And if you ever do see him by accident, run away! Don't approach him. Don't talk to him. Nothing! Not a word or a wave or even a smile. You don't know what could happen."

"You hate him?" Nachum was appalled. "He's my brother!"

"I have to keep you safe; that's my job right now."

"And what about Mendy?"

Shuli stifled her sobs. "Mendy will watch over himself. It's okay that you miss him; I miss him too. But you can't call him or let him know that we're alive. It could be very dangerous. You know how close we were to being killed."

Nachum fell silent, and only his eyes told the story of what he thought now of his older brother.

"What is it you want?" Yochai furrowed his eyebrows, trying to make sense of the man's confused speech.

Minutes before, Meir had burst into his office, shouting something about "people dying from this," and "I can't take it."

"I'm quitting," he continued.

"What are you quitting?"

"The job. The mission. Take your check. It's a lot of money, but I can't take the risk. I won't sacrifice my life for this like the others."

"What others?"

"I read the newspaper. Don't you know that they're dead?"

"Who?"

"Mendy's family! Or Jamil's family. Or whatever you want to call them!"

"I heard. What's it to you?"

"What's it to me? They only happen to be the closest people in the world to Mendy. And who's the next closest person? Me. And I refuse to be the next dead man on the list, or to place my wife and kids in the line of fire, which is what you're trying to do."

"When did I ever say that?"

Mild-mannered Meir looked furious. "Yochai, your dumb questions are doing nothing to calm me down. I refuse to endanger myself or my family. I leave my house, and who's there waiting for me? Mendy. The kid was a wreck after hearing that his family was killed. He was talking to himself, crying, screaming like an *avel* on the first day of *shivah,* which I guess it is. Yochai, I can't take it. Do you know what he wants me to do?"

"To come along with him to a rav, so you can help him convert ASAP?" Yochai responded dryly.

Meir's jaw dropped. "How do you know that?" His eyes flitted anxiously in all directions.

"Meir, I already told you. We're following you. Every single word of yours is recorded. We're watching you and keeping you safe. Your job is very important to us, and you're deep in this already. You can't quit now."

Drops of sweat rolled down Meir's face. "Watch me. I've already gone way too far. If I'd known how dangerous this would end up being and told the rav that up front, then he'd never have allowed me to help you. It's *sakanas nefashos!*"

Yochai remained calm but serious. "Yes, but now he won't permit you to abandon the mission, either. Listen, Meir, I can't waste a security detail on you unnecessarily, and I don't think Mendy is going to stop pursuing you. Suppose I authorize your resignation and hire somebody else to replace you. The problem is, Mendy and his people just aren't going to leave you alone. Right now you're under close guard, and your safety is ninety-nine percent guaranteed – and not just yours, but that of your wife and kids, as well. Even your baby, who's in the Maon Chava daycare center on 23 Yonah Street is protected."

Meir's face turned gray, and he sagged into a chair.

"What else do you know about me?"

"Everything we need to know. That's our job," Yochai replied with feigned modesty. "When you're one of us, part of a mission, we do everything to protect you. But if you refuse to help, we can't waste our resources on you, in which case you'll have to hire your own bodyguards. Listen, if that's what you want, I can't force you to stay on board… I'll find somebody else to befriend Mendy, although I'm not really sure that it will keep Mendy away from you. He trusts you, and he likes you. You're the only person he still has from his old world, but if you insist on leaving… well, I can't stop you.

"So are we calling it quits?" he concluded, picking up the check and toying with it in his hands.

Meir's voice trembled revealingly. "If I quit, you lay off the security detail?"

"Yes, you'll have to engage your own private security firm, if that's what you choose to do."

"But I can't afford that! I'm in *kollel*! I can barely afford to pay the rent."

"It's up to you." Yochai drummed his fingers on his desk, signaling that he was about to terminate the meeting.

Meir rose and replied stiltedly, "Okay. Listen, for now, keep up the security. I'll see what to do. Do you really think that he's a candidate for conversion?"

Yochai looked amused. "I'm not a rabbi, Meir. I've got no idea. That's your department."

"Well, do you think he's sincere?"

"If I knew, I'd tell you; but I can't be sure. To be honest, I couldn't care less one way or the other."

Meir left GSS Headquarters dejectedly, deciding to head straight to *kollel*. When Naomi quizzed him that evening, he would find some way to tell her something that would calm her, without making it clear whether he had left the job or not. One thing was for sure: He would not tell her the reason why he simply couldn't leave. He would deposit the check quietly in their account and withdraw some of the money immediately to repay his outstanding *gemach* loans. Then, he would try to decide what to do next…

It was early in the morning, and Nachum stood at the edge of the moshav waiting for the bus together with Suri. Even at this hour, the arid desert heat coupled with the sun forced them to take cover beneath the bus shelter. As usual, the bus was late.

"It's so weird to have a new last name," Suri commented, drawing circles in the dust with her shoe. "I don't like changing schools so often either."

Nachum murmured something indistinct, knowing that it was his duty to protect his little sister from the truth.

Suri sat down on a large rock and put her chin in her hands. "Nachum, do you think that Mendy is also dead?"

Nachum whipped around to face his sister. "*Chas v'shalom!* Why would you think so?"

"Why? Because Mommy hardly ever talks about him, and when she does, she starts to cry. Just like when she talks about Tatty. Don't you think it's strange?"

"No. I mean, she misses him."

"Nachum, I have to tell you something," Suri whispered suddenly, "but you can't tell anyone, okay?"

"Okay." Nachum felt his heart begin to hammer.

"Yesterday, when you were still in *cheder*, somebody came to the house. He was about Mendy's age, but he didn't look anything like him."

"Who was he?"

"Wait a second. Mommy told me to go outside, and I did, except that I peeked through the window, and I saw that they were talking and Mommy was crying."

"Who was he?" Nachum repeated impatiently.

"I don't know," Suri replied, "but he wasn't wearing a yarmulke." She glanced around the picturesque moshav cottages and made a face. "He was wearing a yellow shirt, and he didn't have *peyos*. He walked all through the house, looking at everything."

Nachum felt his heart beating faster. "Suri, think hard. Did Mommy say his name?"

"No, I don't think so. Oh, but get this – Mommy gave him a *siddur*. He *davened* a little bit, and Mommy was crying."

Nachum was growing more confused by the minute. "What else did you see?" he finally asked.

"Nothing. I couldn't, because I was scared they'd see me peeking, but I did listen to what I could," she added guiltily. "Mommy was talking and she started crying, and then I started crying too, because… maybe she'll switch us too, one day." With that, she burst into tears.

"Suri! Stop crying and tell me what you heard this second!" her brother screamed at her. Never had Nachum been so glad that the bus was delayed.

"Mommy said something like, 'You're my real Mendy, our hope and future… I don't have any more contact with the other Mendy, so you have nothing to fear… He won't hurt you.' Nachum, how could Mommy just switch Mendy? Do you think she did because he went off the *derech*?" Suddenly, Suri looked terrified. "Do you think if I'm bad one day or I don't do well in school that Mommy will switch me too? She always says that grades are very important, and what if she—"

Nachum cut her off mid-sentence. "Of course not! She loves us, and she'd never switch us for anyone. Besides, you said that this other person wasn't even religious."

"Yes, but it looks like Mommy is being *mekarev* him. She gave him a *siddur*, and he *davened*."

Nachum was blown away by his sister's story. "I don't know what to make of all this, but I think we have to speak to Mendy and tell him what's going on. I think that if he knows what's going on, things will change. He'll come back, he'll talk to Mommy, and maybe he'll even come back home and become frum again. Mommy wouldn't just go and switch him! Besides, I don't want any brother besides for Mendy!"

"How will you find him?" Suri's longing for her eldest brother sounded clearly in her voice. "Tatty's not here. Mendy's gone. Our whole family is falling apart. Every day we move and start over again in a new place. We were almost killed in England. What's going on? Who knows what's going to be tomorrow?"

Nachum stood contemplatively for a moment and then replied. "Suri, I've got an idea. An amazing idea. Want to hear?"

"Yes."

"Listen, in two days, my class is going on a trip to Yerushalayim. We're going to *daven* at the Kosel and walk along the walls of the Old City. It's a whole planned trip. When I get there, I'll say that I'm not feeling well, and that I want to go to my uncle's house to rest up."

"We don't have an uncle in Yerushalayim." Suri stared strangely at him.

"I know that, but my rebbi doesn't. I'll tell him that I want to call my aunt who lives in the Old City, and really, I'll call Mendy."

Suri looked skeptical. "What if it doesn't work?"

"It has to," Nachum said fervently. "And don't you dare tell a soul!"

"But Mommy said that you shouldn't dare talk to Mendy!" she argued.

"If Tatty were alive, *he* would tell me to call Mendy. Tatty wouldn't give up so quickly on his son! Mommy's been through a lot lately, and she's not herself. She doesn't realize that Mendy is still good, and that she can't just switch him for someone else." Nachum looked tremendously proud of himself. "And listen, Suri, I'm telling you again that you'd better not say a word – not *one word* – to Mommy. Just watch me! I'll bring Mendy home with a yarmulke and *tzitzis*, and even a hat! He'll go back to *yeshivah*, and our family will be happy again, even without Tatty. We don't need some weird guy as a new brother. Whoever heard of switching kids? Even Mommy knows you can't just switch your kid!"

Suri didn't look convinced. "Nachum, I don't like it. Mommy says that being in touch with anybody from the past isn't good. It's dangerous. Mommy is always scared these days, and I don't like it. Maybe you shouldn't go to Yerushalayim at all."

"I'm going," Nachum said resolutely

"What if Mommy doesn't let?" she challenged him hopefully.

"Then I'll cry and say that I don't want to be different from all the guys in my class. Mommy said that it's important that we fit in. Don't worry, she'll let me go. Wow! I can't wait! Mendy is going to be so happy when he finds out we're still alive! We haven't seen him in ages!" His voice caught in his throat as he was carried back in time to the days when he had led a normal life, with a father and big brother in Bnei Brak… It had been so long…

53

Two days later, on the morning of his class trip, Nachum was astonished to discover that his mother was also traveling to Yerushalayim, to "take care of things." Nachum worried that his mother's presence in Yerushalayim would ruin his plans, but instead, it turned out to his advantage. When, in response to his complaints about strong stomach pains, his rebbi tried to call his mother, she wasn't home to pick up the phone, and Nachum silently thanked Hashem for the *hashgachah pratis*.

The rebbi cast worried looks at the now-groaning boy. "I can't get hold of your mother, Nachum. Do you perhaps have any relatives in the area? Maybe they could help out?" he suggested.

"I have an uncle in the Old City," Nachum gasped, clutching his stomach as he spoke. "He lives just five minutes away from the Kosel, and my aunt is almost always home."

"Really? That's perfect! Do you want to call her and see if you can rest up there?" his rebbi asked kindly.

Nachum took his rebbi's phone, dialed a random number and talked to the sound of a woman's voice trying to get him to understand that he had the wrong number.

"Hi, Aunt Shoshana? It's me, Nachum. I'm on a class trip to the Kosel but I'm not feeling well… Yeah, that's what I wanted to ask you… Sure I know the way… It's only a few minutes away. It's okay, but you really don't have to… I know the way. Yes? You don't mind? Thanks. I'll be over soon. Ugh, I really don't feel good… See you soon."

He hung up before his rebbi had a chance to ask to speak to his aunt. "She said it's no problem, and that she'll meet me at the top of the steps leading down to the Kosel," he told him, still clutching his stomach.

When the class reached the security checkpoint, Nachum pointed eagerly toward a woman standing on the steps overlooking the plaza. "That's my aunt," he lied. "Can I have rebbi's number, and I'll call you later before you leave?"

Rabbi Farber scribbled his cell phone number on a scrap of paper and handed it to Nachum. "*Refuah sheleimah*," he wished him. "Be in touch. We'll be touring the Old City for about four hours. We're going first to the Kosel and then to the Churvah. We also have a tour of the Machon Hamikdash and then we're going to the Kosel Tunnels. If you feel better, call me, and we'll meet up somewhere. Otherwise, I'll call you at your aunt's before we leave. What's her number?"

"Oh, it's okay, I'll call you," Nachum answered hurriedly, starting to climb the steps before his rebbi could protest.

Rabbi Farber watched as Nachum waved toward a figure on the steps and made his way up toward her. From a distance, he saw the boy speak to the woman for a moment, but then his view was blocked by a passing tourist and the class began to pass through the security checkpoint. By the time he got another look, both Nachum and the woman were out of sight, and, satisfied that his *talmid* was in good hands, he continued with his class toward the Wall.

Nachum, meanwhile, hadn't wasted a moment. After asking a random *chareidi* woman for the time, and then following in her direction for a few minutes in case his rebbi was still watching him, he scurried into one of the narrow alleyways of the Old City and started to hunt for a payphone.

A few moments later, he located one, and, his heart pounding in excitement, he inserted a pre-paid phone card into the slot and dialed the familiar number.

The phone rang once, then twice, and then another six times before the voice mail announcement began: "Hey. You've reached Gil. Leave a message, and I'll decide whether or not to call back."

Nachum's heart plummeted to his toes. Who was Gil? Where was Mendy? Were they friends? Maybe, if he left a message for this Gil, whoever it was, it would still reach his brother?

Trying to fight back the disappointment, Nachum spoke into the receiver: "Hello, this is Nachum Brand. I'm trying to get through to my brother Mendy. Mendy, if this is still your phone, or Gil, if you know where my brother is, I'm trying desperately to reach him. I'll try calling again in another five minutes, so if you know where he is, please answer!"

Nachum wasn't quite sure if his message made sense, but he decided to wait and hope for the best. For the next five minutes, he paced up and down the narrow street, biting his fingernails and glancing at his watch. After what seemed like eons, the five minutes were up and he returned to the phone, staring at it for a moment before picking up the receiver.

What if Mendy still didn't pick up? Then what? But he had to try.

He dialed the number again, but this time, it didn't even ring once before a familiar voice shouted, "NACHUM!!!"

Nachum was so startled he almost dropped the receiver. "Who is this?"

"Is it you, Nachum? Is it really you?" This time, the voice didn't shout, but trembled.

"Of course it's me. Who's this?"

"It's me, Mendy."

Nachum exhaled a sigh of relief. "Oh, I thought the phone belonged to somebody named Gil."

"Nachum, is it really you? Can you prove it?"

"Prove it? Why should I prove it? Mendy, of course it's me! Who else would I be? Mendy, I'm in Yerushalayim now. Where are you? Is there anywhere we can meet?"

"I'm in… You're in Yerushalayim? No problem. Tell me exactly where you are, and I'll come get you. One second though – I still need proof that you're really you."

Nachum began feeling uneasy. "What's that supposed to mean?"

"Some kind of proof. I don't know. Oh, I do. What song did we always sing together during *Shalosh Seudos?*"

The question awakened a wave of longing in Nachum. "*Elokai, neshamah she'nasata bi,*" he answered without missing a beat.

"It is you," Gil choked. "Okay, I'm already in my car. Tell me *exactly* where you are."

"I'm in the Old City, near the Churvah."

"Wow. That's going to mean traffic…" Gil muttered under his breath. "Listen, Nachum, I want to meet up with you as fast as I can. Do you have any cash on you?"

"Of course," Nachum grinned. "You know Mommy never lets us go anywhere, even on a class trip, without money, in case we get lost or something. I've got 100 shekels."

Gil silently blessed his mother for her ever-cautious nature. "Perfect. Here's what we'll do. I'm already on the road to Yerushalayim. Take a cab to the first bus stop on Rechov Givat Shaul, which is right at the city entrance, and I'll cover whatever it costs you. Got it? Rechov Givat Shaul. Hopefully, it shouldn't take me more than about forty minutes to reach you. I feel bad about making you take a cab alone, but with city traffic, it'll take me an extra half-hour, at least, to get to you. Later on, I'll take you back to wherever you have to go."

"No problem!" Nachum exclaimed, excited by his impending adventure in an unfamiliar city.

"I'll see you soon," Gil whispered, his voice overflowing with emotion. Mindless of honking drivers and traffic cameras, Gil sped recklessly all the way to Yerushalayim, reaching the Holy City in record time. Less than thirty minutes later, he screeched to a halt at the first bus stop in Givat Shaul and jumped out of the car, throwing his arms around the little boy and lifting him in his arms.

"You're alive! I can't believe I'm seeing you again! What about Suri? And Mommy? Are you all really okay?" he cried.

Nachum was staggered by the embrace of a stranger; it took him a moment to realize that this was really Mendy, his beloved brother, even if he did look totally secular. His eyes were still the same, and his face was streaked with tears. "We're okay," he managed to say. "We barely got out in time, before the explosion. You mean, you really thought we were…" he couldn't bear to say it aloud, and he was also tongue-tied, ashamed to be seen with this secular-looking boy.

"Um, I… maybe we can talk somewhere more private?" he ventured.

"Get into my car," Gil offered. They entered the car, and Gil spontaneously decided to drive to the Jerusalem Forest, which was only a ten-minute drive away and deserted at this early afternoon hour. The ride passed in silence, and when they arrived, they sat down across from each other at a wooden picnic table, facing a breathtaking mountain view.

"Where are you living?" was Gil's first question.

"Down south. I guess you haven't been in touch with Mommy."

"Mommy can't talk to me."

"Why not?" Nachum was pleading for answers.

"She just can't," Gil replied succinctly.

"She cries a lot."

"She cries not because of me, but because of a very painful situation that no one ever anticipated, and she has good reason to cry. But it's not because of me," he repeated.

"It *is* because of you," Nachum insisted. "I know it is. Mendy, we all miss you so much! Mommy also thinks that you blame yourself for what happened to Tatty, but it wasn't your fault. You know that Tatty always said that whatever happens is from *Shamayim*. You weren't even the *shaliach*," he added breathlessly, trying to include everything possible in their brief time together.

Gil closed his eyes. "Please, stop, Nachum. I can't. You're hurting me too much. You can't imagine how much you're hurting me. I just need to know that everyone is okay: you, Mommy, and Suri. I need to know that you're managing on your own, and that no one hurt you. That's all I need to know."

"Okay, I'll tell you what you want to know, but then you promise to let me say what I want to say," Nachum stipulated.

Gil nodded. "All right. You have a deal."

They grinned, and once again, they were brothers. It was just like it had all been a year earlier, before Mendy had left home, before Tatty had died.

"Okay. And, we're all okay, more or less. We were living in England for a while. Suri liked it, but I hated it. The sun hardly ever shines there. I was really glad when we came back to Eretz Yisrael, even though we're living in nowheresville, down south. By the way, Suri knows that I'm meeting you today, and she's *chalishing* for you to come visit."

Gil closed his eyes again, and when he opened them, they sparkled with tears. "How did you know to come now?" he asked in a voice choked with emotion.

"What do you mean? We came back to Eretz Yisrael, and I decided I had to meet you. I couldn't wait any longer. You're my brother! And now it's time for you to listen to what I have to say," he replied.

"Of course. Nachum, you have no idea how happy I am that you called! I thought you were all… gone. I didn't know how I'd ever live again," Gil said softly, trying to suppress the moan of agony that threatened to emerge from his lips.

How could she do this to me? he wondered in anguish. *After raising me, loving me, and davening for me endlessly – how could my mother torture me with the thought that the whole family had perished? She, more than anyone else, should have understood that I've lost everything. Not just my family, but also my past, my future, and my whole way of life. She knows that I'm trapped between two dark worlds with no means of escape. Why didn't she take pity on me?*

"Are you listening?" Nachum interrupted his reverie impatiently.

"Of course," Gil replied.

"Do you remember our old neighbor, Zecharya Klein?"

"Zachi? You mean that nut who always used to chase the cats and had a collection of cockroaches for any rebbi he didn't like?" Gil chuckled at the memory.

"The one and only," Nachum confirmed. "Anyway, there was a time when everyone said he was hanging out and going off the *derech*. They all thought he'd end up totally secular, but you know what? Today, he's married with two kids and learning in a top-notch *kollel*. He came to the *shivah*, and we ended up talking. He said that when people grow up, they see things differently, and he believes that you'll be the same because you have an amazing *neshamah*. See? Even he knows that! And I definitely do! Remember when everyone was yelling at him for breaking the neighbor's car window?"

"Yeah, and his parents couldn't even afford to fix it. I lent him my allowance to help him pay it back," Gil reminisced emotionally, the memories overwhelming him.

"See?" Nachum said triumphantly. "See what a special *neshamah* you have? You always had *ahavas habriyos* and *ahavas Yisrael*! And you were an incredible *masmid*! Tatty was always so proud of you and pointed at you as an example of what I should become. All the rebbis in *cheder* were so excited when they found out I was your brother, not that I'm as smart as you or such a big *masmid*. But none of this is why I made a whole mess just to come and talk to you, and I really hope no one finds out what I did or I'll really be in big trouble." Gil was about to ask his brother about his last remark, but Nachum seemed intent on getting to the point.

Just then, they heard a car approach on the dirt path, and Gil tensed.

"Listen, Mendy, I want you to remember what I'm saying." Nachum stood up and stared his brother right in the face. "They can take everything from you, Mendy. They can take your money, your pride, and your honor. But there's one thing no one can ever take from you—"

Two police cars screeched to a stop suddenly beside the brothers, who both jumped in shock as six officers leaped out of the vehicles with weapons drawn.

"Hands up!" they cried, training their guns on Gil, who turned deathly white and slowly raised his hands.

"I think this is a mistake," he said slowly.

Ignoring him, an officer turned to the younger boy. "Are you Nachum Brand?"

"Yes."

"Come with us, kid. And you're Gil Brand?" he turned threateningly to the older brother.

"Yes."

"You're under arrest for suspected kidnapping of a minor!" he declared and hurried to snap cuffs around Gil's wrists.

"Wait! This is a mistake!" Nachum cried. "He didn't kidnap me! He's my brother, and I called him to come get me!" His voice trembled fearfully.

The police ignored him too, escorting Nachum to one vehicle and dragging Gil quite unsympathetically to the second.

"Stop!" Nachum shouted. "MENDY, WAIT! I'm trying to tell you that they'll never get your Yiddishe *neshamah*! They can't take it away from you! It'll always be yours! MENDY!" he screamed again. "Don't forget your *nesh-*" His cry was drowned into the interior of the vehicle, and Nachum practically fainted when he saw the familiar figure sitting in the back seat.

"Oy, Nachum! What have you done?" she wept, throwing her arms around her son and hugging him tightly as if she'd never let go. "Why did you lead us right back into the lion's den?"

They both wept all the way home.

"Nachum, I told you not to! You knew you weren't supposed to contact him! Why did you do it?" Shuli cried.

"Mommy, do you know how happy he was to see me? He's all alone in the world! If we don't take care of him, who will?"

Shuli fixed her gaze upon her son. Nachum was no longer a baby, and although he was only eleven years old, he was mature far beyond his years. He had taken a rash step, but it had been well thought through. Maybe the time had come to tell him the truth?

"Nachum, many things that may seem like facts are not really so. When you met with Mendy now, you endangered us all."

"Mommy, if there's one thing that's fact, it's that Mendy is my brother!" the boy protested.

"Not necessarily."

The two police officers sitting in the front seats of the car listened silently to the exchange. They had received unambiguous orders from the GSS, but the story itself was totally bizarre. A *chareidi* kid had met up with his secular brother, and now their mother was chasing them both? None of it made any sense.

Noting the officers' interest, Shuli promptly fell silent, realizing that this was hardly the appropriate venue for their discussion. Nachum, however, failed to pick up the hint and continued talking.

"Mommy, I told him where we're living and asked him to at least come visit. You'll see, Mommy, Mendy is going to come back some day, soon, I hope. You're angry with me now, but one day, you'll thank me for it."

Shuli turned pale. "You did what?" she cried out in anguish. "Oh, Nachum, why did you have to go and do that? Why didn't you listen to me when I told you to stay away from him? Oy, Nachum, who knows what's going to be now, and how many more times we'll have to move. We have to leave, immediately, before it's too late."

"You mean, we've been running away from *Mendy?*" Nachum couldn't believe his ears.

"Yes," she whispered tearfully. "Enough, Nachum. We'll speak at home."

The three-hour ride passed in relative silence, interrupted only by occasional sighs that escaped from Shuli's lips as she tried to suppress her tears. At long last, the car pulled to a stop outside their house and they exited, walking up the short path toward the front door.

"Nachum, I have to tell you now," Shuli began hesitantly, "after what happened today… There's something you've always assumed was fact but isn't really so."

"What something?"

"Mendy is not your brother."

Nachum inhaled sharply. Although he had already partially guessed as much, it was still painful to hear it uttered aloud. "You mean he's adopted?"

"Something like that." Shuli preferred to be vague. "So what I'm trying to tell you is that we don't really owe him anything, even though he grew up in our house, and we loved him very much."

"He still loves us, Mommy. I know that."

"Possibly, but he could still be very dangerous for us."

Nachum's eyes were troubled. "You know what? If he's adopted, and you loved him so much, how do I know that I'm not adopted, or Suri? One day, if I *chas v'shalom* go off the *derech*, will you decide that I'm dangerous too, and run away from me?"

"Chas v'shalom!"

"I know, *chas v'shalom*, but will you?"

"Of course not, Nachum. You're my son. Mendy is not. I'm telling you this, and ordering you at the same time never to contact him again. You just got us into very hot water."

As they spoke, a medium-size truck pulled up to the house, and a man leaped out of the cab. Nachum recognized him as vaguely familiar, but Shuli identified him immediately as Yochai.

"We meet again," Yochai murmured in patent discomfort.

"Yes," she replied briefly. Turning crimson, Nachum escaped into the house.

"I'm sure you understand that the truck is here for you. You have two hours to pack before departure."

"Where to this time?"

"Farther south."

"Where?"

"Eilat. It's close to the Egyptian and Jordanian borders."

"So?"

"So in the event of any danger, you can escape through Jordan to another continent."

Shuli lifted her eyes bravely. "Yochai, tell me the truth. How much longer is this going to continue? How many more times will we have to run away?"

"Honestly, I don't think much longer.""Why not?"

"Because it's going to end sooner or later, and likely sooner. Their objective is a massive terrorist attack. As soon as it's over, Mendy – excuse me, that Arab – will be worthless to them, as you will be too."

The information was shocking and relieving at once. Shuli could only bring herself to utter a single sentence: "And then we'll be a normal family again?"

"Yes."

Shuli lifted her chin rebelliously, with courage that she didn't even know she had. "Listen, Yochai. I've had enough. I'm not running away again. We've run away enough times. I can't be blamed for the constant GSS failures, and I can't uproot my children every few days without causing them long-term emotional trauma. They're my children, and I need to worry about their emotional welfare as much as their physical welfare."

"Lady, if you were really concerned for your children's welfare, you would have made sure that your son didn't contact him. We're doing the best we can, and this wouldn't have happened if you'd done your job. Now, I'm picking up the pieces, and it isn't easy. Listen, Shuli, I've known you for many years, which is why I'm willing to go the extra mile for you. But the GSS is not a small operation, and we've got a lot of work on our hands. Half of the department is up to its ears taking care of your family instead of taking care of other important business."

"And it's getting to be too much for you?"

"Honestly? Yes."

"Okay. So you're fired," she replied calmly.

"What?"

"You're fired. Or dismissed, or whatever you want to call it. I don't need protection. Only Mendy knows that we live here in the settlement. And Mendy, even as an Arab, grew up with us and cares about us. I raised him, and I know him as well as any mother knows her child, and I'm telling you that he won't pass that information to his contacts."

Yochai cursed under his breath, and his expression turned harsh. "You're naïve, Shuli. Mendy won't voluntarily relay the information, but his contacts will squeeze it out of him by force, and he's not strong enough to stand up against them."

"He will be. He won't betray us or sacrifice us. I saw his eyes, and… I know him, Yochai. In fact, I wouldn't be surprised if he wanted to convert."

"He does," Yochai blurted out.

Shuli's eyes filled with tears of joy, but Yochai was furious. Why was she risking herself for the sake of an Arab! She'd gotten her real son back in place of that traitor. Why couldn't she suffice with bringing him back to Judaism and helping him come to terms with his past instead of focusing her emotional energies on the lost Mendy?

"He does?" Shuli repeated, her heart overflowing. "I knew it… I felt it… *Baruch Hashem!* I knew there was nothing to worry about…"

"Of course there's what to worry about!" Yochai retorted. "You're in grave danger, and I refuse to take responsibility for this. I promised Shimon I'd protect you. If anything happens to you, I—"

"Many things already happened to us," Shuli replied softly. "Many, many things. What else could happen? How much worse would it be? I prefer to stay here and try to lead a normal life with the kids. I don't think they can take another move now. Let us be. We'll be okay. Assign us a bit of protection, and it'll be fine. You'll see. Nachum won't contact Mendy again."

Yochai didn't look convinced. "Shuli, I can't force you to go, but you realize that you're waiving your rights to safety and protection. It's a grave responsibility."

"I understand that."

"And neither you nor the children may meet Mendy. We made a lot of effort to prevent certain others from following us here, but you're still in extreme danger."

"I know that."

Yochai shrugged helplessly. "If you're sure that this is what you really want…"

"I am."

"Okay, so I'll send the truck off."

"Thank you."

From a distance, he spotted Jamil – the real Mendy – walking toward them. Since Shuli and her children had arrived back in the country, he had met up several times with his mother, who had directed him to a rav and then to a *yeshivah* for *baalei teshuvah* which was located in the same settlement. Yochai hardly recognized the kid, who in concerted attempt to fit into the community, was now dressed in a white shirt, black pants, and *kippah*. He briefly wondered if Jamil was merely trying to ingratiate himself with his new family, or if a Jewish lifestyle actually appealed to him. The thought intrigued him.

"He's wearing a *kippah* already?" Yochai couldn't disguise his astonishment.

"Yes. There's a wonderful rav here who recommended the *yeshivah* at the far end of town. You see? It wasn't just you, but also *hashgachah*, that led us here."

Yochai lifted his arm to wave at the boy, but Jamil only nodded curtly, resentment flitting across his face. He walked right past them without stopping to say hello.

"He says you treated him terribly," Shuli explained, restraining her impulse to rebuke the man.

"Everyone perceives things differently," Yochai muttered caustically. "At least he made it back home hale and hearty, and not in a coffin. That's something, isn't it?"

"I suppose so. Sorry, I guess he didn't appreciate the extent of the danger. I guess we didn't either," she added as an afterthought.

"No one does. Everyone has a litany of complaints, but no one has a clue of what's really going on. They want to cut the budget; they tell us to treat everyone 'humanely.' 'Give, do, bring, go, you didn't do enough.' People have no clue how much we invest from inside," Yochai said, his eyes narrowed. "Whatever," he sighed after a moment. "It's all part of the job. I'm going now. But just remember that if any of you need to leave the settlement, you have to contact me in advance. You're not forbidden to leave," he hastened to add, "but we just need to continually touch base if we're going to keep you guys safe. Okay?"

"Yes. Thank you."

"And you're taking responsibility for this?"

"Absolutely."

Yochai turned to address the truck driver. The two conferred briefly, and then Yochai issued rapid-fire orders into his cell phone, assigning several men to guard the settlement.

A helicopter awaited him not far away, prepared for takeoff. Shuli heard the sound of the rotors, and she waited impatiently for him to leave.

"Goodbye, and lots of luck," Yochai said softly, keeping his eyes low. "Shuli, I'm telling you again that I'm not comfortable with this. Take care of yourselves."

"*B'ezras Hashem*, we will," Shuli replied. She exhaled a loud sigh as the truck rumbled away from the house, and she felt waves of strength and determination fortifying her. She would survive this. Hashem had ordained this bizarre set of circumstances, and she had done her utmost *hishtadlus,* as she saw it. She felt as if she had lived through four years in as many months, and now she was willing to face her enemies from the safety of this house.

"Ima," Jamil approached her after waiting to see that Yochai had left. He had taken to calling her "Ima" when it was just the two of them, and Shuli forced herself to ignore his coarse Arab accent.

"Yes, Mendy?" That was another thing she forced herself to say, and she automatically found herself treating him as if he were many years younger than his real age.

"I've mentioned it before, but I'd really like to meet my brother and sister already," he said confidently. "Don't you think the time has come for us to become a real family?"

Until then, Jamil had been residing in the *yeshivah* dormitory on the outskirts of the settlement, and he would meet his mother occasionally only during the morning hours when the children were at school. Why today, of all days, did he have to start asking difficult questions?

As Yochai had predicted, Gil was waiting for him in his office. He didn't even have to look to know he was there.

"Are you out of your mind?" Gil shouted, his jaw quivering in rage. "How dare you arrest me in front of my brother! What were you guys thinking? And how could you tell me that they were all killed in the bombing?"

"I didn't say anything. You read about it in the paper," Yochai replied placidly.

"And who dictated the article to the media?"

"No idea. You can try to find out if you like," Yochai replied indifferently. "Listen, Gil, or rather, Jamil, the game is up."

The boy lowered his eyes. "What do you know about me? Or what do you think you know about me?"

"Everything there is to know."

"You're wrong. You know nothing!" Gil spat. "And I'm continuing to work here, just to set the record straight."

"It's set straight. Especially because we really need you on the job. You're vital to the GSS, you know."

"Why did you arrest me?"

"You're forbidden to meet him or any of them. That's an order. Not because we think you'd hurt them, but because there are people following you."

"No one's following me."

Yochai's face darkened. "Kid, what do you know about covert operations? You really don't realize that you're being followed? Do you know that for every step you take, we've got two guys on your tail, and so do they? You're nothing but a pawn in a game, Gil, a human time-bomb. I understand that your encounter with your brother, however foolish, was very significant for you, so I'm telling you the painful truth: Under no circumstances should you dare to meet with them again or pass anyone any information about their current location, otherwise the article in the paper will be for real next time."

Gil absorbed the dressing-down silently. "Why didn't you just tell me the truth? You could have spared me the tears."

"You have a lot to cry about, kid. Those tears weren't wasted."

A look of disgust crossed Gil's face, and he spun around and stormed out of the room. It was all over. For the first time, there was no more hope, no more chances. He was completely on his own. The people whom he had thought were his allies – Nachum and Suri – even they would become his enemies eventually. He had no doubt in his mind that his mother would tell them the truth in order to protect them.

There was only one thing left to do. He could still choose the way he would spend the last days of his life.

The yearning for *limmud haTorah* still resounded fiercely within him, and Gil saw himself as a second grader listening, wide-eyed, as the rebbi described how the Torah had been given on Har Sinai, all Jews united with one heart to receive it, with all the souls of future converts present too.

Had his *neshamah* also been there? Surely it must have been, or else he wouldn't be craving Torah. His *neshamah* must have also heard the holy words spoken, "*Anochi Hashem Elokecha*," and fervently declared, "*Na'aseh v'nishma*" along with the others.

He had already made his decision, but with all the commotion of the last few days, he had let it lapse. But now, it could no longer be postponed. In the last days of his life, he would take the final step toward becoming a true Jew. The rav he had approached hadn't rejected him, only listening and repeating the *halachos*, granting him a second chance to choose the peaceful life of a Noahide.

But the only life he craved was that of a Jew.

Why? a small voice sounded in his mind, challenging his convictions. Yet the challenge was quickly rebuffed by a louder, surer voice.

Because Yiddishkeit is eternal. Torah is eternal. And what do I have in this world? Nothing.

When he had met Nachum, he had actually sensed a rush of envy inside of him. Envy, because Nachum was Jewish, and he wasn't. Now, that envy was impelling him to take a dangerous step.

Shuli painstakingly set the small dining room table with her fine china that Yochai had managed to procure from their old apartment in Bnei Brak, along with an array of cakes and decorative miniatures that she had baked in honor of the special reunion.

"Wow!" Suri exclaimed when she returned home from school, swinging her knapsack. "We have company?" She reached to filch a truffle off the tray and gobbled it down to the sound of her mother's protests. "Who's coming?" she asked through a mouthful of luscious chocolate.

"It's a surprise," Shuli replied mysteriously.

"There are way too many secrets in this house!" Nachum declared as he entered the house after his sister. "I can do without the secrets and surprises. I can't take it anymore."

"Okay, so I'll tell you," his mother replied, surprisingly conciliatory. "But you have to realize that this is a secret that you can't share with anybody yet. Anyone in the world. And you both know how to keep a secret. Right?"

"Right," they chorused.

"Okay, so I'll tell you what happened in brief. Almost twenty-one years ago, when Mendy was born, Tatty and I were very happy. We loved him very much, and we raised him. And he was the best brother in the world, wasn't he?"

"He was," they replied.

"Now we only discovered this recently, but what really happened was that when Mendy was born, there was a problem in the hospital, and two babies were switched. Our Mendy with another baby. Our Mendy grew up with a different family, and the Mendy that grew up with us really belongs to another family."

The children stared at their mother in shock mingled with disbelief.

"Maybe… maybe I was switched too?" Suri blurted out, her eyes expressing fear at that possibility.

"You weren't. Unfortunately, in this case, somebody did it on purpose. It's really impossible for such a thing to happen by accident. Babies have name tags and things – usually the system is very secure. That's why it took us so long to find out what happened. It took a lot of hard work, but we finally discovered where Mendy really was all the years."

"But what about *our* Mendy… I mean, the Mendy that grew up with us?" Suri cried miserably. That means he doesn't want us anymore? He'll never live with us again? He won't be our brother? Mommy, don't you still love him?" She looked brokenhearted.

"Mendy grew up with us, yes, and of course we still love him. Obviously, Hashem wanted him to live with us for twenty years and then for us to get our real child back. It's very sad that the real Mendy – my son and your real brother – didn't grow up with us and grew up instead with a different family."

"But our Mendy also grew up with the wrong family," Nachum pointed out. "We're not his family."

Shuli nodded, and her eyes filled with tears which she quickly swiped away. "I know this is hard for you, but I hope, I really hope that in the end, it will be good for all of us. That's why I thought it was time that you met Mendy, your real brother. He should be here any minute."

Nachum and Suri exchanged anguished glances, but before either of them had a chance to react, a knock sounded at the door.

Shuli rose to open it, and Nachum and Suri stared at the person standing there, prepared to find anything but seeing only someone who looked more or less like a typical *bachur*.

"Hello, Nachum and Suri," he greeted them simply. "It's good to meet you finally."

The kids were too taken back to respond.

"Wow," he glanced appreciatively at the table. "You didn't have to go out of your way," he smiled shyly at Shuli.

"It was my pleasure, Mendy," she replied graciously.

His next comment shook them all up. "I'm really not used to that name yet. You can call me Jamil. I think it might be better for everyone like that at first. After all, the children already have a Mendy in their lives, right?"

"*Jamil?*" Nachum gasped, staring at the newcomer. "What kind of name is that? Who calls their kid Jamil?"

"People who live in Arab villages call their kids Jamil," the young man grinned easily.

"Arab villages?" Suri whispered, suddenly terrified.

"Yes, Suri, your brother was raised in an Arab village," Shuli interjected, trying to keep her tone calm. "He was raised by an Arab family, and they treated him very badly."

The children looked horrified and stared at Jamil as if he were a terrorist or suicide bomber.

"So, you're, like, an *Arab*?" Nachum finally asked.

"No. I just grew up in an Arab home, but I'm a Jew, just like you. See? I also wear a *kippah*, like your mother wants."

"Like Hashem wants," Suri corrected him, clearly appalled by what she had just heard.

"Like everyone wants," Jamil concurred good-naturedly. He reached for a chocolate fudge brownie, and a second later, he was chewing it appreciatively. "Delicious!" he complimented Shuli generously. "Nobody in the village knew how to bake like that. All they ever baked was pita and dry cookies with sesame seeds…"

As he chatted on, Nachum and Suri exchanged scandalized looks. Neither had missed the fact that Jamil hadn't made a *brachah* before eating. Although all the cakes had seemed so tempting a minute earlier, by now Nachum felt queasy, and worse still once Jamil began describing his life in the village.

Shuli dexterously drew the conversation to other, less disturbing realms.

"Why don't you tell us about your new *yeshivah*?" she suggested. Jamil nodded and easily changed the topic, and the atmosphere settled slightly. Suri even reached for another three chocolates, but Nachum remained stonily silent.

Suddenly, understanding hit him with the force of a sledgehammer.

"Mommy!" he said suddenly, not even realizing that he had interrupted Jamil mid-sentence. "If Jamil grew up with Arabs, and he was switched at birth with our Mendy… That means that… that Mendy is an Arab?"

The question caused them all to freeze, its implications hanging heavily in the air.

Only Jamil seemed unaffected. "Yes," he replied with equanimity. "He's an Arab, which is why you have be careful. He has dangerous intentions."

Suri burst into tears. "It's not true! Mommy, it can't be! Mendy isn't an Arab! Tell me it's not true!" She ran to her mother and grabbed hold of her, something she hadn't done in years.

Shuli gathered the girl in her arms, trying to calm her.

"Suri, now we have to think of the real Mendy, our Mendy. Not the old Mendy."

"He's not the real Mendy! Our Mendy is the real Mendy!" Suri wept.

Nachum also looked accusingly at his mother and deliberately switched into Yiddish in order that there would be no chance of Jamil understanding what he was about to say. "Are you trying to say that Mendy is a 'cousin'? And that's why you won't let me talk to him! You really think he'd hurt us?! Mommy, how could you? How could you doubt him like that? How could you forget who our Mendy really is? This person," he made a discreet gesture toward Jamil, "he's not one of us, and he never will be. I want my brother back! I want Mendy, the real Mendy. I'm willing to help him. I'm sure he isn't really an Arab… Mommy, how could you do this to Mendy, to our whole family?"

Usually an exceptionally-behaved boy, Nachum uncharacteristically lashed out at Shuli, venting all the pain and frustration of the past months at her, and when he finished speaking, he burst into tears. Not only was Tatty gone, but now Mendy was lost to him forevermore. And Mommy didn't even care.

The only one who remained untouched by the heartrending scene was Jamil, who calmly helped himself to another three slices of cake in the interim. With a forgiving smile, he turned to Shuli and calmly said, "Don't worry, Ima. He'll get used to the idea. He's still a little boy, but when he grows up, he'll understand that life doesn't always work out as planned."

Nachum was tempted to scream and order the impostor out of his house, but when he noticed the tears in his mother's eyes, he struggled to control himself and instead escaped to the privacy of his bedroom where he buried his tears in his pillow for a long, long time.

Meir left for *Shacharis* with a medium-size garbage bag in hand. Naomi had zero tolerance for garbage in the house, so Meir made a twice-daily stop in the tiny room in the corner of the lobby that housed the building's garbage bins. Already during *shanah rishonah* he had perfected his aim, and he never missed a shot even from ten feet away.

He reached the vestibule and opened the door to the garbage room, but the moment the door swung open, something, or rather, someone, sprang out at him. Meir almost shrieked with fright when he recognized the man as none other than Mendy.

"Meir, I've been waiting for you for hours! You didn't take out the garbage last night," he added with accusing eyes that suddenly bore a striking similarity to Naomi's. Meir's heart started to pound in his chest and he forced himself to breathe slowly in order to calm himself.

"Since when do you keep track of how often I throw out the garbage?" he tried to disguise his panic with a note of humor. "If my garbage interests you so much, why don't you knock on the door and offer to take it out?" Nonetheless, even as he spoke, Meir's eyes flitted around in terror.

"You have nothing to worry about. It's sterile here. Well, that is, if you can ignore the stench of garbage for a few minutes."

"Sterile?"

"Meaning, there's no reception in here, so there's no one listening in on us," Gil said as he closed the door to the vestibule. His words did nothing to relax Meir, who felt more frightened than ever.

"You're sure?"

"Positive. Really, Meir, I only wanted to ask you a question. I see you're scared, but please, don't worry. I promise you that I'm not out to hurt you. Did you really think I was?" Genuine pain sounded in his voice.

Meir took advantage of the moment to plead his case. "Listen, Mendy, I'm begging you. In fact, I'm more than begging you. I'm getting down on my hands and knees and pleading with you to please leave me alone! I trust you, but my wife is petrified, and she's terrified for the kids too. I don't know how we got into this mess, but I'm asking you now to please leave me alone, once and for all. Don't talk to me; don't approach me anymore. It's not fair… Please, Mendy… Will you do it for me? It's a huge *chessed*, and *goyim* are also rewarded for doing *chessed*."

"But that's just it. I don't want to be a *goy* anymore. Meir, I'm ready to be *misgayer*."

"So go to a rav! I'm not a rav, and I can't help you with that." The stench in the room was making Meir nauseous, but the need to rid himself of Mendy forced him to remain there.

"I already went to a rav, and he's willing to let me go ahead. In two more days, you'll see me again, but this time, as a Jew," Gil announced.

"Fabulous," Meir said dryly. "Mazal tov, and I hope it goes smoothly for you. I would happily host you, but being that you're almost a Jew, I'm sure you understand that I have to take care of my family first. I really wish you all the best, and—"

"Don't say goodbye yet," Gil stopped him, his expression pained. Meir felt a twinge in his heart as he realized how deeply he was letting the younger man down; it was obvious that Mendy had hoped that his announcement would stir excitement or at least acceptance in Meir.

Gil's heart sank as he saw that his plea had fallen upon deaf ears. How he had hoped that his announcement would open the door to warmth, caring, and assistance. *But that's not the way, Gil,* a voice whispered in his mind, gaining strength as it persisted. *If you convert, it won't be because somebody lent you a hand or offered you help or protection. You'll be converting because it's the Will of Hashem, your Father in Heaven Who loves you and desires you.*

But the rejection still hurt.

"Meir, please listen to me. I didn't come here for nothing. I'm going to convert, to become a *ger tzedek*. I've gone to a rav, but I can't tell him the whole story because it's too dangerous. For me and for him. So why am I coming to you now? Because you already know my story, and there's something I want you to find out for me."

"And what's that?"

"I need to know if a Jew is allowed to sacrifice his life to save another Jew."

"What does that mean?" Meir asked carefully.

"To die for him," Gil answered, leaving no room for ambiguity.

Meir's response was automatic as he quoted the well-known *Gemara*: "*Chayecha v'chayei chavercha. Chayecha kodmin.* When it's a question of your life and the life of your fellow man, your own life comes first."

"Thank you. I learned in *yeshivah* too, don't forget. Actually, my question isn't exactly that, but if it's permissible to save the lives of many people by sacrificing my own. Am I allowed to give up my life for others, if I'm a *yachid,* and they're the *rabbim.*"

Meir was aghast by the question, but he tried to conceal his horror. "If that's all you want, then I'll ask."

"And please tell me the true answer."

Meir stared penetratingly at him. "Why are you asking this, Mendy. Is it really important for you to know?"

"Yes. Meir, I want to convert, but I have to know the answer before I do. Because if the answer doesn't fit with my plan, then I won't be able to convert after all."

"Well, if you're so willing to sacrifice your conversion, then you shouldn't convert in the first place," Meir countered, becoming more confused by the minute.

His words seemed to anger Gil, whose eyes were already turbulent. He narrowed them furiously at Meir and retorted, "Do you have any idea what you're saying? Suppose I knew that someone planned to kill you. Just you. You and no one else, and I wanted to give my life to save you. Can I do that or not? I'd rather do it as a Jew, but if it's forbidden, and I'll be considered a murderer, for having killed myself, a Jew, then I won't convert and I'll save you as a *goy*."

His words hammered into Meir like icy balls of hail, and he paled. "Look, Mendy, I really don't know. I'm not a rav, and definitely not a *gadol*, who's probably the only one equipped to deal with such a *she'eilah*. But Mendy," he added, his voice trembling violently, "is someone really out to kill me and my family?"

Gil was losing patience. "No, *baruch Hashem*, nobody is. But please, I need an answer by tomorrow!"

"Okay, you'll have one, *bli neder*."

"Thank you. Okay, you can go now," the younger man nodded.

Meir opened the door in relief, but on second thought, closed it again. "You know what? I think I'll leave you my answer in a letter, here in this room. Okay? I'll put it there, on the side by the windowsill."

"Please, don't do that. I want to see you," Gil practically begged him. *You're the only one in the world with room left in your heart to listen to me, and to pity me, even a little. I see your compassion, but also your fear. Please, talk to me! I need someone to talk to me!* But of course, he said nothing.

Without another word, Meir nodded curtly and left the tiny room. Gil waited another fifteen minutes before emerging and discreetly leaving the building. In the past few weeks, he had barely stepped foot in his cubicle at GSS Headquarters, having belatedly figured out that one of the junior officers on the staff bore the distinct privilege of being the one to assign him bogus missions, and that his presence in Headquarters provided occupation to no less than eight fellow officers, those who had been assigned to follow him wherever he went.

He drove back to his apartment and tried to calm his frazzled emotions with a long, hot shower, desperately needed after ten hours spent waiting in the garbage room. With nothing else left to do afterward, he sank onto his bed and stared blankly at the walls for hours on end. His Arab operators chose that day to inform him that "zero hour," as he had privately dubbed the mission that would herald his death, was soon approaching. No date was given, just an order to be prepared for the call whenever it came, and Gil just prayed that he would have time to convert before it did in order to die as a Jew.

Meir dragged his feet home from *kollel* at a quarter past seven, physically and emotionally drained. He would be leaving again at ten to nine for *Maariv* followed by his regular night *seder*, but he always made a point of spending the time in-between pitching in at home and helping his wife with the final minutes of the bedtime routine.

He crossed the street to find a shiny blue car parked right outside his apartment building. He couldn't put his finger on it, but his intuition screamed that it boded no good.

As he had expected, the driver honked at him and stuck his head out the window. "Meir?"

Meir glanced at the driver and blushed deeply. Although it was probably just his imagination, he suddenly felt as if all the neighbors' eyes were upon him, observing his exchange with a large, secular Jew with greased black hair slicked against his scalp who was now smiling politely at Meir.

"Hop in. Yochai wants to see you."

"I can't right now," Meir apologized nervously. "I'm on a tight schedule, and I promised my wife I'd help her get the kids to bed now, and—" The man's steely gaze left Meir no option other than to meekly conclude, "but I'll finish as soon as I can. I'll just run upstairs and tell my wi—" The man's eyes choked him. "Okay, I'll call her from the car." Without another word, he disappeared into the vehicle.

The blue car began to glide smoothly out of the congested Bnei Brak residential neighborhood, and, as they turned the corner from his street, Meir noticed Leibel Katz, his nosy neighbor, watching him with astonished eyes. Tuvia and Aharon, two of his *kollel* friends, had also seen him enter the car.

Who knows what they're thinking, he thought glumly. *There's going to be a lot of speculation during Maariv tonight...*

The ride passed uneventfully, without an extraneous word spoken. Meir had been on the job long enough to know that all unnecessary speech was both redundant and unwelcome.

A half hour later, he found himself being ushered into Yochai's office, where the Big Boss himself greeted him with a broad smile.

"Come on in, Meir!" he invited him warmly to be seated. "Fantastic work!"

"What did I do?" Meir wondered in confusion, unable to believe that his conversation with Mendy had been captured by the GSS's advanced listening devices.

"Your conversation with the kid," Yochai intercepted his thoughts.

"You heard us?"

"As if you were sitting right here in the room."

"But Mendy said it was impossible..."

"And you believed him?" Yochai looked surprised. "I thought I'd write you a recommendation for your improvisation skills, but I guess I was wrong. Well, even if you really did believe him, it was to our benefit. We overheard your conversation, and we're very pleased. And we want you to tell him that you asked a rabbi and were told that it's forbidden for a Jew to sacrifice his life to spare another Jew."

"Which rav said that?"

"What difference does it make?"

"It makes a lot of difference. I'm not going to lie. I need to know which rav you asked, because I'm sure Mendy will ask me the same question."

Yochai shrugged. "We didn't ask, and we have no intention of asking. It's irrelevant. And you'll do what you're told, understood?"

Meir rose defiantly. "Sorry, Yochai, but not in this case. There are many things that I'll do for you, and that I've done for you in the past. There are things that you can force me to do, and have forced me to do. But there's a limit to what I can be forced to do, and you've just crossed that line. With all due respect, I will not relay false information that pertains to *halachah*, not to a Jew, and not to a gentile either."

Yochai was taken aback by the vehemence in Meir's voice, and he had been in the field long enough to know that the young man would not be swayed. He sighed disappointedly. "So what will you tell him?"

"Whatever the rav says."

"And what do you think he'll say?"

"Honestly? I don't know. I'm a simple Jew, Yochai. I'm not capable of making decisions that decide the fate of a Jewish *neshamah*. I'll ask, and tell Mendy whatever the rav says in response."

Yochai still looked frustrated. "I don't think you understand the situation fully. Mendy is in a very difficult position, morally and emotionally. His operators know that too, and that's one of the reasons they're doing everything possible to speed up their preparations for this final operation. They've been waiting twenty years for this, and they won't let themselves lose the opportunity." Never had Meir heard Yochai sound so tense.

Meir softened slightly, suddenly appreciating the tremendous weight that Yochai bore on his shoulders, the burden of his nation's security and lives. The man's level of *emunah* was nowhere near high enough to permit him to see that really, the burden wasn't being carried by him at all.

"Yochai," he expressed gently, "I… Besides for this, I'd do anything to help you. Honestly. But there's something else I don't understand. You have no trouble hiding people. Why don't you just spirit Mendy out of the country, change his identity, and save his life that way?"

"You're asking a very good question," Yochai replied tiredly. "One day, I hope to be able to answer you. The only thing I can tell you right now is that our hands are tied. At this point, the GSS can't help Mendy. It's sad, but he's a lost cause. Mendy was right when he turned to you, because you're the only one in the world who is willing to listen to him with an open heart and considers him, as a person in his own right, in this awful game. From our perspective, he's simply an enemy who is threatening Jewish lives. Do you understand? He's a human time bomb, despite whatever wonderful qualities he may have."

"How soon do they plan to use him?" Meir felt sick at the thought.

"Any day. Any hour. Exactly when, I don't know, but very soon." Suddenly, Yochai looked terribly exhausted. He gazed at Meir, and for once, his expression was gentle, as if the dormant Jewish spark within him had been ignited. "Meir, I'm not a religious man, but I do believe in G-d. Still, I've never really prayed, and I don't know how to pray; but that doesn't mean that I don't believe in the power of prayer. Meir, you know how to pray. All I can recommend is that you pray for Mendy, and perhaps more importantly, pray that we manage to avert a terrible disaster for our nation. And pray for me too. My name is Yochai, Yochai *ben* Sarah."

"I will," Meir said emotionally.

"Thank you."

Meir left the office, reflecting that the meeting had been bizarre, but that he and Yochai had shared a moment of truth, and both had been deeply affected by it. It was only at that moment that he grasped the magnitude of the impending tragedy.

57

The thick vegetable soup smelled delicious, but Nachum refused to eat, even though he was hungry. He just sat there staring blankly at the steaming bowl without even touching his spoon. Shuli sat down beside him and put a comforting arm on his shoulder.

"Nachum, *zeeskeit*, please. I know it's hard for you, and it's hard for me too, but this is the challenge that Hashem is giving us now. Everything will work out. You'll see. Even the hardest times come to an end eventually."

"No," the boy's voice trembled. "None of these hard times are coming to an end. They're going to stay with us, forever and ever in our hearts. First we lost Tatty. And now we lost Mendy. He's my brother, and I miss him."

"Of course you do, and I know it's hard, but we have to focus on the future, not on the past."

Nachum's face twisted in pain and anger. "Mendy isn't just in the past. He's still here with us, in our hearts – and he's still alive, not like... Tatty." The little boy swallowed hard. "I can't just forget about him. And I can never replace him with that..." Nachum's voice trailed off. He had wanted to end with the word "Arab," but at the last minute, his sympathy for his mother won over and he held himself back. After all, the guy was his mother's son – which meant that he was his *brother*. The thought made Nachum sick.

Shuli looked at her son pleadingly. "I know, and maybe you're right, for the moment, but please, at least try to understand that he really is your brother, and that maybe one day, you'll even love him. Please?"

Nachum shook his head. "You don't love him either," he retorted, with a clarity that stunned and frightened Shuli. "How can you even *like* him? How can you even *think* of loving him? How can you compare him, in a million years, to Mendy? How can you *call* him Mendy? He's so… He's such a… He's, like, primitive – he grew up with all the trash, and I couldn't even stand listening to the way he spoke."

Shuli turned around so Nachum wouldn't see her tears, but he felt them anyway. How had he, at his young age, discerned the truth so quickly? He was right, so right. But didn't he realize how much it hurt her when he said it out loud? She had a child in the world whom she didn't even feel capable of loving, and acknowledging that failure was most difficult of all.

"Right, Mommy?" he asked pointedly, a note of triumph in his tone.

Shuli turned back to face him. "No, Nachum. You're wrong. You're not thinking straight. Imagine, for just a minute, that the baby fated to grow up in an Arab village was you, *chas v'shalom*. Imagine that you were the child surrounded by a bloodthirsty family that would love to kill you in cold blood, but they don't, just because they're not allowed to. Can you imagine living with a family that had been forced to raise you, but hated you just because you're really Jewish? Nachum, how do you think your brother should have turned out? It's a miracle that he turned out as gentle and kind and normal as he did."

Something in her outburst piqued Nachum's curiosity. "Why couldn't they just kill him? Why did they let him live?"

"Whenever a child, and even a baby dies, the police get involved. The last thing they wanted was the police taking an interest in their family," Shuli explained. "The family are real simple folks, dirt poor and not very intelligent, to say the least. They lived in some forsaken village in the Galilee, but they were specifically chosen for the job so that the plot would never be uncovered. Ironically, they were ordered to take good care of him so that he wouldn't die, so they hated him, but raised him nonetheless, while mourning their own child who had been taken from them. The Mendy that we knew. Your brother – your real brother – grew up in a terribly hostile environment, and he could never understand why he was rejected and hated, even though he thought he was just like them. He suffered a lot in his life, and he deserves a fair chance now. Nachum," she added, "I don't expect you to love him instantly. It's possible that you'll never really love him. But at least open your heart to pity him, as you would any unfortunate Jew. And especially one who was born your brother."

Nachum listened in silence without reacting. Only after she finished speaking did he ask a question that took her completely by surprise. "How could it be that Mendy was such a good *bachur*, if he was an Arab?"

Shuli thought carefully before answering. "The world is filled with all kinds of people. There are good people and bad people, talented people and those less talented. Generous people and stingy people. Mendy is a good person with a good heart, regardless of where he originally came from. Besides, a major part of a person's character is molded according to his upbringing and environment, and Mendy grew up with a frum family that loved him and did everything possible to raise him as an *ehrliche Yid* with good *middos*."

"That's not what I mean. I'm talking about the specialness inside of him."

Shuli took a deep breath, wondering if she should reveal the secret that Yochai had inadvertently disclosed. "Listen, Nachum, things are not always as they seem. There's a lot of confusion in our times, and often people discover things about themselves that they never dreamed could be true. Sometimes, *goyim* can find out that they're really Yidden, and people who always thought they were Yidden can suddenly discover that they're *goyim* and then they spontaneously decide to leave *Yiddishkeit*."

"Really?" Nachum looked scandalized.

"Yes. These things happen, and you know what? It's fine. By leaving *Yiddishkeit*, they're not even doing anything wrong because they don't have that *pintele Yid* inside of them. Then, there are also people who decide to convert, not because logic dictates that it's the right thing to do, but because their *neshamos* were there with us on Hair Sinai. They shouted '*Na'aseh v'nishma*' together with us, and they can feel it. It's not a matter of good or bad; it's just a matter of being a Yid."

Shuli exhaled a deep sigh and continued, "I know Mendy, and I know that he appreciates the *zechus* of being close to Hashem and the beauty and meaning inherent in a Yiddishe life, learning Torah and doing *mitzvos*. You know, until we found out the truth about Mendy, I never thought very deeply into the *brachah 'Shelo asani goy.'* But now, every day when I say it, I feel both sad and happy. I'm sad because Mendy, the son I raised as my own, is not a Yid; and I'm happy because I myself am a Yid. I could have been born to anyone in the world, and I was *zocheh* to be born Jewish. Do you realize how lucky we are, Nachum?"

"So what you're saying is that Mendy's *neshamah* is not Jewish?" the boy concluded.

"Actually, I can't say that for a fact," Shuli replied slowly and then decided to take the chance and share the secret, even at the risk of raising her son's hopes and having them crash down on his head. "I heard a rumor that Mendy might want to be *misgayer*, and I hope it's true. If it is, then I'm sure it's not for nothing that Hashem sent him to us, to raise him. But to be honest, Nachum, I don't think that Mendy is the point right now. The one we have to focus on now is… Jamil." It was hard for her to say his name.

"Why?"

"Because he is already Jewish. He was always a Jew, and he'll always be one. Unfortunately, he was raised in a horrific environment, but now he's here, trying to close the gap of years and searching for family. Nachum, it's a tremendous *chessed*, not to mention *kiruv rechokim*, to open our hearts and our home to him. Will you help me?" Her plea was so earnest that Nachum felt himself soften.

"Okay," he conceded. "I'll try to be nice."

Shuli smiled through her tears. "Look at him like he's a little brother. Not a big brother, like you thought of Mendy, but a little brother who needs your help and guidance. He's literally a *tinok shenishba*, and we have to look at him like he's a newborn who has to learn everything from the start."

Deep compassion welled up in Nachum's heart, but it was too late…

Yochai was fielding four calls simultaneously, three on internal lines and one on his cell phone, trying to contend with the sudden influx of information that had just arrived from Intelligence. Hence, his curt response to his secretary who buzzed him to say that Jamil was waiting to see him was, "Not now."

Three minutes later, however, Jamil barged into the office, shocking Yochai to the extent that he actually ended all four calls simultaneously and gazed daggers at the intruder.

"I said, 'not now.' Who let you in?" he demanded angrily.

"Nobody. I didn't ask," Jamil replied breezily.

"What do you want?"

"I need to speak to you. Yochai, listen, you're the one who decided that I don't belong in my Arab village. You located both my families – my Arab family and my Jewish family. You led me from one world to the other."

"So?"

"But I don't belong in a Jewish world."

His tone was so earnest and sad that all Yochai could think to reply was, "What?"

"I don't belong with that family. Are you sure they're my real family?"

"Sure I'm sure. And I'm also sure that I'm not your shrink. What do you want from me?"

"I don't know. They treat me like I'm a terrorist, and I can't take it. Those kids, who are supposed to be my brother and sister, hate my guts. They think I'm going to try to kill them. And that lady who's supposed to be my mom cries all day long about her son."

"*You're* her son."

"Not really."

"Yes, you are. Jamil, you don't know what's going on behind the scenes. If you did, you'd shut up and just say, 'Thank you very much.'"

"Then, thank you very much, but I don't belong there," Jamil insisted. "I need to find somewhere else to be."

"So go talk to your mother."

"She's not my mother, or at least she doesn't feel like it, and neither do I."

"Talk to her anyway. She's a smart woman."

"The thing is, I do like the *yeshivah* learning," Jamil added tangentially. "It's very satisfying. I don't get why somebody would be Jewish and not take advantage of the learning. Why don't you learn too?"

Yochai had long since lost his patience. "Say, do you see a sign for a psychologist in this room?"

Jamil glanced around. "No."

"Good, so beat it. Why are you asking me these questions? Do you want to return to the village or stay in *yeshivah*?"

"It's better in the *yeshivah*."

"I'm glad to hear it. And you know what? The reason you're tempted to return to your past is only because people are always tempted to return to what's familiar, as terrible as it may have been. If you can overcome that intrinsic pull, you'll become a normal person; because the other option is surrendering to an awful fate. It's your choice, Jamil, and I'm telling you that as a friend, not a therapist – which I'm not."

Jamil nodded in slow acceptance. "I guess the best choice would be to say goodbye to my family and enroll in a *yeshivah* somewhere else. It's too hard to see them on a regular basis, trying to hide their tears or avoid me or whatever."

"Sounds like an excellent plan," Yochai said encouragingly, congratulating himself on his unprecedented show of patience. "Time will pass. They'll recover and get used to the idea, as you will too, and then you'll get to know each other."

"Do you know of a *yeshivah* where—"

Yochai had reached his breaking point. "No, I don't. But I'm sure you can find one if you try hard enough. Now if you'll be on your way, I have a lot to do."

"Okay. Thank you. I was almost tempted to go— Forget it. It doesn't matter." With that, he was gone.

The phones rang persistently, but Yochai was too distracted to answer them, his mind still on the bizarre conversation he had just had with Jamil.

Within several days, arrangements were made for Jamil to transfer to a *yeshivah* for *baalei teshuvah* located in Yerushalayim. Shuli purchased an entire wardrobe for her son and packed everything, along with a huge assortment of home-baked goods, into an oversize suitcase.

"I don't eat that much!" Jamil pointed out, too polite to tell her the truth which was that he really didn't care too much for home-style Jewish coking. He had grown up with a different array of flavors, mostly sharp and pungent, along with endless doses of Turkish coffee instead of that sickly-sweet, soft stuff the Israelis drank. In his opinion, Shuli's menu was either over-spiced or completely bland, two extremes that he couldn't fathom. Although at first he had enjoyed some of her cakes, he had quickly lost taste for them, instead reminiscing about good old baklava.

He felt a twinge in his heart when she stuffed yet another foil-wrapped kugel into his suitcase, regretting that all that good food would go to waste. Maybe he would manage to find someone in his new *yeshivah* who would enjoy it, he hoped.

"It's really okay. I don't need so much. I'm only one person." Jamil was starting to get annoyed by now, worried that the smell of the food would cling to his new clothes. Shuli refused to take back any of the food, however, although she did resist stuffing in another bag of cinnamon buns.

Just before he was set to leave, she opened her wallet and removed a small wad of bills. "Here, this is for you."

"Really?" Jamil stared at the money.

"Of course."

"Can you afford it?" he asked uncomfortably, knowing that as a widow, she couldn't be rich, but still deeply touched by the gesture. "Half of that is more than I need," he added quickly, and he immediately discerned the relief in her eyes. She had offered him the money out of the goodness of her heart, despite knowing that she would have to tighten the belt at home.

"Are you sure?" she asked, concerned, and Jamil had never felt so cared for. Back in the Arab village, no one had ever treated him with such kindness or compassion.

"Absolutely. And if I ever need any more, I can get a job in my spare time. I grew up in a very different world. There, the children work to support their parents; here, you support your own children."

"But you don't have to work. You're one of us," she smiled encouragingly.

"Yes. I'm a Jew." He said this with a strange note in his voice, a blend of happiness and sadness and confusion. Could he really miss his wretched life in the village? *How* could he?

It was time to leave by then, as far as Jamil was concerned, but just before he started to say goodbye, Shuli stopped him and asked him to wait so the children could say goodbye too.

"It's okay," he said firmly. "Just tell them I said goodbye."

"Are you sure?"

"Positive."

He left, dragging his suitcase, on his way to the central bus stop in the settlement. On his way, he noticed curious neighbors peeking out from behind curtains. None of them knew the identity of the newly-arrived widow and her sad, quiet children, and certainly not of the eldest son, who had obviously gone astray but seemed to be on the road back to observance.

Jamil took the first bus headed north, even though it wasn't going to Yerushalayim but rather to Hadera. From there, he would figure out the way to his village, and then make his way back down south to his new *yeshivah*. Once he was enrolled there, it would be far more complicated to make the trip, the trip that his heart was yearning to make.

Finally, after over five hours on the road, he reached the nearest spot he could access via an Israeli bus, and he alighted and flagged down a cab, naming his hometown as his destination. The cab driver stared at him in disbelief. "Either you're kidding me, or you've got the wrong address, because that's an Arab village."

"I'm not kidding. If you don't want to enter, you can drop me on the highway and I'll make my own way in."

"It's very dangerous," the driver warned him anxiously, eyeing the *kippah* on his head. "You're a religious kid, so you should know that it's forbidden to risk your life."

Ignoring him, Jamil opened the passenger door and slipped in beside him. "It's fine. Just go."

Shaking his head, the driver floored the gas. "The only thing I can imagine anyone doing in that place is rescuing some poor kidnapped girl, and I have lots of respect for Yad L'Achim for all they do, but I can't understand why they would think to endanger innocent taxi drivers…" The man prattled on, hardly noticing that Jamil didn't seem to understand a word of what he was saying. "You know, I've been wondering, I don't wear a *kippah*, but I cover my head if I go to a *beit knesset* or a *levayah*. You think that's okay?"

Jamil stared blankly at him. "Huh?"

"I'm wondering about the actual *kippah* thing. I mean, is there a difference between a *kippah* and a baseball cap, or are both okay?"

"Um, I guess," Jamil stammered.

"So why do you folks insist on wearing *kippahs*? Why don't you wear anything else?"

"Listen, friend, I really don't know. I've just started wearing a *kippah* myself, and I don't know too much about it," Jamil confessed.

"Really? Now, that's impressive. It must have taken a lot of courage!" the driver complimented him. "I wish I had it in me. It takes strength of character to search for the truth and to try to live by it. As you can see, I'm not religious, but I do believe in G-d and that the Torah is true…"

Ten minutes later, the cab pulled to a stop on the highway outside the village. Shocking his passenger, the driver put his hands on Jamil's head and gravely recited, "*Yevarechecha Hashem v'yishmirecha…* I may not be religious, but I am a *kohen*, so I hope my blessing means something. How did you get into Yad L'Achim so quickly if you just became religious? You must be really talented…"

Jamil paid the fare, not even trying to make sense of the man's monologue. "Thanks for the ride," he murmured.

"Take care of yourself!" the driver said, his concern showing on his face as he drove away.

Shaking his head at the amusing encounter, Jamil crossed the street and found himself on the dirt path leading to the village. As expected, nothing had changed since the last time he had been there.

It was already spring, but the weather was still cool in the Galilee, even at that hour of the day. A breeze wafted into his nostrils, carrying the odors of fodder and fresh fields that stretched ahead as far as the eye could see. From the distance, he could hear Yasser's whistle as he herded his flocks in the pasture.

These were the smells and sounds of his childhood, and though his childhood had not been replete with happy memories, the place was still home to him.

He hiked up the path, removing his *kippah* as he did and tucking it into his pocket. The village was quiet and empty at this midafternoon hour which many passed with a siesta. It wasn't long before he reached his house, which he was surprised to see was brightly lit and occupied by a young family. *It must have been sold*, he concluded.

He decided to try his luck at the neighboring home, and met Jabbar exiting his house on his way to his storeroom to collect more firewood in preparation for a cold night. Jabbar stopped short when his eyes fell on Jamil.

"You're back?" he gaped in disbelief.

"I came to speak to you, Jabbar."

"What do you want?" the man asked harshly. "You're one of them now. Don't you get it? You don't belong here anymore."

"Is my father in touch with you?"

"He's not your father," Jabbar retorted sharply. "I can't believe you still call him 'Father.' What else do you want him to do before you drop the title? But, to answer your question, I spoke to him about a month ago, and he said that it would have been better if they had been allowed to kill you when you were still a baby. Now he fears your revenge, and Samira does too, even though she didn't always know that you weren't hers. You know, she pitied you at first, but when she discovered the truth, she grew to hate you more than any of us. What are you doing here?"

"I don't know. I really don't know what to do, Jabbar. I don't belong either here or there. I'm nothing. Do you know what I'm saying? They look at me like an Arab, and you guys think I'm a Jew. I'm so confused."

The simple-minded farmer stared at him. "*Ya*-Jamil, do you remember that I always opened my door to you after your father beat you? Do you remember all those times you came to me in tears, and I took pity on you? And you know why? Because it really doesn't make a difference to me if you're an Arab or a *Yahud*. You're a person, as far as I'm concerned. But I'll tell you this now, so that you'll know the truth. Whatever happens, you're better off with them than you are here. You belong more to them than you do to us. Here, you've got nothing. They hate you, and they'll always hate you. Go back to the *Yahud*. It'll take time, but you can get used to it there and have a good life, or whatever's left of it." He stopped short, his eyes flitting about in fear as he belatedly realized that he had said too much.

"What was that you just said?" Jamil asked, his whole body stiffening.

"Oh, nothing. It doesn't matter." Jabbar's tone was unnaturally high.

"You said, 'whatever's left of it.' What's that supposed to mean? That I'm going to die? Why?"

"Because you're a tool, that's all. So is the one who grew up with the *Yahud*. You serve a purpose in this world; each one of you. He has a purpose to kill, and your purpose is to be… Whatever, each man and his destiny," he ended philosophically.

Jamil glared at him. "Talk straight, Jabbar."

"You won't tell a soul?"

"No."

"Okay, so they want to kill you as revenge against the *Yahud*. And you're still coming back here! Now how crazy is that?" He laughed in amusement, but Jamil remained rooted in place, too terrified to utter a word. In the Jewish world, all that awaited him was rejection and disillusionment; in the Arab world, what awaited him was death.

Those were his options.

"*Baruch haba!*" a rabbi greeted him with a broad smile. "I'm Rabbi Feinberg, the *rosh yeshivah*. We heard that you were coming, but we were expecting you hours ago. Did you have a hard time finding the place?"

"Uh, no. I just made a small detour beforehand."

If the rabbi was surprised, he didn't show it.

Jamil glanced around the old, dilapidated building, which despite its physical appearance, exuded warmth and vibrancy.

"Fine, in any case, we're glad you're here. I'll show you your room, and then you can come down to dinner when you're ready. It's this way," Rabbi Feinberg continued, pointing the way and starting to head down the corridor.

Jamil, distracted by the commotion and the newness of everything, somehow managed to set off in the opposite direction, and Rabbi Feinberg turned around in surprise. "Mendy! It's this way!" But if Jamil heard him, he gave no indication.

"Mendy! Mendy Brand!" The *rosh yeshivah* stared in confusion. Maybe the new *bachur* had a hearing disability? Swiftly he headed after him, tapping him on the shoulder until he finally succeeded in getting his attention.

"Mendy, you're going the wrong way. Didn't you hear me calling you?" he asked him.

"No! I didn't hear anything," Jamil replied in surprise.

"That's okay, Mendy. It takes time to get used to a new place."

"I'm not Mendy. My name is—"

Feinberg looked astonished. "You're not? I'm so sorry. Maybe there's been a mistake. I was expecting a new *talmid* named Mendy Brand. That's not you?"

"Oh, yes. I mean, it is. Yeah, you can call me Mendy," Jamil stammered, realizing that going by the name "Jamil" wouldn't do anything to increase his popularity in this new place.

"Okay, so the dorm is this way." For the time being, the *rosh yeshivah* decided to overlook the new boy's strange behavior, attributing it to anxiety and excitement at this major step he was taking in life. He chatted lightly with him, trying to calm his nerves. "Actually, someone came by earlier in the day, asking if you'd shown up yet," he mentioned in the course of their conversation. "He wanted to make sure that you had been given a good room and a suitable *chavrusa*. It's nice that you've got someone out there looking out for you."

"Someone came by? Who was he?" Jamil's voice rose anxiously.

"He said that he was a relative."

"And you told him about me?" Jamil pressed, practically frantic.

"It's okay, Mendy," the *rosh yeshivah* said soothingly, accustomed to high-strung characters. "You've had a long trip. Why don't you settle in, have something to eat, lie down for a bit, and then come to my office for a talk."

"No. Let's talk now," Jamil said forcefully, his voice loud enough to cause a few heads to turn in his direction. Several boys passing by in the corridor looked shocked by his outburst. No one ever dared raised his voice to the *rosh yeshivah* – yet the latter maintained his composure.

"What would you like to talk about?" he asked patiently.

"I want to know who that man was."

"He left me his number, and if I remember correctly, he said his name was Binyamin. He actually seemed quite worried about you, and he said that if you ever need any help with anything, you shouldn't hesitate to call him."

"Give me the number."

Ignoring the rudeness of the request, the *rosh yeshivah* slipped his hand into his jacket pocket and glanced through several small notes before handing one to Jamil. He paused a moment before adding, "He also asked me to notify him if you ever leave the *yeshivah* premises to go on a *tiyul* or for any other reason."

"What's it got to do with him?" Jamil demanded angrily.

"I was also surprised by the request, actually," Rabbi Feinberg admitted, "and I didn't promise to inform him, as I wanted to ask you about it first. Although he did sound very concerned about your welfare," he continued, frowning, "so much so, that at first I assumed he was your father, until he told me otherwise."

"My father died."

"Was *niftar*," Rabbi Feinberg corrected smoothly.

"Whatever. He's not here anymore," Jamil conceded, stuffing the note into his pocket. "Okay, thank you for showing me around. I guess I'll try and settle in now."

"When you're ready, I'll introduce you to your *chavrusa*."

"Thank you," Jamil murmured, waiting with feigned patience for the *rosh yeshivah* to disappear before racing to the payphone in the hall and punching in the numbers on the paper.

An unfamiliar voice answered. "Hello?"

"Who's this?" Jamil demanded.

"Who are you looking for?"

"Binyamin, or whoever came to investigate Mendy Brand."

"Who is this?" the voice sounded suspicious.

"Mendy Brand. Who is this?" he fired again.

"Wrong number," the voice replied and ended the call.

Jamil felt a rising wave of fury and immediately dialed again, realizing he had erred in revealing all his cards during the first conversation. To his surprise, the man actually answered.

"I already told you that you've got the wrong number," he said upon hearing Jamil's voice again. "Don't call back."

"It's not a wrong number. What do you want from me? Who are you?"

"It *is* a mistake, and if you call again, I'll—" The line went dead.

Jami felt ready to explode and dialed a third time, but his call went directly to the voice mail. Determined to succeed even though he knew how pointless were his efforts, Jamil spent the next half hour dialing and dialing again, but his calls always went straight to the voice mail. And all the while, Jabbar's words reverberated in his mind: *They're waiting to kill you. You're a tool in their hands. You'll serve a purpose.*

Jamil was terrified, and he wondered if he should escape this place before it was too late. He attended night *seder* that evening for the first time, but couldn't concentrate. The *rosh yeshivah* patiently explained that it was completely normal, and that even brilliant academic professors were often challenged by their initial foray into *Gemara* – and Jamil felt like screaming at the man.

Finally, at half past ten he made up his mind. After locating another payphone in a more secluded part of the building, he dialed Yochai's number at the office, and the agent answered him on the first ring.

"Yochai. It's me. I'm in *yeshivah*."

"That's good to hear. What do you need?" Yochai replied, always pragmatic and loath to waste time on pleasantries.

"Listen, the *rosh yeshivah* told me that someone came by here to ask about me, but he doesn't know who it was except for the fact that the guy claimed to be a relative. What do you think that means? Am I in danger?"

Yochai was silent for a long moment. "What do you know about this person?" he answered finally.

"Nothing at all except a name, Binyamin. But I do have his phone number."

"Give it to me."

"It won't help. The calls just go straight to voice mail. I tried calling already, tons of times, but whoever it was that answered said I had the wrong number. I kept trying, but after the first few times, the phone was always switched off."

"Just give me the number," Yochai ordered impatiently.

Jamil dictated the number and Yochai scribbled it onto a paper. "Okay, don't worry, kid. And don't you go gallivanting again into Arab villages where you might get yourself killed," he added, to Jamil's surprise. "Better to work on settling down and building your life here."

"What life? They want to kill me! What chance do I have of evading them?"

"No one wants to kill you. You're not important enough to anyone now."

"I've been told otherwise."

"We know everything you're told. But nobody knows where you are right now, except for your mother and us. The person who asked about you is probably one of your bodyguards. But he'll pay big time for his rashness."

"It was one of your men?" Jamil reacted, astonished. "What a fool!"

"Agreed, but we'll take care of it," Yochai replied darkly.

"So I'm not in any danger?"

"No."

They ended the call, Jamil feeling relieved, but Yochai on the verge of exploding.

Grabbing the phone, he dialed the number that he already knew by heart and left a furious message on the answering machine. "Are you insane? What were you thinking? Do you want to get him killed? Do you want to get them all killed? What were you thinking?" he ranted into the voice mail before slamming the phone down angrily.

When disaster struck, they would all return to blame him.

Laser sat at his desk, studying the maps. "That kid is a total mess. He doesn't go to work, and he's not following orders anymore. It's time to finish off this mission once and for all. I'm sorry to say that this won't be on the scale that we imagined, nothing like the Twin Towers, but it will still be something," he added in disappointment.

In his megalomania, Laser had foreseen himself as the next Bin Laden. He had been a passionate supporter of his hero during his lifetime, and had spent the last few years reading every available article and biography of the man in an effort to understand the secret of his greatness and emulate his brilliance. Laser's ultimate dream had been to carry out an attack that would eradicate tens of thousands of people in one stroke, but even twenty years of patient waiting now seemed virtually wasted, and he was desperate to salvage at least something from his brilliantly conceived but poorly executed plan.

"It was a mistake to wait so long," he admitted to his aide. "At one point, I was sure this would be something to rival the Twin Towers, something that would be an even bigger sensation, as it would be carried out by one of their own. But I see that it was a mistake to wait. We should have hit while the iron was still hot, but now, the boy's lost his motivation."

"So what do we do?"

"Plan a smaller-scale attack. There are two reasons for this: First of all, the kid was never trained by the Israeli army, so he's completely unskilled. Second, he's not at peace with his mission, and if we wait any longer, we'll lose him completely. He's already fading on us, but if we lose him entirely, the Israelis win."

"Why doesn't he turn to them for help?"

"He knows that they know that we won't ever leave him in peace, and they're both right."

"But why should he listen to us at all?"

"Because we have his Jewish family in our gun sights, and he'll want to save them. Enough. Down to business. We've got three options, as I see it, and I want you to help me make a final decision." Laser then proceeded to detail the three possibilities to his aide, who acknowledged that all were brilliant, creative, and possible. Yet only one plan – the one that would lead to the largest number of casualties – would be selected.

Naomi returned home from work to find her husband sitting listlessly on the couch. "What's wrong?" she asked in concern.

"I don't know what to do," he muttered, his head in his hands.

Naomi felt her heart begin to pound. What was Meir doing at home at this hour? And what was he so anxious about? Usually, he was so easy-going and confident, regardless of what was going on. A quick glance at her watch told her that it was one o'clock already – the children would be home in fifteen minutes, which meant that they had better find a solution before then. But a solution to what?

"Meir?" she said gently, reminding him of her presence.

Her husband bit his lip. "I went to *kollel* this morning, but then I received a call that the rav wanted to see me. So I dropped everything and went."

"Of course."

"Of course," he repeated.

"Nu, what did he say?"

"Don't ask."

"I already did."

"Don't," he gasped the word as if in genuine pain. Naomi's uncharacteristic silence actually prompted her husband to continue. "Anyway, the rav said that he understands that I'm close with someone who's looking to convert. Obviously, he meant Mendy."

Naomi took a deep breath. "Okay. How terrible is that?"

"Not terrible at all, until I noticed these two guys hanging around the rav's house. Naomi, I can tell who's real and who's not, and let me tell you, those guys were not real. One of them was dressed *chareidi*, but he was wearing sneakers. When I asked about him, the rav explained that he's on the road back to *teshuvah*, and that he started hanging out in the house in the past few days. The other fellow was a gas technician who supposedly discovered a leak several days ago and fixed it, but he's been returning to check it every single day now for the past week. How strange is that? Worse yet, I think he looks like an Arab. Do you know what all this tells me? And, the rav is so innocent of all this, that he has no clue what he's gotten into. What *I've* gotten him into."

Naomi could hardly breathe, and for once, she was silent as she waited for her husband to finish speaking.

"Mendy either realized or didn't realize that he would get the rav into trouble simply by asking him his question. There are two groups who are watching him; the first is Yochai's, and the other are the Arabs. Oh, Naomi, you were right! Whoever comes into contact with this guy gets into major trouble, like me. And now I've messed up the rav too! I should have anticipated this, but now it's too late."

"What did the rav tell you?" Naomi changed direction.

"He spoke a bit about Mendy, and how it's a tremendous *mitzvah* to be *mekarev* him. Naomi, I practically thought I would have a heart attack. The door was closed, but everyone in the house was listening in on us. It's like the rav's house with all its secrets just became a mini-Headquarters."

"I wonder if the Arabs realize that the Israelis suspect something," she mused.

"Why are you wondering about that?"

"I don't know… And, from what you say, I don't think the rav is in any danger."

"That's what you think? Maybe – if only – but I still feel terrible. It's not like I gave him a choice about putting himself in this situation. He simply wasn't aware of the implications of getting involved."

"What can you do now, in any case?" she shrugged helplessly.

Meir shook his head. "I wish I knew. Anyway, do you want to hear the end of the story?"

"Okay."

"As soon as I left the house, who do I meet outside? Mendy. He gave me a huge smile; he was sure that... well, you know, that the rav would give him a warm reception, and Heaven knows he needs the support. Instead, however, I told him that he should be ashamed of himself for putting the rav in danger. If he has any spark of a Jew inside of him, he should just stop playing with fire. Mendy turned white and said, '*You're* the one playing with fire. Just be quiet and do what you're told.' Then, he turned around without even bothering to go in to the rav. Naomi, I don't know what to do anymore!" Meir cried in distress.

Naomi was quiet. "Well, if it's as you say, then Mendy didn't get scared for nothing. I don't think that anyone plans on hurting an old rav, but I do think that he was frightened at the thought that you exposed his Arab trackers. Apparently, the Arabs don't yet realize that the Israelis are onto them."

Meir looked thoughtful. "I guess that's possible," he mused.

"It is. And another thing that's clear is that you can't continue meeting him. As soon as they discover that you're important to him, they'll want to hurt us," Naomi added firmly.

"So what do we do? Later, he called me again and told me that he's coming by tonight to discuss things—"

"And I hope you told him that he can't," Naomi interjected.

"Of course I did, but he said that he's got no one else to help him. Only me."

Naomi sagged at the thought. "So what do we do?" she whispered helplessly.

"I don't know. That's what I've been doing sitting here for the last two hours," Meir confessed. "Trying to come up with a solution."

Naomi sat down next to him on the couch and listened to her husband speak. "I've been asking myself every day why this is happening to me. I tried to help, I tried to do a *mitzvah*, and look where it got us! Into the deepest *tzarah* ever!"

She thought for a moment before replying. "I've actually got an idea."

"You do?"

"Yes. Why don't we disappear for a bit?" she suggested. "We'll go to my grandmother's house in Netivot. He'll never think to look for us there. Then, we'll wait it out until things… resolve themselves, shall we say, and afterward, we'll come back. It's not so easy to arrange with the children and everything, but I hope it will work out. Right now, our primary responsibility is to take care of the kids and ensure their safety."

"So you want to pull a disappearing act?" he asked doubtfully.

"Exactly!" Naomi exclaimed, proud of her idea. "I'll give notice at work that I have to take a long-term leave, and you can do the same at *kollel* and with your private students. The children will be in seventh heaven, and Savta will be even happier. She loves when we come… though, well, I hope she won't mind that we don't exactly have a time frame for this," she concluded doubtfully. "But we don't really have another option, the way I see it."

Meir nodded glumly. Once again, his wife was right. Had she been right all along?

"Okay. I'll call her now," Naomi stood up to get the phone.

"No! Don't call!" Meir stopped her before she left the room. "If you tell her over the phone, we'll lose the opportunity. We have no idea who's listening in to us or recording what we're saying. I say we order a cab and go straight to Netivot without telling anyone beforehand."

Naomi swallowed hard. If her Meir was that worried, then things were really bad.

In the end, they had five hours to put their plan into effect, as Mendy had said he would only be coming by that evening. He desperately wanted Meir's support, and Meir had no doubt that Mendy would search for him, but he was certain that in Netivot, he would never find him. He would knock on the door, call his cell phone again and again at all hours of the day and night, but to no avail.

It wasn't exactly commendable that he was running away from him, Meir knew, but it was much worse that Mendy was intentionally putting his family and children at risk. Admittedly, Mendy was on his own and in terrible distress, like someone drowning in a stormy ocean, clutching at any straw as he tried to overcome the waves. But Meir still had to put his own family first.

Just before they left, Meir stuck a small note to the front door. *Dear Mendy, please don't come looking for us because we'll be gone for the next few months. I believe in you. Be strong. I wish I could help you, but I can't. All I can do, and will do, is daven for you.*

He perused the sign briefly, feeling terribly guilty.

"You can't help it. It's not your fault," Naomi said soothingly. "He may be a special *neshamah*, but our lives still take priority. You know, '*Chayecha v'chayei chavercha…*'"

"I know," Meir murmured.

"Maybe you should refer him to someone else who can help him?" she suggested.

"Like who?"

"I'm not sure."

"Who should we endanger this time?" he rejoined bitterly.

"I don't know," she sighed, appreciating the extent of their dilemma.

The taxi pulled up, and the Landsmans quietly shepherded their family inside. Meir didn't even bother updating Yochai on the change in plans.

Not that he needed to be informed. Yochai had his own ways of knowing these things.

61

Jamil rose early the next morning and smiled in pleasure at the view from his window. Maybe he could make a fresh start here? The possibility excited him.

"Good morning!" a voice greeted him from outside his room, accompanied by knocking at the door.

Jamil opened, and his jaw dropped when he found himself facing none other than the *rosh yeshivah* himself.

"Good morning, rabbi."

"*Davening* and breakfast, Brand," Rabbi Feinberg reminded him with a smile.

"Thanks. I'm just getting up now."

"You'd better hurry if you don't want to miss *Kriyas Shema shel Shacharis*."

"Okay, I won't miss it," he promised. He dressed quickly and hurried downstairs to the *beis medrash* where dozens of boys were already assembled, bedecked in *tefillin*. Jamil had learned how to lay *tefillin* in his previous *yeshivah*, but he still sometimes got stuck when it came to winding the straps correctly. He had attended plenty of classes in the past, but had basically spaced out during prayers. Before he left, Shuli had given him a beautiful leather-bound *siddur* with the name "Mendel Brand" embossed on the cover. He still couldn't identify with the name, but there was something about the Jewish prayers that touched a chord deep in his heart, and he had promised himself that in his new *yeshivah*, he would make a real effort to connect to *davening*.

Fortunately, he had learned how to read basic Hebrew back in elementary school in the village, so he was able to follow along quite easily, although he got a bit confused when it was time to skip pages. A short *bachur* sitting nearby noticed his bewilderment and scooted closer to him, helping him find the correct page and follow along throughout the service.

Even though he could speak modern Hebrew fluently by now, Jamil knew his *lashon hakodesh* skills were not up to par, and he wondered if he would ever feel at home in the prayer book. The beginning paragraphs and blessings were self-explanatory, until he got to *Birkos Hashachar. What's a sechvi?* he wondered.

"*Shelo asani goy.*" A lump formed in his throat as he recited this second blessing. *Your Father in Heaven, the Father of all Jews, made you a Jew, not a gentile. Jamil, you're lucky to be here!* For the first time, Jamil actually felt that he did really want to be where he was, not because of the comfortable conditions or because it opened the door to a new life, but rather because he felt that here, in the *yeshivah*, his Father in Heaven was close by, watching over him, showering love and gifts upon His children.

In the midst of that *tefillas Shacharis* in the *yeshivah beis medrash*, Jamil discovered himself as a Jew.

His inspiration faltered slightly during the ensuing breakfast. He joined a half-occupied table and tried participating in the lively chatter, but the moment he opened his mouth, he was treated to strange looks.

"You're from here?" one of the guys asked.

"Yeah."

"From where? I can't place your accent..."

Jamil's heart sank as he wondered how he would ever overcome this obstacle. Obviously, none of them dreamed that his accent was really Arabic.

Then, the short guy who had offered his assistance during *Shacharis* turned to him. "Are you a *baal teshuvah* or a *ger*?" he asked him casually.

"Why are you asking?" Jamil retorted defensively.

The guy blushed. "Sorry. I just thought that maybe you were an Arab convert."

"Well, I'm not. I've always been Jewish."

"No problem. Hope I didn't say anything out of line. It was just a thought. It's just that my dad has a bunch of Arab employees, and your accent is very similar to theirs. Some of them actually come from Spain, rather than here. Maybe you're Spanish?"

"Yes, actually I am," Jamil replied, without missing a beat. While working in the grocery store months earlier, he had run into several Spanish Jews, one of whom had described the spiritual desert in Spain. The country boasted few Jews, and those few were quickly assimilating into oblivion. It was a good, safe choice, he congratulated himself.

But it also got him into trouble. Later that day, the short guy approached him during a break and said a few words in some unintelligible tongue, clearly proud of himself for his tactic.

"What did you say?" Jamil asked in confusion.

"You said you're Spanish, didn't you?" The *bachur's* tone was accusatory.

"Yeah. What of it?"

"Well, I just spoke to you in Spanish, and you didn't understand a word."

"Oh." Jamil swallowed his humiliation and looked around furtively in all directions to make sure there were no unwelcome listeners. "Listen, friend, I'd rather not share where my accent is from, and I didn't dream that there was anybody Spanish here in the *yeshivah*. Listen… Would you mind…"

The short guy grinned understandingly. "No problem, Brand. Your secret's safe with me. But I still think it's a shame that you feel you have to lie. Lying is a terrible sin, and as Jews, we try to avoid it. By the way," he added as an afterthought, "my name is Yitzchak."

"I'm sure I'm allowed to lie about such a thing," Jamil argued stubbornly.

Yitzchak shrugged. "I don't know. You should probably ask a *she'eilah*."

"How do I do that?"

Yitzchak looked confused. "You go to a rav," he explained patiently, understanding that this young man still had a lot to learn. "Don't worry," he added, "you'll get it all eventually. There are a ton of concepts and *mitzvos* and expectations, but you'll figure it all out… By the way, who are you learning with?"

"I don't know yet. They need to to test me and find out which level I'm on before they assign me someone, so in the meanwhile, I'm learning by myself, with the rabbi assisting me as often as he can."

"So I'll learn with you," Yitzchak offered spontaneously.

"Thanks."

They became fast friends, perhaps because of the secret that Yitzchak had uncovered. Yitzchak was a laid-back fellow, but Jamil still kept up his guard. He made discreet inquiries about the boy and discovered that he had joined the *yeshivah* only a week before him. Yitzchak was considered an all-round great guy. He was extremely eager to learn more about Judaism and to make major changes in his life.

One evening, as night *seder* was winding down, Jamil summoned the courage to ask a question that had been bothering him. "Hey, Yitz, what possessed you to find out about Judaism?"

"Well, I finished my army service and capped it off with a trip to South America like everyone… I was a medic in the army, and I was planning to go to law school. On the outside, life couldn't be better, but I still felt like I was missing something, so I began asking myself questions. And those questions hurt."

"And did you find the answers?"

"So that's just it. I went to an Arachim seminar. Ever heard of it? It's a three-day retreat where they give you Judaism in a nutshell. I found a lot of the answers there, and that made me do a full stop."

"Funny that we came here at exactly the same time."

"I guess."

"Very."

Jamil suspected everyone and trusted no one, even his faithful friend and *chavrusa*, Yitzchak, who dormed in the room next to his. Something in his heart didn't permit him to trust the fellow. Perhaps he was just a bit too friendly, too light-hearted, too ingratiating... Everything was just a bit too much... The fact that he had discovered Jamil's secret but kept it to himself only added to his suspicions. On the other hand, it was nice to have at least one friend in the place, and it was a relief that there was one other guy who was almost as ignorant of the rules as him.

Still, Jamil remained ever vigilant with his finger on the pulse and kept his distance from the guys, including Yitzchak, to the greatest extent possible. Then, after two weeks of progress, he discovered one significant detail that Yitzchak had conveniently forgotten to share...

Yochai folded his arms across his chest and stared blankly at the ceiling. After a moment of listlessness, he reached for the phone and dialed Meir's cell phone number. Not unexpectedly, it rang seven times before Meir plucked up the courage to answer.

"Hey, Meir. What's up?" Yochai's tone of voice was suspiciously smooth and silky, and Meir felt his hair stand on end.

"*Baruch Hashem*. A bit busy. You need something important?"

"What exactly are you busy with?"

"What's the difference?"

"Oh, no difference. Just that somebody's been asking about you, and I wasn't sure if I should tell him that you're vacationing down south or not."

"Who's asking?"

"A friend of yours. Someone you've been seeing a lot of lately. Get my drift?"

"Mendy?"

"Well done, Meir! How did you guess so quickly?"

Meir held onto the phone with hands suddenly slippery with perspiration, gazing unseeingly out of the window of the taxi, oblivious to the stunning scenery they were passing. Naomi was sitting at his side, smiling and relaxed as Meir hadn't seen her in months. They each had a child on their lap, and another one between them, all of them fast asleep. They had been so sure that they were on the road to freedom and peace of mind, but that illusion was now being swiftly shattered.

"Yochai, if you dare breathe a word about where—"

"Oh, you didn't want to me to tell?" Yochai feigned innocence. "All I said was that you're on your way to Netivot to visit your grandmother, and not to get too upset by the note you stuck on your door. I reassured him that you've still got a heart of gold and that you won't turn him away."

"Stop it. You're lying."

"Lying? Me? Meir, seriously. Would I lie about something as serious as this?"

"So then tell me it's a good joke."

"The only jokester here is you."

"What's that supposed to mean?"

"You don't abandon a mission in the middle, do you understand that?" Yochai retorted sharply, abruptly reverting to true form.

"I didn't ask for this mission, and I never wanted it in the first place, so I'm perfectly entitled to walk out whenever I please. I'm on my way to Netivot now, and the only person with power to harm me is you. And if you dare to lay a finger on me, I'll take you to court."

"Ooh, I'm scared."

A cold hand clutched at Meir's heart, strangling him in fear.

"You gave him the address? You really did that?"

"I sure did."

"Don't you get that they're following him wherever he goes? Do you know that? Why are you risking my life? How dare you endanger my wife and kids?"

"*You're* the one who put yourself in danger, Meir. Until now, everyone was sure that your only connection with him was Judaism, and your fanatical desire to get him to be *chozer b'teshuvah.* But now that you're running away, you've proven that you know other stuff too. Not very intelligent, my friend. You're in a taxi right now, aren't you?"

"Yes," Meir confessed.

"Look to your left. See a black car?"

Meir's head whipped to the left, and his heart plummeted. "Yes," he rasped.

"Take it easy. Those are our boys. But look to your right. See a blue car, ancient model?"

"Yeah."

"That's them. Get it?"

"No!"

Yochai sighed in frustration. "Look, now that you've abandoned ship, they're onto you, and they're not going to leave you alone. You'll be much better off if they think you're only going away for a short visit rather than planning a major escape. Stay with Grandma for a few hours, maximum overnight, and then you'll head back home. Got it?"

"Yochai…" Meir sounded like he was on the verge of tears, and the seasoned officer felt himself soften.

"Look, Meir," he said gently, but firmly, "I agree that none of this is your fault, and that you didn't ask for this. But I'm telling you honestly that the solution right now is not to jump ship. You'll only endanger yourself and us. Do your best to minimize the damage and come home ASAP. Just forget about that note you left for Mendy. Because if you don't, I can't continue taking responsibility for your safety, if you know what I mean." With that, Yochai ended the call.

"Who was that?" Naomi asked, although she already knew.

"Yochai. He said we should go back home."

"And you explained that we can't?" Naomi hadn't managed to grasp the gist of the conversation just from hearing one side of it.

"I said that we'll visit Savta for the day and then return home."

"WHY?" she cried, aghast.

Suddenly, Meir understood that the less Naomi knew, the better it was for both of them. "Because I was reading the situation wrong," he found himself lying to his wife for the first time in his marriage. "I thought we were in danger, but we're not really. We can't just uproot our lives because we're being paranoid. You have a job, and I have a *kollel*, and who knows if either of us will have that whenever we decide to come back. Besides, Savta is wonderful and all that, but she's not really up to hosting our family for more than a day or two. I know you packed enough for a year, but I'll help you unpack – don't worry about that."

Naomi narrowed her eyes, clearly skeptical. "Meir, you can't lie to save your life," she muttered, but then stopped short. Perhaps she, too, understood that there were some things that she was better off not knowing.

The conversation took place outside, in the small garden bordering the dilapidated *yeshivah* building.

"How exactly did you end up in this particular *yeshivah*?" Jamil asked his friend. "Why didn't you pick somewhere closer to where your family lives, up north?"

"Oh, it's a long story," Yitzchak took a long drag from his cigarette, a habit that the *rosh yeshivah* hadn't yet managed to talk him out of. "I went through a lot in life before I ended up here."

"Like what?" Jamil's curiosity was piqued.

"Oh, you know. Like I told you once before, I was living it up. I had friends, money, a great career in the offing."

"Law, you said."

"Uh huh."

"But the career choice was a mistake," Yitzchak began to say.

"Why?"

"I was idealistic about it; I thought I'd change the world, you know, that kind of stuff. Until I saw that all you do is either deal with dead people's money or defend low-life criminals and work to get them lighter sentences when what they really deserve is to spend their lives behind bars."

Jamil grinned self-deprecatingly. "I can think of worse mistakes."

"Like what?"

"Like the mistake I made which was growing up with the wrong family."

"What?"

"Whatever. Forget about it."

"It's good to talk about it, Mendy," a warm voice sounded behind them, interrupting their conversation. It was the *rosh yeshivah*. *"Da'agah b'lev ish yasichena,"* he added and then, noticing Jamil's blank stare, explained, "A person should talk about his troubles."

Rabbi Feinberg joined them on the bench. "I've heard that you've been through a lot in life, and I know you're anxious, but you can rest assured that here, at least, you're safe. *Hakadosh Baruch Hu* watches over us, and in this case, sent us a fantastic *shaliach* – Yitzchak. Yitzchak," he turned to the other young man. "Did you ever tell Mendy about your past?"

"He was just starting to tell me now," Jamil replied, noticing with sudden suspicion that the color had drained from Yitzchak's face.

"I'm glad that the two of you are close enough to share your 'past lives.' So Yitzchak told you that he used to work for the GSS?"

"WHAT?" Jamil choked.

"Yes. He was involved in many secret operations, but *baruch Hashem*, one day, he discovered the truth, and that's how he ended up here," the *rosh yeshivah* concluded with gratification.

"He discovered the truth?" Jamil repeated in disbelief.

"Exactly."

"I thought you said you were planning to be a lawyer!" Jamil turned accusingly to his friend.

"He was, but that was only the beginning of the road," Rabbi Feinberg replied. Just then, his cell phone rang. "Excuse me, *bachurim*, but I have to take this call." He strode quickly back toward the building, leaving the two young men staring at each other in wary silence.

"So I started to tell you about what I was doing," Yitzchak continued quickly as if nothing had gone awry. "Halfway through law school, I was approached by the GSS and offered a job there. I advanced quickly in the ranks and was sent on a mission that nearly cost me my life, but *baruch Hashem*, I survived it. And that was a turning point in my life when I discovered Hashem."

Jamil stood up stiffly. "Tell me the truth, Yitzchak, or whatever your name really is. You think I'm such an imbecile? Just admit that the GSS sent you here to spy on me. I hate liars."

Jamil had never been taught the art of rhetoric and the word "subtlety" was not in his vocabulary. Without mincing words, he confronted his erstwhile friend, his feelings of betrayal clearly evident on his face.

To his surprise, Yitzchak shook his head. "I did tell you the truth. I started out with my eye on the courtroom. Then I ended up with the GSS. It was all one long miracle, but that's how I ended up here."

Jamil sank heavily back onto the bench. "What's the difference, I guess?" he said wearily. "You guys held me down in chains over there. Now that I'm free, you're still spying on me. I guess that's your job. And my job is to just live."

"Exactly. And, to be honest, it hurts me that you don't believe that I'm here because I believe that the Torah is true."

"Whatever. I'm getting sick of this conversation," Jamil spat. He stood up and stalked off toward his dorm room, slamming the door behind him. He stared out of the window at the rolling hills far beyond, and suddenly, a terrible thought occurred to him. *Maybe they sent me here purposely? Is this my private jail? Is this whole place one big farce with everyone collaborating against me? If I ever want to leave, will they let me?*

How would he ever manage to escape when he was being tracked by so many eyes?

He dug deep into his closet and retrieved the envelope with the money that Shuli had given him. Then, without stopping to think about the ramifications of his decision, he walked out of his room, out of the building, and down the path that led to the nearest bus stop. He would take the bus to Teveria, and then? He himself wasn't sure, but maybe a first step would be to visit the tomb of Rabbi Meir Baal Haness. He would pray there, and then set out to try to uncover the truth that Yitzchak was hiding from him. He strode quickly along the path, making good time – and he wasn't in the least bit surprised when he heard the sound of running footsteps from behind him.

"Mendy! Mendy!" a familiar voice called out him to stop. Jamil didn't have to glance behind him to know it was Yitzchak, who was sprinting toward him at an impressive speed. Jamil quickened his gait but deliberately decided not to run, which allowed Yitzchak to close the gap between them in about two minutes.

"Mendy, wait! Mendy! Would you stop for a second? Jamil!" he called. The last word caused Jamil to whip around suddenly; he had told no one his real name.

Yitzchak's face was red from exertion. "I need to tell you a few things. First and most important is that I never lied to you. I really am here because I believe that the Torah is true. And I did start out in law school, but then I made a career change. My life was saved miraculously, which was what impelled me to do an about-turn. I became a believing Jew, and I came here to learn. None of that contradicts the fact that I'm also here on a mission."

Jamil looked impatient. "How much should I wager that your mission involves me?"

"Well, of course it does. I became a *baal teshuvah*, got married, and asked for low-risk assignments because I couldn't afford to hurt my family. All I'm doing here is keeping an eye on you to make sure you stay safe. That's it. Nothing more and nothing less. I guess I'm not as good as I used to be if you exposed me so quickly. If you want to destroy my career and future, you can go and make a whole hullabaloo and storm into the GSS offices. Call Yochai and tell him that you exposed me. I can't stop you, although it would mean an end to my career and livelihood. But,

Mendy, you're here learning in a *yeshivah* which is founded on the twin principles of *bein adam l'Makom and bein adam l'chaveiro*. Please, do me a favor and let me continue doing my job. I have a family, a wife and two kids, and I can't afford to lose my job. Please keep this between us. You know as well as I do that if my cover is blown, I'll lose my job."

Jamil stared at him, unimpressed. He had endured far worse hardships and didn't really pity the man. The only thing that aroused his compassion was his mention of two small children.

"I don't understand how the *rosh yeshivah* knew all this," Yitzchak continued, "or why he thought it would be a good idea to tell you. It was a dangerous error, and something I'll pay for, big time."

Jamil still didn't reply, but finally conceded. "So, what do you suggest?"

"We can just continue as if this conversation never happened. What's the big deal? All in all, I'm just keeping an eye on you to ensure your safety. You're not a prisoner here or anything. What's the difference? All I ask is that you don't spill the beans."

"On one condition," Jamil said slowly.

Yitzchak's eyes flickered in fear. "What's that?"

"That you tell me who sent you."

The young man looked relieved. "If that's all, I'll tell you. It was Yochai."

"Yochai? You're sure about that?" Jamil seemed to have a sixth sense, and he didn't miss the tiny quiver in Yitzchak's voice.

"Yes, Yochai, and one other."

"Who?"

"I don't know. Honest. He never identified himself, but we did speak on the phone. Somebody who's very concerned about you."

"My mother?"

"No. It was a man, but I really don't know who it was. I spoke to him, and also to Yochai, and I got the impression that this other person is in contact with Yochai and perhaps works in the department that's dealing with your case."

"Find out who it is. It's important that I know."

"Why?"

"I don't know exactly. Maybe he's connected to my life or something. There's so much that I don't even know about myself yet. I can't even figure out what the danger to my life is all about."

"I can't really help you there," Yitzchak admitted. "My orders were to keep an eye on you, and I don't even want to know anything more about your story."

A long silence passed between the two.

"Okay. Listen, I'm going to Teveria. Want to come along?" Jamil asked, almost amiably.

"What are you doing there?"

"Going to pray."

"Prayer is always good," Yitzchak grinned.

They shook hands and continued along the path side by side. They boarded the bus, and while Jamil was waiting to get change from the driver, Yitzchak quickly called Yochai at Headquarters.

"You know what they say. If you can't beat 'em, join 'em," he chuckled.

"Good job," Yochai congratulated him. "But I'm warning you, Itzik, don't let that kid play you for a fool. I want to put an end to this story already."

"Agreed," Yitzchak nodded and ended the call, smiling placidly at Jamil who sat down beside him. Jamil managed a half-smile back, maintaining a nonchalant façade even as he grasped that if he was in danger, then his family must be, too.

The drive back home the next day was quiet, with Naomi still bewildered, unable to make sense of what was going on in her life. Meir, sitting beside her, was like a different person, suddenly reserved and cool-headed, weighing every word before he spoke.

"Meir, please tell me what's going on," she pleaded eventually, turning to him with imploring eyes. "I can't take this much longer."

"And you don't have to take anything," Meir replied confidently. "All we have to do is start following directions instead of thinking we're smart. Yochai knows what he's doing, and he understands what's going on. We don't, so it just makes sense to rely on his judgment.

"And, in any case," he continued, "I felt terrible abandoning Mendy. I really can't believe that Hashem put this *mitzvah* into my hands just for me to run away from it. He has no one else but me! I'm only doing this for him – I don't get anything out of it for myself – so surely '*shluchei mitzvah einam nizokin*' applies to me, right?" he concluded. "Hashem will protect me as His messenger, just as the Torah promises."

"Well, I certainly hope so," Naomi replied slowly. "Because this is no simple *mitzvah*, that's for sure. And I'm still not convinced that we're not in danger because of this oh-so wonderful Mendy. I mean," she added quickly, noting the disappointment in her husband's eyes, "that... well, he isn't doing this because he wants to. He's just as compelled as we are."

"You know what, Naomi?" Meir suddenly suggested. "How about we just drop the whole subject from here on? I'll take care of whatever needs doing, and you won't ask questions. I really think it's better that way."

Just then, their bus stopped at a red light, which matched the shade of Naomi's face at that moment. "Don't even think of it!" she lashed out at him. "No such thing. There are no secrets in marriage."

"Not secrets! It's just that you won't ask, that's all. It's for your own good," he pleaded. "And, I never want to have to lie to you," he added from the depths of his heart, begging for her to understand. "So, I'm asking you to please trust my judgment, even though it's hard."

The light turned green, and the bus continued on its way. Tears sparkled in Naomi's eyes. "Okay," she conceded eventually, much to her husband's relief. "Don't tell me anything anymore, but promise me that you won't do anything too dangerous. You can help Mendy as long as there's no significant risk to yourself. And I'll *daven* for you. For both of you," she added quietly.

"Agreed," Meir said gratefully. They shared a meaningful look, both appreciating the significance of the moment. As if on cue, as they crossed the Coca Cola bridge into Bnei Brak, Meir's phone rang. Naomi wasn't at all surprised to hear that it was Mendy, nor did she protest when she heard her husband arrange to meet him later that day in a local shul before proceeding together to the home of Rav Mechel Kroizer, who was renowned as an address for converts.

The final meeting was scheduled for Friday afternoon, immediately after prayers in the mosque. All the plans had been completed, and now Laser issued clear instructions. The next stage would be revealing the program to Gil, but that wouldn't happen until the following Thursday, Laser explained.

"I think that's too risky," Aziz argued. "He needs more time to prepare, to anticipate any problems that might crop up. After all, he's the insider, and he knows more about the terrain than we do. I vote we give him a whole week to get ready."

"No, it's better that he finds out the details at the last possible minute," another defended Laser. "That way, he doesn't have a chance to get cold feet. And, in any case, he has plenty of time from Thursday until Sunday to warn us of any pitfalls."

"Right, and he's hardly the typical *shahid*, in any case," Laser settled the discussion. "We all know that he's not motivated by any higher ideal. He's just a human bomb – that's all." Laser chuckled, his eyes glinting malevolently. "Note that I want security to be tighter around everyone this week, most of all around the woman and her children. Also, one of our moles found Jamil. He's in Yerushalayim in a Jewish academy. We need to get one of our men over there too. At the moment of truth, Gil will be staring reality in the face. Either he dies along with all those Jews around him, or his family goes."

An evil smile appeared at the corners of Laser's lips, but he wouldn't allow himself to laugh until the mission was complete. Israel's General Security Service was convinced that they had the situation under control, but little did they know what Hamas knew; and now was the time to reveal all those cards…

"Should we call in Gil?"

"I thought you said that he wouldn't be briefed until Thursday?" one of the men spoke up.

"Final details will be issued then. For now, it's just the basics. And let's call him Jamil, not Gil. He's one of ours, after all. Everyone is dismissed. We'll meet again on Thursday," Laser announced.

The men dispersed, leaving Laser alone with his assistant, Aziz, who made the call to Gil and ordered him to hurry to the improvised Headquarters in the Hebron Hills area. Meanwhile, Laser retired to his private room to conduct an important phone call, and when Gil arrived reluctantly with the dull eyes of a condemned man, Aziz greeted him cheerfully.

"Hey, what's up, *ya*-Jamil?"

"Fine."

"Getting ready?"

"Yes."

"You know, you're a lucky one, Jamil. When we pick our boys for these missions, we pick from a whole line of eager young men who each long for this opportunity. I can think of no less than 100 boys who would jump at the chance you've just been offered!" Aziz tried to encourage him.

"Of course," Gil replied dryly. "They've got nothing to lose. I visited some of your decrepit villages and saw what they have to offer. What other options do you give them in life, other than hunger, poverty, and hard work?"

"They do it because they want to, not because they're forced to."

"With the illusion that there's some kind of paradise waiting for them after their rotten life down here. You're forgetting that I have a lot to lose by this. Only someone with nothing to live for is willing to give his life," he said sharply.

"Do you doubt their faith?"

"I don't doubt anything. What do you want from me?"

"To tell you to prepare yourself, because the time is approaching."

"Great. I told you I'm ready."

Laser appeared just then, cold and calculated as ever. "This week, you'll be receiving notice of the final plan – the time and the place. We've been waiting nearly twenty-one years for this day, Jamil. Twenty-one years. Good luck, my boy. I know that you won't disappoint us, because if you do, we'll disappoint you."

Gil didn't reply.

"If you do as you're told and kill a bunch of Jews, your family will survive. If not, we'll kill them, and you as well."

Gil still didn't move a muscle.

"And you know who's ready to stand in for you in case you chicken out?" Aziz spoke up suddenly.

"Who?"

"The boy who grew up with us. Jamil."

"What about him."

"He'll be there too. Your failure means his immediate death. We'll have our gunsights set on him."

"Why should I care if he lives or dies?" Gil asked apathetically.

"Because you care about your mother, and your mother cares deeply about him. She waited twenty years to reunite with him. What do you think of that?"

"I don't think anything about that."

"*Ya*-Jamil, just do all of us – and yourself – a favor, and do what you're told. We gave you a good life on a golden platter with a Jewish family. Now you can have eternal life too. Say thank you."

"Thanks."

"Not that kind of thanks. Show us your gratitude for what you're getting: a golden life in this world followed by paradise."

Gil didn't deign to reply. Laser returned to his study, but Gil had no doubt that he was listening in on the conversation, as was later proven.

"Listen, *ya*-Jamil, whether you like it or not, you're one of us," Aziz continued his lecture. "We want you to stay in the general area during the next few days, meaning you go no farther than the Gush Dan region. That way, we can summon you at a moment's notice."

Gil pierced the man with blazing eyes. "Tell me just one thing: What do you gain by my death? Why can't I just dump the stuff and get out of there?"

Laser's laughter bubbled from inside his office, and he emerged again to face Gil. "You little fool! Do you really think you could have a good life after killing a whole bunch of them? Your death is not just for our good, but for yours, as well!"

A heavy silence settled between them. "So, as agreed, we'll see you sometime this coming week. Be prepared." Laser ended the meeting, and Gil shuffled out of the room with all the apathy of a man on death row.

Once he was out of earshot, Aziz spoke up. "He doesn't look good. I fear for the success of the mission."

Laser was indifferent. "You have nothing to fear. As soon as it's all over, *everything* will look good, especially with Jewish blood splattered everywhere. We'll get through this week and have much to celebrate. This will be the pinnacle of our careers."

64

"Do you have any need for a gardener?" a man wearing a wide-brimmed hat and old, faded clothes knocked on Shuli's front door, his voice raspy as if he were recovering from the flu.

"No," she replied, caught off guard, "but maybe the director of the moshav needs someone – it's worth a try."

"I was hoping that *you* could help me out," the man said, tipping his hat back slightly as he spoke.

Shuli jumped a mile and practically shrieked in terror. "Mendy! What are you doing here?" Her eyes filled with tears, and Gil wished he knew if they were tears of longing or of fear. "How many times have I asked you to stay away? You're endangering us!"

"I'm not endangering anyone, Mommy. They already know where you are. All those security measures Yochai so prides himself on are worthless."

A wave of longing filled her, longing for a world that had once been, for her family that was no longer. Yes, she had grown to appreciate and love the new Mendy, the real Mendy, the Mendy who had grown up among Arabs and still insisted that she call him Jamil. She had grown to pity him and love him after everything he had suffered in his young life. And yet, all that love couldn't come close to comparing to the love that she felt for this Mendy, for the son she had raised for twenty years only to discover that he wasn't her flesh and blood at all.

"Mommy," he whispered.

"Please, Mendy. Stop it. I can't. Don't you see that I can't do this? That I don't have the strength for this? I can't even invite you inside, even if I wanted to."

"You're right, Mommy." He seemed to relish the sound of the word on his lips. "And I don't want to come in, anyway."

"So why are you here?" she demanded angrily. "Why?" For over a year, he had been the source of so much upheaval and anguish in her life. Her husband was gone, her family was irreparably shattered. Why had he returned? Just to stir up old, painful memories?

"I'm here because I have something important to do."

"What?"

"To say goodbye."

"You're going somewhere?" Her expression was so yearning that Gil's heart melted.

"I'm leaving. I'll never see you again, or Nachum, or Suri..." his voice cracked painfully. "I... I want to say goodbye to them too."

Shuli didn't know what to say. "They're upstairs. Playing chess."

"Tatty taught me how to play chess," Gil's face lit up nostalgically. Those were the days... On Chol Hamoed, the family rarely went on trips, but they spent hours in close company, playing board games and especially chess, Shimon's favorite. Sometimes, the games could stretch for three hours or more, and the older Gil grew, the longer the games became, with the little ones watching from the side, learning the tricks.

But now all that was gone, lost forever.

"I'll call them. I'd prefer it if you stayed outside," Shuli said, her eyes apologetic. She herself wasn't sure that she was being fair, or why she refused to allow him to enter. He was her son, but he was a stranger; he was the child she had raised, but he was now an Arab. Just where his loyalties lay, she didn't know.

A moment later, Gil heard the sound of running feet, and Nachum and Suri were suddenly there in front of him.

Suri wanted to throw her arms around her brother, but Shuli forcefully held her back. "Mendy is going away, and he wants to say goodbye."

"Where are you going?" Suri asked.

"Far away," he said, his voice husky with emotion.

"When will you be back?"

"I won't. That's why I came to say goodbye now."

Suri's face fell, and her eyes filled with tears. Nachum, standing at her side, gazed seriously at his older brother. "I'd like to speak to you in private," he said suddenly to Gil, turning pleading eyes toward his mother. Shuli hesitated, but finally emotion overcame logic, and she nodded her agreement.

"Okay, go ahead and talk," she sighed, knowing that this would probably be the last time. For a moment, she was tempted to remain and listen, but sensing the boys' eyes upon her, she turned and went inside. What could Mendy tell Nachum in just a few minutes, anyway?

The two boys sat down on a rusty double swing that stood in the yard, a relic left behind by the previous owners.

Nachum was the first to speak, and his question almost amused Gil. "What does it feel like to be an Arab?"

"Nothing special, trust me," Gil replied dryly. "I didn't choose this, Nachum. Next time you say, *'Shelo asani goy,'* you should dance for joy. And not just next time, but every time."

Nachum looked at his feet, chastened, and Gil felt bad for hurting him.

"Nachum, this is the last time we'll be meeting. I've come to say goodbye. Forever," he continued.

"Where are you going?"

"To a place of no return. But there is something I want to tell you, and I want to tell it to you, and not to Mommy, because you're almost bar mitzvah, and able to look at the world logically. Listen carefully, Nachum. There will come a day when people – and you, too – will judge me. You'll ask yourselves what sort of person I really am..." Gil's voice was heavy with emotion.

Inside the house, Shuli stood beside the window where she could hear everything, without being observed. She was afraid to leave Nachum alone with Mendy, and she felt that it was vital that she hear what was being said between the two.

"...you might think that I did terrible things, but you won't understand what happened behind the scenes. You...you might go crazy when you find out what happened, so I'm telling you the truth now, before it happens. And when it happens, you'll tell this to Mommy."

"I don't understand," Nachum interjected, his eyes confused, frightened.

"You don't have to understand yet. Just make sure you remember everything I'm saying, okay? Please, Nachum, it's very important. Maybe when you're older you'll understand, and maybe you'll never understand, but you do have to remember this: I did what I did because I love you and I want to protect you. You hear? I love you and I want to protect you... And you also have to know that what you read in the paper is not necessarily true, okay?"

"I don't understand," Nachum repeated.

"Like, sometimes, you read in the paper about a terrible car accident where someone was badly hurt, right?"

"Right."

"But maybe there wasn't really a car accident, and no one was really hurt."

Nachum shook his head. "If there wasn't an accident, and no one was hurt, why would they write about it in the paper?"

"Because someone wanted you to think that there was."

"Okay. If you say so," Nachum's tone was skeptical.

"Please remember this," Gil pleaded. "You'll remember?"

"Yes."

"And even if they show you the place where the accident happened, and the car that was destroyed in the crash, you'll still remember that?"

Nachum looked more confused than ever. "I guess so. If you say so."

"Okay. Thank you, Nachum. I appreciate it. I have to go now, and this is goodbye forever. You were the best brother in the world, and… take care of Mommy."

"I will."

"Be big and strong, and don't cry."

"Okay."

Inside the house, Shuli wept. Hot tears rolled down her cheeks as she absorbed Mendy's sincerity. This was really and truly goodbye. He had come to them with love, caring, and devotion; it was written all over his face. Until now, his love had been mixed with frustration, disappointment, disillusionment – but now all the other emotions had evaporated, and what remained was only pure love and a desperate desire to be remembered positively by his family.

Shuli wiped away her tears and swallowed hard before exiting the house and walking slowly over to the two boys. "Can I join you?" she asked with a sad smile.

"We're finished," Nachum rose from the bench. "But…" he turned back to his brother. "Maybe you'll at least stay for a meal, just for a few more hours?"

This time, it was Gil's turn to hesitate and Shuli watched his face as the battle raged inside him. It was so tempting – just for a few hours… for a few hours, he could forget the miserable facts of his existence, forget the life to which he would soon be returning, and lose himself in the warmth of what had once been his family. It was so tempting… but he knew it would only cause more emotional torment, both for him and for Shuli. He couldn't do that to her, and neither could he do it to himself.

"I would love to, Nachum, but I can't. I really shouldn't be here at all, to be honest, and I have to leave immediately."

"So you're really going?" Nachum asked in disappointment.

"Yes." It was so final.

Suri joined them as well before the final parting, her eyes welling with tears. "I'll miss you, Mendy."

"I'll miss you too, but don't cry," he smiled encouragingly at her.

"You're really going so far away that you can't come back?" she asked sadly.

"I'm going very, very far away," he nodded. "But you'll always be with me in my heart. You're still my family, and I'll do my best to make sure that you're happy and safe. From now on, I'll do everything I can to ensure that. Okay, Suri? Will you remember that?"

The little girl nodded, feeling just slightly better.

"And you?" Gil turned to Shuli, who didn't even try to hide her tears.

"I will," she whispered.

Taking a deep breath, he added gravely, "Also, I'd like you to know that the fact that I haven't yet converted is also because of you. Regardless of that, I'm keeping all the *mitzvos*, even though I'm not obligated to do so. I *daven* three times a day, and I keep Shabbos, except for one minor thing, which as a *goy*, I'm obligated to do. Inside my heart, I'm still a Jew. Everything that you taught me is still within me, and will forever remain there."

"So why don't you convert?" she asked suddenly.

Gil lowered his eyes. "One day, you'll understand," he replied heavily. "Maybe in a week, maybe in a month, or maybe in twenty years. Who knows? Maybe you won't understand until we meet above in the *Olam Ha'emes*. But there, you'll understand everything."

Shuli gazed at Gil with wide, frightened eyes, but Gil shook his head, indicating that he would not explain any further. As he turned to leave, she called out to him softly, "Take care of yourself, my son. May Hashem watch you and guide your footsteps."

"Amen," he choked, and slipped back into his car.

They waved until the car disappeared around the corner. What they saw next shook them all up. The moment Mendy's car reached the corner, two cars burst into the street out of the shadows and began following him. A third car then turned off a side street and joined the chase, followed by a fourth car that appeared and disappeared as quickly as the others.

"That's so weird! This place is usually so quiet. I never saw so many cars on the streets here at once," Suri noted.

Shuli's heart sank. Not only was her Mendy an Arab, but he was also a hunted man. How had fate turned so cruel upon him? How much longer would he survive? And, what had he meant when he told them that he was going to a place that was so far away that he would never be able to return?

65

Yochai nodded curtly at the young man with the tortured eyes.

"What's doing, kid?"

"Not much. What's on my agenda for the week?"

"Only one assignment. But it's an important case. Dror will brief you on what you need to know."

"I'm sure it's *extremely* important, like all the other assignments you give me," Gil replied dryly.

"If that's how you want to look at it," Yochai shrugged noncommittally. "Is there something you want?"

"I need a week off."

"Take it," Yochai exhaled a small sigh of relief. The less people wandering around his department at this sensitive time, the better; and the less brainpower he had to invest into fabricating missions, all the better too.

"You're happy about it?" Gil didn't miss a beat.

"Happy? I'm actually very annoyed!" Yochai lied. "And I expect you to make up your hours, understood?"

"Funny, funny."

"What's funny?"

"It won't be any vacation for you. Listen to me carefully, Yochai. You need to take this week very seriously."

He spoke with such intensity that Yochai instantly grasped the message hidden in his words, and his face suddenly bore a distinct similarity to the color of the walls.

Zero hour was approaching.

Rabbi Feinberg stared, astonished, at the latest arrival. "What did you say your name was?"

"Moshe."

"And your last name?"

"Bensoussan. Moshe Bensoussan. Wasn't the *rosh yeshivah* informed that I was coming?"

"No, I wasn't," Feinberg replied.

"I don't understand. I spoke to several people, and I understood that there wouldn't be a problem. I came all the way from America to join this *yeshivah*."

"From America? How do you speak such good Hebrew?"

"My mother is Israeli, so she spoke Hebrew at home. My father is French, and he teaches French at Harvard. My parents are liberals, very anti-religious, but I'm their only child and they don't want to lose me. So they sent a donation to the *yeshivah*." The young man proffered a signed check.

The *rosh yeshivah's* gaze flitted momentarily to the check, and his jaw dropped. He had never encountered such a bizarre situation. He ran a small *yeshivah* for select *baalei teshuvah*, and he never accepted a *talmid* without making inquiries first. On the other hand, the *yeshivah* was always in difficult financial straits, barely making it through the month and usually in arrears when it came to paying the teachers' salaries – and here, this *bachur* was presenting him with a signed check for fifty thousand dollars!

The sum was enough to blind most people, but not Rabbi Feinberg, who took the *chinuch* of his boys very seriously and was in no hurry to accept a boy who could end up causing more trouble than any amount of money was worth. "That's a very generous donation, Moshe," he said slowly, the question in his voice obvious.

The boy grinned self-consciously. "My parents really are very generous people," he agreed, "and I guess they wanted to make sure that I'd be well taken care of."

"We take care of *all* our *bachurim*," Rabbi Feinberg said firmly.

"That's what I heard," Moshe replied.

"How did you come to hear about our *yeshivah*, Moshe? Is that the name you went by in America?"

"No. My parents named me Macy. But here, I want to be Moshe. When I came to Israel, I went straight to the Wall, where I saw guys from all over the world, and that was the beginning of my journey..."

Moshe's explanation was vague and disjointed, and the *rosh yeshivah* didn't quite understand how "meeting guys from all over the world" had led this Bensoussan to discover either Judaism or the *yeshivah*. On the other hand, the boy looked exhausted, and Rabbi Feinberg couldn't bring himself to turn the boy away. He agreed to admit him, if only as a gesture of *hachnassas orchim*.

"Look, I'm not sure how this misunderstanding happened, but maybe it's from *Shamayim*. In the meantime, I'll accept you, but only on trial basis. I hope you'll understand – usually, I make extensive inquiries before I accept a *bachur*."

"I understand – no problem. And, thank you. I really appreciate it."

"I believe there's an empty bed in Room 304, on the third floor," Rabbi Feinberg continued. "You can settle in and then come down to the *beis medrash*, while I make arrangements for a *chavrusa* for you. And by the way, Moshe, I don't intend to cash the check yet," he added.

"Whatever the *rosh yeshivah* decides," the young man replied respectfully.

Rabbi Feinberg poked his head outside his office, summoned a passing *bachur*, and asked him to show the new arrival to his room. Shaya Goldsmith, a longtime student, welcomed Bensoussan with a good-natured grin, swung his duffel bag over his shoulder, and motioned for the newcomer to join him. Rabbi Feinberg followed the pair with his gaze, wondering what he would uncover when he began investigating this new student's past. The boy, if one could call him that, gave the impression of being in his late twenties at least, giving him plenty of years during which he could have been in many more places than the Kosel.

From the distance, the *rosh yeshivah* spied another pair of *bachurim,* walking in his general direction. Squinting, he identified them as Mendy and Yitzchak, his other recent arrivals, and he grew pensive. Yitzchak, he was confident, would go far and make quick strides both in *limmud haTorah* and *mitzvah* observance – his motivation was high and he was tenacious enough to keep going even when the going got tough. Mendy, on the other hand, had arrived at the *yeshivah* with one percent willpower and ninety-nine percent despair, but he had been progressing beautifully in the short while he had been with them, and was starting to feel a real sense of gratification from his learning.

On the spur of the moment, Rabbi Feinberg decided to approach them with his idea. He left his office and walked quickly to meet the pair.

"Good evening, rebbi," they greeted him respectfully as he approached.

"Good evening. Where are you coming from?"

"We went to the *kever* of Rabbi Meir Baal Haness."

"Very special. May you both merit *nissim* and *yeshuos*!" he blessed them from the bottom of his heart.

"Amen. We mentioned you in our *tefillos*, as well," Yitzchak added.

"If you're on your way to supper, I'd like to ask you to fulfill the *mitzvah* of *hachnassas orchim*. A new *bachur* joined us today, and he could use some help getting to know the place and feeling at home here."

"Another new *bachur*? What's his name?" Yitzchak asked in pleasant surprise.

"Moshe Bensoussan."

"Really? The *rosh yeshivah* didn't mention anything about a new *bachur* coming."

"I didn't know a thing until he arrived," Rabbi Feinberg admitted. "There seems to have been some misunderstanding, and I'm beginning to wonder if he even showed up at the right place. He insists that he made all the arrangements in advance, but that's impossible. I would have heard something from the secretary."

Jamil nodded and replied, "No problem. I'll introduce myself." He was hungry after his long day out and eager for a hearty supper.

"One second, Mendy," the *rosh yeshivah* stopped him as inspiration hit him. "He's a nice boy, this Moshe, but clearly lacking background. What do you say about learning with him *b'chavrusa*?"

Uncharacteristically, Yitzchak interrupted the *rosh yeshivah*. "So, how exactly did he end up here, rebbi? We all know that it's a fantastic *yeshivah*, but it's not very well known."

"I really don't know, but I would like to find out," Rabbi Feinberg confessed. "In the meantime, he's here on trial basis only." He deliberately omitted any mention of the check burning a hole in his pocket.

"He's Israeli?" Yitzchak was strangely persistent.

"American, but his father is French and his mother is Israeli."

"How's his Hebrew?"

"Actually, it's very good. He said his mother spoke Hebrew at home."

"He's really American?" Yitzchak asked sharply.

"Why don't you go introduce yourself?" the *rosh yeshivah* suggested, somewhat taken aback at Yitzchak's interrogation. The usually mild-mannered *bachur* had suddenly become distant, cold, and calculated. Unnoticed by Rabbi Feinberg, his hand automatically slipped into his pocket where he kept his tiny weapon.

"Where is he now?" Even his tone of voice was unfamiliar.

"I would guess the dining room. I told him that we'd speak again tomorrow. I'm not at all sure that I'll accept him, but I do want to give him a chance, and in any case, it's too late at night to send him away. I'm sure he wasn't anticipating this," he continued, more to himself than to the two boys, "given the size of the donation..."

The *rosh yeshivah's* last sentence sent Yitzchak's mind into high gear. "A donation?" he repeated tautly.

Rabbi Feinberg himself wasn't sure why he was revealing so much to Yitzchak, who was still a relative newcomer to the *yeshivah*, but with his background in security, the young man didn't seem such a poor choice right then. "He presented me with a check for fifty thousand dollars," he confessed. "I have no intention of depositing it, for the time being, although it's certainly very tempting," he sighed, "given the *yeshivah's* current financial situation."

"I understand," was all Yitzchak said before nodding respectfully and practically grabbing Mendy by the arm and dragging him after him.

"Hey, Avner!" Yitzchak greeted a fellow *bachur*. "Did you meet the new guy yet?"

"Yeah, just now in the dining room. He's a friendly fellow. Moshe's his name."

"Is he still there?" Yitzchak demanded.

"Not sure, but probably. He had tons of questions, and wanted to know if we thought it was worth joining the *yeshivah*. How weird is that? Why did he come if he doesn't want to join?" Avner asked.

"What else did he ask?"

"I don't know… People's names. He wanted to know if the guys go by their Jewish names or not. Like, he asked if there are Jakes or Yaakovs or Mikes or Mendys. We all laughed because he was right on target with every one of those names, and we told him that everyone chooses how they want to be called, and that the *rosh yeshivah* just wants everyone to feel comfortable and go at his own pace."

Yitzchak didn't seem have heard the last part of the sentence, too anxious was he upon hearing that Bensoussan had specifically asked about a Mendy. *It can't be coincidence,* the thought resounded like a siren in his mind.

Yitzchak tightened his grip on his gun and, once Avner was out of earshot, turned to his friend. "Listen, Mendy, I don't like the sound of this guy one little bit. I've got no idea who he is, but something doesn't smell right."

"What could be the problem?" Jamil dismissed his fears. "I know Yochai can make anyone nervous and even paranoid, but what's the big deal about a new guy at a *yeshivah*?"

Yitzchak's eyes narrowed. "You may laugh, but I've been in the field long enough to sense when something isn't right, and even though I've haven't even met this guy yet, he already reeks to me." Jamil chuckled, but his friend was completely serious.

"Listen, Mendy, do me one big favor. Just for an hour."

"What?"

"You know the little enclosure behind the building?"

"Where they store the garbage before it's collected?"

"Right."

"*No way!* Don't even think about asking me to hide in there!" Jamil reacted in horror. "You're nuts. Yochai's nuts. Just let me live, will you? I'm safe here – even Yochai told me so – and I finally feel like I'm starting to get somewhere in life. Why do you have to go and stir everything up for no good reason?"

"Hey, take it easy!" Yitzchak interrupted the tirade. "I didn't ask you to go *inside*, just to hide behind the garbage shed. That's it. Do twenty minutes of *hisbodedus* or something, and I'll soon be back to give you the all-clear."

"Can't you come up with somewhere that smells better?" Jamil grumbled in annoyance.

"Will you?" Yitzchak asked pointedly. "It's not somewhere anyone will be inclined to search so quickly."

"All right! All right," he conceded. "If that will make you happy..."

Yitzchak tightened his grip around his pistol and strode quickly toward the dining room, knowing that time was short, as Jamil's patience would wear thin very quickly. From outside the room, he could already hear voices, one of which sounded suspiciously foreign.

France was a hotbed for Moslem terrorists; Arabs emigrated there like ants, and Islam was blooming like mushrooms after the rain. Maintaining a cool façade, he pasted a pleasant smile on his face and entered the dining room, which was nearly deserted at that late hour.

"Hi, Yitz! Meet Moshe, our newest arrival!" Aharon, a heavyset fellow with rimless glasses, waved him over.

Their eyes met, and Yitzchak sized him up. As he had expected, Moshe was completely nondescript and wore a placid expression; they nodded politely at each other.

"Anything left to eat?" Yitzchak looked around.

"Probably in the kitchen," Aharon replied.

"I've had a long day," Yitzchak flopped theatrically onto a chair. "Maybe bring me some grub, Aharon, and I'll entertain the newcomer?"

Aharon grinned good-naturedly. "Alright, Yitz, but you owe me one." He walked quickly toward the kitchen, suddenly wondering why the temperature in the room seemed to have dropped to zero.

66

"What's your name?" Yitzchak asked.

"Moshe. Macy. Whatever you like." Macy stabbed at his schnitzel, suddenly eager to eat.

"How did you end up here?"

"You know, like everyone else and you too. How did you end up here?" He took a big bite of schnitzel and made a face. "This stuff is nasty."

"I learned a lot beforehand," Yitzchak replied to the question. "Where were you before here?"

"France."

"Oh, that's neat. I spent some time in France too." Yitzchak suddenly spoke a few words in a foreign-sounding tongue, keeping his eyes glued to Moshe as he spoke, watching like a hawk for his reaction.

Moshe's face paled, but otherwise he failed to react, preferring to take another bite of food and chew it slowly and deliberately.

"Well?" Yitzchak fired at him.

Macy rose quickly from his seat, making an effort to appear relaxed. "Well, what?"

"Why don't you answer?"

"I'm eating. You want me to choke?"

Yitzchak narrowed his eyes. "Choke? Oh, certainly not. So why don't you just answer me when I ask you a question, instead of panicking?" he challenged.

In the blink of an eye, Macy leaped out of the open window, and a second later was sprinting away. The dining room, which was located on the ground level of the building, featured large windows, and not to be bested, Yitzchak followed suit, landing easily on the soft grass and aiming his weapon at Macy.

"Stop or I'll shoot!" he shouted.

Macy stopped in his tracks. "Be quiet! What's the matter with you? You don't understand anything!"

"Well, I'm trying to understand."

"Sure doesn't look like it." Macy drew his own gun and trained it on his opponent. Both of them trembled from the tension.

"You're lying!" Yitzchak seethed. "I have no idea where you come from, but it's not France or America. Tell me what you're doing here and why you're trying to bribe the *rosh yeshivah*."

"I don't have to tell you anything!" Macy shot back.

"Fine, but you're coming with me!"

"I'm not going anywhere."

"Oh, yes you are! Unless you want to be my target practice."

"I'd rather you were mine."

Yitzchak laughed aloud, and before Macy could react, he unleashed a powerful kick that sent the newcomer sprawling, and his gun skidding on the grass. Yitzchak had both guns trained on Macy before the other could even recover.

"Where do you want me to go?" he gasped for breath.

"Exactly where I tell you." With both guns trained on Macy, Yitzchak led him around the back of the *yeshivah* building where they were both surprised to find Jamil walking toward them.

"I told you to wait for me," Yitzchak said tightly.

"What's going on?" Jamil retorted.

"Go inside the building," he ordered him while Macy studied him carefully.

"I'm not going anywhere until you tell me what's going on."

Yitzchak waved him away as if he were an annoying fly. "Mendy, just listen to me for once. You're only making a mess of things."

"Why?"

Yitzchak lost his cool. "Mendy! I said to get lost! Stop causing problems for once, will you!"

Jamil's expression hardened. "I don't like it when people talk to me like that. And now, just tell me what's going on, okay?"

Yitzchak softened his tone. "You'll understand soon enough. I'm asking you now to please do what's smart and go back inside the building."

"I'm coming with you wherever you're going!" Jamil insisted with the obstinacy of a two-year-old.

Yitzchak paused momentarily, weighing his options, and decided not to react. He continued walking with Macy at gunpoint and Jamil trailing behind.

"You're turning my life into a nightmare. You guys are all nuts!" Jamil repeated again and again. "Why won't anybody just let me live? I've already been through more than enough in life, and all I want now is some peace and quiet, but nobody will let me! Not the Arabs, and not the Jews either." Yitzchak, noticing how carefully Macy was paying attention to every word Mendy spoke, briefly debated giving his friend a not-so-friendly incentive to leave, but managed to restrain himself.

Ten minutes later, they reached the far edge of the *yeshivah's* campus where a small garage was located. A dusty car was parked outside.

"You're my guest this evening, Macy," Yitzchak announced with feigned geniality and opened the door. He grabbed something from the glove compartment and before Macy could see what was going on, his hands were cuffed behind his back.

"Is this really necessary?" he asked grimly.

"Oh, very."

"You guys are nuts. You're all nuts!" Jamil repeated, and entered the car without bothering to ask permission.

"Where are we going?" Macy asked nervously.

"To someone who'll be very happy to meet you," Yitzchak replied festively.

"Who?"

"To someone who'll be very happy to meet you," Yitzchak repeated.

Macy's eyes blazed, but he didn't say another word. He seemed to draw comfort from Jamil's muttering in the back.

After about an hour's ride, Yitzchak called someone on his phone. "Hey. I'm on Highway 2. We'll meet at the Red Point? Yeah, I'd appreciate it if you came along. There's someone I'd like you to meet… A fat fish?" he cast a sidelong glance at Macy. "A fish, yes, but I'm not sure yet how fat."

He ended the call and began whistling a happy tune. In the backseat, Jamil closed his eyes and fell asleep, tired after his long day. Ten minutes later, the car pulled to a stop in a deserted lot occupied by one other car.

A familiar figure emerged from the other vehicle and leaned over to the driver's window.

"Hey, Yitzchak. What's up?" Yochai asked.

"I brought you your fish," the operative replied. He exited the car and theatrically circled it, opening the passenger door with a flourish to expose his catch. "You can come out now!" he called teasingly.

Macy emerged, his eyes downcast. Yochai's jaw dropped in disbelief. "*Macy?*" he roared. "Already? But I just sent you today!"

This time, it was Yitzchak's turn to look surprised. "You mean… you know him?"

Macy's face was crimson, and he was too mortified to say a word.

"Hold it!" Yitzchak exclaimed angrily. "You mean, you sent two of us to guard Jamil, and you didn't bother to tell us? What is this, kindergarten?" In his fury, he didn't hesitate to direct his complaint at Yochai, his superior.

Macy finally summoned the strength to defend himself. "Yochai, I tried... He was just too suspicious. No matter what I said, he jumped on me."

Yochai was unimpressed. "How?"

"First of all, you told me to say that I speak French!"

"So?"

"So you didn't tell me that Yitzchak is fluent in French!"

"You are?" Yochai was too astonished to reply with any of his usual cynical remarks.

"Not a word," Yitzchak said calmly. "I just saw that the boy was lying through his teeth so I spoke some gibberish with a bad French accent to catch him on it. The expression on his face was all I needed to know that I was right."

"Good job," Yochai complimented him reluctantly.

"I wish I could say the same for you," Yitzchak retorted, his expression wounded. "Why don't you just say it like it is, Yochai? You don't trust me, right? Otherwise, you wouldn't have assigned a second guy to the same job."

An uncomfortable silence passed between them, and the only sound was the roar of passing cars on the highway.

"I'll explain later," Yochai murmured. "Macy, you're finished. You're going home, kid. And Jamil," he turned to the young man who had just emerged from the car, "I can't, for the life of me, figure out what you're doing here. You're going back to *yeshivah* with Yitzchak, and don't leave the campus again." Noticing the fury in Jamil's eyes, he relented. "Okay, I don't mean that you can't ever leave, just that you should stay on the *yeshivah* grounds as much as possible in order to stay safe.

"Look, Jamil," he added, "I'm not jailing you, but protecting you. I can't say more, but this is going to be a very critical week. Yitzchak, keep up the good work. If anything looks even remotely suspicious, let us know. We're still hoping that they don't know where he is, but in any case, this whole situation should be over in about a week or so. Then, Jamil, you'll be free to do whatever you like.

"Believe me," he turned back to Jamil. "We gain nothing by wasting our resources on you, but we're committed to keeping you safe. Just do what you can to stay out of trouble and cooperate with Yitzchak. He's a good guy."

Jamil spun around, the disgust in his eyes speaking louder than words. He was sick of Yochai, sick of all the secrecy and suspicions, and sick of the macabre game that had become his life. Suddenly, Yochai seemed as much an enemy as those intent on hunting him down.

Yitzchak slipped back into the driver's seat, but Macy issued a protest.

"What now?" Yitzchak asked apathetically.

"Take the cuffs off!"

Yitzchak laughed. "Oh, right." He emerged very slowly from the car and tinkered with the cuffs binding the young failure of an agent until they clicked open.

"Good luck!" he added caustically, before disappearing into the night.

Macy massaged his sore wrists and turned, shamefaced, to follow Yochai into the latter's car, the silence between them so thick that it could have been cut with a knife.

The knocks on the door were too familiar, and Naomi turned to her husband. "It's him," she said unnecessarily, her tone tense, even fearful. "If you don't mind, I'm going to bed. Wake me up if one of the kids needs me, okay?"

"Okay," Meir smiled encouragingly at her and waited for her to disappear into the bedroom before opening the front door, still wearing a smile. "Hi, Mendy. Come on in."

"I hope it's not too late and that I'm not disturbing," Gil said hesitantly.

"Not at all!" Meir lied. "What's up?"

"I need you to come with me to the rav now."

"Again?"

"Yes. Can you come? It looks like I'll have to go to him every day, at least for this coming week."

"Really? Why?" Meir asked curiously. It was already eleven-thirty, and he knew that the rav usually learned alone every evening from eleven until two in the morning. Nonetheless, the moment Gil arrived, he closed his *Gemara* and devoted himself fully to his guest, spending as long as an hour in deep discussion on matters of *emunah* and other related topics.

For some reason, Gil always insisted that Meir accompany him, despite the latter's protestations that he was totally redundant.

"The rav will agree to see you even without my introduction," he pointed out, but to no avail.

"Please Meir, I need you to come with me, even without understanding why," Gil always replied. "And, in any case, you won't have many more opportunities to do *chessed* for me."

His words, spoken so plaintively, never failed to bring about the desired effect, as they did that evening.

"Okay – but just give me a minute," Meir excused himself, "while I tell my wife where we're going."

Gil nodded absently, pacing the floor of the living room while Meir held a whispered conversation with Naomi, who resignedly agreed to let him go – after all, they were only going to the rav's house. Then, Meir grabbed his hat and jacket and accompanied Gil outside. "I really should be getting home within the hour, though," he added as they walked down the stairs and exited the building.

They entered Gil's car, and Gil turned out of Meir's residential street onto the main boulevard. "I recently discovered a shortcut to— Oh, no!" he cried, shutting the engine abruptly.

"What happened?"

"I think the tire just went," Gil replied. He opened the car door, adding, "Stay inside. If I need your help, I'll call you." As he stood up, he deliberately dropped a sheet of paper onto the driver's seat.

Meir stared at the paper, which was clearly intended for his eyes only. Lifting it, he scanned the hastily penned lines.

Meir, this is very important! I need your help! I need to go somewhere and make sure that no one will follow me there. You'll say something about having to drop something off for a friend who just happens to live nearby, and I'll head for a certain building – you don't have to know the address.

After I park the car, you'll give me your hat and jacket and put on my cap. Then, you'll wait in the car for me – it shouldn't take more than fifteen minutes or so.

Please, Meir, please do this for me! You have no idea how much it will mean.

If you agree, and you've understood, then get out of the car and ask me if I need help.

Meir took a deep breath and weighed his options. Once again, what Gil had initially portrayed as a simple undertaking was turning out to be downright dangerous – he could sense it. The idea of taking Gil's place, even for just fifteen minutes, petrified him. Who would be watching him, and listening to every sound he made, during that time?

A second later, he felt overcome with guilt. *Meir, you're afraid of pretending to be Mendy for fifteen minutes – can you imagine the fear he must feel every minute of the day? How can you turn him down? He has nobody else but you, and you know it.*

Now firm in his resolve, and determined to act on it before he got cold feet, Meir opened the car door and called out to Gil, "Need some help?"

Gil turned to him and flashed him a brilliant smile that radiated joy and relief. The obvious intensity of his emotion made Meir wonder what Gil was planning, and whether he had just willfully stepped into a deadly arena.

"Actually, it looks like the tire's still okay. I think we can continue," Gil replied. They both got back into the car, and Gil turned the key in the ignition, after casually pointing to the note he had written.

"Uh, Mendy," Meir began hesitantly, before making an effort to sound more natural. "My wife asked me to drop something off on the way to a friend of hers. Would you mind? It's not a big detour and it won't take long."

"Sure, no problem," Gil replied. "Which way should I go?" he continued, as he started to drive, inclining his head to the left and tapping with three fingers on Meir's shoulder as he did so.

"It's the third street on the left," Meir told him, unsurprised when Gil turned the car around in a rapid U-turn and sped off in the opposite direction. Within ten minutes, Gil had pulled up outside a three-story building that looked relatively new and featured an underground parking lot. Meir could sense his excitement as Gil parked the car, his eyes narrowed in concentration, sparkling in anticipation. Then, in a swift motion, Gil donned Meir's hat and jacket, giving the latter his baseball cap to wear instead, and motioned toward his lips.

Meir returned a quizzical stare, and Gil gestured again to his lips, a bit more frantically this time.

"Ah, I'll be two minutes, maybe a bit more," Meir said in a loud, unnatural voice. "I hope you don't mind waiting."

"Not at all," Gil replied. Slipping past Meir, he motioned for Meir to quickly move over to the driver's seat, which Meir did, before he exited the car through the passenger door.

Meir remained seated in the car, his heart pounding and glancing at his watch every fifteen seconds. If it had been up to him, he would have told Gil no more than thirty seconds – or even three. Alone in the thick darkness, every second felt like an eternity. Though only two minutes had elapsed, Meir felt like he was beginning to lose his mind.

After another minute came and went, Meir began to wonder if and how he would survive another twelve minutes of this torture. Just then, he heard the crank of the gate to the parking lot opening and the hum of a car driving in. For the first time in his life, he understood what it meant to have one's blood freeze in his veins, and his lips went white. Glancing frantically toward the backseat, he noticed a newspaper tossed haphazardly on the cushion. He grabbed it quickly and buried his nose in the paper, slouching down as low as possible in the driver's seat. He had no doubt that whoever was following Mendy had just entered the lot, even at this late hour. His eyes flitted across the newspaper, but he saw nothing; he was too terrified. He was tempted to call Mendy and demand that he return when he noticed the car pull into a space across the lot and watched a man exit the vehicle before forcing his eyes back to the newspaper, fearful that the stranger would sense that he was being watched. Still, he couldn't help but look toward the man every so often, who had opened his trunk and seemed to be looking for something inside.

Just as his heart rate finally began to slow to a normal pace, the crank of the gate sounded again, and another car glided into the lot, this time, parking right beside him. The two men in the front didn't even pretend to busy themselves with anything else, and their eyes bored right into Meir. Before he could count three, the gate opened again, and a third car joined his pursuers. This one had four men sitting inside and loud music blared from its open windows.

Meir thoughts flitted to his wife, and he wondered if she sensed that he was in danger, and what she would do in such a situation. It didn't take long for him to recall that level-headed Naomi would have refused to place herself in such a situation in the first place.

Goosebumps broke out all over his body as the door to the adjacent car opened, and two men stepped out in perfect synchrony. One of them rapped on Meir's window, motioning for him to open it, and Meir responded with a questioning gesture.

"How do you get to Herzl Street?" the man asked him, but Meir pretended not to be able to hear through the closed window. Opening the window just a crack in order to answer something innocuous, Meir froze as the man stuck the barrel of his revolver through the narrow slit and aimed it directly at Meir's head.

"Open the door," he commanded, and a trembling Meir complied. "Don't make a sound while you move over to the passenger seat," the stranger said in a dangerous voice.

Meir raised his hands to show they were empty. "Wh-what do you want from me?" he asked in a trembling voice. "I don't have any money on me."

"Move over and be quiet," the man answered crisply, and Meir suddenly realized that his eyes were coal black and his mouth was almost invisible under a thick black mustache. There was no mistaking that coarse accent.

"I said move over," the man whispered harshly. "If you don't, I might find some use for this little toy."

While Meir climbed into the passenger seat, two things occurred simultaneously. The first was that a short man suddenly burst out of the third car and leaped into the backseat, right behind Meir; the second was that the Arab who had been training his gun on Meir slipped behind the wheel, gunned the engine, and sped out of the parking lot toward the street.

It took less than a moment for it to dawn on Meir that he was witnessing a kidnapping, and that the one being kidnapped was none other than himself.

While Meir was living through the nightmare of his own kidnapping, Gil was making his way quietly up to the fourth floor of the building. He took a deep breath and stared at his reflection in the elevator mirror. The face that stared back at him was strangely familiar, as if even the events of the past months had failed to leave a permanent imprint on him.

"Look at yourself, Gil," he spoke aloud, briefly wondering if he was starting to lose his mind. "All you're missing are the *peyos*. Do you still remember that world? You could have just stayed there, remember…"

He smiled bitterly at himself, fighting back the tears that threatened to well up in his eyes. Clearing his throat, he forced his regular air of indifference back onto his face.

The elevator doors swished open and he walked down the corridor until he found himself facing an ornately-carved door. He knocked politely, and then quickly swiveled around in order to ensure that anyone peering through the peephole wouldn't be able to identify him.

"Who's there?" The question startled him, and a tremor went through him at the sound of the voice.

"Courier service," he replied tonelessly, pulling his hat down lower over his eyes as he slowly turned around.

The door opened immediately; apparently, the resident was accustomed to receiving packages at all hours of the day and night.

Gil had done his research well and knew that a *chareidi* disguise would grant him entry – and he was right.

Taking a quick step inside, he slammed the door shut behind him before the man had a chance to push him out. Then, he removed his hat.

"Mendy!"

The man's eyes widened in terror, though he struggled valiantly to maintain a calm exterior. Gil immediately noticed that he looked older, weaker, and sadder than ever before. But the eyes were undeniably the same.

"Tatty."

They faced each other in shock, and Gil wondered if this was how it felt in the world of truth, when two people confronted each other again after being certain that death had parted them forever. This time, however, it seemed as if both of them had somehow managed to elude the Angel of Death – so far.

"Baruch mechayeh meisim!" Gil pronounced with a wry smile.

Ten long seconds of silence passed between them before Shimon recovered sufficiently from the shock to pose his first question. "Did anyone see you come?"

"No. I know that for a fact. But, don't I at least deserve a 'hello,' Tatty?"

Tatty. Never had the word sounded so sweet. Despite it all, they were still Tatty and Mendy, a father and his son.

"You're endangering my life. Each minute you remain here, I'm in greater danger of them discovering that I'm alive." Shimon's eyes so clearly expressed his torturous dilemma – how could he let Mendy stay, but, on the other hand, how could he send him away?

Gil shook his head. "Why didn't you tell me? Do you know what I went through thinking you were gone? The worst of all was that I couldn't even *shivah*. And I'm sure you know that I blamed myself."

Shimon glanced anxiously at the door. "Are you sure no one saw you enter?"

"Positive."

"Why did you come?"

"I wanted you to know."

"Know what?" Shimon did his best to preserve a sense of distance between them, battling against all his instincts in order to do so.

"I wanted you to know that… that it's almost over. What I call 'zero hour' is almost here. Just a few more days."

"A few more days until what?"

"Until our problems are solved," Gil said, so calmly that Shimon stared at him incredulously.

Gil returned his gaze, drinking in the sight of Shimon's features and trying to imprint them on his mind. Nearly a year had passed since he had seen him last, but only recently had he begun to suspect that Shimon was actually still alive. Painstakingly, he began to gather clues, pieces of information, until finally, he was convinced that his theory was correct.

The next step had been to accost Yochai and present him with the evidence he had uncovered. Surprisingly, Yochai hadn't even attempted to deny the accusation, readily admitting that the months Gil had spent working for the GSS had given him the tools he needed to launch his own independent investigation. If Yochai was dismayed at the thought that Gil would most likely soon be paying his father a visit, he didn't show it.

"How did you find me?" Shimon finally asked.

"I went home, a few days ago. I wanted to see how everyone was doing," Gil ignored the question.

"Why are you endangering them?" Shimon demanded sharply.

"I'm not. They know where they are without going to the trouble of following me there, but they're irrelevant at this point. They no longer have any intention of harming them. In fact, I went to see them on their orders; they still want me to maintain contact."

"Why?"

"Aren't you going to ask me how I'm doing, Tatty? Don't you care about me anymore? Are you still my father? Don't you mourn the fact that I'm about to die the way I mourned you?" Gil demanded suddenly, the anger that welled up inside him surprising even him.

Shimon placed a comforting hand on his son's shoulder.

"Calm down, Mendy," he said softly. "This isn't the time for recrimination. Especially with… with zero hour approaching, as you term it. Mendy – do you really intend to carry out the attack?"

Gil's shoulders sagged. "I don't have a choice in the matter, the way I see it. They found a new way to threaten me. They don't know about you. Yet. But they found someone else to threaten."

"Who?" Shimon asked sharply, his eyes frosty.

"Jamil. You know who I mean, right? He's your son."

Shimon's eyes narrowed, and his hand slid off Gil's shoulder. He began pacing the length of the room.

"How do they know where he is?"

"They know. He's in some *yeshivah* in Yerushalayim, I gathered, from what they told me. Yochai's trying to keep him safe, but it's pointless."

"No. It can't be. Somebody has to stop them," Shimon whispered weakly.

"They have their hands everywhere, Tatty. If not me, they've got hundreds of others waiting their turn to be a *shahid*. But they *davka* want me."

"Because…"

"Because their handlers in Damascus have promised them a massive injection of funds if they pull this off. And they know their chances of succeeding are much higher if they use me."

"And Yochai… does he know?"

"He has some idea, and some vague plan, but it's pathetic compared to what they have in store. He still thinks he can save me, but I know the truth. No one can save me." Gil's voice caught in his throat.

"But if Yochai's men are following you, then there's no way you'll be able to carry out the attack," Shimon argued, but Gil just laughed caustically, a mirthless laugh.

"Don't worry. They've got their ways of getting around such obstacles."

Shimon gazed at his son in shock. "You've really lost hope, haven't you?"

"Yes. There is no more hope for me, although Yochai thinks otherwise."

"Do you know things that we don't?"

"Yes."

"Like what?"

"Like, no matter what happens, it's either me or Jamil. Your son. If I don't do what they want, your son is dead. Do you understand what I'm saying, Tatty?"

Shimon lowered his head.

Gil gazed for a long moment at his father's features, as if trying to commit them to memory. "I have to go now, Tatty," he said after a pause. "And, I also wanted to thank you for everything you've done for me. No matter what happens, I'll always love you so much."

"I'll always love you too." Shimon's voice was a mere whisper.

"Even as an Arab?"

"I'll always love you, because of the unique *neshamah* inside of you, Mendy. You probably think that I curse the moment that I laid eyes on you, but it's not like that at all. You have beautiful character traits and… and a good heart, and I thank Hashem for granting us the *zechus* of raising you. That doesn't mean it doesn't hurt me that I didn't raise my own son, and my heart breaks when I think of the suffering he endured, but that's got nothing to do with your suffering right now. Mendy, as I see it, I have two eldest sons."

"I was never *misgayer*," Mendy noted hesitantly, turning a fearful gaze to his father.

"I know. Why not?"

"I have my reasons."

"Such as..."

"I spoke to a rav, and he told me not to," Gil replied quickly.

"Really?" Shimon looked surprised. "That's strange."

Gil glanced quickly at his watch and paled. "Wow. I'd better go. Someone's waiting for me downstairs."

"Which someone?" Shimon's voice rose fearfully.

"Don't worry. Someone completely uninvolved. A *chareidi* friend of mine. His name is Meir Landsman."

"Mendy, please try not to involve innocent people in this mess. And please don't come back, because I won't be here anymore. Five minutes after you leave, I'm off to a new hideout." Shimon pointed to a concealed exit. "I've got my own private parking lot and a motorcycle. You'd never recognize me."

"So I guess this is goodbye," Gil said in a husky voice.

"Mendy, take care of yourself," Shimon whispered.

"I will. You too, Tatty."

"I mean, take good care of yourself. You can never know, Mendy. Things could change... Don't give up. And please, Mendy, don't... You know..."

"I don't know anything, Tatty. Not about their plans and not about Yochai's plans. I'm just a pawn in this game – I don't get to make my own decisions. But now I really have to go, Tatty. Please believe me that none of this is my choice."

"No, Mendy, it is!"

"Goodbye, Tatty," Gil opened the door and was about to leave, but Shimon stopped him.

"Mendy, you're not worth less than any of my other children! Please, take care of yourself."

Gil looked quizzically at his father. "What do you mean by that?"

"I won't tell you to sacrifice yourself to save any of my other children. That's what I mean." Shimon's voice cracked, betraying his emotion. "Mendy, you're just as much my son as the others, and—" His father's face crumpled, and Gil watched him break down in tears.

"It'll be okay, Tatty. You'll see," Gil whispered. Without waiting for his father's reply, he closed the door gently behind him and raced down the steps, not even bothering to wait for the elevator. His fifteen minutes had come and gone, and Meir was probably frantic. He ran into the parking lot and toward the space where he had parked twenty minutes earlier to find it empty.

The car was gone.

Meir was gone.

Who would be next?

69

It was one-thirty in the morning, and Meir still wasn't home. Naomi felt her heart constrict in fear as she stared frantically out of the window, waiting for his familiar figure to appear in the distance, willing him to come home. She had called him no less than thirty-five times on his cell phone, but he hadn't answered even once, and each time the voice mail clicked on, she suppressed a scream. Why? Why hadn't he listened to her? Why didn't he have the sense to stay out of this? Why did she have to suffer – yet again – from his impossibly good heart?

Naomi sighed, and a stray tear escaped her eye. *Oh, Meir, please, just come home!*

In a subconscious effort to escape the tension of the present, her thoughts flitted back through the years, to when she had been a young girl of eighteen, presented with her first suggestions for *shidduchim*. It had been such an exciting time, and all the more so as the prospect of marriage became more and more real.

Meir had been the first serious suggestion her parents had fielded, and after making extensive inquiries, they had brought her into the picture. She could remember that evening like it was yesterday, the evening when her father sat her down at the kitchen table and detailed everything he had found out about Meir Landsman.

"He's a solid boy, an excellent learner from a respected family," he had begun. "He's a real *yarei Shamayim* and a *baal middos*, but there's one thing I've heard that surpasses even that. He's got a real heart of gold – that's what people say."

Naomi had dimpled in pleasure. "That's sounds really special." How impossibly naïve she had been…

Her father had looked slightly uneasy, "Naomi, the thing is, that with every *middah*, there has to be a limit. There's a fine line between having a good heart and allowing oneself to be exploited."

"I can't imagine how a good *middah* could be a problem," she had dismissed her father's concerns. "Someone who has a good heart will treat his family well, and, with all his other qualities, what more could a wife ask for?"

"Well, when the Torah commands us '*V'ahavta l'rei'acha kamocha*,' there's a *mitzvah* to love ourselves too, and not to love others more than ourselves. Did you ever hear that *peirush* before?"

"No."

"So you're hearing it now, Naomi. The point is that a person shouldn't let others take advantage of him, and I'm worried that this boy tends to do precisely that."

Naomi had silently absorbed her father's words, and, ultimately, both sides had given the go-ahead. Before long, the couple was happily engaged.

Already during the first week after their *chasunah* Naomi had become aware of the ramifications of her *chassan's* heart of gold. They had been preparing to leave for *sheva brachos*, and as Naomi put the final touches to her outfit, she noticed her husband fishing around in his jacket pockets.

"What are you looking for?" she had asked.

"A check."

"Which check?"

"The one that we got from Rubin, my father's friend."

"Oh, the big one?" she had smiled. She easily recalled the name, the one signed at the bottom of a check for five thousand shekels. "Why are you looking for it?"

"Because I don't want to have to look for it in front of all the guests," he had explained, as if it were self-evident.

"What do you need it for now? Don't you think it would be better to leave it in a safe place until we deposit it in the bank?" she had asked.

"Well, I was actually thinking that we could do something special with it," her *chassan* had replied thoughtfully.

"Like what?" Naomi had automatically assumed that the money would be put toward the down payment on the apartment they hoped to buy one day, but clearly her husband had something else in mind.

"You remember my friend, Yerachmiel Cohen? The one who came last night to *sheva brachos*? I told you he got married a few months ago."

"Oh, yes. *Nebach*. What a story!" she recalled sympathetically. Meir had told her that his friend, newly-married, had a father who was ill, a sister who had just gotten engaged, and a brother in a wheelchair. His mother, the sole breadwinner, had just lost her job, and Yerachmiel had taken on the burden of paying back the debts incurred from his wedding expenses, no small endeavor for a *kollel yungerman*. "What about him?" she asked as an afterthought.

"I happened to hear him asking around if anyone had five thousand shekels to lend him, and I told him that we did. Can you think of any better way to start off our marriage than with such a *chessed*?"

Naomi gaped. She may have been young and naïve, but she was still coldly logical. "Meir, you said that he's in major debt, didn't you?"

"Yeah. Something to the tune of a hundred thousand shekels, if not more, from what I understood."

"So how will he be able to pay us back when *we* need the money?"

"We don't need it right now."

"No, but when we hopefully buy an apartment, we will. And that could be anytime in the next few months. You know that."

Meir looked chagrined. "I hear what you're saying, but what can I do now? I already told him that I'd lend him the money, and I could see the relief on his face."

Ultimately, Meir had indeed extended the loan, but Naomi had determined to retrieve it within a half year, and luckily, she was successful. However, she wasn't always able to intervene so directly, neither was she able to soothe Meir's hurt feelings on the occasions when even he realized that he was being taken advantage of.

The issue had been one of Naomi's greatest challenges in her marriage, but she admitted that at least it was something like this, and nothing worse. This time, however, she felt completely powerless, as well as terrified to the core. Her insistent warnings to her husband not to get involved had been to no avail, and now the whole family was paying the price.

She watched the hands of the clock turn steadily, counting the minutes as they crawled by. By two o'clock, Naomi knew without a shadow of a doubt that her husband was in grave danger. Something terrible had happened to him, and he needed help. With trembling hands, she went to search through her husband's drawer, to see if maybe, just maybe, he had left his little phone book inside. For all his faults, Meir was extremely organized if slightly old-fashioned. He copied down all important information into a little directory, refusing to rely on the memory in his phone which, as he said and rightfully so, could easily be lost.

She practically cried in relief when she saw the little booklet with its dog-eared pages. *Who do I call now?* She flipped through the book until she found two numbers which were both possibilities; one was Mendy's, and the other was Yochai's. Presumably, Meir was still with Mendy, meaning that it was probably a waste of time to call him. And, it was Yochai who had ordered her husband out on this perilous mission, meaning that he certainly owed it to the family to guard his life.

To her surprise, her call was answered immediately, and the voice didn't even sound sleepy.

"Yes?"

"This is Meir Landsman's wife—" she began in a trembling voice.

"Oh, okay. He'll be home in about fifteen minutes," came the calm reply.

"Are you sure?"

"Absolutely."

"He's not answering his ph—" Naomi stopped short, realizing that she was speaking to herself. Her sigh of relief was accompanied by frustration and anger. She couldn't wait for this nightmare to end.

Gil looked around in confusion. The car clearly wasn't there, and neither was Meir. He walked slowly out of the lot, realizing that there was no chance in the world that timid Meir would have dared to hijack his car and escape. Realizing what must have happened, he broke out in a run, exiting the parking lot and scanning the street with frantic eyes.

Not surprisingly, the neighborhood was deserted at this late hour; everything was eerily silent, and Gil looked around, feeling powerless. His choices were non-existent; he couldn't return to his father's apartment, neither could he leave without locating Meir.

It suddenly struck him that for the first time in ages, he wasn't being followed. There were no eyes pursuing him, tracking his every footstep. He was free! Free!

His exhilaration was fleeting, however, when he reminded himself that Meir was almost certainly in grave danger, and that it was his obligation to see to it that he was all right. His immediate reaction was to call a cab and head straight to Headquarters, but he quickly dismissed the notion.

Where can I go? he wondered miserably. The thought echoed in his mind for a full ten seconds before he heard the sound of an approaching vehicle from behind and spun around, intuitively knowing that they had returned for him.

As expected, the car sped toward him quickly on the empty streets and pulled to a neat stop directly beside him. "Hop in," commanded a voice in Hebrew. Gil sagged in relief; it was one of Yochai's men.

As if to confirm his thoughts, the man continued, "Yochai's waiting for you."

"Where's Meir?" Gil asked suspiciously.

"Who's that?"

Gil himself couldn't know if the man was being truthful, but any further attempts to question him were ignored, and he resolved to wait until his meeting with Yochai, whom he met exactly twenty minutes later in the parking lot of a cheap convenience store located near the city limits.

Yochai folded his arms across his chest as soon as he laid eyes upon Gil, who stifled a smirk. Recently, he had noticed that while most people traditionally shook hands with those they met, Yochai had a quirky habit of folding them, especially when he was determined to assert his superiority.

"Well, there you are! Dropped Meir like a hot potato, eh?"

"You know where he is?" Gil was genuinely anxious.

"What's the question? Of course we do. You think we'd trust you to keep him safe?"

"Where is he?"

"Well, actually, Arabs tried hijacking the car first, but our guys got them, and now they're in our custody."

Gil turned white. "They'll blame me for this."

"I doubt it. We'll let them out soon enough. They know nothing about us."

"I hope not."

"In any case, here is your one chance to talk openly without worrying about people eavesdropping on you or knowing where you are," Yochai continued. "We're delaying Meir a bit longer to make this possible, and as soon as we finish our tête-à-tête, we'll bring him back to where we found him."

"So, what do you want to talk about?" Gil got straight to the point.

70

"Me? I thought *you* would want to talk," Yochai replied. "But, if you have nothing to say, then just take this, and we'll say our goodbyes." He pulled a popsicle stick – or what looked like one – out of his pocket and handed it to Gil.

Gil fingered it cautiously. "What's this?"

"Your protection."

"What do you mean?"

"Not only does this tell us exactly where you are and allow us to listen in to everything you say and hear, but we can even see everything in your vicinity, up to a radius of about two hundred meters," Yochai told him. "It's an expensive toy, worth tens of thousands, but well worth it. And, it's virtually indestructible, despite its flimsy appearance. It also has a wide range of other capacities, but those don't need to concern you."

"Like what?"

"Like X-ray capacity. If you see a bag, for instance, we see what's inside."

"Neat."

"Cut the sarcasm, Gil. We're trying to help you."

"No, you're not, Yochai. You know the truth, and so do I. You're helping yourself. My dad is helping himself. My mom is helping herself. The GSS is out for itself. Occasionally what's good for me happens to coincide with what someone else wants, but nobody really cares about me in the slightest."

"You'd be surprised," the older man retorted sharply.

"About what?"

"About how important you are to us. To us, and even more so, to your family. And that's one reason I'm so concerned. We know that they're threatening your family, and that you're aware of that."

Gil shrugged, his face expressionless.

"Gil, we're taking responsibility for you, for you and for your family. But when the moment of truth arrives, we don't know how much you'll be willing to sacrifice for our people."

Gil stiffened. "Thanks for the vote of confidence, Yochai. Nice to know that you think that I'd throw away twenty years of upbringing in a wonderful family and all my connection to Torah and the Jewish People for a bunch of murderers, just because I happen to technically be one of them."

"Well, you know what they say. Blood is thicker than water. And, you haven't converted," he added pointedly.

Tears sprang into Gil's eyes and rolled down his cheeks, but he made no attempt to hide them. "Believe me, Yochai, if I could be a Jew, I would, in an instant. I would give anything, *anything*, to have been born Jewish, although I don't expect you to understand that."

Yochai's eyes narrowed in anger. "Look, kid, I may not be religious, but I still wouldn't sell my Judaism for all the money in the world. And I don't expect *you* to understand that either.

"In any case, let's just drop this, shall we?" he continued, his tone of voice reverting to its usual even keel. "We have more important matters to discuss." He paused for a moment, before adding, "We need you to trust us this time. To stop thinking and acting like you know better."

Gil froze. "You're not saying that for nothing."

Yochai's face paled slightly. "What do you mean?"

"I mean that you have a reason for what you just said. What happened, Yochai? Tell me!"

"Nothing happened."

"I want the truth," Gil spoke harshly.

"Nothing happened! But I still need you to trust us fully. That's it, okay? Now, I think you should head back so we can let Meir out. Our guys are watching him in the meantime."

"What exactly happened to him?"

"I told you. Your friends hijacked the car."

"They're not my friends, and you're crazy, Yochai!" Gil shot back furiously. "Meir isn't to blame for what's going on. Don't play games with his life. He's a man with a heart of gold who's motivated only by the desire to help his fellow… man. That's something you've probably never experienced in your life."

Yochai bristled. "Then, perhaps you would like to explain why I put my life on the line every minute of the day?"

"You earn a nice, fat salary every month. Should I count the zeros at the end?"

"Money can't compensate for everything, as I'm sure you know by now," Yochai retorted.

"Yochai, I couldn't give a hoot if you're motivated by money or the thrill of adventure, but whatever it is, please don't put Meir in danger again. He's okay, right?"

"Oh, he's fine, except for managing to faint in the middle of everything."

"Poor guy."

"He is. You can go cheer him up now, if you like. And do me a favor and take him home because somebody over there thinks we're his babysitter and that we should be providing hourly updates on his welfare."

"Cut the cynicism, would you? If only any of us were worth half of what he is. If only you had a fraction of the compassion he has in his heart for me."

“I do, Gil. I really, really do.” For once, Yochai seemed to actually care what Gil thought of him.

And with those words, the two parted ways. Yochai slipped into his car and disappeared down the dark street, while Gil remained alone with his morose thoughts.

“Meir!” Naomi shouted in relief when she heard the knock on the door and hurried to unlock all three bolts. “Where were you all this time? Do you know that it’s three in the morning? Do you have any idea how worried I was? I was frantic! I didn’t know what to think anymore! I was—”

“I know,” Meir replied succinctly, and Naomi suddenly realized that his face was a pasty white.

“What happened over there?” she asked anxiously.

“Not much,” Meir sighed. “Only just like always when I go places with Mendy. We got a bit delayed and… let’s just say he didn’t exactly tell me where we were going. I’m beginning to see that both Mendy and the GSS are using me as a cover for whatever it is they’re doing – and I just don’t know why they picked me for the job.” Even as he uttered the words, Meir realized that he knew exactly why he had been picked for the job, but Naomi, thankfully, was gracious enough not to remind him.

“So just call it quits, or at least demand a salary!” she burst out in frustration. “We can’t continue like this!”

“A salary?” Meir’s voice rose. “I don’t want a monthly salary! No amount of money can compensate for what I just went through! I want out!” Sinking down onto the couch, Meir exhaled all his pent-up fury and reverted to his usual calm demeanor. “In any case, it’s almost over, regardless,” he told his wife. “That’s what Mendy told me. He said that his mission will be complete sometime during this coming week, and after that, we won’t be seeing each other again.”

"Really?" Naomi's relief was mingled with confusion. "Suddenly this is all going to be over? How?"

"I didn't ask. I'm sure he wouldn't tell me anyway, not Mendy, and not Yochai either. I don't even know whose mission this is anymore, nor do I care! I just want to go to sleep and forget about it all." He didn't have the emotional strength to share all that he had endured that night – the terror of his kidnapping and the subsequent humiliation when he had passed out in the car. The GSS boys had rolled with laughter, and his shirt was still wet from the water they had poured on him to get him back to his senses.

"You still haven't told me exactly what happened tonight," Naomi pointed out, torn between her sympathy for her husband and her anger at him having willfully exposed himself to such danger. "How do I know that tomorrow won't be a repeat performance? What are you hiding from me?"

"Lots."

Her expression thoughtful, Naomi replied slowly, "Look, you don't have to tell me what you don't want to. I understand that you'd rather not scare me, but maybe I can actually help you out with this. The more I'm thinking about it, the more I realize that the end of this mission – whatever it is – equals death. I don't know whose death, but this whole thing is going to be on someone's account, that's for sure. The way I see it, the GSS will protect their own people; they won't risk losing one of their agents. To them, people translate into money. How much do you think it costs to train one of their boys?"

"I have no idea."

"Tons, right?"

"Most probably, yes."

"And that's without accounting for the money they'd have to pay in compensation to the family of whoever ends up a victim."

"Naomi! What are you saying?"

"What I'm saying," she replied in feigned indifference, "is that it's much more worthwhile for Yochai to risk somebody cheap –

like you, for instance, whom he views as disposable. If something goes wrong, who'll know you were ever connected to the GSS? You never signed a contract with them. There's nothing tangible linking you to them at all. Something happened? You volunteered! Something went wrong? Your problem. Bye bye."

Meir gazed at his wife with newfound respect. *She's right,* he realized in sudden and awful clarity. *They endangered me just now, and they laughed at me, and they won't hesitate to do it again.*

"Let's take it a step further," she forged ahead mercilessly. "Look at Mendy. In the end, he decided not to be *misgayer,* and now he's talking about a final mission. Who's he loyal to? Definitely not to you. He's walking all over you, using you like a *shmattah*, and then he'll leave you hanging dirty on the line. You yourself just admitted that he needed to go somewhere and used you as his cover," she reminded him. "You won't tell me what happened, but I know that whatever it was, it wasn't good! Who's going to put his life on the line to rescue you at the end? Who'll save you? Yochai? Mendy? Do you really think they would? I, for one, sincerely doubt it. So, who cares about you, Meir – who?"

"Who?" he repeated.

"Me. Only me! Your wife and your family." Tears sparkled in her eyes, but she continued, her argument gaining momentum. "And that's why I've had enough of this already! No more! I can't take this any longer, and why should I? So, you know what I'm going to do? I have an idea that will get you out of this once and for all, if what Mendy told you is true and there really is only another week of this to go."

"*You* can get me out of this?" Meir's voice was dubious.

"Yes! Tomorrow morning, you're going to have a special breakfast. Your usual bread and salad, with a peanut on the side. Just one, and you'll blow up like last time, not dangerously but enough to make you wheeze. I'll call an ambulance, and they'll keep you in hospital for a week under observation, just like that time when you ate that cake at a *simchah* and there was peanut butter in it. You'll feel awful for a few days, but believe me, it will be worth it."

The volume was on full blast, and Naomi's voice resonated clearly in Yochai's office. His eyes blazed in astonishment mixed with fury, and he banged his fist down onto the desk.

"Just one more of her bright ideas, and our whole operation is finished!" he exploded.

"She's not bad. We should hire her," his aide smirked.

Yochai pushed a button on his desk. "Nir, send a car to get Landsman this minute! I can't have his wife feeding him any more ideas. I need him here, pronto!"

The loud knocks at the door at four a.m. were more irritating than frightening. Meir was already fast asleep, and angry at being woken so soon.

"What do they want from me?" he grumbled, only half-awake. "Tell Mendy I'm asleep, in the middle of a dream… Wait a minute…" Meir suddenly sat bolt upright. "It must be important if he's knocking now. I have to open, Naomi, I'm sorry. But you go back to sleep. I'll invite him in, and there's no way I'm going anywhere with him now, so don't worry."

Naomi's eyes were wide with fear and she nodded slightly to her husband, before he left the room. Then, she closed the door behind him and pressed her ear against it, listening intently.

She heard the door open and a man apologize politely for the rude awakening.

"Good evening. My name is Nir. Yochai sent me to—"

Meir stared at him. "It's not Mendy? So what are you doing here? You can tell Yochai that—"

"No, you can tell him yourself, because you're coming with me," Nir smiled deferentially.

"Now?"

"Now."

"Are you out of your mind? I'm not going anywhere at this hour. If you want, you can call the police and take me there in handcuffs, but then I'll tell the world what's going on, so I'd suggest you leave now before this turns unpleasant." Meir's voice, which he kept to a whisper to avoid waking the neighbors, didn't particularly impress Nir who deliberately raised his.

"Listen, friend. If you want handcuffs, I can bring those too. I can even bring a whole crew of boys in blue uniforms, but right now, I come in friendship. Let's go, before it really does turn unpleasant."

Meir's mouth went dry, understanding that this guy meant business. "Okay," he said slowly. "Let me get dressed."

"Get dressed?" Nir repeated hesitantly.

"Yes. Get dressed. And put on shoes. You don't expect me to go in pajamas, do you?" Meir retorted harshly.

Nir glanced at his watch. "You've got five minutes." He stepped into the house without invitation. Naomi, trembling behind the closed door, had heard every word. She quickly opened the door and joined Meir in the living room.

"What now?" he asked despairingly.

Naomi was as tense as a coiled spring. "I'm going to the kitchen to get you a drink and something to eat. You hear? Eat it on the way and get it over with. It won't be pleasant, but you'll get over it…" She stared meaningfully into his eyes.

Meir nodded, understanding exactly what she was alluding to. As he prepared to leave, she discreetly slipped a peanut into his jacket pocket.

"I'll just take a coffee, and we can be on our way," he said to Nir.

"You'll get your coffee over at Yochai's," Nir promised, and Meir capitulated and followed him down the steps.

"Just one second. Yochai asked me to do something before we leave…" Nir suddenly remembered. In a flash, he grabbed hold of Meir's jacket and rifled through the pockets until he found what he was looking for. "Here you are!" he exclaimed jovially, grinning at the solitary peanut. "I knew I'd find you somewhere!" With that, he popped it into his mouth and chewed it with evident satisfaction.

"Just for your information, people don't just eat one peanut. You eat them by the handful, but I guess you wouldn't know that if you're severely allergic to them!" he chuckled.

Meir's shoulders sagged in despair. "Okay. I get it. You know everything about me. What else do you want?"

"To inform you that you'll be staying with us until further notice."

"I don't owe you guys anything."

"That's an order from Yochai, and nobody, *nobody,* says no to Yochai. If you try to, he can find other, far less pleasant ways of getting to you. Meir, for your own good – you live in a quiet, residential neighborhood. Do you really want to create a stir?"

It was the most persuasive threat that Nir could have used against Meir. The last thing he wanted was for people to start talking about him being under arrest, something that could easily destroy his reputation and jeopardize his children's future. Just then, Naomi appeared outside; she had overheard Nir's last sentence and understood exactly what was going on.

"I just want to give him something for the way. Okay?" she pleaded.

"It's not necessary, ma'am. We'll provide your husband with everything he needs," Nir replied pleasantly.

"Okay, so at least for the journey," she persisted.

"The journey is a grand total of thirty minutes in daytime, and ten minutes at night."

Naomi looked like she was about to throw a tantrum. "You need a coat in this weather," she added, turning to her husband.

"It's not cold tonight, ma'am," Nir countered.

"Not for you, maybe. But my husband needs a coat."

"As you wish, ma'am." Nir remained the perfect gentleman. "What we don't do to keep our wives happy!" he joked, but Meir didn't smile. Naomi raced to the kitchen and returned less than a minute later with a water bottle and Meir's coat and wallet. "Here, you should have your wallet, so you won't need any favors from them to get back home. And talk to Yochai, okay? Don't give in to him. Make him sign a contract with you. Please!" Her eyes filled with tears.

Meir nodded, though he already surmised that it was a lost battle.

Just before they entered the car, Nir turned to Meir. "May I?" Without awaiting a reply, he grabbed Meir's coat and checked the pockets, emerging with another two peanuts.

"Two, this time. I'd call that progress!" he exclaimed cheerfully. "And now, on to Yochai! Since I knew you'd be accompanying me, I even downloaded some chassidic music!" He pressed the play button, and Mordechai Ben David's voice blasted "*Mashiach, Mashiach, Mashiach. Oy yoy yoy yoy yoy yoy.*"

But all Meir could think was "*Oy yoy yoy.*" *What does Yochai want from my life?*

Yitzchak didn't dare utter a word, knowing that anything he said would be used against him. Yochai paced his office, not even deigning to cast a glance at his agent, now revealed as totally hapless, in his eyes.

Finally, Yochai swung around and pierced Yitzchak with a penetrating gaze. "Just tell me how it happened. No excuses, no explanations, just facts."

Yitzchak cleared his throat, trying to buy some time, even an extra second. "So, it's like this..." Noting Yochai's glare, he hurriedly continued, "There was a technician in the building, to repair the washing machine. It must have been him. I watched to see that he was actually doing a repair job, and he was. Jamil was in his room, and when the repairman finished, I went to check on him, and he was still there – Jamil, I mean. I watched out of the window to see that the repairman had left, and I even saw him leave, alone. But when I went back to check on Jamil again, he was gone. There were only about two minutes between the times I checked on him," Yitzchak tried to defend himself. "I really don't understand how it could have happened."

"That's not your job, to understand," Yochai retorted. "You were supposed to protect him, not to understand how he was nabbed from right under your nose. As I'm sure you're aware, you'll pay dearly for this… but that's not going to help now." Yochai exhaled sharply in frustration. "At least we got Meir in time," he muttered under his breath. "And you," he turned back to Yitzchak, "can go and get some sleep now. At least while you're on extended vacation you won't be able to do any damage."

Yitzchak nodded sadly and turned to leave, almost colliding with someone entering Yochai's office as he did. It was a young, pale-faced *chareidi* with a terrorized expression, with Nir, Yochai's assistant, at his side.

"Hey," Nir greeted them. "I brought him."

"Thank you," Yochai nodded and dismissed him. As Nir returned to his desk, he realized he was still humming *"Mashiach, Mashiach, Mashiach!"*

Not a bad song, he thought.

"Hi, kids. I'm home!" Shuli called as she stepped into the house.

"Hi," Nachum greeted her, picking his head up from his homework.

"Anyone call?" she asked nonchalantly, even though her heart beat rapidly every time she asked the question, never knowing what the answer would be.

"Uh huh."

"Who?"

"The guy from the fruit store."

The color drained from Shuli's face. "Oh?" she mustered as calmly as she could. "What did he say?"

"That the vegetables came, except for one sack of potatoes that got lost somehow."

"He said what?" she asked, her voice shrill.

"I didn't get it either," Nachum replied with a shrug. "Big deal. A sack of potatoes. Do you want me to buy them from a different store?"

She ignored the question. "Did he leave a phone number?" Her voice trembled violently.

"No."

"Did he say anything else?"

"He said that all the vegetables are in a safe place, except the potatoes." Suddenly, Nachum noticed that his mother was shaking and that a tear was trickling down her cheek.

"What's wrong, Mommy?"

"What?"

"Why are you crying? It's only a sack of potatoes! If you need them for supper, I can run to the store now or borrow from a neighbor."

"No. No! Stay home. It's okay. Where's Suri?"

"Playing at the Rosenbergs."

"Can you run and get her?" Shuli stopped short. "You know what? On second thought, I'll go. You stay home. Or… you know what? You come with me. Maybe we'll visit the Rosenbergs for a while."

"Do you mind if I stay? I don't have any friends there, plus I have a lot of homework and a huge *Gemara* test tomorrow."

"I'd rather you came," Shuli said firmly. Nachum sighed reluctantly, but joined her at the door.

"Oh, wait. I forgot to tell you," he remembered suddenly.

"What?" Shuli wondered how much more her heart could withstand.

"The guy from the fruit store said that he's sending someone to pick up the money for the order."

"When is he coming?"

"Sometime in the next hour. Maybe I should stay home to wait for him?" Nachum asked hopefully.

"No! You go and get Suri. But carefully, okay? I'll wait for him."

"O-kay," Nachum sighed again. He understood enough to grasp that his mother's fears were probably not baseless, and that fetching his sister was a grave responsibility.

Less than a minute passed between the time that Nachum left the house and the knocking on the door. Shuli recognized those knocks; she'd heard them hundreds of times, and tears of relief sprang instantly to her eyes.

She opened the door to find herself facing a deliveryman with a bushy orange beard. The eyes were unmistakable, though.

"Shimon!" she whispered incredulously.

Shimon smiled, but Shuli couldn't mistake the anxiety etched into his features as he heaved a large box of fruit and carried it into the kitchen.

"What happened? Where's Ja-Mendy. Where is he?" she finally stammered, having never really figured out the best way to refer to her son.

"He disappeared into thin air. He was under close watch, with three of our boys guarding him, but somehow, they managed to grab him regardless."

"Is he… alive?"

"In all likelihood, yes."

"Why?"

"Actually, the answer is definitely yes. Yochai even knows where he's being held. They can't smuggle him out of the country.'

"Why did they take him?"

"The conjecture is that Mendy… Mendy…" he stopped short, still feeling responsibility and love toward the son he had raised. "Their purpose is to force Mendy to carry out an attack, and they're threatening that if he doesn't comply, the other Mendy will pay the price."

Shuli paled. "So… so there's no way out of this?"

"That's not what I said. But we do have to *daven*. *Daven* hard. You know, Mendy came to see me after he visited you, to say goodbye."

"How did he find you?"

"How? I don't know – it doesn't matter. I moved on since then, in any case. They didn't catch on to me. But… he's not in an easy position."

"At least he's free, whereas Jamil—"

"He's not free," Shimon sighed. "He is in a terrible trap, with no clear way out. Yochai seems to think he can help him, and I hope he's right, but it's not simple."

Their conversation was interrupted by a knock at the door,

and then it opened to reveal Nachum and Suri. Shimon promptly turned to leave, studiously avoiding the children's gazes.

Nachum gazed curiously at the deliveryman as he left. "He looks a bit familiar, doesn't he?" he murmured.

"Yes. I thought so too," Shuli struggled to maintain an even tone.

"Did he bring the potatoes?"

"No, but he said he'll bring them tomorrow or later in the week."

Nachum nodded, well aware that his mother was hiding something from him but knowing that she wasn't about to divulge the secret. Shuli managed a weak smile at her children before disappearing off to her room, where she could be alone with her thoughts.

Never had she dreamed that her husband's former profession would return so dramatically to haunt him. As far as she had been concerned, his years of working for the GSS were firmly relegated to the past, and suddenly she found her mind wandering back to that day, so many years ago, when Shimon – then Yotam – had first revealed his secret.

They had already been dating for a few months, and one afternoon, Yotam suggested that they go on a hike through a nature reserve. Shuli, known as Sheila back then, had automatically assumed that Yotam had chosen that setting in order to propose marriage, but it was a different kind of proposal entirely that she ended up facing.

The revelation was completely unexpected. Yotam wasn't a nature-loving photographer, as he had led her to believe, but rather a GSS operative. She was shocked into speechlessness, and it took her a while to overcome her feelings of betrayal and muster a response. How could he have lied to her for so long? Didn't he trust her? What kind of basis was that for a relationship?

They had been sitting on the bank of the river, and Sheila stared into the rushing waters, trying to figure out how to react. It didn't take long for her to overcome her initial angry reaction and see things in a different light. If she married Yotam, she would be marrying someone with a mission, someone with principles who was willing to sacrifice for them. Slowly, she nodded her acceptance of this new reality, and listened to what he had to say.

"It's not necessarily how you think it is," he had warned her. "Working for the GSS isn't about glory or prestige, and nobody gets to choose his assignments. And, you have to be aware that there are many personal risks involved. I can't ask you to enter into a lifetime partnership with me without knowing this. Please, don't answer me now. Give me an answer tomorrow, or in a few days, or even a few weeks if you think you need the time."

In the end, she had given him her answer the next day, and they were married only a few weeks later. Two months after they were married, Yotam had disappeared for a week, and it was only then that she fully grasped what she had taken on. During that week, she had no idea where he was – or even when he was coming back. He reappeared as abruptly as he had disappeared, gently reminding her that this was going to be a recurring pattern, and gradually, she had become more accustomed to her new life.

It wasn't easy for him, either. Although sometimes he returned from a mission with the fire of success burning in his eyes, on other occasions, he dragged his feet into the house and burst into tears.

"No one will ever know what happened," he would mourn. "Nobody will ever even recognize their sacrifice…"

After becoming religious, Shimon submitted his request for early retirement from the field. After giving over a decade of his life to his nation, all he wanted was to learn more about his heritage and raise a family. For twenty years, he had succeeded in forgetting his past and keeping it totally apart from the present; but now, the past had returned to haunt them, and once again, Shimon was gone. Since his staged death, they had met just three times, and never for more than a few minutes on each occasion. Those moments were never spent crying or lamenting the past – time was too precious, and instead, they focused on preparing for the future.

By all accounts, Shimon's "death" had been one of Yochai's most masterful operations. The moment that he received word that Shimon had been admitted to hospital, he began to devise the plan. He headed straight for the hospital and conferred briefly with the head of the department to make the necessary arrangements, and the level of secrecy surrounding the operation was such that Shuli only learned the truth an hour before the *levayah.*

She had been furious at Yochai, and at her husband too, for causing her such intense suffering, but once her anger cooled, she had realized that there was really no other choice. If she wanted to maximize the safety of her family, she was going to have to make sacrifices, and living as a widow was a small price to pay in place of actually becoming one.

Now, however, things had taken a frightening turn, and despite Shimon's efforts to reassure her, she knew that the situation was grave. The more she thought about it, the more she realized that Shimon no longer trusted Yochai. Although Yochai himself still preferred to present a confident front, events had proved that he had lost control. Jamil-Mendy was being held by the other side, and although Shimon insisted that he was only a temporary hostage in order to ensure that the other Mendy followed orders, Shuli doubted that the Arabs would release him once the operation was over. Why should they? What did they have to gain?

No, she didn't trust the Arabs, nor Yochai, nor any other human being, for that matter. And neither did Shimon.

Suddenly, it dawned on her that Shimon had come for one purpose only. He had been hinting that he was entering into action, but for once, not under the auspices of the GSS.

He was planning to go it alone.

He was going to try to save Mendy – both Mendys.

Jamil sat on a hard-backed wooden chair in a locked room, his voice hoarse from shouting. After unleashing all his fury upon his Arab guards, he felt somewhat better, even though he had to admit that he had achieved absolutely nothing with it. He was still a prisoner, and his guards were even less fond of him than they had been previously.

He hated to admit it, but Jamil actually enjoyed speaking Arabic again. Despite being at the mercy of his enemies, somehow he felt secure in the familiarity of it all – the food, the language, even the coarse shouting… He knew what to expect, and even after living for many months with the *Yahud*, he still didn't feel that level of comfort with them.

He asked to be let out for a few minutes to take a walk and get a breath of fresh air, but was, unsurprisingly, refused.

"Sorry, *ya-habibi.* We're not authorized to let you out, not even for a moment. Sit tight and say thank you that no one's killing you," one of the guards replied, their previous clash already forgotten.

Jamil balled his hands into fists and started pacing the floor. "Why me?" he complained, for probably the thousandth time since he had been kidnapped. "What do you guys want from my life? I'm just a dumb village kid who no one ever cared about. Why is everyone suddenly out to get me?"

Nobody answered. The two men in the room continued their game of backgammon while Jamil groaned and lamented his sorry fate. Only occasionally did they yell at him to shut up.

"Hey, did it ever occur to you guys that I could actually cooperate with you?" Jamil asked suddenly.

Finally, he had their attention, even though their initial response was to snort contemptuously and turn sneering gazes upon him. Jamil wasn't deterred.

"Of course I can be of use. I'm fluent in Hebrew by now, and they're starting to see me as one of them, even though my loyalties will always remain with the Arab nation," Jamil lied effortlessly. "I always hated them, and I threw rocks at them hundreds of times," he bragged, even though it was hardly possible given that his family hadn't let him out of the village.

Finally, one of them approached him. "What exactly are you proposing, brother?"

Jamil grinned disarmingly. "Think about it. I can walk around freely, dressed as a *Yahud*. I can go anywhere, and no one will stop me. I don't have to tell my family anything. They let me come and go as I please – and yet, they waste tons of resources taking care of me, resources that they can put to other uses when they know that I'm safe here with you."

The two guards exchanged meaningful looks, and the second one replied, "Look, we don't have the authority to make any decisions. But we'll pass the message on to our superiors. The only thing that's not clear is why you would want to help us. Stop all the nonsense about the 'Arab nation,' okay?"

Jamil shrugged. "Let's just say it works out because we both get what we want. I get my freedom, and you get what you want: a successful strike against the enemy."

The Arabs burst out in raucous laughter. "You're quite a character! But you've got good ideas. Sit quietly and don't talk too much, okay?"

Jamil didn't join in their laughter. Over the past few months, he had come to despise the people and covert activities taking place all around him. He saw himself as nothing but a pawn, and he wanted nothing more than to escape – from the Arabs, the Israelis, and everyone else. He wanted a new life, a life of freedom and choice; and he felt that it wasn't long before he would attain it. All he needed to do was wait for the opportune moment. His knowledge of the language and culture would serve him well. The moment he detected even the tiniest breach, he would escape, to finally become his own master.

Despite Yochai's threat, that Meir would be kept under lock and key until the operation was over, in the end, Meir was dismissed – Yochai having correctly surmised that he would think twice before trying to escape again. He was home by nine the next morning, catching Naomi by surprise. The children had already left for school and nursery, and although the house was a wreck, it would have to stay that way for the time being, as Naomi had to leave for work in less than twenty minutes.

"Is it you?" she asked in disbelief, searching for signs of an allergic reaction on his face and forgetting to even say hello.

Meir smiled weakly. "It's me."

"You didn't eat the peanuts." Her words were a statement, not a question.

"I couldn't. They confiscated them before I had a chance," he replied apologetically.

Naomi's face darkened, but Meir was quick to reassure her. "But I'm happy that I didn't. I have other, more important things to do now."

"Like what?" She faced him with her hands on her hips.

"I can't tell you everything, but, Naomi, I need you to be with me on this. One hundred percent. Yochai is letting me tell you one important point, and he's certain – and so am I – that as soon as you hear this, you'll appreciate the magnitude of what I'm doing."

Naomi folded her hands across her chest. "Okay. I'm listening."

"Okay, so it's like this. Jamil, you know, the guy who grew up with Arabs, was just kidnapped."

Naomi's instinctive reaction was a horrified gasp, but a moment later, she reverted to her innate suspicious self. "I didn't see anything about it in the paper this morning. How do you know it really happened?"

Meir had to restrain himself from rolling his eyes. "Naomi, this is top secret stuff! It's classified – the man on the street knows nothing about any of this. What they release to the media is all for a purpose, and with this operation, there's no purpose in having anyone know about it."

"Except you," Naomi reminded him. "I still want to know why Yochai insists in keeping you involved."

"I'm getting to that. Well, actually, you know already. Mendy needs a listening ear this week, more than ever, and Yochai promised me that this really will be the last week."

"Oh, really?" Naomi sounded unimpressed. "And we're supposed to believe that?"

Meir was about to answer, but before he got a chance, his phone rang.

"Hello? Hi, Mendy… Yes, I'm home. Sure you can come up," he said, before ending the call.

"What does he want?" Naomi demanded.

"To learn."

"But he's not even Jewish yet!"

"He wants to convert," Meir reminded her.

"I thought he changed his mind."

"Kind of, but not really. I think it depends on the outcome of the mission."

"He doesn't need you to learn. He can learn in any *beis medrash*," she said obstinately.

"Naomi," Meir looked her in the eye, imploring with her to show some understanding. "Please, be patient. Just another week, I promise you."

"Okay! Whatever you say. In any case, I'm going to work," she replied, her frustration evident.

"That's a good idea," he said calmly.

Naomi put on her coat, grabbed her pocketbook, and stormed angrily out of the house, almost bumping into Mendy as he made his way up the stairs.

"I hope I'm not disturbing," he said to Meir as he entered.

"Not at all."

"I was hoping we could learn for a while."

"Of course. That's a great idea," Meir replied, briefly wondering how he was going to explain his repeated absences to his *rosh kollel.*

"I'm going to be very busy this week, but I still want to try my best to keep to a regular *seder*," Mendy added. "By the way, I spoke to the rav again last night—"

"And?"

Mendy smiled, but it was a smile laced with tears. "We spoke for a long time, and I finally came to a decision."

Meir sighed in relief. "I'm so glad to hear that. It must have been so hard for you, not knowing what to do."

"Meir..." Mendy said seriously, "don't jump to conclusions so quickly."

"What do you mean?" Meir looked surprised. "This is what you want. No one has to convince you of it; it's who you are."

"Yes, but after speaking at length to the rav and asking my questions without getting into details that I can't reveal, I reached a final solution. It's not the ideal, but it's the ideal in my situation."

"Meaning?" Meir's voice rose in angst.

"I can't convert. If I want to save *Klal Yisrael*, I'm not allowed to. And the way I see it, the nation comes before my puny little life." Mendy broke down in tears.

Meir gazed pleadingly at the younger man. "Mendy... I don't understand."

"Don't you get it? I can't convert! If I become a Jew, then I'm obligated to save my own life first, because *chayecha kodmin.* But if I'm not bound by this *halachah*, then I can save other people's lives. And... I prefer to save their lives over mine."

"But..." Meir was shocked, but struggled mightily to muster a response. "What... what are you trying to tell me?"

Mendy smiled again, this time without tears in his eyes. "I'm trying to tell you that I want to learn with you, while I still can. That's one thing that I'm allowed to do, so let's get started. Do you have any idea how much I missed learning, or *davening*? And... whatever. That's not the point now. Just remember that I really miss being a Yid, because after... everything, people will have a million-and-one things to say about me. But at least someone will know the truth, and that person will be you."

He fell silent, and Meir intuitively grasped that this was Mendy's way of saying goodbye, and thank you.

Laser was satisfied. "Three days are over, and they've been tough days, but we've gotten past them. Just another four days to go, and then the week will be behind us. We'll get there. Where's Gil?"

"He should be here within the hour," Aziz, Laser's aide, told him, hoping that his boss wouldn't become infuriated at the delay.

"An hour?" Laser's eyes narrowed. "Can't you do anything quickly? Well… just make sure that everything's ready for when he gets here. And as for Jamil, tell him and his guards to get ready for a trip. I want him out of the way, maybe even to Jordan, before the operation begins."

"And afterward?" Aziz dared to ask. "What's going to happen to Jamil then?"

"Then? He'll die like the dog and traitor he is. But for the meantime, we can let him live," he added magnanimously.

"You want his guards to finish him off? The Israelis are liable to seek revenge," Aziz pointed out.

"So they'll kill the guards in revenge. Big deal. That's what those street kids are for," Laser replied dismissively.

Aziz paled. Those "street kids" just happened to be his nephews, and he had used his connections to get them appointed to the coveted position of bodyguard in the first place, knowing that they would be well reimbursed. Laser's funds came straight from Damascus; his staff didn't have to wait for the cumbersome Palestinian bureaucratic machine to get paid.

Yet, when Aziz considered his own sizeable salary and then looked at his own position with clearer vision, suddenly it seemed so much less appealing when he realized that he was likely destined to share the same fate as his young relatives.

Laser spent the next hour closeted in his office, reviewing every single detail of the plan. Finally, Aziz knocked gently and informed him that Gil had arrived, but Laser deliberately made him wait. Twenty minutes later, he exited his office and stared intently at the young man who looked even younger than usual beneath his baseball cap. His face was pinched and white, as if he hadn't eaten in days.

"Welcome, *ya-habibi!* Why the long face? The *Yahud* aren't treating you well?" he greeted him with false joviality. "You should be happy! You're a hero, and in just a few days' time, you'll prove it to the world! Your soul will ascend to the heights of Paradise, to enjoy the wealth and bounty of kings! Smile, boy! Aziz, bring him something to eat and drink before he passes out."

Aziz hastened to bring a tray of pastries to the table, but Gil paid it no attention.

"What do you want? Where is everyone else?" he demanded.

"Today, we're having a private meeting. Call it a tête-à-tête, if you will. Today, I'm going to tell you everything you need to know, because in three days from today, you're coming back, and you won't be leaving again until the operation begins. Understood? So here it is, black on white, and in Hebrew, for your convenience." He handed him a sheaf of papers which Gil rifled through quickly, skimming through the main points.

"There?" he asked in disbelief, and to everyone's surprise, started laughing. "That's the grand location where you plan on executing your plan?"

"Precisely," Laser replied calmly. "Official police estimates are that there will be around eight thousand people at the event. You'll find your way in, which shouldn't be difficult with you dressed up like one of them. Get rid of the baseball cap and switch it for one of those black hats of theirs. You'll drag in the stuff and tell them that it's refreshments for the guests. That's it. Simple as can be."

To his consternation, Gil continued to laugh.

"What's so funny?" Laser demanded angrily. Aziz's eyes flitted anxiously between the two men.

"You want me to blow myself up at a *hachnassas sefer Torah*, and you expect me not to laugh?"

"So laugh. Go ahead." Laser shrugged, changing his approach. "Listen well, *ya-habibi*: We have Jamil, the son of the *Yahud*, with us as we speak. We also have your mother targeted, as well as your brother and sister. Don't think we'd leave them out of this. We've got three people on each of their tails, so don't imagine that you have a choice in this. If you so much as dare to deviate one iota from the plan, your family that you love so much is 'poof,' goes up in smoke. And you can end your days as a despised, loathed creature without a place to call home, shunned by Jew and Arab alike. Well, what do you have to say, my dear Gil? Still finding what to laugh about?"

There was no trace of a smile left on Gil's lips.

"You have the boy?" he asked weakly.

"He's not exactly a boy. He's actually your age, almost to the minute," Laser reminded him.

But he was a son. He was the true son of Gil's parents, and Gil's face turned even whiter than before.

"You have him?" he repeated again dumbly, his eyes flitting in their sockets as if he were on the verge of collapse. Aziz gave him a light shove to return him to the present, while Laser smiled, an evil smile.

"Yes, Gil, he's with us. He's safe and sound. For now. What are you so surprised about? Didn't you know that already?"

"When they told me, I thought… I thought…" *I thought that*

they were just trying to pressure me – that it was just another one of their lies...

But what was far worse was what Yochai believed. He still thought that there was reciprocity. If Gil obeyed his Arab masters, then they wouldn't harm Jamil; if he refused them, they would kill him. Gil, however, who had spent a full year in the company of these Arabs, knew that Jamil would never escape with his life, regardless.

"A *hachnassas sefer Torah*?" Naomi countered in surprise. "In Yerushalayim? Why all the way there?"

"It's supposed to be incredible. There's going to be something like ten thousand Yidden there."

"You have some kind of connection with this?"

"No."

"So why shlep all the way to Yerushalayim?" she repeated, and then the realization dawned on her. "Meir, tell me just one thing: Does this have something to do with Mendy Brand?"

"Yes." Despite everything, Meir was still unwilling to lie to his wife.

Naomi bit her lip. "Meir, if this has something to do with Mendy, then why shlep us all there? What if it's a *sakanah*? Why put the kids in danger?"

"It's not dangerous at all." Meir couldn't understand her fears. "Mendy wants to go there, unrelated to everything else that's going on. It's going to be a huge event, and he doesn't want to go alone. He wants to come back, to become a Yid, but he feels that something is preventing him. He's hoping that this will change things, and give him that feeling of connection. He practically begged me to accompany him, so I agreed. What's the big deal? Why not go? We agreed to help him, after all."

"We agreed that *you'd* help him. I never said anything about me or the kids. You're changing the rules in the middle of the game, Meir."

"Okay, so I apologize. Look, Naomi, I'll tell you the truth: I'm scared to leave you alone these days, which is why I'd much rather you came along rather than staying behind without me. Please?" Finally, Naomi found herself listening and not just hearing.

"But Meir, why do you think he wants you to come along with him?"

"I already told you. And in any case, why not? It'll be an amazing event, a real *kiddush Hashem*."

"But Meir," she continued to try to rouse him from his self-imposed stupor, "last week, Mendy told you, 'one more week.' Why now, of all days, does he suddenly want to run off to Yerushalayim?"

Meir shook his head, wondering why his wife insisted on being suspicious of absolutely everything in sight.

Naomi sighed. "Look, Meir, I'm willing to come along, but I'm not willing to put you, or I, and definitely not the children, at risk. So this is my condition: Either Mendy tells you exactly why he so badly wants to go and needs you to come along – and not some fudgy story about wanting to be inspired by a massive *kiddush Hashem* – or none of us goes anywhere near that place. Agreed?"

Meir nodded slowly; it was fair enough. "Agreed."

Yochai slammed his fist into his desk again, a bad habit that, of late, he found himself doing with increased frequency. "Why does he get his family involved in every part of the plan?" he cried in frustration. "He's jeopardizing the success of the entire mission!"

Guy Arbiv, a colleague who was listening in on the conversation along with Yochai, simply laughed. "She's a sharp one, that wife of his. And, it really is unethical of us, Yochai. If anyone gets wind of the fact that we risked civilians in such a dangerous mission, we'll both lose our jobs, not to mention probably spend the next two decades in jail."

"Feh! This isn't dangerous at all," Yochai said dismissively, but Guy made a face.

"Yochai," the junior officer tried again, "this Meir may be a father of three, but he's a baby in these matters and completely untrained. Imagine that he was your son. Would you still put him in this same position with the same confidence that he'll emerge from it unscathed?"

Yochai didn't reply, and Guy silently celebrated his victory.

"She's right," Guy repeated. "And you should take heed, sir."

Yochai's face darkened. "You're out of line, Arbiv! Get out of my office this minute! You think she's right, huh? Thousands of lives are at stake! If I cancel the event, our enemies will find a different venue to carry out their plan, but this time, they'll leave Gil out of it and we'll be clueless. Here is our one and only chance to nab them all. Don't you get it? We're talking about saving thousands of people!"

Guy shook his head. "You have a son, Yochai, and so do I, so I know what I'm talking about. How many people would you sacrifice to save your own son? You're putting Meir in harm's way, and his life is no less valuable than anyone else's. He doesn't have the slightest idea that he's walking into a death trap, and what we're doing isn't just unethical and immoral, but it's probably downright illegal too!"

Yochai narrowed his eyes dangerously at his junior colleague, and he suddenly resembled a poisonous snake on the verge of attack. Hoping he hadn't just lost his job, Guy fell silent and fled his boss' office.

"You're out of your mind," Aziz said, but Gil didn't reply. "You're nuts. You're just making it more likely that Laser will get rid of him."

Gil smiled thinly. "More likely than one hundred percent? If so, then what do you care? Stop making trouble, Aziz, and let me go in, okay?"

The Arab moved aside reluctantly. "All right, but if Laser hears about this, then I had nothing to do with it. You went in of your own accord."

Gil nodded brusquely and headed swiftly down the corridor, turning left, and then right, until he reached the room he sought. Outside, an armed guard sat, looking bored, but his demeanor stiffened as he saw Gil approach and his finger slid along to the trigger of his gun.

Aziz, coming up behind Gil, nodded at the guard. "Let him in." The guard stood up and drew a bolt in the door, standing back to let them pass. Aziz led Gil down a long corridor where they encountered another two guards who retreated at the sight of Laser's personal aide, allowing them access to a staircase that ended in another door.

"Here you are. You can go in, but remember to tell him that this was your doing, not mine. Is that clear?"

Gil nodded in assent, and Aziz unlocked the door. Gil entered the room, and Aziz locked it behind him.

The room was windowless but brightly lit. As soon as the door opened, Jamil jumped to his feet and treated Gil to an antagonistic look.

"Another one to torment me?" he whined. "What do you want? When are you going to let me out of here already?"

Gil watched the boy dispassionately. This was the boy whom he should have become, the boy who had lived his miserable life in a squalid village, suffering for a decision taken by others and now about to pay the price – a price he seemed to be as yet unaware of. Didn't he realize that he would likely never see the light of day again? Was he really so naïve?

"I can't let you out," Gil replied, his eyes still locked on Jamil.

"Who are you, anyway?" Jamil finally remembered to ask.

"I'm Mendy."

"Who?"

"Mendy."

Jamil looked astonished. "My Jewish name is also Mendy," he said slowly.

"And my Arabic name is also Jamil," Mendy replied quietly.

Understanding sparked in Jamil's eyes like a bolt of lightning. "So it's you! You're the one who messed up my life! You're the one who…" Jamil didn't even know how to describe what Mendy had done to him.

"You could say so," Mendy sighed and sank wearily onto the only chair in the cell, leaving Jamil on his feet.

"It must have taken a lot of courage for you to come here," Jamil said, with more than a touch of admiration.

"Yes."

"After everything you did, after everything you did to our family, after you ripped your mother's heart to shreds and basically killed your father… You still had the guts to come here."

"After everything *I* did? Do you remember how old we were when they switched us? How much choice do you think I had in the matter?" Gil countered.

Jamil's eyes flashed angrily. "It's still your fault that I have no life. Even when the *Yahud* realized I was one of them, they still wouldn't leave me alone. They still didn't trust me."

"They were trying to protect you," Gil told him, his tone grave. *Did the kid really not get it?*

"From what?"

"Death."

Jamil laughed caustically. "Death? The Arabs won't kill me. I talk their talk and walk their walk. I'm one of them."

"You're mistaken, Jamil. Mendy. Just like I'm not a Jew, you'll never be an Arab." Gil spoke so softly that Jamil had to strain to hear his words. "They don't view you as one of them; they see you only as a pawn in the game of death and destruction that they're waiting to play."

Jamil was struck dumb. "So why are you here? To save me?"

"I wish I could, but they don't trust me. They're listening to every word we say here. Believe me, every word is being recorded and listened to."

"So why are you here?" he repeated. "To laugh at me? To mock me? To see the Jew who was once an Arab, sitting in a cell while you walk free?"

"No. Actually, I came to see how you're doing."

Jamil glared at him. "Oh, really? Well, in that case, you can leave already, now that you've seen."

"I will do, soon. But first, I just wanted to say a few words to the son who took my place, the one who has my mother's prayers now instead of me. You're the one who…" He couldn't bring himself to continue, and Jamil stared at him in undisguised interest.

"You really love your Jewish family, don't you?"

"Of course I do. What about you?"

"They're nice people," Jamil replied guardedly. "I can't complain. The kids are petrified of me, but otherwise, they're not so bad. Especially the mother."

"Yes. She is." Gil's voice cracked.

"She cries a bit too much, if you ask me, and I don't see why. Doesn't she realize that tears get a person nowhere?" Gil merely shrugged, so Jamil continued. "I don't miss my other family. Your family, that is."

"I paid them a visit, and I know what you mean."

Despite his words, a look of longing suddenly sparked in Jamil's eyes, and he took a step closer to Gil. "Did anyone ask about me?"

"No," Gil replied indifferently. Jamil sank sadly onto his bed and buried his face in his hands. "I'm just a nothing," he moaned. "Nobody could care less about me. I should have stayed in America and had a life. Here, I have nothing to live for."

"You do," Gil said forcefully. "You have a family and a nation and a special religion. I came here, Jamil, to see you one time – because this is the first and last time we will ever meet. It breaks my heart to stand here, and believe me, I would give anything, *anything*, to trade places with you, to be your parents' child, to be a son of the Jewish nation..." Gil fell silent under the weight of Jamil's shocked expression, but he took a deep breath and forged ahead.

"I don't know if either of us will get out of this alive, but if you do, there's something I want you to know. I already heard you're very bitter about your lot, but you should be happy. Because you're very, very lucky."

"Happy? Lucky? For what?"

"Did you ever *daven* in *yeshivah*?"

"Yeah. I learned some of the Jewish prayers."

"Did you learn *Birkos Hashachar*? Do you say the *brachah 'Shelo asani goy?'*" Tears sparkled in Gil's eyes.

"Yes."

"And did you *daven*?"

"I told you I did!" Jamil was getting annoyed by the questions.

"Did you ever sing? Did you ever experience the *simchah* of Shabbos, or Yom Tov? Did you rejoice when you recited that *bra-*

chah? Did you dance for joy to know that you're a Jew? When you said that *brachah*, '*Shelo asani goy*,' what did you feel?" Gil practically shouted the words.

Jamil retreated. "Um… I don't know… I never really thought much about it…"

"So think, my friend! Think! I don't know how much more time you have left to think about it, but I came here to tell you one thing, Jamil-Mendy. You're a Jew! You're my parents' son, the son of a family that gave me twenty wonderful years. But you're the one who shouted '*Naaseh v'nishma*' at Har Sinai, not me! Do you understand what I'm saying? Your *neshamah*, your soul, was fashioned beneath the *Kisei Hakavod* and dwells beneath the *Kanfei Hashechinah,* and…" He stopped short, suddenly realizing that Jamil was staring at him in complete bewilderment.

"Whatever," Gil sighed. "You might not understand all that I'm saying, but the point is that you're a Jew. And there's nothing better than that! If you do manage to escape with your life, maybe try to salvage your *ruchniyus* – your spiritual soul – as well. And if these really are destined to be the final days of your life, then I hope I did something to help you live them with meaning."

He rose from his seat, preparing to leave.

"*Shelo asani goy?*" Jamil repeated after him.

"Yes, Jamil-Mendy. Rejoice because Hashem did not create you a *goy*."

A goy like Laser, like Aziz, like Jabbar or even Samira… Yes, Jamil had no desire to be like any of them, and, if what this Mendy was saying was true, then he really wasn't like them. He was cut from different cloth, and for that, he was indeed truly grateful.

Jamil stretched out his hand to Gil, who grasped it. "Thank you for coming, brother," he told him quietly. "I have to think about what you told me."

Gil nodded. "Think about it, Mendy. For as long as you have left."

Naomi was having a rough morning. Naftali didn't want to go to *cheder*, and Rachelli complained of a tummy ache. To top it off, the baby woke up with an eye infection. Naomi grimaced as soon as she saw it; there was no way the director of the daycare center who stood at the front door to greet all the children as they arrived would let her pass. Pedantic Mrs. Felder was a stickler for rules and hygiene, and she would kindly but firmly instruct Naomi to take her baby home with her, with warm wishes for a *refuah shleimah*.

She had three kids wailing, and a long morning ahead of her.

She hurried to dress the kids, and then sat the older two at the kitchen table to wait for her while she went downstairs with the baby to get the newspaper. There was a lone envelope sticking out of her mailbox along with the newspaper, and Naomi immediately sensed that there was something strange about it, for two reasons.

First of all, it had no stamp. Second of all, it had arrived before the mailman.

She climbed back up the stairs to her apartment with her baby in one arm, the paper and envelope in the other. Then, she sat down opposite the older children, dispensed bowls of cornflakes to all, and opened the envelope, removing a single sheet of paper containing a few lines that had obviously been scribbled in haste.

Every word in this house is being recorded. Don't talk about it aloud, but under no circumstances should you go with Mendy

to the hachnassas sefer Torah. Your lives are in danger if you do.

The letter was unsigned. Naomi inhaled a sharp breath and clamped her lips tightly together. Fortunately, Meir chose that precise minute to enter the house and was astonished to find all three children still home.

"Hi. What's up?" he greeted her in surprise.

"Yanky has an eye infection. Rachelli has a stomachache, and Tulli, I don't know, but he doesn't feel good either," Naomi replied, while gesturing silently at the letter. "I went downstairs to get the paper," she added, handing him the letter and placing a finger to her lips.

Meir stared back at her, perplexed. "What's this?"

"The newspaper," she replied naturally, and unfolded the letter for him to read.

Meir skimmed the lines and, to her astonishment, grinned.

"This is for real?"

"Totally. What the newspaper writes is usually true," she replied meaningfully, glaring at him.

"Oh, come on, Naomi. You take things way too seriously. Who do you think has time or patience to eavesdrop on—"

She interrupted sharply. "I also saw that article. The point is that we can't go to the *hachnassas sefer Torah*."

"Oy, Naomi..."

"My grandmother was just hospitalized, and my mother asked me to stay with her tomorrow night. I told her I would, and I thought you could come along with me."

"What do you need me for?"

"You know Bubby. She always likes to see the couples together. It's a *mitzvah*, after all."

"Why tomorrow night *davka*?"

"I have no idea, but that's what my mother asked me, and she sounded so stressed that I couldn't bring myself to turn her down. It sounded like she didn't have anyone else who could do it," she replied nonchalantly while waving the letter furiously under Meir's nose.

Then, grabbing a pen from the counter she scribbled furiously on the paper, "I won't let you endanger yourself or us! You promised me you wouldn't!"

"What about Mendy?" Meir asked reluctantly.

"Just tell him the truth. That you have to come with me to the hospital," Naomi replied triumphantly.

"All right..." Meir sighed. "Even though I really think that... Okay. I'll come along with you. Does that make you feel better?"

"Somewhat."

Meir cast a sidelong glance at the kids munching their bowls of cereal and smiled. "I guess until we come home to greet the aftermath of a babysitting disaster!"

Yochai was in a temper. Again.

He dialed his office, and was immediately put through to one of the computer staff.

"Find out if and where a Mrs. Gittel Barer, who lives somewhere in Netivot, was hospitalized. I need an answer on the double!"

"Yes, sir."

The answer wasn't long in coming, and it was negative. Yochai seethed in fury.

"I knew it! How are we going to get him to accompany Gil there? What else can we do?" Yochai didn't have much time left to plan. Gil was scheduled to pay him a visit in the next fifteen minutes, and he showed up right on time, his expression grave.

"Hey, Gil. What's up?" Yochai tried to smile.

"I met Jamil," Gil replied bluntly.

Yochai couldn't contain his surprise; such an encounter had never been part of the plan. "You managed to get authorization to do that?"

"No, not exactly. But that doesn't matter now. The main thing is that I met him."

"What for?"

"I wanted to. I did it for my parents, not for me or you."

"What was your impression of him?"

"He… I don't really know. He doesn't seem to get what's going on. Neither do you guys, for that matter."

"What's that supposed to mean?" Yochai retorted sharply.

"That you don't get that as soon as I die, he dies too. The first victory shot is going to be aimed at him."

"Gil." Yochai rose from his chair, and Gil followed suit. The GSS chief looked the young man in the eye, and only then did he notice how gaunt he appeared. Yochai was shocked to see how much weight he had lost in just one short week, and how pale his face was, and how dull his eyes.

"Gil, would you like me to tell you the truth of what I think?" Yochai asked gently.

Gil nodded mutely.

"The way we see it, you're a double agent. You're working for us, but also for them. Even now, I don't know who you'll be loyal to at the very end. You clearly harbor a great deal of anger and hatred toward us; I read it in your eyes, in your demeanor. Likewise, you love your Jewish family very much, but you're also angry at them. Am I right? You left them of your own accord at some point.

"I don't know what's going to happen at the last minute, what you'll choose, who you'll betray, who you'll serve. I'm telling you exactly what I feel right now, exactly what I think."

Gil remained standing ramrod straight, his face impassive.

"Why don't you deny it?"

"It's what you think. How can I deny what you think?"

Yochai was momentarily taken aback.

"I can't contest your feelings. All I can say is, that tomorrow, you'll know the truth. What I do ask of you until then, though, Yochai, is to arrange a rescue operation to save Jamil. Do you agree?"

Uncharacteristically, Yochai found himself nodding his consent, while Gil continued speaking in a quiet, commanding tone, as if he were the superior. "And another thing, Yochai. I heard that you're trying to keep Meir from joining me at the *hachnassas sefer Torah*. Nothing you told me right now is news to me. In fact, your attempts to hold him back from joining me are proof enough of your distrust."

"It's not us, Gil. It's Meir's wife. Believe me, it has nothing to do with us," Yochai protested feebly.

"Whatever you say," Gil said wearily. "It doesn't really make a difference where the opposition's coming from. But I will tell you one thing: If Meir doesn't come with me to the *hachnassas sefer Torah*, the operation is off. Yes, I admit that he'll be endangering himself, but I refuse to go without him. If he's not with me, it's all off, and you'll be held accountable."

Yochai almost fainted when he heard Gil's words. "Look, Gil, I can tell you two things: One, he'll come; and two, don't you dare try to threaten us. We have our ways of threatening you too, and don't test us. Have we reneged on our word to you even once so far?"

"On many words," Gil replied coldly. "Yochai, you stand on one word alone, and it's called advancement. You're not an intrinsically bad guy, but you have no problem trampling on others in order to reach the top."

Yochai was chastened into silence.

"And one more thing, Yochai. Meir stays with me throughout the entire operation." With that, Gil turned on his heel and walked out of the office. Instinctively, Yochai ran after him.

"Why?" he called after him. "Why do you need him? I can give you a dozen guys, a hundred others. Why do you need that Landsman, for Heaven's sake?"

"He'll protect me," Gil replied simply.

"*He'll* protect you?" Yochai repeated derisively.

"Exactly." Unexpectedly, Gil burst out laughing. "Look at yourself, Yochai. Just look at yourself, along with all your fancy staff. You're all busy playing cops and robbers. Our country is hardly the size of a dot on the giant globe, surrounded by the most virulent enemies. Look what's going on in Syria, Egypt, Jordan, Lebanon… Look how much blood is being spilled in all those places. And you think that you guys are strong enough to protect us? You think you're strong enough to prevent the destruction of our tiny country? Tell me, Yochai, if all our enemies join forces in simultaneous attack, who'll protect us? Should I tell you Who?"

Stunned by the intensity of Gil's outburst, Yochai didn't reply, and Gil forged ahead.

"I'll tell you Who and what. The Torah. The same Word that states that this country belongs to us will protect us. And if you don't believe in that Word and in that protection, then you don't really believe that this country belongs to us and that we have a Divine right to live here. So instead of joining you in your pathetic games, I want to know that I have the one man beside me who has a load of merits that outweighs the entire GSS arsenal. I want the man who believes that those engaged in performing *mitzvos* won't come to harm, and I promise you not to do anything to endanger him."

Yochai exhaled a sigh, and responded only to Gil's final statement. "Your promise will have to be delivered to his family, not to me. As far as I'm concerned, you're welcome to have him as your escort; it's his wife who opposes his participation in the plan."

"But you can take care of that quite easily, can't you, Yochai?" Gil noted, before turning his back on the man and walking away.

Jamil was livid. "You can't just move me!"

"Why not?"

"Because I'm not a puppet that you can drag from place to place, back and forth from Arabs to Jews to Arabs again. I'm a human being with free choice!"

His two captors burst into loud guffaws. "*Ya*-Jamil, we're moving you whether you like it or not. You can try resisting us, but it won't get you far. You're much better off cooperating."

They opened the door with a flourish and led Jamil into another room where one of them blindfolded Jamil and the other began to tie his hands behind his back.

A phone rang in the next room.

"It's probably Laser," one guard said to the other. "Answer it."

"You answer it," the other replied reluctantly.

"So we'll both go," the first one compromised.

Jamil was too angry to think twice. Perhaps one day, men would say that he was courageous, daring, cunning, a true son of Yotam, former GSS agent; but the truth was that he was just angry and desperate, and he wasn't using his head.

The rope binding his hands hadn't been tied tightly, and he quickly wriggled his hands out of it and yanked the blindfold off his eyes.

The door to the room was unlocked, but a quick glance outside revealed a third bored-looking guard sitting close by. Pulling his baseball cap low over his eyes, Jamil strode confidently out of the room.

"Shu hada?" * the guard challenged him, suddenly sitting up straight.

"I'm Rashid. I came in a few minutes ago to bring the prisoner his food. Didn't you see me? Sleeping on the job, eh, *ya-habibi*?" Jamil accused.

The guard trembled. "Sleeping? Me? No, I remember you, of course." He opened the door, and Jamil stepped straight out and strode away, turning at the very first corner and then again, walking as fast as he dared and then breaking into a run as soon as he thought it safe.

Not a minute passed before he heard furious shouts in Arabic and he realized that the chase was on. He flagged a passing cab and was relieved to see that the driver looked Jewish.

Pulling open the door, he dove into the passenger seat, keeping his head low. "Fast! Just get out of here!" he told the startled driver, his voice urgent. "They're after me!"

"Who? Who's after you?" the driver queried, looking at him strangely.

"Just get me out of here!" Jamil cried. At that second, a gunshot shattered the rear window, and the driver screamed in fright as he floored the accelerator. The car jerked and swerved violently as he sped away, the driver glancing into the rearview mirror as he drove.

"What are you doing getting me into your gang wars?" he shouted furiously at Jamil. "Why didn't you tell me you're an Arab? I'm stopping in one minute, as soon as I get away from whatever crazy's after you."

"I'm not getting out of the car, and I'm not an Arab! If you don't continue driving, man, you'll be dead meat like me!"

* Who are you?

The driver was about to slam on the brakes and order his customer out of the car when a second shot was fired, prompting him to drive even faster and make a series of perilous turns in an attempt to shake off his pursuer.

"I'm going straight to the police!" the cabbie shouted, beads of perspiration appearing on his brow. "I won't forgive you for this!" He swung the car around another corner, and then sighed in relief. The reckless driving of the taxi and the car pursuing it had evidently already attracted the attention of the police, and, slowing down, the taxi driver watched as two squad cars managed to get the second car in the chase to stop.

"Don't slow down – get out of here!" Jamil urged the driver on. "Do you want to be arrested too?"

The cabbie paled, and stepped down hard on the gas. "You just tell me where, and I'm getting rid of you as fast as I can. But not before you pay me in full," he glared at Jamil. "For the ride, and for the window."

Jamil turned around in his seat and viewed the shattered rear windshield. "Yeah, I'm really sorry about that. But... You know what? Take me to this address," he fished around in his pocket to find Meir Landsman's street name and number, "and I'm sure they'll be happy to pay you."

The driver didn't look convinced, even after Jamil listed the address.

"Where's that? Bnei Brak? At least there, no one's going to shoot at us..." He shook his head in aggravation. On the way over, he called his garage to inquire about the price of a new rear window.

Jamil exited the taxi leisurely and told the driver to wait downstairs. "All right, all right, leave the meter running. What are you so worried about?" He climbed the steps and knocked on the Landsmans' front door.

Naomi opened and looked curiously at the stranger. "Can I help you?"

"Is Meir home?" he asked politely.

"No."

Jamil placed his hand nonchalantly inside the doorframe, to prevent the expected slam of the door in his face.

"Don't you recognize me? It's me – Jamil – but now they call me Mendy. You saved me once."

"Meir's not home," she repeated bluntly.

"I understand, but the thing is that I need your help again. I came here by cab, and I don't have the money to pay."

"Oh."

Naomi disappeared momentarily into the house and returned with twenty shekels. "Here," she proffered the bill.

Jamil swallowed uncomfortably. "Uh, the thing is that it's not really enough. I need a blank check."

"You need what?"

"I feel really bad, but I need a blank check. I'll work to pay you back as soon as I can. I was in the cab, and somebody fired on us and shattered the rear window. The driver's demanding that I compensate him, and I need the money right now."

Downstairs, the cabbie honked impatiently.

"If we don't hurry up, he's going to barge up the stairs and start screaming," Jamil warned.

Naomi turned white. "Hold on," she gasped. "I'll call Meir."

To her chagrin, Meir didn't answer his phone, and Jamil was right. Less than a minute later, the driver came stomping furiously up the stairs and began screaming about *chareidim* collaborating with Arabs to murder innocent Jewish citizens. Startled neighbors peered through the cracks of open doors, and the pattering of small feet was heard from the lobby as curious children gathered to watch the spectacle.

Naomi was at a loss. "Listen, sir. This has nothing to do with me. I'll give you a check, but I'm capping it at a certain amount.

If you still have a problem, you can call. All right?" she addressed the irate driver.

"I won't call. I'll come," he threatened.

"As you wish, but please, without shouting. I really have nothing to do with this!" With trembling fingers, Naomi signed the check which the driver snatched before disappearing down the stairs.

Jamil seemed inordinately relieved. "Wow! Thanks so much! You really saved me. By the way, would you mind giving me something to eat?"

"Um, well, I don't really have anything in the house right now, sorry." Naomi was trying valiantly to keep her wits, and she blocked the doorway with her body. "Here, take this," she handed him the twenty shekels again. "It's enough to buy a falafel and a drink."

"When will Meir be back?"

"He's in *yeshivah*. He'll be back in about two hours."

"Okay, I'll go visit him there."

"No, you can't! He learns with *bachurim*, and you mustn't disturb him."

"He'll be happy to see me," Jamil protested.

"I'm sure he will be," Naomi replied bitterly. "But you can't disturb him now. Go eat something and come back later."

"Can I borrow another fifty shekels? I'm desperate for a smoke. I was kidnapped and I didn't have anything normal to eat or drink in days…"

Without a word, she handed him a hundred shekel bill.

"Wow! Thanks! You guys are really great! You remind me of my Jewish family. I really hope I didn't disturb you too much," he said cheerfully as he waved jauntily and headed down the stairs with a merry whistle.

The moment he stepped outside, his smile died on his lips.

"No!" he said resolutely to the two men who faced him and

gestured for him to enter the waiting car. "Tell Yochai I said no. No means no. I'm a free man, and I'm not going – not with you or with anyone else. Got it?"

He spun around and strode down the street in the opposite direction toward the falafel store at the end of the block.

They reached a compromise, but Naomi still felt uneasy.

"So what do we gain from this? You're still in danger!"

"First of all, what we gain is that you and the children are safe," Meir answered soothingly. "And I also promise you that I'll find some excuse to keep a distance from him during the actual event. There will be thousands of people there, and it won't be hard to 'lose him.'"

"Please, Meir. Do it right away. Don't linger for too long. And do you really have to go along with him in the car?"

"That's part of the plan."

"But do you know why he needs you?" This was the part that disturbed Naomi most. "I can't stop thinking about it. He's a very serious boy, with real intentions – even I admit that. And it obviously hurts him that he can't be *misgayer*. But why does he need you with him all the time? The only thing I can think of is that he's still wavering between two loyalties, and they're attempting to brainwash him on the other side."

"I don't think so," her husband disagreed. "He's not wavering. His *neshamah* is clearly Jewish."

Naomi was unimpressed. "If that were so, then surely he would convert. But… that's not even the point now. Back to what we were saying: You'll go with him in the car, but as soon as you get out of the car, you separate and keep at least fifty kilometers away from him!"

Meir grinned. "I think you meant to say 'fifty meters.'"

"No, I didn't!" Naomi replied seriously, and they both laughed.

"It'll be okay, Naomi," Meir said encouragingly. "After tomorrow, everything will be behind us. Yochai promised."

"And I'm sure he's *very* reliable," Naomi remarked, but her next comment wiped the smile off Meir's face. "If only the Jamil story were behind us too."

The Jamil story was only just beginning, Meir feared, after hearing his wife's account of the morning's events. Although it had been a relief to hear that Jamil had escaped his Arab captors, he was mortified at the thought that his neighbors, and indeed, probably half the neighborhood, had witnessed the drama, culminating in Jamil being forced into a car by three plainclothes officers, easily identifiable as Secret Service operatives. As yet, nobody had dared to confront Meir and ask him what was going on, although the strange stares and whispers were already beginning to catch up with him and he had no idea what he would reply when the first nosy neighbor plucked up the courage to ask him who exactly Jamil was and how he was related to him.

Yochai paced his office like a caged lion.

"Hey, boss. Why don't you call it a night? You haven't left the building in days. Think about your wife," said Shai, who would be overseeing the operation the following day.

"She's visiting her parents in London."

"In any case, some shut-eye wouldn't hurt," his colleague hinted gently.

"I can't stop worrying if I'm really going about this right," Yochai mumbled to himself. "Maybe I should have just arrested Gil, thrown him in jail, and then spirited him out of the country to some safe haven somewhere. I'm giving myself a heart attack with this. It's dangerous. How should I know what he's going to do when the moment arrives?"

Shai debated whether to respond, but decided to take the chance. "Yochai, if it's not Gil, then it'll be somebody else. You know that as well I do. Here, we have a golden opportunity to get our hands on Laser and a bunch of the others as well, the brains of Hamas, if that stuff in their heads deserves to be called brains. He's the mastermind behind twelve major attacks, but we've never had anything solid on him. Now we do. We can get him, sir! We'll have our revenge, and better yet, avert dozens of other attacks that he would have plotted in the future. You're doing right, sir. You're just nervous, and rightfully so. If you weren't scared, then you wouldn't be worthy of your position."

"Scared isn't the word," Yochai finally confessed his fears. The responsibility was more than he wished to take upon himself. He knew that if the mission succeeded, he would take the credit – but the praise he would receive no longer held any appeal for him, given the immense danger associated with even the tiniest glitch in his planning. If anything went wrong, people would die – a lot of them.

His lips were dry when he admitted the truth. "Shai, I'd never let my wife or my children anywhere near that place. How can I risk so many innocent people?"

"It's either those innocent people or other ones. This way, we have a reasonable chance of stopping those terrorists and averting the disaster. But if they change the venue and take Gil out of the picture, we won't know a thing, and it will be a calamity! This is a risk we have to take, sir! There's no other way."

"And no other way of protecting the other kid, either?"

Shai shook his head. "As long as we keep him indoors, he's safe, but the minute he leaves… We know they're watching him. I don't see a solution," he confessed. "And he's already complaining about being locked up again, even though by now he must realize why we're doing it. Something about growing up in their decrepit villages must cause their brains to rot," he concluded dismissively. "The kid has no sense, none at all, just like the rest of those filthy Arabs."

"I wouldn't underestimate them," Yochai replied. "They do seem to know what they're doing, after all, and they have us backed into a corner. As always, the most desperate of our enemies, with little or nothing to lose, are the most dangerous. Are any of our men so devoted to the Service that they would risk everything? No, because our men have families, community, meaning in *life*, not just in death. And Hamas knows that."

A long, heavy silence filled the room.

"So you won't try to get some shut-eye tonight?" Shai finally returned to his original point, after fully grasping the situation.

"Not tonight. But you go to sleep, Shai. It's been a long day."

Shai wished his boss good night and exited Headquarters, leaving Yochai alone. For his part, Yochai stared sightlessly out of the window. From his office on the thirteenth floor, he had a stunning view of the Mediterranean, sparkling blue by day. Now, it was a formidable black, almost invisible against the dark horizon.

His eyes drifted heavenward to the night sky and to the stars, few of which were visible on that cloudy night. Nonetheless, he knew they were there, just as he knew that above them was their Creator, looking down on the world He had brought into being. For the first time Yochai actually found himself praying.

The kitchen cuckoo clock chirped six times precisely as Gil's black car pulled to a stop outside the Landsmans' building. He didn't honk or even call Meir to tell him that he was waiting downstairs, but rather waited for his older friend to appear at the prearranged time, confident that he wouldn't let him down.

Naomi peered out of the living room window and wrung her hands in anxiety. "He's here, Meir."

"Of course he is. It's six o'clock. Okay, Naomi, I'm going now. Bye."

"Meir!" she was suddenly seized by panic. "Don't go! *Please* don't go. You can still change your mind. Eat a peanut or something…"

"Naomi," he said calmly, "it'll be all right. I promise. I'll be back no later than eleven, *b'ezras Hashem*. Then, it will all be behind us. Mendy promised. So did Yochai," he reminded her.

"I don't trust either one of them!" she reverted to her previous arguments.

"Don't worry," he mustered an encouraging smile.

"Famous last words," she muttered. "At least promise me that you'll answer the phone whenever I call."

"If I can hear anything over the music," he grinned. "Bye."

"Bye."

With a final wave, he left, closing the door softly behind him. Naomi rushed to the window and watched her husband emerge from the building and then enter the car, her vision blurry through teary eyes. Where would her husband's good heart lead him this time?

Downstairs, Gil smiled when he saw Meir appear. "Thanks for coming along. The weather's supposed to be nice tonight," he greeted him.

"Great. Maybe we'll even have time to stop by the Kosel for a few minutes on the way?" Meir suggested. "It's been a while since I was last there."

"Sure. Why not? I think we can still make it in time," Gil replied generously. A few minutes later, when they started to encounter traffic, he glanced at his watch again. "On second thought, I'm not so sure. I can't afford to be late."

They made slow progress along the first stretch of the highway, chatting about nothing in particular to pass the time. Two cars trailed them throughout the ride, making no effort to disguise their presence, until even Meir couldn't help but notice them. He knew without a doubt that one was from the GSS, and the other, from Hamas.

It took an hour for them to reach Yerushalayim and pass beneath the String Bridge at the entrance to the city. Gil sighed and rolled down the window, allowing a cool breeze to waft inside the car.

"Ah. Fresh air!" he said. "Breathe, Meir! When do we ever breathe air like this in Tel Aviv or Bnei Brak?"

"Never!" Meir agreed with a laugh.

Gil switched on his GPS. "Okay, now let's figure out exactly where we're supposed to be going." He switched lanes and slowed down, almost as if trying to delay the inevitable. After fifteen minutes, pedestrian traffic swelled, and they saw hundreds of men, women, and children headed in a general direction.

"I should probably park here, because who knows where else I'll find a spot," Gil remarked as he began to search for an available space. "There are tons of people here," he sighed.

"This is just for starters. The *hachnassas sefer Torah* isn't supposed to begin for another half hour. There'll be hundreds, if not thousands more people here by then!" Meir exclaimed, suddenly infected by the excitement in the air. "Mendy, thanks for schlepping me along!" he added spontaneously. "This is going to be an event to remember. Do you know which *rabbanim* are supposed to be coming?"

"No," Gil replied shortly. "You can ask someone if you want to know." He spied a parking space and pulled into it before anyone else could nab it. "Let's go," he ordered Meir.

Meir opened the door and stretched after the trip. Meanwhile, Gil got out and walked around to the trunk, from which he removed a giant backpack.

Meir's eyes widened. "What's that?"

Mendy smiled, a bone-chilling smile, and Meir froze. It was as if a *dybbuk* had suddenly entered Mendy, and he had literally become a different person. His eyes seemed out of focus and his expression was that of one possessed. Meir shuddered, and instinctively turned away.

"What do you think it is? You know why you're here," Gil replied vaguely.

"Mendy… What's up with you? What are you doing? You promised you wouldn't do anything dangerous! What have you got in there? Mendy, don't do anything stupid, or I'll call the police!"

"Oooh, I'm scared. Cut it out, Meir, will you?" Gil replied derisively.

Meir paled, and his hands trembled. "Listen, Mendy, I need to run into a store for a second. I'll be right back."

"You're not going anywhere." The voice was harsh, commanding.

"Excuse me?"

"You're not going anywhere." Gil slammed the trunk shut and took a step toward Meir, his expression menacing. Meir noticed a small wire dangling from one of the side pockets of the backpack, and cold sweat broke out all over his body. Gil, in contrast, remained totally apathetic in the face of his terror.

"You're coming with me, or else I might just choose to blast us both to a better place."

"You're out of your mind!" Meir whispered, his lips quivering in fear. "Naomi was right. I should never have come. Mendy, you're acting like a crazy. What are you doing? *What are you thinking?* You promised me that we'd go to the *hachnassas sefer Torah*, and that would be it!"

"Exactly. I told you that I'd be carrying out my last mission, and this is it. Afterward, I disappear for good, because I'll be dead. I didn't lie."

"But you didn't explain it like that until now!"

"Of course not. If I had done, you'd never have agreed to accompany me, and I need you at my side, a typical, average *yeshivah* guy who'll smile at everyone like you always do. We'll hang out together and keep the questions away. If anyone asks, you'll say that I was on my way to *yeshivah* with my stuff, and that you persuaded me to join you. Understood?"

Meir was too horror-struck to reply.

"Stay away from me with that. I'm not walking anywhere near your bomb!" Meir finally croaked.

Gil threw him a harsh look. "Meir," he said roughly. "Either you walk together with me, or… you get the gist, don't you? Take a deep breath; it's great air. Here, why don't you have a drink too? Make a *brachah*, say a *perek Tehillim*. Let's go! The crowd's over there."

Meir choked. "You mean you're taking that bomb into the…"

"Yes."

"But… you always said that you're a Yid, Mendy, that you've got a Yiddishe *neshamah* inside you!"

"I know exactly what I said, and I meant what I said. And now I also mean what I'm saying, and what I'm saying is that you're coming with me. Right now."

Meir stood facing the younger man, frozen in fear, his eyes wide with terror. "Mendy!" he whispered, his expression shattered. "Please! Tell me that you're on our side! I'll come with you, but tell me that you're one of us. Tell me that you're a Yid, that you have a Yiddishe *neshamah* and that you're planning to convert."

"I have nothing to tell you. What you have to do is follow orders. Either you come with me now, or we're both headed to the place of no return," Gil repeated his previous statement. "If you want an explanation, talk to Yochai. Only G-d has the words to explain how he let you endanger yourself like this. Let's go!"

They walked, merging into the giant crowds. Gil's huge bag elicited several strange stares, as it contrasted sharply with his black and white yeshivish dress, but nobody asked any questions, and nobody seemed to notice how stiff and awkward Meir was as he trailed behind Gil, his mind frozen and numb.

"Need some help?" a *bachur* offered generously.

Gil nudged Meir to reply. "Uh, no thanks," he stammered hoarsely. "He was on his way to *yeshivah*, but I convinced him to stop at the *hachnassas sefer Torah* first."

"It's worth it!" the *bachur* exclaimed. "This is going to be an event to remember. The *rabbanim* are supposed to be arriving really soon."

Standing beside them, an older man turned to Mendy with a warm smile. "I live right across the street. You're welcome to drop your stuff at my house until afterward."

Gil gave that grotesque smile again, causing Meir to shudder. "Thanks, but I'm okay."

"Where are you going?" Meir whispered fearfully, noticing that Gil was heading deeper and deeper into the crowd.

"Stop asking so many questions," Gil replied harshly. "Just stay with me or it's all over."

"Meir!" somebody called from behind, causing Meir to spin around to find his cousin Ari Schechter. Ari pumped his hand vigorously. "It's been ages! How are you? How's the *mishpachah*? What brings you to Yerushalayim?"

Gil grimaced, realizing that he couldn't drag Meir away from his long-lost relative so quickly. Meir managed to conjure up a weak smile for his cousin. "*Baruch Hashem*, Ari. How are you? It's so good to see you! Uh, you can go ahead, Mendy. I'll catch up in a minute."

"That's okay. I don't mind waiting," Gil replied tightly.

"How many kids do you have these days?" Ari asked Meir, nodding politely to Gil.

"Four," Meir mumbled, pushing four on the speed-dial to call Yochai. His heart almost stopped beating when the voice mail clicked on at the first ring. Why was Yochai's phone switched off at a time like this?

"Four! Already!" Ari reacted in amazement.

"Four? No, I mean, I've got three kids," Meir mumbled.

"You're still learning or you're working?" Ari continued.

"Working? No, it's not working at all," Meir said in frustration. "It was great seeing you, Ari," he added quickly, suddenly noticing the furious expression in Gil's eyes. Ari watched his cousin wander off like a drunkard, wondering what in the world had happened to easygoing Meir Landsman.

"Don't you dare try anything like that again," Gil whispered into his ear, his voice cold as ice. "And don't try calling Yochai again, either. He got you into this mess, and I doubt he'll help you now. You're with me until the very end, Meir. And if you really want to know where we're going, it's right to the center of things, where the crowd is the most dense. As I said, either you're with me here now or… or you're with me someplace else."

Meir's heart sank as he thought of Naomi, of Naftali, Rachelli, and Yanky, all waiting for him to come home…

Gil and Meir maneuvered themselves deeper into the crowd until they found themselves almost unable to progress further among the thousands who had gathered to honor the Torah.

Meir heard an excited father tell his children, "From here, we'll have a great view of the *rabbanim* on the dais!" He clutched their hands tightly to keep them from wandering off and getting lost in the crush of people. Meir turned pale, his thoughts of what was about to happen to those children making him feel nauseous. Suddenly, another thought almost made him retch. In the tightly packed crowd, Gil's bag was constantly being pushed by one person or another…

"Mendy, people are pressing against your bag!" Meir hissed to him. "What sets it off?"

"Keep your voice down. Do you want the whole world to hear you?"

"So tell me what you're planning!" Meir turned around to face him. He wanted to stand in place, but the surging crowd pushed him ahead, and he had no choice but to continue walking if he didn't want to get trampled.

"Oh, there he is…" Gil's voice was suddenly filled with relief.

"Who?" Meir looked around, searching for the elusive "he."

A car was inching forward, progressing carefully through the throngs of people. Meir's heart practically stopped beating as it slowed down beside them and Gil leaped inside, still wearing his bag. In the driver's seat sat another young man with facial features practically identical to Gil's. Clearly, a full staff of makeup artists had labored to create a perfect replica of Mendy Brand. Now the driver leaped out of the car, holding a bag identical to Gil's. The men's eyes locked, and the look they exchanged was so filled with meaning that Meir could almost see rays of energy passing between them. To any observer, they were identical twins greeting one another, but Meir saw so much more.

"Meir, you stay with him!" Gil whispered from the car. "This is as far as we go together. They'll get you both out of here at the right time. But for me, this is goodbye. Goodbye, my friend. And thank you, forever." His voice cracked, and all the harshness of minutes earlier vanished instantly, revealing Gil's innocence, vulnerability, and also courage. His eyes sparkled with unshed tears.

"No one in the world will know that I did what I did to protect other Jews. They'll curse me forevermore; they'll say I was an animal, a traitor, the scum of the earth. Even you, Meir, will only know part of the truth, but never again will I see you or threaten your safety. Goodbye, my friend."

Crouching low in his seat, Gil switched his black hat for a baseball cap and donned large sunglasses, altering his appearance in a split second. At that moment, Gil's double resembled him more than he resembled himself.

In shock, Meir watched the car continue down the street, and in a split second, he understood exactly what was happening. The car stopped about fifty meters further down, and Meir saw Gil emerge and heave his bag back onto his shoulders. He turned a corner, and a moment later, he was out of sight.

"Mendy!" Gil suddenly heard his name being called. Gil jumped in fear and looked around frantically. Who knew he was here? Who had managed to identify him?

His jaw dropped as he found himself facing Shimon, his father.

"Mendy! Don't do it! I won't let you!" Shimon panted to catch up with his son.

"Tatty, please go. It's dangerous!" Gil begged, his voice cracking in agony, but Shimon ignored his son's pleas.

"They told me that you… Yochai said… Tell me if it's true!" he demanded. "You're my son, Mendy. Not the son that your mother gave birth to, but still our son! We raised you. We love you. Don't do anything crazy just because Yochai told you to! Listen to me, Mendy! I'm your father!"

Gil lowered his eyes, unable to meet his gaze.

"Tatty!" he whispered, his words saturated with tears. "Tatty, I would do anything to be accepted back into your family. You know that more than anyone. But I have to do what's right, and this is what's best for everyone – me included."

"Best? To end your life before it's even started?"

"They're prepared for it. It's a controlled blast. None of the damage will be real. Hatzolah is already here, ready to deal with all the faked casualties. Everything will be okay. No one will get hurt."

"Except for you."

Gil nodded slowly. "It's the best way. The only way."

"No, Mendy! It's not. Mendy, you don't understand, and they don't understand, because the GSS views you as an operative, not a person. But I care! Mendy, you're my son, and I won't let you do this."

"Don't try to change my mind, Tatty. Please, it wasn't easy for me to come to this decision, but I know that it's for the best." A tear escaped Gil's eyes, and he made no effort to hide it.

"But why? Mendy, I'm telling you that you have a right to live!" Shimon cried out in anguish. "You have a right, just as much as anyone else. You told Meir Landsman that you want to convert. I heard it loud and clear. You told Meir that you wish you could be a good Jew, that you yearn for the moment of connection to

Hakadosh Baruch Hu! Mendy, as the father who raised you, I'm telling you now: Don't give up! You can still make things work out."

"Tatty, please! I'm asking you to give up. You're just making it harder for both of us. Go, Tatty! Go quickly!"

Shimon was pale. "I gave up so much already, Mendy! For months, I've been wandering from place to place, a dead man. But I'm alive, and I have no peace."

Gil shook his head and started to walk away.

"Where are you going?"

"The controlled blast is supposed to take place over there," Gil pointed ahead in the distance. "And there will be another fake blast, with no casualties at all, so nobody will be able to pinpoint exactly where it took place. Don't worry. Everything is arranged."

"Mendy, there's no such thing as a controlled blast where you're at the center of it! Save yourself, Mendy! Run away and save yourself!"

Gil couldn't bear it any longer. He had so longed to spare his father the anguish. The last thing he wanted to do was present him with the dilemma that he himself had been forced to confront and make him choose, as well.

But his father was leaving him with no choice, and in this moment of vulnerability, Gil wavered.

"Tatty, there are things that you don't know," he said finally.

"What do you mean?"

"Jamil escaped. You must know that."

Shimon nodded. "I heard. So until this is all over, Yochai's men are standing guard over him to protect him."

"Tatty, it's not so simple. There are sharpshooters there, ready to fire as soon as they're ordered to. If the operation fails, then he'll be the first one to pay for that failure. If it's deemed a success, then there's a slim chance that they'll let him go. But otherwise – no chance of it. They need casualties, a lot of them, and me among them. And so, there's no other option. Somebody had to choose between me and Jamil. So, I did."

Shimon shook his head in disbelief. "No. It's not true. Yochai can keep him safe somehow," he protested. "It won't happen like that."

"Tatty, this is what I've been dealing with for the past two months. It's me or him. Jamil is your Jewish son, the real Mendy. It's a question of his life or death, and his life is no less important to me than the lives of the rest of the family that I love so much." Gil was weeping openly by now. "Please, Tatty. Don't make this any harder on me. My time has come."

Shimon, still shaking his head, found himself unable to speak.

"There's nothing else I can do," Gil continued, his voice barely above a whisper. "If I save myself, then Jamil dies. I'm not a Jew, but Jamil, your son, is. Tatty, you know the *halachah* as well as I do. Who comes first?"

Shimon's face was as gray as a corpse; his mouth opened, but no sound emerged.

"If I had chosen to be *misgayer*, I could never have made this choice," Gil continued, tears streaming freely down his gaunt cheeks. "But I didn't, and in this way, I'm giving you back a Jewish life for the beautiful Jewish life you gave me. Thank you, Tatty. Thank you for everything. Thank Mommy too. And don't mourn me too much… I did what I had to do, and hopefully, I'll get my reward in the Next World, if such a thing exists for *goyim*… Put your efforts – the same efforts that you invested in me – into Jamil. Inside, he's a good person, and I'm sure that, one day, you'll have *nachas* from him. Don't give up on him. He had such a wretched childhood, and it left its mark on him, but everyone should be given the chance to do *teshuvah*, and he can do it. Pity him, because the more you pity him, the more you'll grow to love him…"

With these last words, he mustered a small smile and began to hurry to the destined site.

Shimon ran after him.

"No, Tatty. This is as far as you go," Gil said firmly. "Security won't let you past this point anyway. My time has come. Please, ask Mommy to still *daven* for my soul…"

Out of nowhere, two men appeared and guided Shimon firmly away. Gil strode directly ahead, not even looking back.

Held back by the two GSS operatives, Shimon sagged in anguish. Could he allow himself to save his son – his real son – at the expense of Mendy? Could he allow Mendy to die in order to save Jamil?

There was no time to think or act, because less than a moment later, he watched Mendy break into a run. The joyful music of the *hachnassas sefer Torah* was drowned out in the blast of a sudden massive explosion followed instantly by the terrified shrieks of men, women, and children.

People ran in all directions. Panic ensued. Shouting. Screaming. Tears.

Sirens wailed. Rescue teams and emergency vehicles sped to the scene of destruction, with lights flashing and sirens blaring. And still the awful screaming and horror continued.

Shimon sank lifelessly to the ground. The grief-stricken cry of a father bereft emerged from his throat and was swallowed into the wailing and hysteria all around him. "*M-E-N-D-Y!!!*"